Where Wild Birds Shriek

Where Wild Birds Shriek

Christian Lea

British Library Cataloguing in Publication Data

A Record of this Publication is available from the British Library

ISBN 978-1-914199-22-6

This edition published 2022 by The Red Telephone
Manchester, England

And others hurried to and fro, and fed
Their funeral piles with fuel, and look'd up
With mad disquietude on the dull sky,
The pall of a past world; and then again
With curses cast them down upon the dust,
And gnash'd their teeth and howl'd: the wild birds shriek'd

—*Darkness*, Lord Byron

To be told of such hills
To be held in such spots
To behold such warmth

—*Pleader*, alt-J
(Reprinted by permission of alt-J)

Map of Gallows Village and surrounding area, Cumbria

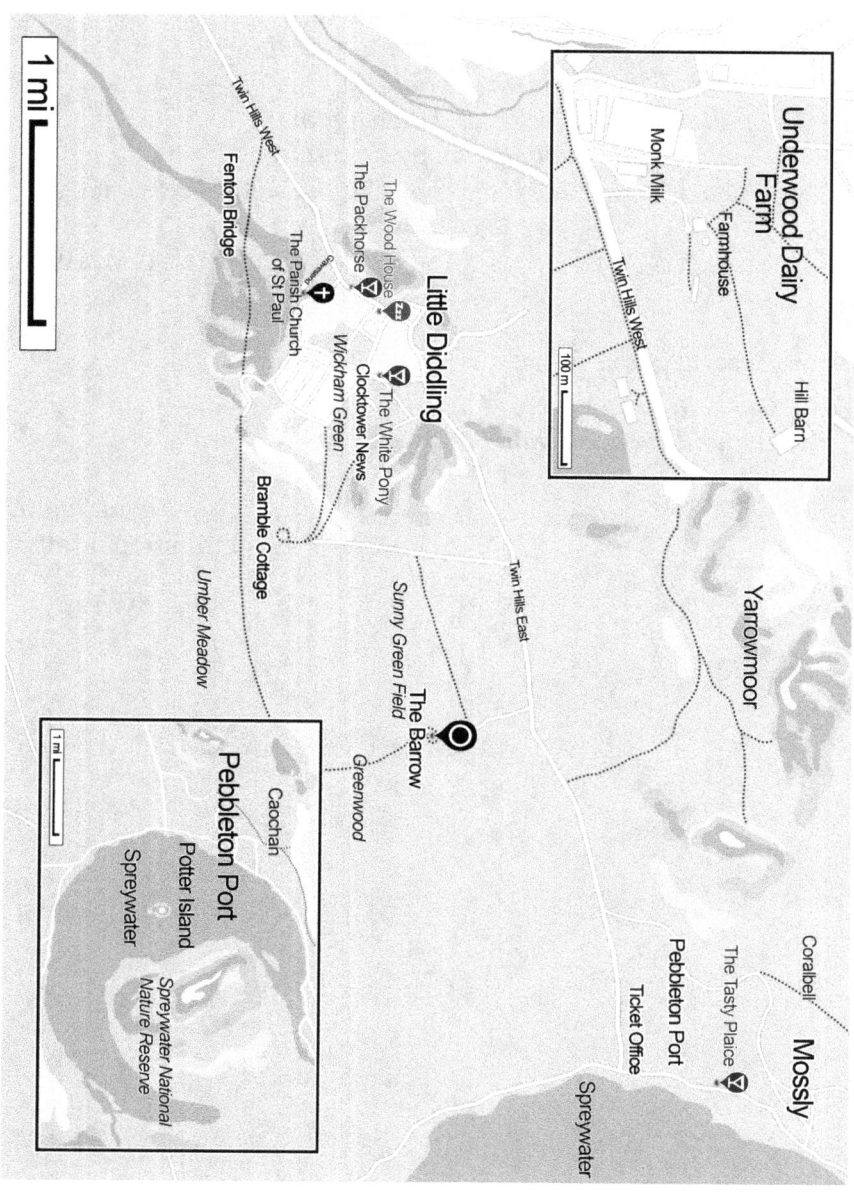

Part I

Chapter 1

London smelled like a dead thing. And it occurred to Charlie Bloom—who stood wearing only a bath towel and looking through the grey square of kitchen window as whole gallons of rain came teeming from the rooftops outside as thick and heavy as steel girders then crashing to the concrete in waves—that it might just never go away, that smell.

It was of brown runoff Thames water. It was of sulphur and bloated corpses. It was of black water sewage and fire and brimstone and death and it swirled around in the estuary that had once been the road outside his door.

He lived on Milk Street, half a mile north of the river where the handsome townhouses were like slices in a long white cake. The kitchen was at the back of the house and looked onto a miserable courtyard. Four stone walls, a birdbath and a hint of shrub. Charlie had the window open an inch and the bitter air nipped at his face. But he didn't mind. This was as close to the outside as he had been for a week and a half—and that was only to fetch the milk from the doorstep.

He pushed the window open further and noticed his hand was shaking. He had grown so neurotic that he flinched every time the apocalyptic growl of London thunder rumbled across the city and its fantastic spiders of lightning exploded like blue flowers through the dark. Their static glow bounced around the walls of the courtyard and made all the shadows dance. It was only midday but a convoy of iron storm clouds had moored up like warships sometime last week and they completely blot out the sun. It was hard to believe this was spring.

But Charlie knew that it was hardly the weather depressing him. That honour went to his roommate, Harry Burden.

Harry was incredibly bright. Harrow educated and from a well-to-do family. He claimed to be descended from Lord Byron—and acted like it. And he had grown up on an estate quite unlike the one Charlie had. Blye House wasn't owned by the council, for one thing. For another, it came with a butler. And while Harry could recite for you the complete works of Shakespeare and conduct whole conversations in Latin, he couldn't tell you how much a loaf of bread cost. He was classically handsome, wildly eccentric and fiercely intelligent—but at the same time, the single biggest nitwit Charlie Bloom had ever met.

Presently, Harry was up in his bedroom making a bloody awful racket without a care in the world for Charlie's hangover. They may have been best friends but Charlie still hated the stupid bastard with all his heart.

Christ! His heart! It felt like it was being juiced by a big hand. Why had he agreed to move in with the silly prick? They had lived together back at university and that had almost killed him. Now he was certain Harry meant to finish the job. It was a natural side effect of their living together. Harry didn't *mean* to cause trouble. It just had a way of finding him.

'What are you doing up there you bloody fool?' Charlie groaned as more monstrous banging shook the ceiling and caused the chandeliers to rattle.

He doubted very much that Harry had heard him, but was relieved to find the banging did subside.

'*Thank* you,' he said, looking around the kitchen wearily.

God was he fed up. For a minute or two he considered doing the dishes, but the state of them depressed him more than Harry ever did. The plates were stacked so high by the sink they touched the ceiling and were crusted over with something like barnacles. And by the back door, a deflating mountain of bin bags coagulated into a puddle of black treacle.

Charlie was quite certain theirs was the only house for a mile in every direction you would find in such despair.

He turned back to the courtyard outside. *Concentrate on the birdbath*, he told himself. *Yes, just watch the birdbath*. A pool of mercury whose ripples were all he wanted to contend with that morning, the ripples, which spread from the barrage of rain-like arrow fire and bubbled on the surface like magma. The storm was hypnotic and he watched as the courtyard began to flood. He watched the pools eddy round the drains; he watched a cyclone tear through puddles; he watched the water level rise, first in inches, then in feet, then lap at the rooftops. He watched as ships dipped and soared across the back of a rising tsunami. As a forty-gun frigate opened fire on a fleet of Portuguese schooners. As cannonballs tore through the gun deck, while hail, as big and round as boulders, came down in a meteor shower, crashing through the deluge of swirling black ocean and sending explosive geysers of froth a hundred and forty feet into the air. He watched as a thousand rearing seahorses led the Kanagawa rogue wave across violent tempests and were consumed by the mouth of Charybdis on the Italian strait—

Something smacked hard into the window and Charlie's eyes sprung open like roller blinds. He had fallen asleep and awoke in time to catch a puff of black feathers evaporate into the air. He put his head to the glass and saw a little blackbird outside, twirling through the courtyard like a downed bomber. It swooped up before it crashed into the shale and landed awkwardly beneath the birdbath with a broken wing. The basin above had flooded and a waterfall pinned the bird to its stone ankle like the bars of a cage.

'One for sorrow,' Charlie muttered to himself. 'You and me both, Mr Magpie.'

The walls shook again and bits of plaster dropped heavily across the dining table. He felt like he was in a warzone. The thumping subsided. The sound of a door opened above, footsteps stormed the landing and came charging downstairs, before the clatter of an almighty crash exploded at the foot of the stairs.

'*Ow!* You swine!' a voice cried out.

The door swung open and Harry burst into the kitchen, rubbing his leg. He spotted Charlie and thrust a thumb over his shoulder.

'Tripped over the bloody boar head again,' he explained.

At the foot of the stairs the trophy mount of a tusked boar sat looking quite unhappy to find himself stuffed and discarded so unceremoniously. Harry had stolen the thing from his father's estate, Blye House, the week before, then promptly aborted any plans he had for it.

'Charlie-Boy, I'm in the throes of a most violent hangover,' he said, collapsing into an empty chair and throwing an arm across his forehead dramatically. 'I saw off the end of the turps last night. Have we any ice?'

Charlie looked Harry over; he was gangly and foppish and had a few too many teeth in his mouth, but he was handsome regardless, in an old-fashioned kind of way. He reached for debonair but was several inches too short. And presently the whites of his eyes were a fatty yellowish colour.

'Christ, you look a picture,' Charlie said.

'Nonsense. I'm the paradigm of man,' he rebuffed. 'Besides, I'm coming down with pneumonia or something. I nearly coughed up a fucking lung this morning. You're hardly a painting yourself. Have you slept? Why are you only wearing a towel?'

'My clothes are in the wash. What was all that banging about?'

Harry wasn't listening. He was lost in his own head, sitting cross-legged on his chair, with eyes shut tightly, drilling fingers into temples.

He started to hum.

'What are you doing?' Charlie asked.

'Regenerating liver mass. *Omm…*'

'And what was all that banging about?'

'*Shh*. Meditating. *Omm…*'

Charlie rolled his eyes. He noticed Harry was still in the old brown suit he'd had on three days ago and it was stained about the lapels from drink or vomit or both. Only now it was below an attractive military greatcoat with a high, stiff collar.

'Where did you get that coat from? It looks warm.'

'This old thing?' Harry smirked. 'I *repurposed* it from my father's last winter.' He had started referring to the things he stole from his father as "repurposed" recently. It had become a catch phrase. It drove Charlie quite mad. 'Forgot I had the bloody thing until I received *this*.' His devilish smile faded. 'It concerns you. Here.'

He had pulled a letter from thin air and shoved it under Charlie's nose.

'I can't read this. I've got a migraine like a tumour. Who's it from?'

'My father. Give it here, then.' Harry got to his feet and cleared the throat. '"Dear Harrington,"' he read, '"I remember a boy on the green in plus fours and a beret at the close of last summer, strenuously promising to apply himself this year. So why is it you've not shown up for a single day with van der Sar—?"'

'Who's van der Sar?' Charlie interrupted.

'A great fat puff from The Times. I was meant to be his assistant. My father scheduled the whole affair. Didn't I tell you? I met up with the bugger on New Year's Day and he tried to roger me without so much as a whiff of foreplay. When my father told me I was to work *under him* I hadn't realised he meant it quite so literally. Well, he can fuck his job sky high if he means to sell my arse for it.'

Charlie noticed how Harry was grinding his teeth and looking off into the corner with a fixed glare. He shook his head and said, 'I'm getting off pace. His letter continues. "It's unbecoming to have such ill regard for one's future, and"—Christ, listen to *this*—"Burden Boys are made of better stuff..."'

'Blimey.'

'Blimey indeed. It goes on and on like this for some time. I'll skip ahead. *A-ha*! Now this part is fantastic—I ought to have it framed for posterity: "From the moment that twee midwife severed your umbilical cord, you've been edging toward the limit of my patience. But until this year you had always toed the line. Now you've given up on the toe and stuck the whole bloody leg across."'

'He's got a point,' Charlie reasoned.

'Well of *course* he has! But it doesn't mean he's not a total bastard for *saying* it. The *gall* of the man! And then he manages to write *another* three paragraphs without actually *saying* anything. But there's more, this is the important part, listen to this: "I was deadly serious when I said I would cut you off if you failed at this job. You've left me no choice but to follow through on that promise. I will not continue to *mollycoddle* you through life."'

Harry snorted sarcastically. He balled the paper up and threw it on the table in front of Charlie and held his arms out to the dishes.

'My father ladies and gentlemen. What a cunt. *Mollycoddle*

me? The man's effing *insane*. He had old Sallow take me fishing, the chef cook all my meals, and the nanny change my nappies. Paying our bills is just about the closest thing to affection he's ever shown me. I half-believe the van der Sar episode was another of his attempts at love-by-proxy.'

Charlie had un-balled the letter and ironed the creases out with the palm of his hands. He read through it again, quickly. It was signed *Richard Burden*. Below was a postscript: "You wouldn't happen to have seen my greatcoat?"

Charlie shook his head, troubled by the thing.

'This is bad Harry. Really bad. This is not, er, y'know—'

'Good?'

'Exactly. This is not good.'

'I know darling. He's severed all ties with me. He's stopped paying our bills. Stopped my allowances. He's denying me access to my trust fund. I'm now officially poorer than *you* and you're a food bank baby for crying out loud and from the north of England! I mean no offence, Charlie, but it's a bloody classist *joke*.'

'This is why you finished off the turps?'

''Fraid so. Didn't have the stomach to tell you he'd written last night, so I tried to get abso-blotto first. Must've passed out before I could muster the will.'

'You've been up there for days. What've you been *doing*?'

'Getting my affairs in order.'

'And all the banging?'

'I'm building a bird table. We've a family of crows living on the roof.'

The light flickered overhead. The two of them moved in to watch as it sparked on and off. Charlie held his breath with worry. The lump in his throat metastasised as a particularly brutal knot in his stomach. He was being infested by his own neuroses. The bulbs gave a final cackle of light then cut out and the room darkened. The only light now came from down the hall, but it was a grey and spectral kind of light and it was strobed with the shadow of the rainfall.

'That *bas*tard,' Harry growled.

'He's done it,' Charlie whimpered. 'He's cut us off.'

'That's it then. I'll have to kill myself. Where's the revolver?' He pulled open the kitchen draw and rooted through it.

'You lent it to Mad Eric Wardle for a gram, which turned out to be sugar. I used it in my tea.'

'I did? Why on Earth did I do *that*?' Harry stopped rooting through the draws and fished a mug from the sink.

'It was during one of your episodes. You'd insufflated some hairspray. Look, don't use that mug, I found a creature living in it this morning.'

Charlie doubled over suddenly with intense pain. The knot felt like some bastard ventriloquist had an arm up his arse and was honking his internal organs like horns.

'Christ! What are we going to do about this, Harry? Things are getting desperate around here as it is. There's toxic goo dripping from my bedroom ceiling. I woke up to Chinese water torture. I told you this place was too much for us when we moved in. Didn't I *tell* you it was too much for us when we moved in? You *promised* your father would cover the rent. That was all I asked. I just quit my job for God's sake. This is bloody *Knightsbridge*, Harry and I'm from the north. I'm hyperventilating. Ow. *Ow!* I've given myself a hernia—'

'Calm down,' Harry said.

'I *knew* something like this would happen, but I let you talk me into it. Oh *why* did I let you talk me into it? Our halls were never this bad at uni and I almost contracted cholera in first year. I think I've got hives or carbuncles or *something*.'

'Charlie, you're being hysterical,' Harry said, edging away. 'Take a breath.'

Charlie rocked back and forth on his chair, breathing heavily and scratching imagined fleas all over his naked torso. He was working up to that breakdown he'd promised himself.

Harry waited another moment until Charlie's breathing had steadied, and then he asked, 'What does Mad Eric Wardle want with my great-grandfather's old service revolver? He's not going to do a crime is he?'

'*I* don't know, he's mad isn't he?'

Harry turned the tap on. It made a long, rattling sound and he squatted down to watch as a stream of brown sludgy water trickled out.

'Right. That's it!' he decided. 'I'm going to do something.'

'Good! Thank God. We can't go on like this. What will you do?'

'I'll write to my father,' he said. 'Take a note, Charlie-Boy!'

Charlie scrabbled around the table for something to write on.

'"Dear Father",' Harry began. '"What a funny little man you are. Sincerely, Mr Burden, your son. Dictated but not read." Be a darling and post it before the last pick up, would you Charlie? Send it with a dead mouse—we've plenty around.'

Charlie compared the two letters in front of him—if theirs could even be *called* a letter. It was scribbled in Charlie's spidery handwriting on a torn sheet of yellowing paper with a cigarette burn in its corner and a spot of mould by the margin. Richard's was on a thick letter-headed cardstock with the family crest and a dated stamp and a series of important-looking initials trailing his name.

'I'm not convinced this will help with our plight,' Charlie said.

'Of course it will. I can just imagine the look on the bastard's face when he slits it open with that ruby inlay letter-opener he's so fond of and discovers such devastating contents. Besides, it's the best I can do, short of grovelling.'

'Then grovel!' Charlie slammed the letters on the table, startling Harry. 'This place is killing us. Look at me; I haven't eaten in three days. I've got a potbelly like a starving African. And I can't sleep. All we do is give ourselves hangovers. It's not *usual*, Harry.'

'Relax, Charlie. Sit back down, take a Valium. There's some in the draw, I think, by the unguent for the carbuncles.'

Harry was going through the fridge now. It was depressingly empty. Two expired cartons of orange juice, a bottle of milk, sprouting cress through its foil lid, and a pack of butter. He closed the door and looked down at Charlie. The boy was a wreck. Unshaven, with red eyes, ringed by that eternal darkness. He'd stared too long into the abyss. And he was only dressed in a bath towel.

'Why are you wearing that towel?' Harry asked again. 'You're covered in goose pimples. You'll catch your death.'

'My clothes are in the wash,' Charlie groaned, utterly defeated.

'What, *all* of them? You didn't keep *spares*?'

'I was drunk! This is what I'm telling you. I'm not functioning properly. I've got a brain like a fried egg. Do you know who does their washing when they're drunk? The winos two doors over! That's who. I'm on the verge of a mental breakdown, Harry. I need to get out of this place, it's killing me. *You're* killing me. Country air, that's what I need.'

''Tis but a minor setback, Charlie-Boy. Fear not. There's a suit in my wardrobe with your name on. Savile Row, don't you know.'

He tried to sound upbeat and wore a weak smile, but edged away from Charlie and occupied himself opening cupboards. They were all empty except one, which had been stocked with twenty cans of soup and all the beans you could eat what felt like yesterday. Now it held just one solitary tub of something the colour and texture of molasses and it sat below a cobweb watched over by something with twenty red eyes.

'There's another of those creatures in here,' Harry noted.

Charlie gave up. He slumped over his laptop on the dining table like a marionette without a puppeteer. When he noticed, Harry slid over and prodded him in the cheek.

'Are you still breathing?'

'Unfortunately so,' Charlie mumbled.

'Good. Try not to die. I don't suppose you've written anything today?'

'No I've not,' Charlie said. He sat up and slammed his laptop shut. 'I've not written anything since *God knows* when. And neither have you, I'll wager. If I wasn't so fucking miserable I would laugh. For a couple of writers, we never actually *write* anything, do we?'

'I've been trying to write my memoirs,' Harry said, scratching at his jaw. 'I'm just having some trouble with the main character.'

'Oh?'

'Yes, it's that he's insufferable and I wish he would piss off and die.'

Harry took the molasses from the creature and read the label.

'You see? We're useless,' Charlie said. 'This isn't how writers should live. I should be on an Italian hillside, hammering away at an old Remington, chasing the elusive novel through the long winters. But here I am. With you. Didn't someone say "Hell is bad company" or something? We're useless...'

'We're not useless. We're just... I have writer's block—'

'Yes and you just so happen to have had it for twenty-four years.'

'What about you? You wrote that stage piece, didn't you? Hm. Best before April. What month is this?'

'March. Yes, I did,' Charlie said. 'And I've yet to see a penny for it. Those fuckers from the Comedy Store are trying to shaft me.'

Harry unscrewed the lid and sniffed inside the jar. He threw his head back and retched. 'Dear God! This must be from *last* April. I'm going out. We've nothing to eat. Or more importantly *drink*. Do you want anything?'

'Yes. Some nourishment. I haven't eaten in three days. I almost had a go at the butter before.'

'But it's *green*!' Harry was appalled. 'Leave it to me.'

He dashed from the room but made it only so far as the door before he turned back around with his long greatcoat cutting a figure eight behind him.

'Oh, er... I don't suppose you have any money?'

Charlie got up and followed Harry down the hall. The rain had eased off a little bit and the spectral light that fell in through the frosted glass was now speckled with gold. Somewhere over London there must have been a rainbow.

Charlie took the wallet out of his coat pocket and emptied it into his palm while Harry wrestled with a golf umbrella. The boar head watched the two of them in judgment as the umbrella sprang open.

'Don't do that!' Charlie said. 'It's bad luck.'

Harry raised a brow. 'Yes and our lives are otherwise just *brimming* with good luck, aren't they?'

'Things can always be worse.'

Harry snorted. 'They surely can't,' he said. 'Death is preferable to our current situation. I should reclaim my revolver and end all this.'

'Don't talk like that,' Charlie snapped. 'Not after everything that happened last month.'

Harry blushed. 'Sorry, yes.' He nodded. 'I just mean this is ridiculous, that's all.' And then tactfully changing the subject, he asked, 'Have you spoke with Emily today?'

'No. Why?'

'She left a message. Said she had something *exciting* to tell you. God I'll *bet* she's pregnant,' Harry scoffed. 'You realise you can barely look after yourself don't you? The bastard will starve.'

'She's not pregnant. And I can look after myself just fine,' Charlie grumbled.

'Oh really?' Harry said. 'Did you know you've got pepperoni in your hair and no clothes on and you haven't eaten in three days?'

'I'm chasing the elusive novel into the winter—'

'Yes, yes. Look, forget all that,' Harry decided, changing his mind. Clearly this was not the time to get into any of the old bickering. Alcohol beckoned. 'Should I get us vodka or a couple of four packs? Lager's *cheaper* of course but you can't argue with percentage.'

Charlie sifted the coins about in his palm. 'I've only got about one pound sixty or a twenty.'

Harry plucked the twenty-pound note out of Charlie's fingers and unbolted the door. He pulled it open and almost bowled into Emily on their doorstep. She was dripping wet with her hair plastered to her face and her arm raised about to knock.

'Speak of the Devil and she shall appear,' Harry whispered before he dashed out under the golf umbrella. 'Bubye lovers!'

Chapter 2

Charlie went into the dingy bathroom to find a towel for Emily. The sink and bathtub were blackened with molluscs and he knew better than to expose her to it. He picked up a damp flannel and sniffed it. 'Ugh...'

He found a towel on the back of the door—this one only partially invaded by the mould—and took it down to the kitchen for her.

She was sat on the work surface, rolling a cigarette across her knee when he returned. She hopped down to towel-dry her hair while Charlie had a go at the washing up. He had changed into one of Harry's suits and pulled a pair of Marigolds over the sleeves.

Neither of them spoke for a moment. When Emily had finished drying her hair, she cracked the window open an inch and lit her cigarette.

Charlie watched her and smiled. He'd almost forgotten how to use those facial muscles. He'd become the chrysalis of a creature somewhere between man and beast in the last few days, but Emily made him resolve to change all of that. She was an English rose—and all of its thorns. When he was around Harry for too long, he almost forgot how it felt to be normal.

After blowing a smoke ring out of the window, Emily said, 'My *word*, Charlie, I couldn't even *begin* to tally the amount of penises I've seen this week.'

The glass Charlie was scrubbing shot into the air leaving a vapour trail of suds. He scrabbled to catch it and placed it on the draining board as she smirked.

'I *mean* it,' she went on. 'It's enough to put a girl off. I'll bet I've seen more naked men than a prostitute in a lifetime. And I mean a *good* prostitute too. An Italian courtesan. Not one of Soho's "models."'

'It's an occupational hazard,' Charlie said.

'But I'm a junior doctor not a *urologist*,' she stressed. She stood with her back to the window and held her cigarette over a shoulder like a fifties starlet.

Charlie was having no luck with the washing up. It was foolish to have even attempted without a hazmat suit. He dropped the mug into the bowl and the water swallowed it up.

'It's like today,' she said, 'we had this American gentleman in, from Texas, I think. Easily two hundred and fifty years old and he was just *masturbating* in his bed. Completely oblivious to his audience while partaking in the unholy alliance.'

She paused and flicked a column of ash into the plant pot on the windowsill. 'His little chap was sprouting like an old potato,' she went on. 'It was really something. And of course, *I* had to deal with him. The matron was naturally AWOL and the nurses were all off doing their rounds leaving this young first-year girl on her own down there and *she* was in the midst of a freak-out.

'So I was called to the ward and I approached the chap, who was strangling the turkey—with its pink head and drooping wattle—and I said to him, "Excuse me sir, you can't be doing that in here!" and he had the *audacity* to tell me the nurse *told* him to! I said, "What do you mean the nurse *told* you to? I don't believe that *any* of the nurses here told you to start masturbating, sir." But he's insistent, this old cowboy. "She did, missy," he says to me in his brash American way. "She told me to lie down and make myself comfortable and to take off my pants and jack it."'

Charlie howled with laughter. Emily just shook her head.

'There were five other patients staring at him in sheer horror. Old people just don't have shame the way you or I do. It's quite empowering, when you think of it.'

'I hope you got him a hearing aid before he was discharged.'

Emily stubbed her cigarette out and walked over to the wall. 'We kept him in overnight,' she said, flicking the switch up and down. 'But he had already *discharged*, so to speak.'

She pulled open the door to the fridge and stuck her head inside. 'Do you know your electricity is out?' she asked.

'The Old Burden's cut us off,' Charlie said miserably.

'*God* this house is depressing. The hospital mortuary is livelier. Come on. Leave a note for Harry and let's go to the Nag. I've something exciting to tell you!'

The Nag's Head was an anomaly in West London. It was a run-down little pub with weeds growing up it like ivy and all its plaster flaking off. The two front windows had been boarded up for a decade and out front, a chalkboard boasted a beer garden—five square feet of one, with four stone walls to keep the sunlight out. And here in the early afternoon it was already crawling with women in pink feather boas and bridal veils, high on mimosas.

It was the kind of place you wouldn't find it odd to see vomit permeating the Axminster carpet, Charlie thought, and, in fact, he didn't find it odd when he sat down on a wobbly table and saw somebody else's dinner enveloped in their bile.

'God the Nag,' he grumbled. 'This is the kind of place you end up on the wrong side of midnight; look, we're shoulder to shoulder with the English Defence League.'

He nodded at a gang of skinheads monopolising the dartboard in full QPR regalia.

'I like it here,' Emily said. 'We came here all the time when we were students.'

'Exactly.'

'It keeps one grounded, a place like this. You're letting that house of yours turn you into a snob, Charlie Bloom.'

Charlie sank back. There was a fruit machine in the corner with an 'Out of Order' sign around it. He thought the whole place could do with an 'Out of Order' sign around it. 'Closed for fumigation' maybe. Tent the place—with everyone still in there.

'We've had good times here,' Emily went on, smiling. 'Do you remember when Harry was thrown out for gluing the snooker balls to the table?'

Charlie chuckled. 'Actually,' he said, 'that was at the George and Dragon.'

'Was it? Are you sure?'

'Mm, because you remember when he got thumped?'

A wrinkle appeared at the bridge of Emily's nose. 'By that big biker bloke with the facial tattoos?'

'Exactly. Well that bloke was Sheila, the Dragon's landlady. Plus,' he continued, 'I don't think it's possible to get barred from here. A man tried it once in the eighties and they put up a blue plaque for him.'

'Well *I* like it here,' she said. 'It has character.'

Charlie watched as a stumbling drunk at the bar attempted to molest one of the hens. It has *characters,* he thought to himself.

'So, you had something exciting to tell me?'

'Oh, I do,' Emily said sitting up. A thought appeared to come over her and she settled back down slightly. 'But first, while we're alone, I meant to ask. Have you got round to telling Harry yet? About Greenwich?'

Charlie's heart skipped a beat. He hadn't told him a thing. He hadn't even mentioned they were looking, never mind that they had found a place. He believed his fear of telling Harry was partly responsible for his nerve having given up on him last week. It was no coincidence the two things occurred within an hour of each other.

'Christ, Charlie,' Emily said, as if she could read his mind. 'The longer you leave it—'

'I know!' he admitted. 'Be*lieve* me, I know. It's just, Harry— he's not like you or me, he's—'

'Unstable?'

'He's not *unstable*. He's just—well, okay, perhaps he *is* unstable. The point is, he can't live in that house without me. I once caught him trying to make toast in the microwave. He thought a dovetail joint was something you smoked. You have to understand, Emily, he grew up with a valet—'

'And how lucky he was to meet you, then, to fill that vacant position.'

Her face turned hard. She crossed her arms and pretended to find the menu fascinating.

'I will tell him,' Charlie said. 'Soon. I promise. I'm just waiting for the right moment.'

Emily didn't answer him. He watched the drunk at the bar for a while. The hen wised up to his antics and gave him a face full of her gin and tonic.

Charlie cleared his throat. 'Come on then. Don't leave me in suspense. What's this exciting news?'

Emily uncrossed her arms and rolled the straw of her drink between her finger and thumb.

'We've been invited away for the weekend,' she said, without making eye contact.

'Oh? Where?'

'To the Lake District. We would leave on Friday.'

'Friday? *This* Friday? Blimey, Em, that's a bit short notice isn't it? Who invited us?'

Emily pursed her lips. Charlie could tell she was reluctant to answer, preferring to fold a napkin across her knee. But eventually she did.

'Rose.'

Charlie pulled a face. 'Rose? I don't Know, Em. I'm not sure it's a good idea for me to go away with your sister for the weekend. Not after everything that's happened.'

Emily rolled her eyes. 'You might be Harry's friend, but they broke up almost a year ago. I really don't think even *Harry* would be so petty as to demand you never see my sister again on his behalf.'

'*I* think you're overestimating his maturity,' Charlie grumbled. 'But I'm not talking about Harry. I doubt Rose wants to see me after what happened last time.'

Emily looked confused. 'What happened last time?'

'She almost scalded me with boiling hot water. And all because that pet rat of hers found its way under my foot.'

'You know full-well that was her *dog*, Charlie. And it was an accident. Rose happened to throw her coffee over you because you stomped on the poor thing's tail and it startled her. That's just how she is. She's dramatic! She is an *actress* after all.'

'Mm, and she doesn't let a minute pass without announcing it to the world. Must've picked *that* habit up at RADA.'

'She didn't *go* to RADA. She went to Italia Conti—'

'Where she took courses on "Shakespeare", "ballet" and "How to be an unbearable pain in the arse",' Charlie sneered.

'Charlie Bloom!' Emily said. 'That's my *sister*.'

'You weren't under any illusion that I *liked* her were you? You know she has a screw loose. No, more than a screw, her head rattles like a toolbox.' He had sunk into his chair and now raised his shoulders in exasperation. 'Why has she invited *us* anyway? She hardly likes *me* any more than I like *her*.'

Emily lifted up her glass and wiped the wet table beneath it with her napkin. 'She wants us to meet her new boyfriend.'

Charlie felt his eyebrows fly up his head in surprise. 'And who's the poor bastard she's sunk her teeth into now?'

'His name's Tom Darrow,' said Emily, ignoring his remark quite diplomatically. 'He's a personal trainer, on quite a good salary, too—or so Rose tells me. Apparently he could've played rugby for England but he got some kind of injury and went into fitness. That's how they met, you see. At the gym.'

Charlie was silent for a moment. He was considering the invitation. He had been telling himself all morning that he needed to get away from Milk Street—to get away from *Harry*—and now an opportunity arrived wrapped up in a bow and he found himself hesitant. But not without reason. Going away with his best friend's ex-girlfriend and her new boyfriend felt something like a betrayal. And the last thing Charlie needed right now was to get on Harry's bad side when he still had Greenwich to tell him about. The slither of ice where Harry's heart should be might just melt.

But still. The countryside. Fresh air. Peace, away from that maniacal flatmate of his. It sounded good, even if it did mean living with Rose.

'Where would we stay, on this trip?' Charlie asked.

Emily smiled. She turned to her bag and took out a pink Post-It Note and slid it across the table.

It said: *The Barrow, Fri-Mon* in flowery handwriting, with its tittle dotted with a little ink heart.

'Tom wrote this, did he?' Charlie joked. 'The Barrow. This is a lake house?'

'That's right. It's by a village called Gallows. Oh, *come* on Charlie. This will be good for you. You're stagnating in that house. And you always talk about going camping. Leaving our phones behind and using a battered old A-Z roadmap, like our parents would have done. We could *do* that!'

Before Charlie could reply, a pint slammed down on their table, startling him.

'God it's like buffalos at the watering hole over there, isn't it?'

It was Harry. He plonked himself down on a stool in a flap of coattails and thrust his thumb over at the football fans by the dartboard who appeared to be racing to finish their pints first.

'You got our note then?' Charlie asked.

'Yes. Thought I'd join you for a swift one. What are we talking about?'

Charlie blushed and looked up at Emily uncertainly.

'Er, well...' Charlie began, 'we're going away for the weekend. To this place in the Lake District.'

'Oh, yes?' Harry said disinterestedly. He looked down at the Post-It and turned it round to read. Then he seemed to come over quite different. 'Friday? Is that *this* Friday?'

'That's right.'

'Friday, you say,' Harry repeated, in barely a whisper now as if speaking to himself. 'My, my, what a coincidence...'

'What's a coincidence?' Emily asked.

Harry jerked out of whatever trance had come over him and flashed his teeth. 'Oh, nothing. Nothing. I mean, er, to do some housework Friday, that's all.'

He picked up his pint and drank thirstily while Charlie watched him closely. In the ten years he had known him, Charlie had not once seen Harry do any housework.

Chapter 3

In the small hours of Friday morning, Charlie loaded up Emily's little blue car and they left Milk Street. He had agreed to drive, but immediately regretted this decision. The old jalopy was terminal. It rattled like a rickshaw with half a dozen lights lit up across the dashboard and the exhaust backfired six times before the car finally growled to life. Emily told him not to worry about it. That it ran just fine. And then she promptly fell asleep before they had even made it out of London.

Harry hadn't come down from his room to see them off—but as Charlie got into the car, he glanced up at Harry's bedroom window and spotted his shadow skulking behind the curtain.

He had been extremely reticent for the last few days. Ever since his strange response to their news at the Nag's Head he had begun a routine of theatrical moodiness. But Charlie was content with that. The way he saw things, if Harry found it a *coincidence* they had been invited away on Friday, that could mean only one thing: Harry must somehow know Rose would also be in the Lakes that day. And that spared Charlie the ordeal of having to bring her up—or Tom Darrow, the new boyfriend.

By the time they joined the motorway, daylight was breaking. The darkness beyond the cat's eyes gradually turned into fields of green. Cows and sheep grazed on the hillsides while ponies stood in the metal feet of electricity pylons, chewing the long grass.

An hour before sunrise, the motorway had been empty. Now, it was cluttered with early commuters. First, enormous delivery lorries appeared. Then horseboxes and tractors. Then came caravans and trucks hauling livestock, muddy four-by-fours, Jeeps towing speedboats, cars with sunroofs open, windows down, hands poking out holding cigarettes, with watches catching the light the way it caught a line of wing mirrors that twinkled like indicators. The sun bore down with such intensity it was difficult for Charlie to recall the ballistic rain from only a few days previous. That dreary Wednesday afternoon stood in the kitchen in his towel felt like a lifetime ago.

Charlie took an exit and drove into the heart of Cumbria, winding through several small hamlets until he spotted a sign for the long A-road, Twin Hills.

He had studied a map of their destination and knew that Twin Hills serviced the nearby village of Gallows and then continued on to a small woodland where The Barrow, their home for the weekend, nestled. Further east he would find a little port by a large lake called the Spreywater. He had even learned that 'Twin Hills' was named for the two large mounds in the area. The village of Gallows was built around the smaller of the two, while the Yarrowmoor Mountain, a handsome and imposing sight with a distinctive flattish top, stood somewhere between the village and the lake.

Twin Hills took them through a valley. At the edge of the road, the banks sloped into a bottomless ravine of larch trees. Great orange drifts rose up behind them with a shimmer of water in the distance.

'The Spreywater,' Charlie noted to himself.

It was still some way off. He drove through the valley for a few more miles before an avenue of trees brought them into a wide and flat area of farmland. Up ahead, the road began its incline through the first of the twin hills. The minute village buildings of Gallows sparkled under the sun like silver.

Charlie braced himself as he started up the road. He doubted very seriously whether Emily's car would even make it up the tor.

And he was quite right to doubt it, too. At no more than five degrees the car groaned. He managed to force it up to a point where the road levelled, but he couldn't see how it could climb any steeper. The main road seemed to wind all the way up to the clock tower at the top of the mound before it snaked back down toward The Barrow on its other side. He thought about waking Emily. She hadn't stirred once on the drive. Her dark head was pushed up against the window and her mouth was open slightly. He slid the A-Z from her lap and struggled to see where about in the spine he'd driven them.

Going off the grid, leaving their phones behind and using a

battered old roadmap had *sounded* like a good idea, but Christ, Charlie would've driven the rest of the way naked if he could just follow a satnav. There must have been a way around this bloody hill and yet Twin Hills looked to be the only road for miles. He threw the map onto the back seat and sighed. Gallows was a handsome village and quaint. The buildings were all pastel and colourful flowers were everywhere—in window boxes, in hanging baskets, in arrangements spelling out WELCOME TO GALLOWS at the edge of a small green. Bunting zig-zagged from Victorian streetlamps and everyone who passed had a smile to share. If Charlie was feeling cynical, he might have expected to wind up burning on a wicker pyre before the weekend was through.

Two figures crossed the road in front of the car and he thought about asking for directions. Before he had chance, they entered a chalk-white pub called The Packhorse.

He turned the engine off and Emily stirred.

'Are we here?' she asked.

'Not yet. I'll be back in a tick.'

Chapter 4

Charlie got out of the car and cupped his eyes to the window of The Packhorse. It was a very traditional village pub, with copper pans dangling from four large casks on the wall and hand-carved buttresses around the bar. But what surprised Charlie was how busy it was. It was only half past six in the morning, the place surely wasn't open, and yet it was practically full.

All of the tables had been pushed back against the walls to make space for the thirty or so people, seated in the middle of the room where an assembly of chairs had been arranged around a large stone fireplace. A lectern was set up on the hearth and the red-faced man behind it tried in vain to quell the mob.

When Charlie slipped into the back of the room, lots of beery-voiced men were yelling 'hear, hear!' while others booed and jeered.

The red-faced man at the lectern wore a striped butcher's apron, spattered with blood, and he looked positively distraught at the ruckus he had caused.

'Settle down, settle down,' he implored. 'I'm jus' saying, if we put a fence up, say twenty foot or what-have-yer, between Foxwood and Underbank, the kids would have a lot harder a time getting on there in the first place.'

'A fence won't do diddly, Glen,' someone argued. 'They'll just move to another field. What are you suggestin'? That we cordon off the whole bleedin' countryside?'

'No, but Underbank—'

'You only want a fence round *Underbank* 'cause your garden's on the other side!'

'Hear, hear!'

A few disapproving murmurs passed through the crowd.

A big, butch woman said, 'You don't think a fence'll really stop them kids drinkin' and litterin' any more than I've got three tits!'

The crowd had started to boo again and Glen looked positively defeated. He tried to quiet them, but before he could, a short, rotund man with a great, bushy beard stepped up onto the hearth beside him.

'Come on now, calm down you lot.' He turned to the butcher and placed a sympathetic hand on his shoulder. 'Is that it, Glen? That your only policy? A big fence?'

'Colin, please—'

'I'm sorry, Glen,' Colin said. 'I'd give you my vote, but I doubt this lot will swear you in if *that's* your solution to these vandals.'

Glen shuffled off the stage looking miserable, while Colin, who appeared to be running the meeting, scanned his clipboard.

'Right then, that's about everyone, I think. You can cast your votes before you leave and I'll tot 'em up and let you all know the results by Sunday morn.'

A loud metallic clanging sound rang out around the room. Then another. Then another. A few heads turned to locate the source, which came from a man stood only a few feet from Charlie at the back of the room.

He was a slender, bent-backed figure, half draped in the shadow of a wooden beam. His left leg was bolted into a metal cage-like brace, and he was swinging it back and forth into one of the ornamental copper pans.

Most of the audience had turned round by now and Charlie noticed a few of them, after spotting this strange man, tut their lips or roll their eyes. Somebody whispered something to her neighbour, who chuckled. It was clear to Charlie that the villagers didn't much care for this character.

When the murmuring stopped, the strange intruder set his leg back on the ground, heavily. He took a step forward into a shaft of sunlight and a shiver ran down Charlie's spine. There was something unearthly about his appearance. He had an impressive set of wiry eyebrows and a beard of steel wool and the little hair he did have around his balding head was lank and greasy. But most notably, the man had only one eye. His empty socket was purple and wrinkled like an old prune, and the cheek beneath it glistened with yellowish fluid.

He stood very still for a moment observing the crowd and it looked, to Charlie, as if he was pleased with the affect his appearance had on people.

He made his way down the aisle—all the while, the leg in the metal brace remained completely stiff, and the brace gave a heavy, metallic *clunk* with each step.

As he passed, his stench caused Charlie to recoil. It was like rotten cabbage. Even the crowd seemed to wilt around him like weeds under poison.

Colin looked frightfully nervous as this man approached the lectern.

'Now just what d'you want Mr Monk?' Colin asked in a thin voice. 'You're too late if you mean to run for Alderman. Sign-up closed Thursday last.'

The one-eyed man, Monk, didn't answer. He swung his stiff leg up onto the hearth and stepped up after it and almost knocked the wooden lectern right over as he stumbled. A few laughs passed round the crowd.

'Still gettin' used to the surgery,' Monk spat, pointing at his empty socket. 'Thing about havin' only one eye is, it diminishes the depth perception.'

He steadied himself and put a gnarled hand on Colin's chest and pushed him aside without a word.

'Very clever of yer,' Monk said, in a gravelly snarl, 'to arrange this election behind me back. Is this what yers resort to now Alderman Bibble's dead? Holdin' secret sign-ups and schedulin' meets at the crack o' dawn like a bunch of vicious snakes?'

'Let it go Monk,' someone heckled. 'We wouldn't vote for you even if you'd signed up on time.'

Monk glared at his interrupter until the man flushed pink.

'I know yers don't like me much round here—'

'Hear, hear!' someone yelled to a flutter of laughs.

'I know yers don't like me,' he repeated. 'An' that's okay. Yers don't *need* to like me. But yers must agree I care more for this village than anyone. I've been here longer than any of yers—'

'Aye, because you were born in eighteen-thirty-odd,' someone called and another titter of laughter dispersed around the crowd.

Monk smiled and somehow, Charlie thought, he looked more repulsive when he did. His teeth niggled like loose tombstones.

31

'*Point is*,' Monk pressed on decidedly, 'we all want the same thing. Diff'rence between someone like Glen here, an' someone like *me*, is that *I* can get the job done.'

Glen, the butcher, looked down at his feet.

'These kids've been trespassin' on our property, graffityin' our walls, an' leavin' a trail of broken glass an' cans an' condoms fer as long as I remember,' Monk growled. 'An' even when yer beloved Bibble was still with us, he couldn't get much of anything done.'

Somebody booed and Monk shrugged as though it was simply a matter of fact.

'We all liked Bibble,' he said, sounding as if he did not like Bibble very much at all. 'But he were a crappy Alderman an' you all know it.'

'We were village of the year three years ago,' a woman on the front row said.

'Aye, we were, aye,' Monk agreed. 'He had you all paint yer front doors and threw a scarecrow competition. *Hurrah* for that. But he din't sort out any of yer business did he? Didn't end any feuds. Or deal with the pumpkin thief? Or how about when Mr Greenbottle poisoned the ducks of Sowerberry?'

'There weren't no proof that were Jimmy Greenbottle.'

Monk grumbled something unintelligible. It was obvious to him he wasn't winning the crowd over.

'All's I'm supposin' is this: yer let me be yer Alderman fer one month. Two tops. An' if yer don't think I'm doing a good job of it, I'll resign.'

'Oh, just let him join the ballot, Colin,' someone said. 'I've got an appointment coming in at eight and I need to get home for the school run first.'

'If yers put me on that ballot not one stinkin' one of yers will vote fer me,' Monk hissed, banging his fist on the lectern. 'An' since yers went about this all sneaky-like, I'm askin' fer a fair chance to show yer what I can do. Let me be yer Alderman, jus' fer a week. If yer not happy, you can continue wi' this pony election an' I won't interfere none.'

There was some dissatisfied mumbling from the crowd. A few people looked to Colin for guidance. Meekly, he got back up behind the lectern and scratched at his beard.

'We-ll,' he said slowly. 'I can't just make your Alderman, even honorary as this position is. It must be a group decision, plain and simple, an' the final say comes from the council at Penrith. But what I *can* suggest is this: we're in much agreement the biggest threat to the reputation of this village is these kids, vandalising our property—'

A ripple of agreement passed through the room.

'So I put to you a challenge, Mr Monk.' Colin paused while Monk glowered at him. 'We're a small village and word gets around easy enough. I think if we can catch some of these kids in the act, stick 'em in a cell for a night, scare 'em a bit to make an example out of 'em, then it'll make the next lot think twice in future. If you can catch them, Mr Monk, we'll have a serious talk about instating you.'

There was some outcry to this proposition, but Colin silenced the audience.

'It's only fair,' he insisted. 'If Monk does a good job, we should let him do it. It's not about friendship or popularity. We need someone who's got the best interest of Gallows at heart. And I do believe Mr Monk has that.'

Monk didn't look at all pleased with this agreement, Charlie thought. But he clearly didn't have much in the way of leverage.

'Fine,' he grumbled, shaking Colin's hand roughly and then leaving the lectern. He made his way back down the aisle, dragging his bad leg across the wood, apparently in a hurry to leave before Colin could change his mind.

Monk shoved past Charlie on his way to the door. His empty socket secreted a globule of pus that he collected in his arthritic fingers and flicked on the ground as he stormed outside.

Colin looked sheepishly at the congregation and held up his hands in apology. They had erupted once more into bickering, and Charlie suddenly realised he had been here for over five minutes and had had no opportunity to ask for directions.

Now, he decided, was as good a time as any. So somewhat tentatively, he stepped forward and cleared his throat.

'Excuse me…'

A few people looked round but the bickering went on.

'Excuse me!' he called again.

Colin held the clipboard up to his eyes and squinted over.

'Can we help you, young man?'

More heads turned now.

'Our car won't make it up the hill,' Charlie explained. 'I was wondering if there was another way around the village?'

A man sat close by stood up. He was easily seven foot tall. His dark hair was greased back into a quiff and thick sideburns clung to his chin.

'I'm headed that way myself, just now I am,' he said in a thick Irish accent. 'And I've had enough of this twaddle. Come on, I'll run ye over.'

'Great, thank you,' Charlie said, following the man outside into the bright sun. 'I'm heading to a place called The Barrow. Do you know it?'

'Know it?' the man smiled. 'I own the place. Name's Murphy.'

Chapter 5

Jim Murphy lived in a little thatch-roofed cottage beside the parish church. It was just a two-minute walk from The Packhorse, so by the time Charlie had filled Emily in on the events of the pub—about Mr Monk, the village meeting, bumping into The Barrow's landlord—and then turned the car back round, Murphy was sitting in his pickup truck, waiting to go.

He led them round the edge of the graveyard along a dirt road where a lime-green truss bridge pulled into view. Murphy's arm popped out of the window and he pointed to a sign: FENTON BRIDGE – CLOSED. Instead of crossing it, he led them along the banks of the river for a mile or two until the river disappeared into the earth and they could cross to a dirt road on the other side.

Charlie peered over the edge at the water as they passed. It was so thick with freshwater algae it looked like pea soup. He had a sudden mental image of the car tipping into the bulrushes, twenty feet below. He wasn't certain how good an idea this off-roading was. The car might have struggled going uphill, but cutting across such bumpy terrain felt just as hazardous.

Eventually, they passed a small cottage and found paved road again. This led them back onto Twin Hills East where the road plateaued. They had successfully bypassed the Gallows tor.

The end to their journey was much less problematic. Over on the left, the Yarrowmoor Mountain loomed, while a bright, grassy field flanked along the right. It soon filled with trees that became a thick wood.

'That must be Greenwood,' Emily said, reading the map. 'And that field we just passed is called Sunny Green.'

Murphy slowed at the edge of the wood where a path ran into its heart. His hand reappeared from the window again to warn Charlie of a pothole, cleverly disguised as an enormous gorge. A sign in the treeline said, *Welcome to The Barrow – Beware of pothole!*

The truck turned into the wood and Charlie followed close behind. It was dense, the trees were old and wide and the canopy was thick. But life still managed to thrive on the floor. What looked like a pink brick road was a carpet of petals. It reminded Charlie of The Mall and he imagined Murphy's truck in front was his escort, and The Barrow, which they soon reached, was Buckingham Palace.

The truck stopped on the driveway and its tires crunched on the gravel. The engine died and Murphy got out.

The mud-spattered windshield of Emily's little blue car provided their first view of The Barrow. It was a rustic and old-fashioned cabin, partially recessed into an ancient gully but elevated from the ground on several feet of brick with decking built of a rich, sturdy wood. At the foot of the porch steps was an old barrel with *The Barrow* painted across it.

They got out of the car and admired the place with smiles. Above the clearing was a wash of bright blue sky and its light permeated the wood wherever the canopy wasn't. Although they were in the middle of such a dense wood, the treeline made a wide circle around the house and large driveway so that plenty of sun found its way through.

Charlie had just opened the boot to take out their suitcases when Murphy called him over.

'Fella. C'mere.'

Murphy leaned over the decking and pointed to a black, metal box screwed to the barrel with his cigar. 'I've put a spare key in that wee lockbox there. Code's nineteen-sixty-six. Should be easy enough for an English fella to remember, eh? I'll leave you with this one.' (He handed over another key). 'Now if there's any problems, you've my number don't ye?'

'Rose has it,' Charlie said. 'She'll be here soon.'

Murphy nodded. 'Course. Well ye know where I live? Street's called Gravesend, by the church. Have a grand time now.'

He got back into his car. Charlie thanked him and in a cough of black exhaust fumes, the truck disappeared down The Mall.

'What did he say?' asked Emily. She was busy unloading crates of alcohol from the back seat of the car.

'Said he lives by the church on the other side of the village and he's put a spare key in the lockbox.'

'You should have asked him which way the Spreywater is.'

She yanked the car keys from him and went to the boot of the car.

'Goodness!' she shrieked. 'You scared me half to death!'

Charlie leaned round to see what had startled her. At the foot of the car, staring up at them, was a dopey-looking beast. He was a gangly thing with long, thin legs like a baby horse, but was ostensibly a dog. He cocked his head and a globule of drool poured from his mouth.

'Where've you come from?' asked Emily, stroking him while looking around the clearing.

'Trev!' A gruff voice called out. 'Trevor? Where're yeh boy?'

Twigs snapped behind them and a tall man appeared in the gap between the trees, leaning on a long stick. If he was surprised to find other people in the clearing, he didn't show it. He cleared his throat and reached down for his dog.

'There ya're, Trev. What yeh doing here, boy? You know yeh not to be round here. Let's be 'aving you.'

'He's a gorgeous dog,' Emily said. 'What is he?'

'Trouble, that's what. Come on Trev, let's get you home.'

He clipped a lead onto Trevor's collar and headed back into the wood.

'Wait,' Emily called after him. 'Do you live near here?'

'Aye,' the old man called back without turning round. 'Little cottage, other side of Sunny Green. Must be off.'

'Wait,' she said again. 'Maybe you could help us?'

The man hesitated. He was a towering figure, but doing his best to blend in with the foliage. Green Wellingtons, green dungarees, green jacket, a white shirt—though checked with green lines—and an old green flat cap. He didn't look the type to solicit company.

'Alright, alright,' he said gruffly, stepping back over. 'How can I help yehs?'

'Great. We've just arrived for the weekend you see. We'll be here until Monday,' said Emily.

'Okay?' The old man scratched at his whiskers and wondered how he fit in to all of this.

37

'My name's Charlie Bloom,' said Charlie, 'and this is Emily Seymour.' He held his hand out and the old man shook it.

'Bramble.'

'How do you do?' asked Emily.

'We were just wondering if you could give us some sense of the land. Where's the closest lake, for example?'

Mr Bramble leaned back on his stick. 'Well, yehs're in Greenwood now.' He pointed the stick back along The Mall out of wood. 'Back through there yeh've got main road. Watch for the pothole, mind. Size of an Olympic swimming pool. At the road, tek a right. *That's* your way t'nearest lake. Spreywater it's called. There's a harbour and a few places to eat and what have yeh— providing you like seafood, that is. And then there's the big mountain—'

'Oh, yes, we saw it on the drive in.'

Bramble tipped his hat and spat into the weeds. 'That's the Yarrowmoor,' he said. 'Round here it's known as the right tit.'

'The right *tit*?'

'Aye,' he pointed through the wood in the general direction of Gallows village.

'Gallows is the left tit, Yarrow's the right. Geddit?'

'I see.'

'Mm. Now t'get to Gallows, yeh wanna tek a left at the pothole. 'Bout a mile away. There's two boozers there. The Packhorse and The White Pony.' He sized them up again. 'I recommend The *Pony* for you.'

'Right. I passed through The Packhorse before. Stumbled into a village meeting. This strange, one-eyed man was talking about an election.'

'One eye? At The Packhorse? Talking elections?' Bramble cackled with delight. 'That'll be Fletcher Monk.' He wiped away a dribble of saliva that had accumulated at the corner of his mouth. 'Mean sort is old Monk. Owns a dairy farm back yonder the village. Big red barn in Underwood. Let me give yeh a piece of advice. Yeh'll do well to avoid it. D'you understand me? Monk don't like bloody tourists.'

'He doesn't like *much* from what I heard,' Charlie agreed.

'Aye. He's a mean old bugger. Despises kids. But not without reason. Group of 'em keep wanderin' onto his farm. Cow-tipping, you know. So I'll say it again. Yeh'll do well to avoid his farm all together.'

'What will he do?' asked Emily, with some fear in her voice.

Mr Bramble looked at her as if he thought it a queer sort of question. 'Eh?'

'If someone was on his land,' she said. 'What will this Fletcher Monk fellow do? Shoot them?'

'Shoot 'em? Ha!' Bramble cackled again. He looked like a man who hadn't enjoyed a good laugh for a while. 'Don't be daft, lass. This en't the Wild West. This is Cumbria! Just stay away, d'yeh hear me? Big, red barn an' a sign for his "Monk Milk".'

'Crikey. Does he lactate it himself?'

'Wouldn't be surprised. Queer fella,' Bramble said.

'And what about shops?' asked Charlie. 'Are there shops in Gallows?'

Bramble looked annoyed by the question. 'Aye there's shops. D'you think we're backwards or sommet? There's a school, a church, couple of caffs and on most Sundays, a market. There's even a library. Believe it or not, lad, some of us can read.'

'Oh, I didn't mean anything by it, I just—' Charlie cut himself short because Bramble was already off, with Trevor following him through the wood, his tail swinging low from side to side. 'Thank you!' Charlie called after him. 'I'm Charlie Bloom, by the way. And this is Emily Seymour. We'll be here until Monday!'

'So you said,' the old man called back.

Emily flashed her crooked smile. 'Well! The locals certainly seem a welcoming bunch now don't they?'

39

Chapter 6

The Barrow was open-plan. The kitchen and living area constituted the main space, with a corridor leading off to two bedrooms at the other end of the house. A narrow staircase led up to an attic, though this was being used for storage and Charlie found he could barely fit in amongst the old dressers and wardrobes that blocked the top of the stairs.

He went back out to the car and brought in the last of their alcohol, standing the crate on the large, kitchen island. It was made of Corian and reminded him of an autopsy table.

Emily had already brought in her suitcase and was admiring the hot tub through a set of dazzling patio doors at the end of the living area. It was built into the decking outside and surrounded by a cubicle of trellises, with ivy and fairy lights threaded through the holes of the lattice.

The living and dining area had a rustic, cosy feel to it. A few old settees covered in knitted blankets were grouped around a coal fireplace. Attached to a bracket on the wall was a plasma TV. Charlie flicked it on and the yellow phosphors had burned into the screen giving everyone the appearance of having jaundice.

The two bedrooms were identical, except for being mirror images of one another. Both had an en suite, and while Emily unpacked her clothes across the bed, Charlie dotted his toiletries around the sink.

'What time are they getting here?' he asked.

He noticed he looked tired and unshaven so he took his razor out and laid it beside his toothbrush over a flannel.

'I'm not sure,' Emily answered. 'Rose said they planned to set off an hour after we did but I've never known Rose to be on time for anything in her life.'

'Mm,' Charlie nodded. 'What do you know about this walking steroid, then?'

'*Don't* call him that,' Emily said, looking at Charlie's reflection in the mirror through the gap in the door.

'Why not? All I know about him is he played rugby and works at a gym. I'll bet he's got shoulders like a gorilla.'

40

She rolled her eyes and went back to folding her clothes.

'I don't know much about him myself. Just a few things Rose said.'

Charlie turned on the tap and let the sink fill with warm water. 'Such as?'

'That he's got a fantastic salary. That he drives this big expensive car, which he apparently loves more than anything, *including* my sister. I don't know the model but it's one of those big, black four-by-fours. And she *also* said his Little Tommy is quite unsuitably named.'

'She doesn't like to *brag* though.'

Emily came over to the en suite and ran her finger along the striking plate of the lock.

'Well, it wasn't *all* bragging. She did say they argue a lot and about *everything*. He's got a ferocious temper, and Rose... Well, *you* know what she's like. It sounds very volatile.'

'Great,' Charlie grumbled. 'When's the wedding again?'

He spurted a handful of shaving foam into his palm and started to smear it across his jaw.

'I know it's dysfunctional but this is Rosalind we're talking about! Could you really imagine her with someone that *doesn't* talk back to her? She'd eat him alive.'

Charlie unbuttoned his shirt and wrapped a towel around his waist.

'Oh and *you* should get along with him!' Emily added as if something just came to her. 'He's a northerner!'

'From Manchester?'

'Yorkshire, I think. Anyway, you can ask him all this yourself when we go on this reconnoitre later.'

'Reconno-what?'

'Toire. Didn't I tell you?' She seemed to be playing coy, as if it had slipped her mind. 'We're going on a walk when they get here. It'll be a good way to get to know the area. And each other.'

She put her finger on Charlie's jaw to wipe away a dollop of excess shaving foam.

'Oh *don't* look like that,' she said. 'It'll be fun.'

41

'Yes,' he said. 'Fun.'

He turned back to the mirror and put the razor to his face but cut himself and a little droplet of blood hit the water and turned it milky pink.

When he was shaved he left Emily to unpack and wandered back along the hall to the kitchen. It had taken Emily forty-two hours to pack and he knew it would be a bloody miracle if she finished unpacking before it was time to go back home. Comparatively, it had taken Charlie just thirty seconds. He had placed his suitcase under the lips of his washing machine and let it vomit his entire wardrobe directly inside.

After he put all of their alcohol away, he decided to have another look upstairs. It was a cluttered mess, with cabinets, mirrors and wall-art stacked up against the roof beams all along one wall, while a clunky desk took up most of the other. In between was an assortment of bin bags, chairs and a chest of old records and everything was blanketed in two inches of dust.

However, it was a lot lighter in the loft than he expected. The triangular roof had just one window, but the roof rose up above the canopy of Greenwood—before Charlie had even navigated the maze of old furniture, he recognised the flat-topped Yarrowmoor, perfectly framed by this window. He wondered whether this whole cabin had been built with such a view in mind.

He made his way through the sea of debris until he reached the window and was pushed up awkwardly against the glass while a flirtatious coatrack caressed him. He scooted back and wiped a layer of grime from the window.

'Don't look down,' he said, swallowing.

But he couldn't help himself. He peered over at the woodland floor below and his legs buckled. It wasn't really all that high, but he wasn't good with heights.

'It's okay,' he breathed.

He had closed his eyes and when he opened them again, he was looking dead-ahead at a tall and skinny tree. Its long branch seemed to be reaching out to him. There was even a face in the knots of the trunk.

'Charlie? Where are you?' Emily called.

She made him jump and he whipped round, sending the flirtatious coatrack spinning. One of its arms swung into a vase, resting on top of an old stack of Radio Times magazines. It wobbled on the spot for a second. Charlie lunged to grab it but it slipped through his fingers and shattered on the floor. A thick rust-coloured puddle bled out.

'Oh, bugger,' he muttered, looking round for something to mop it up with.

He pulled a pair of old, velvet curtains from a pile and began dabbing at the water, but it quickly drained away through the floorboards, leaving him to dab at the dark red residue with his fingertips.

Chapter 7

Charlie and Emily were in the hot tub when Tom Darrow's Mercedes pulled onto the drive at ten o'clock.

They had the radio on, trailing from the house through the patio doors, and were on their second bottle of Champagne. The bubbles frothed around them as he unwound the muselet with six small twists. The coil and cage came loose and he turned the bottle. It gave a sigh and the cork popped out as a breath of white fog escaped.

Charlie poured two flutes and leaned across the tub to stand the bottle on the table. As he did, he heard the powerful roar of the V6 engine. He cocked his head to the side like a dog.

'What is it?' Emily asked.

With some irritation, Charlie answered. 'They're here.'

He hopped out of the tub, towel-dried himself and slid the patio doors open, but stopped on the mat so as not to drip water through the house.

The front door opened at the same moment and Rose burst into the house. For such a petite woman she demanded a great deal of attention. In a lot of ways, she was very similar to Emily. Both had wide expressive eyes and the same crooked half-smile. But where Emily was a level-headed brunette, Rose was an over-the-top blonde.

She hadn't noticed Charlie standing there. She marched straight to the kitchen sink, gripped the edges of it as if she were about to collapse and threw her head over the bowl.

'You're okay Rosie,' she told herself, wiping the corner of her eye with a palm. 'Just add it to the tower, that's what you should do. Just add it to that tower of resentment we're building.'

She filled a glass with water and drank the whole thing in two gulps.

Tom came in then, scowling after her. He was a hulking figure and he carried two enormous travel bags in one hand and a crate of beer in his other.

'You daft bloody cow, are you stupid or summat?' he barked. 'Jumping out a moving car like that! You've lost your fucking head.'

Rose spun back around and wagged an admonitory finger at him. 'Don't you use that sort of language with me, Thomas Darrow!'

'Well I don't speak any other. I could try it in French if you like.'

'Oh, har-har! You're positively *hysterical*!'

'None of this is my fault, y'know,' Tom shot back. 'It's that stupid fucking farmer! If there's so much as a *dent* on the Merc I swear to God, Rose—'

'Oh, I wish you'd just let it *go*! I'm fed up of *hearing* about it!' Rose wailed.

'Let it go?' he scoffed. 'I just got her back from the garage last week and now she's making that chugging sound, like a chainsaw fucking a tractor.'

Rose looked up at him quite severely with her bottom row of teeth jutting out and when she spoke, it was in a screamed whisper: 'We've done nothing but argue for the last fifty-eight miles and I've had just about enough of it thank-you-very-much! We're *here* now and there's not much you can do about your stupid car until we get back to London—'

'If we even *make* it back. Do you have any idea how much it'll cost if I have to have her towed? Course you don't 'cause you don't pay for bugger-all, do you?'

They locked eyes for a moment, like two animals across the watering hole. On one side, Tom Darrow was a particularly hairy ungulate. He reminded Charlie of the tusked boar that sat at the foot of their stairs on Milk Street. On his other side, Rosalind Seymour—petite and delicate, but never fragile—stood tense, like a lioness. Her thick, blonde hair was scraped back into a ponytail and the fly-aways stuck out by her ears like whiskers. She clacked her long, pink nails against her water glass like talons, before suddenly hurling it at Tom like a cricket ball.

He managed to dodge it with some impressive reflex and the glass shattered across the doorframe behind him.

Rose seemed to regret throwing the glass the very second it left her hand because she covered her mouth with her fingertips and uttered a quiet, 'Oops!'

Tom wore a monstrous scowl as he turned back round. Charlie half-expected dragon's smoke to come leaking from his nostrils.

'Clear that up *now*,' Tom said in a deep, but calm, voice. 'Before the dog cuts his paws on it.'

'The *dog* has a name,' Rose said, trying to remain prickly herself, but turning a little pink in the face.

'Just get it cleared up,' Tom said, dropping his crate of beer onto the kitchen island. 'And while you're at it, let me tell you summat else. If I ever see that one-eyed little prick again, I'll fucking kill him for what he's done to the Merc.'

'*That's it!*' Rose snapped. 'If I have to hear one more thing about that silly car of yours, I'll go out there and put my keys to it myself, do you hear me?'

Tom went to argue back, but before he could, the patio door slid open behind Charlie and something furry brushed his leg. A huge, fluffy white dog pounced into the room and it caught Tom's attention. He looked over and noticed for the first time that they were not alone.

Emily followed behind the dog and Rose spun round too. Her face contorted from anger to elation as she spotted them by the mat.

'Oh! Emmy!' Rose shrieked.

She whizzed straight past Charlie and almost toppled her sister in a hug. She cradled Emily's head close to her chest and shut her eyes tightly. 'My *word* it's been *far* too long, Emmy.'

'It's only been… three days…' Emily wheezed.

'*So* sorry we're late,' Rose said, finally releasing her. 'I was trying to call you; didn't you get my messages?'

'No, we didn't bring our phones remember,' Emily said. 'We're "off the grid". How were you calling me? Did *you* bring your phone?'

'Oh, no,' Rose shook her head vigorously. 'Tom's car has this thing. It can call people. Anyway, he got us lost and we asked this farmer—'

'I were just the chauffeur,' Tom called over. '*You* were doing directions. Or meant to be any road.'

'He absolves himself of all guilt,' Rose explained, rolling her eyes. 'It was *my* fault of course. I *made* him drive like an idiot. It's that ridiculous car. Every time he gets behind the wheel he thinks he's Jeremy Clarkson.'

'Bullshit.'

'It most certainly is *not*. Whenever you're behind the wheel of that car you drive ten miles per hour too quickly and become a smidgeon more racist,' she turned back to her sister. 'He's in a foul mood. We needed directions and we spotted this horrible little one-eyed fellow back along the main road there and he tried to send us off a bridge! Tom's just absolutely *furious* about it.'

'Of course I am. Them tyres weren't cheap.' He cracked open a can of lager and took a swig.

'You've only yourself to blame,' Rose told him, wrinkling her nose. 'He bought himself these ugly boy-racer wheels that make him feel like he's in the Formula One. Remind me how much they were, babe? A thousand pounds for five, wasn't it?'

'*Tyres* were a grand. *Wheels* were double that.'

'See? It's com*plete*ly barmy.'

'A grand's barmy for *tyres*,' Tom smirked, 'but it's alright for a bloody *handbag*, innit?'

'It is when it's Mulberry!' Rose gasped, failing to see how he could compare the two things. 'And my handbag didn't just get itself stuck trying to go over a bridge, thank-you-very-much!

'It was truly awful,' Rose continued. '*I* had to try and reverse while *he* pushed. Me! In control of a car that size! You remember how many times I failed my test, don't you Emmy—?'

'Fourteen, wasn't it?'

'What did Daddy use to say? That I'd wind up in the Guinness World Records before I ever passed. And now my feet are absolutely *killing* me! Goodness, I'm all cramped up. I didn't get time to do my yoga this morning and the Merc is *not* as spacious as it looks.' She feigned humility then by blushing. 'Gosh, would you just listen to me! You probably think I'm just *terrible* complaining about the Merc when you drove up in that funny little thing! You really ought to get yourself a new car, Emmy, it's practically falling apart. How long have you been here?'

47

Christ, she had been here for thirty seconds and already given Charlie a headache.

'Since seven,' Emily told her. 'We left early. But I think Charlie met that one-eyed farmer of yours.'

Rose opened her mouth as she turned to Charlie, only just noticing—or *pretending* to only just notice—that he existed.

'Oh, *Charlie*!' she said. 'Where did *you* come from?'

'Out there,' he pointed through the patio doors.

'How *are* you? My goodness, you must think I'm so rude, mustn't you?'

'Unreservedly.'

'No you *must* do!' Rose said. Her face had contorted into something she imagined was compassion. Her eyebrows were pulled back and she pursed her lips like a duck's bill. 'Am I just completely, one hundred per cent awful?'

'No you're just—'

'I *am* though, *aren't* I?' she shook her head. 'Oh Charlie. Charlie, Charlie, Charlie. I *do* hope everything's okay between us after, well, you know... *that weekend* and all the... unpleasantness?'

'Of course,' Charlie said, feeling his cheeks burn.

'I wouldn't want it to cause any unpleasantness *this* weekend,' she said. 'Especially considering Pepper and all.'

'Pepper?'

'My Chihuahua!' Rose squeaked. She smacked Charlie playfully on the arm. 'But you said you were sorry and Pepper had a long life—even if the vet *did* say her spine never fully recovered. But look, that's all in the past now, isn't it? And I just *know* you'll get along with Teddy! I don't think it would be possible for you to stomp on *him*.' She kneeled beside the enormous dog so he could lick her all over the face. 'My Teddybear's the best doggy in the world, *aren'ju boy*? Yes you are! *Yes* you are.'

Charlie could hardly look away. When Rose stood back up, a matt of blonde hair was glued to her cheek with dog saliva.

'And how's...' she stepped closer and whispered, 'How's *You-know-who*?'

'Harry? He's... you know. He's Harry.'

She tilted her head in a pitying smile. Then whipped her head back toward Emily.

'You've got yourself a keeper there, Emmy,' she said. 'I bet Charlie doesn't give you *half* the headaches Tom gives me. My head was like a split watermelon this morning.'

'And it had nowt to do with that bottle of rosé you polished off, did it?' Tom winked.

'I won't tell you again Thomas!' Rose snapped, turning on him. 'He's been an unbelievable nightmare the whole drive.'

'*I* have?'

'Oh! But where are my *manners*?' she said. 'I ought to introduce you! Ding, ding, ding!' She pretended to ring an invisible glass with a non-existent fork. When they moved in around her, she clapped her hands together giddily. 'Now, this is Charlie Bloom—'

'Good to meet you.'

'And you mate.'

'Tom's from *oop north*,' Rose said in a failed impression of a Yorkshireman. 'I don't even think they have *schools* where he's from, or if they do, nobody seems to have attended one. It's a dull little place filled with shutters and brothels.'

'And *she* thinks she's Mary Poppins.' Tom rolled his eyes. 'But I'll bet you could hear the Bow bells from where you were born, couldn't you?'

Rose looked appalled at the very idea. 'I most certainly could *not*!'

Tom winked again. 'Well it's good to meet you,' he said, disappearing Charlie's hand inside his great mitt while Rose scowled.

'And *this*,' she said, trying to smile again. 'Is my beautiful sister, Emily.'

Tom said, 'I were starting to think she didn't *want* us to meet the family or summat. Good to meet you, Emily.'

'Now then. Why don't you go and do something useful like bring our things in, hm?'

Tom took the last swig of his lager and planted the can down on the kitchen island, then went out to the car with Teddy padding behind.

Charlie noticed something drip into the can from above. He looked at the ceiling and saw a small red spot had formed, with another little icicle ready to drop. It looked like blood.

'He is driving me *bonkers* Em!' Rose whispered when Tom disappeared outside. 'Just absolutely stark-raving mad!'

'I know. But you've had a long drive,' Emily said. 'Cooped up for hours. Why don't Charlie and I go and dry off and let you two settle in? We can all meet back here before the walk?'

'All right,' Rose agreed. 'But I really ought to do my Tai Chi first. I had no time to do my yoga this morning and I'm all cramped up. Is… he okay?'

She meant Charlie. He had slid the barstool from under the island and was climbing onto it.

'What are you doing?' Emily asked.

He wiped away the red spot on the ceiling with two fingers and they turned moist with a gritty residue.

'Charlie? What is it?'

'When I was in the loft before—I knocked something over, a vase or something, and this rusty water poured out. It must be coming through the ceiling. It looks like the house is bleeding.'

He looked back up and the mark had faded.

'Looks like it's gone now,' Emily said. 'I wouldn't worry about it.'

Teddy led Tom back inside, who set down three hot-pink suitcases.

'We've taken the room on the left,' Emily pointed down the hall. 'We'll meet back here in… Shall we say, an hour?'

Rose agreed and they said their goodbyes before Tom led her down the hall. Emily started off after them but turned back round to find Charlie was still on the kitchen island looking at the blood-red spot.

He wasn't sure why but something about it troubled him. It felt like an omen.

Chapter 8

The four residents of The Barrow went off to get ready for the afternoon's walk. Tom and Rose started rowing about something before their door had even closed. Emily just rolled her eyes.

'It's going to be like this all weekend, isn't it?' Charlie asked.

'I sincerely hope not.'

Charlie pulled on a clean shirt and decided to go and sit in the kitchen where it was quiet. He took a stool beside the island and was staring at the ceiling in a daze when Tom came in from down the hall.

'Sorry 'bout her,' he said, looking a little bit embarrassed. 'She were in a mood before we even set off. But she'll calm down when she's done her makeup and had summat to drink.'

Tom had brought a milk crate of spirits with him and he stood over it trying to choose what to drink. From the look on his face, he was about to give himself an embolism. But before his thick temple vein had chance to burst, he grinned and plucked a bottle of whisky out.

'Twenty-five-year-old Glendochart,' he said, more to himself than to Charlie. 'Single-malt Scotch. I were saving this for a special occasion—or an emergency. What d'you say? You a whisky drinker mate?'

Charlie had barely been listening. He tore his eyes from the red stain on the ceiling to the grin on Tom's face and then to the whisky in his hand and realised he was being offered a drink. 'Oh, yeah, sure.'

Tom poured them a finger each and slid one across the island.

'Summat the matter?' Tom asked.

Charlie's eyes were back on the ceiling.

'What does that look like to you?' Charlie asked.

Tom looked at the mark and squinted.

'Does it look like a skull?' Charlie wondered.

'Uh. Not really,' Tom said.

From the look on his face, he was starting to think Charlie was a bit weird. He had a sip of whisky and they sat in silence for a while until Teddy woke from his nap on the rug and plotted over, his great paws clattering on the wood.

Tom poured another finger and held the glass out for the dog, who stuck his tongue in and lapped at it.

After an uncomfortable silence, Tom said, 'So, uh… Rose tells us you're a writer?'

'In… theory,' Charlie answered slowly.

'What d'you mean by that?'

'Only that I never actually write anything.'

Tom chuckled and his broad shoulders heaved. 'I knew you'd do summat like that, you know. I can see it in you. You're obviously not a Hemingway, man-of-adventure. You're the brainy, quiet type. But you *look* like a writer, if you know what I mean.'

'What does a writer look like?'

Tom thought about it. 'I dunno. Curly-haired, about five-ten. Obsessed with the bloody ceiling.'

Charlie had been staring up again. He laughed, feeling himself blush a little, and sipped his whisky.

Tom topped them both up and raised his glass.

'To new friends,' he said. 'And a weekend of peace and quiet.'

Charlie had to wonder if anything in that toast would wind-up coming true. He raised his glass and they chinked together.

After a few minutes, Tom got to his feet, trying to hide a mischievous grin. 'Come with us,' he said. 'I've gotta show you summat.'

He led Charlie out of the house. His Mercedes dwarfed Emily's little blue car. It was matte black with custom plates and chrome spinners with red stripes around the rubber of the tyres. More sunlight was pooling in from the gap in the canopy and it twinkled from the glass of the windows in the way Emily's didn't. Charlie cupped his eyes to them and looked inside. It had racing seats and red panelling and LED lights along the dashboard.

Charlie tried his best to be polite. 'Wow, yeah, that's certainly, you know, a car.'

Tom took him round to the back, looking smug. 'This way.'

He opened the boot and slid a polypropylene case across the

floor of the car. He unfastened an overlapping interlock and held it shut for a moment to manufacture anticipation while he beamed at Charlie.

'You ready?'

He threw back the lid.

'Jesus,' Charlie breathed.

Tom was elated. He reached into the case and lifted a rifle out.

'That's a—a *gun*?' Charlie said.

'Don't shit yourself, Dickens. It's only an air rifle. But you wouldn't know it from just looking, would you?'

It was silver and brown with iron sights. In one quick motion, Tom snapped the barrel forward, which startled Charlie whose mouth had gone a little dry. Tom was grinning from ear to ear. He pointed down the neck at the joint. 'Air goes in here. Pellets this side.'

He held the rifle over his forearm where it bent at the barrel and he reached back inside the case. He took a box of BB pellets out and rattled them.

'Point twenty-fives,' he said. 'When I was fifteen I were about to go pro. Rugby. Donny Knights were *this close* to signing me. One of these nasty little fuckers killed my career.'

He glazed over behind the eyes for a second. He put his foot up on the back bumper and rolled his shorts over his knee. There was a little bump the size of a garden pea under the skin by his kneecap, and he wobbled it with a finger.

'Lucky for me this one's just plastic,' he said. 'The ones I've got here are made of lead. Get hit with one of these? Well... Let's just say there ain't a great deal of difference between a shotgun slug and a lead BB.'

He shook the box of pellets again and dropped it into the case. He took his foot off the bumper, snapped the barrel of the gun back upright and put it in Charlie's hands, who took it awkwardly, like a new father with a baby.

'Well hold it properly then!' Tom barked.

'How?'

'Just hold it. There you go, that's it, Lock-Stock. Try it out. There's a couple of squirrels up that tree, get one of them.'

'I can't do that!' Charlie said. 'Aren't they, I don't know, protected under some sort of… Wild Animal Act or something like that?'

'Nah, they're vermin. Bushy-tailed little cunts. It's actually *illegal* to let them live. It's every Englishman's duty to immediately destroy them on sight.'

Charlie watched the squirrels on the branch. He imagined they were married with kids. They were in the middle of a divorce, sure, but he didn't want to be responsible for making orphans of the twins.

'I don't think I can do it!' He lowered the gun.

Tom chuckled and snatched it back off him. He laid it down on its bed of foam while the squirrels ran off into the tree.

'It's alright. You've never fired a gun before,' he said. 'But that's summat every man should do if he wants to call himself a man. What d'you say we put you right this afternoon?'

Chapter 9

At midday, the four of them and Teddy left for their walk. They wound up the hill through Gallows village and stopped briefly to take in the views.

Tom carried the polypropylene case, which held his rifle, the pellets and a canister of CO_2. It also held a row of targets. He had decided they would be having a friendly competition before heading back to The Barrow that day and announced it to great indifference.

On their way down the other side of the tor, they came up to The Packhorse. When Charlie mentioned it was the pub in which he had met Fletcher Monk, Tom's one-eyed-farmer, Tom dropped the rifle case on the ground and stormed inside looking like he had murder on his mind.

'Now, really! Just *what* does he think he's going to do?' Rose groaned. 'He's more mouth than muscle.'

They waited for a few moments until Tom stormed back out, his jaw twitching. 'Wasn't in there,' he mumbled.

He picked the case back up and went on ahead.

They kept on straight. At the foot of the hill was a sign for Gravesend. Charlie paused at the kerb and looked down the cobbles. There were just two buildings at the bottom. One was the old Parish Church of St Paul, which appeared to be sinking into the marshy graveyard, causing its spire to point crookedly back up the tor. The other building was Jim Murphy's thatch-roofed cottage along Gravesend, with a white picket fence around a vegetable patch.

They swapped the main road for a winding country lane. Rose let Teddy off the lead and he chased butterflies and then clouds and then ducks across the road. A tractor rolled by and an old Scotsman shouted, 'Get that wee dog on a lead!' so Rose clipped his lead back on until they arrived at the edge of Underwood into a field of yellow grass.

The girls fell behind and Tom showed no sign of slowing as he led them straight into the sun. Charlie trailed a few paces behind him while trying to think of something to say, but his imagination had died a death. He looked over the field on the right. It was part of a farm and dotted with cows, surrounded by a chest-high fence.

Tom had stopped walking to lean on the fence. The little farmhouse was only visible as a smudge on the sky. Its chimney was smoking. There were a few stone buildings dotted around it with a mesh enclosure of chicken coops to the side, but closest to the road was a deep-red barn.

'What's the matter?' Charlie asked, noticing the look on his face.

'That one-eyed farmer, who tried sending my car into the drink. You said he was called Monk?' Tom pointed at the large red barn. A sign along its outer wall read: MONK MILK. 'This must be where the bastard lives.'

Charlie swallowed. He saw how Tom's temple vein was slithering around again, and his knuckles were white where he gripped the handle of his rifle case. He was half expecting him to storm right up to the farmhouse and confront the man.

But he didn't. After a second, Tom spat on the ground and said, 'Come on. Let's keep moving.'

They walked for another hour, first through a valley of rocks that sparkled like silver, then along the banks of an old watermill, which pedalled through a lazy river before they came across a convoy of sailboats that drifted across a small lake like clouds through the sky.

Eventually they rested under the only tree in a wide meadow, another mile or so from Monk's farm. There was an upturned log thirty feet away.

'There. I'll set up the targets,' Tom said.

Teddy hopped around him while he kneeled in the long grass to unfasten the case. He took the row of targets out and stood them over the upturned log. Five metal discs were fitted at equal intervals, each on a hinge. When one was hit with a BB pellet it would flip back against the log.

Tom took the rifle from the case and held it over his forearm with the barrel open. The other three lined up under the shadow of the tree like cadets ready to be drilled. Charlie had the feeling Tom was enjoying his role as General.

'Don't put your finger over the trigger unless you mean to shoot,' he instructed. 'And never mean to shoot if there's someone in front of you. If you mean to shoot, you mean to hit a target. I couldda gone professional with rugby. Donny Knights were *this close* to signing me till I got tagged. So *be careful*.'

Charlie thought he saw Rose roll her eyes.

'Now there's a slight bitta recoil—that's the air releasing. So watch your shoulder for the kick and keep your eye away from the sight. Unless you wanna shatter your cheekbone.' He stepped back and pointed at the targets on the log. 'There's five targets on there. We'll take it in turns. Girls v. boys. First team to twenty wins. What d'you say?'

They agreed and he handed them each an orange hunting vest from the case.

'Put these on. Rose? You're up first.'

'Okay, but I'm *not* wearing that,' she said. 'It doesn't go with my outfit.'

She indicated her bright, white tracksuit, which was topped off with a pair of furry white ankle boots.

Tom waved round at the endlessness of the landscape. 'And who's gonna see you out here? You think there's paparazzi up the tree? What you wearing *that* for anyway?'

'What's wrong with it?' she asked.

'It's white, for starters.'

'*This*,' she said, snatching the rifle from him, 'is Balenciaga.'

She held the gun well. Tom circled her like an inappropriate golf instructor. He lifted her arms higher and slid her left hand down the forestock.

'That's it,' he said and stood back.

Rose aimed the barrel at the first target. She closed an eye and looked down the iron sights. Everyone behind leaned in to watch.

'Ready?' Tom called out. 'Set. Careful of the kick. Fire!'

Rose took her shot. The gun made a pathetic little sound but the lead pellet hitting the target echoed around the field. The target flipped over on its hinge and Tom's smile faltered for a second.

'Oh my goodness, I got it! I *got* it, Emmy!'

'Woo! Go Rose!'

'Easy, killer,' Tom said. 'You've got four more to go yet.'

Rose lifted the gun back up and looked very serious. She took aim, closed an eye again and then fired. She missed the second target and Charlie caught the relief dance over Tom's face. But on her third shot, the sound of contact echoed back around them and the target flipped over to join its brother. She remained still and moved her arms an inch to the side and fired again. The third target went down. Tom turned almost as white as her tracksuit. She took a deep breath and pulled the trigger and the fourth target went down. Rose stared at the set of targets as if she didn't believe it herself and then threw her arms in the air, screaming with delight.

'Can you believe it, Emmy? I'm a *sharp*shooter!'

'Alright, Annie Oakley,' Tom said, snatching the rifle from her. 'Beginner's luck, that's all it were.'

'Hardly, fatso,' she teased. 'I'm just a natural.'

'A natural disaster,' Tom spat.

'Let's see what *you've* got, then.'

Tom went off to reset the targets. When he came back he handed the rifle to Charlie.

'Alright, Dickens, you're up.' There was sweat running down his temple. 'Don't let me down now. We've got this in the bag.' He leaned in closer so the girls couldn't hear. 'Between you and me, it tapers a few degrees to the right.'

The girls crowded behind as Charlie got ready to shoot. He held the rifle to his eye. He had no confidence in his ability to fire a gun. He couldn't even tell if he was pointing at the first or second target from where he stood. He held his breath and pulled the trigger.

58

Chapter 10

Tom was in a foul mood as he packed the gun away.

'Sorry Tom,' Charlie said. 'Now we know not to give *me* the gun in an emergency.'

'You can say that again,' Tom mumbled.

He locked the case and then marched on ahead in a sulk.

They stopped off at a little pub called The Hungry Horse for a bite to eat and even there, Tom only spoke in monosyllabic grunts. By the time they left, it was starting to get dark and when they reached Monk's farm again, the sky was orange with purple streaks and then it was purple with orange streaks. The cows were like black boulders against it.

The girls had fallen behind and Charlie was trailing Tom thinking of something to say to break the ice. But he didn't need to. Tom had stopped quite suddenly in the road and Charlie almost bumped into him.

'What is it?' he asked.

'Sh. Look.' Tom pointed ahead. A hare was chewing on something in the middle of the road in the spotlight of a street lamp.

Tom laid the case in the grassy recess by the road, a devilish look coming over his face.

'Get down,' he urged.

Charlie knelt beside him and could feel the bats in his stomach start to flutter round their cave.

'Alright, Dickens,' Tom said, as he tied Teddy to the fence post by his lead. 'I'll show you how to *really* shoot.'

He unfastened the lid of the case. The hare's long ears twitched for a second and Tom froze, but the hare went on chewing. He slid the rifle out and put it in Charlie's hands. It felt heavier that it had before.

'Don't let me down now. Shoot like Hemingway.'

'You know Hemingway shot *himself*, don't you?'

'Aye, but he also shot a fuck-tonne of big game before that, didn't he?'

Charlie lifted the gun up. He didn't want to shoot the thing. He didn't even want to hold the rifle. But he pointed it at the hare regardless.

'Easy,' Tom whispered by his ear. 'Easy does it. Make sure you can see him through the sights before you shoot. Remember it tapers.'

Charlie squinted down the barrel through the iron sights. He lined the hare up but closed both his eyes before he squeezed the trigger. He could feel the pellet whizzing along the length of the gun. It zipped straight over the hare's head and tore up the grass two feet behind it. The hare stuck its head up and looked around, then leapt off the road into the recess by the fence.

'C'mon!' Tom said. 'He's getting away.'

There was a hole in the fence and the hare hopped through. Tom vaulted it as the hare made off toward the enclosure by the farmhouse, but Charlie hesitated. Teddy was up, watching Tom, and the girls were still a way off, just black silhouettes against the orange streaks of sunset.

'Oh, God,' Charlie moaned. 'What am I doing, Teddy?'

The dog cocked his head in pity and whimpered.

'Christ!'

He hoisted himself awkwardly over the fence and dropped onto the other side. A couple of cows looked round at him, chewing the cud.

''Scuse me,' he said, saluting one.

Tom was low in the grass, twenty feet from the enclosure. The henhouses lined the back wall, their pop-holes were open and the chickens were out, clucking noisily inside their mesh prison. The hare was nestled in the grass by the gate.

Charlie swallowed, looking over at Monk's farmhouse and praying the old farmer didn't appear at the window.

'C'mon, you can do this Charlie,' Tom said. 'It's not hard. Just aim for the eyes. That's the trick.'

'Alright,' Charlie agreed. The rifle was slung over his back. He swung it round and lifted it again.

He felt he had a lot to prove by now so he pointed it at the hare with sweat pooling down his neck. He closed an eye and pulled the trigger. The pellet hit the mesh enclosure, which rattled and caused a few chickens to squabble and flap about in disarray.

'Why did you do that?' Tom snapped.

'I didn't do it on purpose.'

The hare stuck its head back up and its nose twitched at the air. Then it was off again, back the way it had come. Tom snatched the rifle out of Charlie's hands and followed it with the barrel impatiently.

'I'll show you how it's done.'

The hare was halfway across the field when Tom fired. The pellet whistled over the hare yet again and struck one of the black boulders.

No, not a boulder. A cow.

The cow staggered back letting out a horrific, mangled howl. Then she zig-zagged left and right for a few paces before crumpling into a heavy pile.

'Oh, Jesus,' Charlie said.

'Oh, fuck,' Tom groaned.

They dashed over. In the middle of the cow's head, between her wide-eyed stare, was a small, dark hole. From the hole seeped a line of blood.

Yellow light spilled across the lawn. Charlie thought a floodlight had activated until he spun round and saw the farmhouse door had swung open. A familiar, bent-backed figure stood silhouetted against the light.

'Who's there?' The man called.

'It's Monk!' Charlie hissed. His heart was hammering. He was thinking back to the meeting he had witnessed at The Packhorse. Monk had been tasked with making an example of the kids that broke onto his farm. And now Charlie found himself on the other end of that task.

'Leg it!' Tom screamed and they shot off back toward the chest-high fence.

Teddy was barking with his front paws up on the wood. He was almost big enough to climb over.

Behind them, Monk was hollering. 'Bastards!' he screamed. 'What've yer done to me cow? Get back here! *Bastards*!'

Suddenly a deafening bang resounded through the field.

Charlie caught a glimpse of something silver in the old man's hand. Christ! The neurosis he had meant to leave on Milk Street must have found its way into his luggage and was now crawling up his chest like two hands trying to wrap themselves around his throat.

Monk was after them, dragging his caged leg across the mud with fierce determination. A great burst of sparks exploded from the barrel of his rifle and its great boom echoed round the far-off mountains again.

The chickens screeched, the cows howled and the daffodils swayed with a shudder. Over by the fence, the girls had rushed over and were untying Teddy from the post frantically.

'Run!' Tom shouted to them, waving his arms in the direction of the road. 'Run!'

'Come back 'ere! I'll kill yers! Kill yers all!' raged Monk.

He fired into the air again. Compared with the parp of Tom's air rifle, his went off like a cannon. The two boys dropped their heads and kept on running at a crouch.

'Go, go!' Tom said as he reached the fence.

He vaulted it easily and joined the girls on the other side. He stuffed the air rifle away in its case and hoisted it up by the handle. By the time he was back on his feet, Charlie hadn't even got over the fence yet.

'Come *on* Charlie!' Emily said hopping impatiently from foot to foot.

'What are you doing?' Tom roared. The tendon in his neck was as thick as a baby's arm. 'Get over!'

Charlie had one foot hooked over the fence and his arms clung to the top post, but his torso hung like a bag of wet sand on the farm side. Monk was slowly advancing on them.

Tom leapt back over the fence and shoved Charlie across, into the grassy recess where he was whipped in the face by Teddy's helicopter blade tail.

'Get back 'ere!' Monk roared. He fired the gun a fourth time but he wasn't aiming into the sky anymore, it was pointed toward the band of trespassers and the bullet zipped close enough that it struck the fence post.

The thing about having only one eye is, it diminishes the depth perception. If the farmer had had two, he might have just made a hole in Charlie's head.

'Jesus!' Rose squealed. 'The old man's gone all country on us!'

'If I find out who yers are, I'll kill every last one of yers! I'll find out where yers live! An' I'll *kill* yer!'

The four and their dog ran back along Twin Hills, all the way up through the village of Gallows, and back down the other side, and they didn't stop or speak until they entered the wood that led up to The Barrow.

Chapter 11

Tom stormed into The Barrow first. His face was grim and red.

'I cannot believe you'd be this selfish,' Rose said as she led the other two inside. Tom had walked over to the patio doors with fingers locked over his head. 'And over a hare! A *hare*, Tom! What would we have even *done* with a hare? *You* don't know how to skin one.'

'Charlie,' Emily said as she closed the front door, 'Mr Bramble *specifically* warned us about Monk's farm. What were you *thinking* going over there?'

'We just got caught up in the hunt. And it's not like it was signposted: "Trespassers will be *shot*."'

'But Bramble *warned* us—'

'Yes, and he *laughed* when you suggested Monk might shoot us, didn't he?' Charlie reminded her. 'He said this wasn't the Wild West.'

Rose was pacing up and down with worry. 'What if that horrible little man finds out where we live?' she asked. 'He said he would *kill* us!'

Tom shook his head gravely. 'He won't find us.'

'But what if he *does*?'

'How's he gonna do that? Is he gonna knock on every door in the Lake District?'

'You asked him for directions this morning!' Rose reminded him. 'When he sent us across Fenton Bridge! What if he recognised you? You *are* the size of King Kong. He might rally up his horrible little friends and come down here and barge on in. We might be sleeping and he might murder us all in our beds. Have you *even* considered that, Thomas?'

'He won't murder us in our beds.'

'But how do you *know*?'

'Because I'm not that lucky!'

She stared at him severely. 'Don't you dare try to be funny, Tom,' she warned. 'You are trying my patience.'

'Oh give it a rest! The Little Miss Princess routine is doing my head in. Why don't you give us all five minutes of peace and quiet and go and get changed out of that stupid fucking yeti costume?'

'*This*,' Rose howled, shaking with anger and pointing to her fluffy tracksuit, 'is Balenciaga!'

Tom didn't respond so she took a breath and closed her eyes to compose herself. When she opened them again she was calm. 'Now I *am* going to go and get changed as it happens. I'm positively *crawling* with insects and I need to take another shower. But when I get back, I expect there to be a very large glass of something sitting on that table for me!'

Her long blonde Heidi plaits swished through the air as she stalked off down the hall leaving muddy cub-sized footprints behind. She didn't notice Teddy padding after her and she slammed the bedroom door in his face.

'Well I don't care *whose* fault all this is,' Charlie said, crumpling onto the settee, 'that man needs to be sectioned. He tried to *shoot* us.'

'Aye and should he even own a gun, having only one eye? Don't it affect your depth perception and that?' Tom asked. 'Fucker deserved it anyway for what he did to me, trying to send the Merc off a bloody bridge like that.'

Tom chuckled then. Emily looked round at him, not finding it the least bit amusing. 'And what's so funny?'

'Nowt. It's just your boyfriend,' he said wiping away a tear. 'He's the worst shot I've ever—*ever*—seen. Charlie, no offence or owt, but you shoot like a *girl*.'

Emily scoffed. 'If he shot like a *girl* maybe the two of you would've actually won the competition today, hm?' That wiped the smile from his face. 'I'm going to go and get changed,' she added. 'And Charlie? *I'd* like a large glass of something when *I* get back, too.'

She walked off down the hallway and closed the bedroom door quite firmly behind her.

Tom chuckled, hyper from the adrenaline and light-headed from the laughter.

'Christ. Someone's old bleeder must be waking up,' he said turning to Charlie—but Charlie had dozed off on the settee, leaving Tom alone with his ineffable wit.

Chapter 12

An hour or two later, Charlie was dressing again after having taken a shower, while Emily hopped in, when Rose knocked on their door.

'She's just got in the shower,' Charlie said, as he finished buttoning up his shirt.

'Yes—actually, it's *you* I wanted to see,' Rose said, quietly, which took Charlie by surprise. He sensed a tinge of sadness in her voice. 'Perhaps you could come through here?'

She was whispering. He could see along the corridor that Tom was over in the living room, banging the side of the plasma screen with the flat of his enormous hand and swearing to himself. Charlie nodded and followed Rose into her room where she quietly closed the door.

Rose sat down at her dressing table. She was in a hot-pink towel with her hair wrapped in a matching turban. She unravelled the turban and shook the dark blonde curls down her back and then ran a comb through them, all the while staring distantly at her reflection in the concertina mirror.

'Is everything okay?' Charlie asked.

She snapped out of her trance and put on a big smile.

'Peachy! I was wondering if you…' she paused. 'If, um, you could help me pick something to wear! Yes, that's right.'

'*Me*?' He wasn't sure what he was expecting, but it certainly wasn't to give fashion advice.

'Yes, why not?'

Charlie looked round the room. Rose's tracksuit and fluffy ankle boots were positively black with mud, and she had strung them across the radiator by the bed. Along the floor beneath her window were twelve different pairs of shoes and eight of them were heels. He opened up her cupboard and slid each hanger across the pole idly.

'Er—how about this one?' Charlie suggested, plucking something down almost at random.

It was a wine-coloured slip dress. Rose's eyes lit up when she saw it and she grinned. 'Perfect! Thank you, Charlie.'

'No problem.' He started to leave, but Rose reached out and put a hand on his arm.

'Listen,' she said quietly, looking at the gap in the bedroom door. 'Tom doesn't know about Harry and I,' she said. 'And I'd prefer not to get into all of that right now. You didn't... mention him at all today, did you?'

'Who Harry? God, no. I'm happy to have gone all day without having to worry about him for once.'

'I know what you mean,' Rose said, and still, her face was tinged with tragedy. 'I still care very much for him, you know.'

'I know,' Charlie said, although he did not know that at all. He hadn't seen Rose once since she broke up with Harry. And Harry wouldn't even tell Charlie *why* they broke up, leaving him to assume something awful happened. Where Harry was concerned, it was always safe to assume something awful had happened.

Charlie decided if he was ever to ask, now was the best time.

'Why exactly *did* the two of you—'

She held up a hand to silence him and dabbed the corner of her eye with a knuckle. 'You mustn't make me cry,' she said. 'I've just done my makeup.'

'Alright,' Charlie said. He tried to change the subject. 'And everything's okay with you and Tom? We didn't mean for that old Cyclops to try and shoot us all, you know.'

Rose smiled a really beautiful smile, with the little pearls of her teeth catching the light. 'I have matured, Charlie,' she said. 'While applying my mascara just now, somewhere between the first and last brushstroke, do you know what I did? I said to myself, "I will shelve my annoyance with Tom. It's a little red brick and I'll add it to the awful tower of resentment we've steadily been building." And then I did. It's a hundred feet tall and starting to sway.

'After all,' her smile faltered, 'what choice do I really have? If I *don't* forgive him then *I'm* the one driving a schism between the group, aren't I? I can't let his childish behaviour spoil the weekend for *all* of us now, can I? So I must move past it—and smile as I do.'

She tried to smile again but her lip wobbled and then she fanned her face with her fingertips. 'Mustn't cry,' she said breathing in.

Charlie didn't know how to respond. He put an awkward arm around her shoulder and patted her back like she was a well-behaved dog.

'Come on,' he said trying to sound upbeat. 'You can't smudge all that makeup now, can you?'

Rose wiped another tear away. 'You're right. And I'm fine. Really, I am. I'm just being silly.' She turned back to the row of shoes against the wall. 'Now then. Which heels will break his stupid heart?'

Emily knocked on the door then and came in to help Rose finish getting ready. Charlie slipped out and went along the hall to find Tom.

He had been busy transforming The Barrow for the evening's party. He had dimmed all the lights, lit candles around the hearth and set up a pair of disco lights he had found, stashed away in an airing cupboard. They cast an ethereal glow around the walls, the way reflections of water dance across canal bridges.

Tom was still fiddling with the cables at the back of the plasma screen and muttering expletives to himself. Static filled the screen like a thousand blackbirds swarming through a white sky.

'Come on you bugger. Let's 'ave you.' An image flashed across the static at last. But the yellow tint was worse than ever— making the newsreader on screen look less like he suffered from jaundice and more like a paint bomb had exploded in her face.

'Dickens!' Tom said, when he noticed Charlie behind him. 'Here, come and try this.'

There were dozens of bottles of spirits, liqueurs and wines on the island and Tom had been midway through mixing a jet-black cocktail into a pitcher. He appeared to arbitrarily pluck at the bottles like some mad alchemist before stirring the thing with a straw and testing it. He winced and sputtered and then poured Charlie a glass, who studied it carefully.

'Listen, I'll drink anything—you can ask Emily,' he said, holding it up to the light. 'But this looks like it will kill me.'

It was thick like oil, and where the light came through it shone with all the colours of the rainbow.

Tom laughed. 'It just might.' He watched as Charlie took a pained swig, his face doing all the expected revulsions before straightening out again.

'You know...' Charlie winced. 'That's not bad!'

Tom picked up the pitcher about to pour himself a glass, but he froze, staring at Charlie with a serious expression.

'What?' Charlie asked, failing to read it.

Tom craned his neck to look along the hall toward the bedrooms. There was no sign of the girls so he said, 'Come here, I wanna show you summat. C'mere Ted.'

The dog leapt up and Tom led the two of them outside to the drive and over to his car for the second time that day.

'I know I can trust you not to say owt,' Tom said matter-of-factly, 'but I do have to warn you what'll happen if you so much as breathe a word of this.'

He opened his car door, sat on the driver's seat and then reached underneath it feeling around for something.

'First I'll rip your bollocks off,' he grunted as he leaned in further under the seat—but then found whatever he was looking for and grinned. 'Then I'll feed your bollocks to the dog. And when they come out the other end I'll have whatever's left of 'em boxed up and sent to your mam's house. D'you understand?'

'Thoroughly.'

'Good lad.'

He put something into Charlie's palm. It was a little velvet box with a sliding lock. Inside was a ring with an enormous cluster of diamonds.

'D'you think she'll like it?'

'You're going to *propose*?' Charlie said in shock. 'This weekend? To *Rose*?'

'No, to the Queen of old Blighty,' he snatched the box back. 'Of course to Rose. That's why I needed you and Emily here. I can't propose on my own, I've got no idea how she'll react. I needed a sort of... *buffer*. Truth is, I were worried we'd come here alone and I'd bottle it and never pop the question. That's why I asked her to invite you two.'

'*You* asked her to invite us? I… er, well, congratulations?'

'Don't congratulate us yet,' he smirked. 'She still might say "no". *C'mere* boy.'

Teddy tottered over with his long tongue sagging out the side of his mouth. Tom felt around the fur of his neck for his collar and held a little loop out for Charlie to see.

'Got this ring box off the net. It's made to fit on a dog's collar. See?' He latched it onto the collar and gave it a little tug. 'Now we wait.'

'Wait?'

'Aye. Wait for Rose to find it. The way she fawns over him it won't take her long.'

Chapter 13

At quarter to nine, Rose stalked into the room like a model on the catwalk.

Tom had been informing Charlie of 'the best way to turn a six-pack into an eighter,' as if Charlie were anywhere approaching the cusp of such a feat. And Charlie knew full well that he was just seconds away from being exposed to Tom's washboard abs if he didn't divert the conversation to something else.

Fortunately, Tom trailed off mid-sentence and stared open-mouthed across the room.

Rose had stopped at the end of the hallway; her bronze thigh caught the flicker of the candlelight where it slipped through the slit in her wine-coloured dress. She sat on the barstool at the island and swished her long blonde hair in a wave down her back, ignoring the slack-jawed expression of her boyfriend.

Charlie had to push Tom's jaws back together for him.

'Well fuck me sideways,' Tom breathed, shoving his tumbler at Charlie and making his way over to her.

Emily had slipped into the room and she came over to stand with Charlie as they watched the other couple by the island.

'What's happening?' Charlie asked.

'She's decided to forgive him,' Emily whispered. 'But she doesn't intend for *him* to learn that quite so easily.'

Tom was twirling about unsettled and began tracing a pattern across the Corian surface with his finger. 'I'm sorry, Rosie—'

'What for?' she snapped before he had even finished saying her name.

He was caught off-guard.

'For... you know. All that nonsense on the farm today.'

'Oh, you mean for almost having all our heads blown off one by one? Is *that* what you're sorry about?'

When Tom blushed, his neck and arms had a way of turning pink and blotchy.

'Aye, for that,' he said. 'Look. I've made you summat. To say sorry, like.'

He turned round and stuck the oven mitts on. Rose peeped at him, curiously as he opened the oven and pulled out a pizza. He slid it over a rack on the island and Rose giggled.

Charlie and Emily moved in to see why.

He had reorganised the olives to make the letter 'R' inside a pepperoni love-heart. It looked, to Charlie, like a four-year-old had made it. But that was, he admitted, part of the charm.

Rose struggled to maintain her stoicism. She fought off the advancing smile but her eyes sparkled with laughter.

'Okay,' she said. 'I will forgive you. *If only* for the sake of peace. But I'm warning you now, Mr Darrow. If you derail this weekend with any more tomfoolery I will take that air rifle of yours and do you know what I'll do with it?'

'What?'

'I will insert it somewhere so very far that you'll only be able to talk in lead pellets. Now, I do believe I requested a large glass of something?'

Tom took the pitcher from the fridge and Rose groaned as he poured a cocktail each for them.

'Oh not *this*,' she protested. 'It's essentially poison. I wouldn't advise any of you to drink it.'

'Don't listen to her,' Tom said. 'Charlie likes it.'

'*Charlie* will drink anything wet,' said Emily, bumping him with her hip. 'He's hardly a reliable barometer of taste.'

'Suit yourself,' Tom said, taking a big swig.

Emily peered uncertainly into her glass but then wrinkled her nose and sipped it.

'Ugh!' she almost spat it back out. 'What's *in* this?'

'You've got vodka, gin, rum and Peach Schnapps—'

'Blimey, it's no wonder—'

'Hang on. There's Baileys, Gomme syrup, Blue Curacao, grenadine. The colour comes from the Coke. And then there's a smidge of absinthe for good measure. And a quarter bottle of Perrier-Jouët. I invented it when I worked at a bar back in uni. We used to put a sprinkle of chilli powder in too, but I haven't done that here.

'I just called it "Petrol".'

Emily took another swig. 'It's actually not bad,' she admitted. 'There's a sweet aftertaste.'

Rose pulled her face.

'When I asked you to make me a *drink* of something,' she said, lifting her glass and watching the thick liquid sift about like tar, 'I meant something along the lines of a *wine*.' She took a tiny sip and her lips peeled back from her gums. '*Ugh*, it's even viler than I remember. I most certainly will *not* be drinking this.'

But she did drink it and the Petrol soon claimed four victims.

Chapter 14

By the following morning, all Charlie would remember of that evening would be from unwanted flashes that came back to embarrass him. Flashes of dancing. Of drinking bottomless Petrol. Of bleating some awful tosh of a karaoke tune along to an old music channel. Of feeling drunker than he'd been for a good time—even living, as he did, with Harry. Of staggering outside, where Emily was smoking, and then toppling head-first into the hot-tub beside her.

But he would also remember, in more vivid detail, his dream. If it *was* a dream…

Tom and Rose climbed into the hot tub. The bubbles frothed around them like magma; the water spurted up in a volcanic eruption and they melted in silent anguish. Charlie stared through the patio doors, like they were the windows of an aquarium. An aquarium filled with jet-black water. But filled with tropical things of every colour, not unlike the luminescence of a gasoline puddle, or the depths of the Petrol. A school of iridescent fish swam by. Pink dolphins and shimmering jellyfish and narwhals that sparred with their tusks. A giant squid wrapped its tentacles around a ballistic missile submarine and snapped it like a pencil. The squid dissolved and the sea was still and silent and dark. Tremors shook through the water and the enormous shadow of a primordial behemoth rose up from the murky depths. Its yellow eye snapped open, as tall and wide as a Ferris wheel and it filled Charlie with sheer horror.

He managed to force himself up. The house was still. No water. No broken glass. No primordial behemoth. The radio filled the room with static. The television was on, but muted, and yellow-tinted people bickered in an old comedy repeat. Emily was on the other side of the settee, asleep, but Tom and Rose were nowhere to be seen.

Charlie hobbled over to the island and pulled out a barstool. It was twenty feet tall and he climbed until he could sit on top. The work surface spread out like an ocean of onyx. He planted his hands across it and it squirmed beneath his fingers like clay. He was in the land of the lotus-eaters; time was diluted and everything stretched away from him and sparkled and convulsed. The kitchen was so vast! And it swayed like he was at sea. The ethereal glow from the disco lights swam up the walls and he followed the light across the ceiling until his eyes fixated on that spec of red above the island. But now—it was no spec.

It was skeletal and bigger than before and it was *moving*.

Charlie froze up. He couldn't breathe, his skin crystallised. Despair bubbled through his veins. He imagined his blood had turned black and he wanted to cry but couldn't. He couldn't cry, couldn't breathe, couldn't move or look away. He was frozen, staring at the blood-red spot and watching what it did: it morphed into a V shape. Two long black things unfurled through the earholes of the skull and stretched out like the wings of a bat. Charlie blinked his disbelieving eyes. He heard a distant crack of thunder as a rapid tide began to rise up his leg. It flooded the kitchen; he could feel it, warm and sludgy against his ankles, his shins, his thighs, rising up around him till he was submerged in its quicksand, just a head in a jet tar. And in the tar were a thousand eyeballs, all rotating individually, yellow eyes with red pupils. The tar moved up the walls like a sea of snakes, swirling to the ceiling, all the time closing in on that dark winged creature above the island. The rest of the room was consumed, and now Charlie could see what they were:

Not a sea of snakes, or a tide or a tar or a quicksand, but a murder of *crows*. Ten thousand of them, with angry yellow eyes, swarming with wings like tattered leather. They opened their beaks and gnashed their teeth and screamed in thunderous birdsong till the sound of the ocean was drowned out by the deafening shriek of those wild birds.

Chapter 15

Charlie woke up to voices.

'See—what *is* that?' Rose hissed.

'I don't know,' Tom said. 'Just be quiet.'

'Where is it coming from?' asked Emily in an urgent whisper.

Charlie lifted his head from the cold island. It weighed a ton. The digital clock on the cooker bled through the gloom like neon. 06:05. It was otherwise dark in the house. The disco lights were off and all the candles had melted down to puddles of hardened wax. The only real light came from the moon, which fell in through two porthole windows, one either side of the front door. It lit up everybody's skin like opalescent marble.

'It came from the loft!'

'It's *inside* the house?'

'Don't be daft, it's on the driveway.'

Fear corrupted their voices and Charlie recalled his dream— the dark spot above the island... the sound of leather wings... the flood... the crows! He looked up at the ceiling, but all was normal. The small red spot looked no different than it had the day before. That steadied his nerve. Somewhat.

But nervous energy buzzed round the group and it was contagious. It made itself at home in the pit of his stomach. He could see the same look of uncertainty on everyone's pearly face. But what were they so frightened of?

There was a noise outside. Only something faint, but it *was* something. Tom was at the front door with his ear to the wood.

Emily took Charlie by the hand. 'You're awake,' she said.

'Christ, you're ice-cold,' he answered. 'What's going on?'

'*Sh!*' Tom pointed at him. 'Not a word, Dickens.'

Nobody spoke. They listened for whatever they were listening for until Rose couldn't take it any longer. She held her face in her hands and sobbed loudly.

'Rose, shut *up*,' Tom hissed.

He turned his ear to heaven and started carefully pacing the length of the house. They all stood in silence while he conducted his studies. After a few laps he stopped at the entrance and offered a smile.

'See, there's nowt there,' he decided. But he kept his voice low and it betrayed him. 'Probably just an animal or summat.'

'An *animal*?' Rose squeaked. 'What sort of *animal* do you—'

'Well maybe a tree or summat. Trees make all sorts of—'

Someone banged on the front door and Rose leapt six feet sideways.

'That's *some* tree,' Charlie whispered.

He could see even by the ghostly light how the colour drained from Tom's face.

It banged on the door again. Loud, specific bangs, made by a fist. It was no animal. No tree. There was a person out there separated from them only by the wood of the lodge.

'Do something Thomas!' Rose murmured.

Tom sprang into action. He performed another lap of the house, pulling the curtains across the patio doors and shutting all the blinds on his way round.

'Where's Teddy?' Charlie asked.

'We locked him in their bedroom.'

There was a third bang at the door and whoever was out there was saying something. It was hard to hear what, but it sounded like curses. And it was a deep, male voice.

'Oh God!' Rose wailed, 'it's that *farmer* isn't it? Felcher what's-his-face? He's found out where we live just like he said and he's come to murder us! Do you see what you've done Tom? You've *killed* us all, oh I *do* hope you're happy with yourself.'

Charlie crawled over to one of the portholes by the door. They were made of frosted glass, but he caught the swish of a man's coat whip round the corner.

'Christ, she's right!' he choked.

'You mean it *is* the farmer?' asked Emily.

Charlie's heart was beating through his shirt. Perhaps it was a side effect of his dream or some early on-set hangover, but deepest despair coursed through him.

Rose hopped from foot to foot. 'I knew it, I *knew* it,' she chanted.

'What did you see Charlie?' Tom asked. 'You saw that farmer bloke?'

'Don't know,' Charlie said, breathing heavily with his back to the wall. 'Man—dark coat.' He was wide-eyed and sweating profusely.

'Fuck all this.' Tom went down the hall into his bedroom. He came back with the air rifle and a box of BB pellets. Teddy trotted in after him.

There came more banging at the door, frantic now, and the stranger's voice, muffled and aggressive. Teddy started barking aggressively, drowning out whatever the man was saying.

'Have a look through the spy-hole,' Rose said.

Tom loaded the gun with a magazine of fifteen pellets. 'There isn't a spy-hole.'

Charlie watched the magazine slide in and it made a resonating metal clunk like the cog of a huge machine. It infested him with fear.

'No, you can't Tom,' he said, crawling across the entrance and pulling at Tom's T-shirt. He could feel the horror; it was back like a phantom; its black shawl was wrapped around him. 'Listen to me, I've thought about it, it's not going to work. You'll antagonise him further and then he'll really kill us. Perhaps if we just go out there and *apologise*—'

'Get off the floor, Charlie, you're embarrassing yourself.'

'But Tom,' Charlie sobbed, his top lip and brow line were damp. 'We'll buy him a new cow. Tom, *Tom.*'

Charlie clung on tightly to Tom's shirt and was dragged three feet across the ground.

'Stand up, Charlie,' Emily said, pulling him to his feet.

Charlie shook his head; the despair… the horror… the crows… He could almost hear their wings. If that front door swung open now, he was certain the birds would swarm in like bats or he'd be confronted by a man with the head of some terrible blackbird—a giant worm, the size of a constrictor, dangling limp from its beak. He couldn't bear it.

Tom herded the group behind him. He locked the barrel of the rifle into place and pointed the gun at the door. His arms were boughs of yew and if he was nervous he didn't show it.

'Eek!' Rose pointed at one of the little windows. The silhouette of the stranger there blot out the moonlight. He had cupped his eyes to the glass to peer inside.

'It's alright,' Tom said. 'He can't see us, it's dark in here and that glass is frosted.'

They waited until the stranger gave up. He stepped back and the beam of moonlight fell back in. They listened as his footsteps left the porch and retreated across the gravel.

Charlie sighed with relief.

'Is he gone?' asked Rose.

Nobody answered. Tom readjusted his fingers on the forestock and held the gun higher with those great arms, arms the work of Italian sculptors.

There was no sound of the stranger. There was no sound at all, except the syncopated beating of four hearts and the growling of the dog at their feet.

'I hear the fucker,' Tom said.

He was right. Someone was still out there. Something heavy was being dragged across the drive and it made a resonating thud as it bumped up each step. Charlie supposed it was Monk's leg brace. Whatever it was, it came to a stop outside the window. The stranger climbed on top of something so he was level with the porthole.

Tom turned his shoulders so the rifle moved from door to window. The others shuffled round in his shadow.

The stranger drew his leg back and kicked with the flat of his foot. The glass rattled in its frame and made each of them jump. He drew it back and went again and the whole front wall shook.

'If so much as a toe comes through that window...' Tom warned them under his breath. He flexed the fingers of his trigger hand.

The glass cracked. The stranger's leg went back like a pendulum and then came down a third time, even harder. The wooden frame split and the window fell inwards like a pocket watch, hung for a second, and then snapped off, crashing into a pile of glass and splintered wood, leaving a circular hole in the wall.

'Quickly, Tom, shoot him!' Rose screamed.

Tom pulled the trigger. A pellet zipped across the entrance and hit the stranger in the top of his leg. The man cried out and grasped at the wound, froze up and then toppled like the statue of a deposed dictator.

Tom clapped his hands together triumphantly.

'Grab summat to tie him up with.'

He slung the rifle over his shoulder and whipped a blanket from the back of the settee. He pulled the door wide open and leapt outside.

Charlie could only see the stranger's legs, which writhed about in the moonlight. But there was something oddly familiar in his mangled groan.

Tom pinned the stranger down with his big knee, and bound him in the blanket. 'Charlie,' he shouted. 'Come here.'

Charlie followed behind like he was still asleep, trapped in a lucid dream. He peered round Tom's bulk. The man beneath him was convulsing under the blanket and his arm rolled out across the decking.

'Now I'll be honest,' Tom said quietly. 'I've ingested my fair share of mushrooms tonight. But there *is* someone under me, right? I'm not tripping?'

'If you are then so am I.'

'Give us a hand with him.'

Charlie paused. Something caught his eye, glinting through the dark. He put his foot lightly on the stranger's arm and rolled it over. The arm was under the sleeve of a long greatcoat and Charlie recognised the Montblanc cufflink that was fastened through a French cuff.

A whole new feeling engulfed his paranoia. It wasn't relief so much as astonishment. And it hit him like a Japanese wave.

'I don't be-*fuck*ing-lieve it,' Charlie squeaked. 'You mad bastard, I could jump for joy. It's Harrington!'

'You've *got* to be kidding!' shrieked Rose, flying out onto the decking behind them.

Emily followed and gasped. '*What?*'

'Just who the fuck is *Harrington* when he's at home?' Tom asked.

Emily laughed. 'Harry is Rose's—'

'*He's my housemate!*' Charlie interrupted, throwing Emily a silencing glance. 'We live together in London.'

Everyone was crowded round the figure on the porch now and Teddy trotted over to see what all the fuss was about. Charlie had to hold him back by the collar so he wouldn't pounce all over Harry.

'Is he still breathing?' Emily asked.

Harry had stopped squirming and was now completely limp. Tom eased up his big knee and whipped the blanket off Harry's head. His face turned this way and that, gasping for air. It was all purple and the tendons in his neck were thick like tree roots.

'I say!' Harry howled. 'He got me! The great brute shot me in the cock! I'm bleeding out! I'm going to fucking die, right here like this!'

Tom stood back giving Harry the space to start writhing around like a dandy prat all over again.

'Charlie!' He wailed, when he noticed his friend stood over him. 'Thank God! Help me. Oh, and Emily! Dearest *Emily*! I'm dying. I need help!'

'Harry,' Emily sighed, 'I've not got the PhD for the type of help *you* need.'

Part II

Chapter 1

Harry was a mess. He was in a bottle-green tuxedo beneath his father's repurposed greatcoat, but it was flecked with dark stains and mud. His hair, usually combed back, now fell long and straggly across a sallow face, wet with cold sweat.

Charlie flicked a switch and filled the house with bright yellow light. Rose perched timidly on the arm of the settee like a little bird while Emily cleared a space on the coffee table. Tom carried Harry in his arms, like a wounded soldier. He kicked the front door shut forcefully and laid him across the table.

'I'm dead,' Harry muttered. 'I'm dead, aren't I? This is Hell isn't it? He got me and now I'm dead... Oh! *Lament* for me.'

'Listen to me.' Emily clicked her fingers in his face. 'You're *not* dead. You're just a drama queen. But you *have* been shot with an air rifle. So you have two options. You can writhe around in pain feeling sorry for yourself, *or* you can let me remove the pellet from your leg.'

'Remove it!' He gave a short, sarcastic laugh, but it pained him and he lay back down again. 'Charlie, your woman's gone quite insane!'

'Let me make something clear,' she said an inch from his face. 'I'm *nobody's* woman. But I advise you to let me remove it. Aside from being a foreign body stuck inside you, it's a *lead* pellet. When that decomposes into your blood it will poison you.'

'Poison me? One little pellet?' Harry sat up. 'I say, you're stark raving mad, doctor.'

'So you want me to leave it?' Her eyebrows arched high up her forehead. 'Is that your final decision? As a—and I use this word loosely—*competent*, adult man?'

'Yes,' he nodded ferociously. 'I've been poisoning my body for years with great success. Why stop now?' He swung his legs round and got to his feet but his leg buckled. He gripped Charlie's arm for support while his spare hand clutched his ribs instinctively.

'Harry, you really should think about this,' Charlie said. 'Emily's a doctor. She knows what she's doing. It won't hurt.'

'If he keeps his mouth shut,' Emily added.

'I must have missed that clause in the Hippocratic oath.' Harry winced.

'Come on Harry. Be reasonable.'

'Balls to reasonable!' he said, pushing through the opposing crowd. 'All I need's a stiff drink. I demand methuselahs, whole bathtubs filled with the choicest vintage. What have we in?'

'We?' Tom positioned himself between Harry and the fridge.

'Yes, something stimulating,' Harry said. 'A Jäger perhaps.'

'We haven't got any Jäger,' Tom said firmly.

A malicious smile spread on Harry's face. 'Then a bitter. I'd bet money you lugged a barrel of tasteless brown ale up here with you—?'

'Just sit down for a minute will you?' Charlie begged. 'Talk to us. Why are you here? How did you even *get* here?'

Harry's boots and trouser legs were caked in mud. If Charlie didn't know that the stupid bastard could barely get up the stairs without giving himself a stitch, he would've believed it if he said he'd ran all the way from London.

'Aren't you happy to see me?' Harry asked, and it did not escape Charlie's attention that he had avoided answering the questions.

'No, I'm not. And how did you find this place? It was hard enough in daylight.'

'You gave me the address,' Harry said. 'On that Post-It Note. But answers tomorrow. Yes. Tonight: booze and sleep and a fag. Now, come on old chap,' he turned back to Tom, 'surely there's a drinky or two back there for me? I've a callous bogthumper and I've had an awfully long night, you've really *no* idea. I must have some whiskies or a little bit of gak or a key. I'll settle for a bottle of Calpol.'

'I'll get you a drink,' Charlie said, 'if you let Emily remove the pellet from your leg.'

'Are we back pummelling the corpse of *that* old horse?' he said, feigning a yawn. 'Awfully sorry, must decline. Nothing against your expertise, Doctor Seymour, but I'll have one of my father's specialists see to it back in London. Doctor McSurgeon. From the Royal Medical Hospital of England up on Fixit Hill. High class. Private, you know.'

He made a sudden dash for the fridge and was reading the label of a bottle of Champagne before anyone could so much as blink.

But Tom had the advantage of height. He plucked it from Harry's hand and set it down on the island.

'What did you say your name was?' he asked with an air to intimidate. 'Don't think I caught it.'

'I didn't, darling. It's *Arthur*,' said Harry as he sifted through the bottles on the counter. 'I do say I recognise *you* though. Didn't I see your picture in the paper recently? *Ape Escapes Whipsnade* I think the headline ran.'

Tom chuckled. 'He's a cheeky fucker, isn't he? I shoot him in the leg and he gets up and insults me.'

His smiled disappeared. He launched at Harry, who leapt over the island in a flap of his greatcoat. Tom crashed into the kitchen cupboards and almost put his mitt through the microwave door.

'Stop this!' Rose cried. 'Honestly, the two of you are behaving like a pair of children!'

Harry stood looking at his feet.

'Now Harry,' she said in a mothering tone of voice. 'What are you *doing* here?'

Still looking at his feet, he shrugged his shoulders like a scolded toddler.

'I'm not here to cause any trouble,' he said. 'Thought you'd be happy to see me. Aren't you?'

Rose gave him a pitying sigh.

'If I could only have a drink—'

'Look, *mate*,' Tom said, placing the edge of a large paw on Harry's bony chest. 'I dunno what you've come all this way out for, but I think you oughtta piss off back to Never Neverland or wherever you've flown in from.'

'Fresh out of pixie dust, I'm afraid, but procure me some absinthe and I will be happy to make a deal with the green fairy Mab.'

'Jesus Christ, what language is that?'

'Why *English*, my good man! English,' Harry said. 'There may be a syllable or two more than you're used to wedged in there but it's hardly iambic pentameter.'

He cast a look at his audience. He didn't exactly have them in the palm of his hand, that much was clear. Charlie didn't know what Harry could have been expecting. But whatever it was, this could not have been going worse for him. He had broken the window, got himself shot for the trouble, and immediately instigated a bitter rivalry with Rose's new boyfriend. If it had been Charlie in his position, he would've crawled right back out of the window and died of embarrassment.

But Harry was a law unto himself. He decided, instead, that he was all in.

'I must say, Rosie, I thought you had better taste. This thing never quite evolved with the rest of us. He's the broad shoulders, big teeth and brow line of the Homo erectus.'

'Homo *what*?' Tom said, taking a step forward. 'Are you calling us queer?'

'It means "upright man",' said Harry, thoroughly enjoying himself. 'Though I'm quite mistaken in your case. You still drag your knuckles across the floor when you walk. I wonder, is there a portrait of you in an attic somewhere, growing prettier?'

'Eh?'

'Alright, Harry, time out,' Charlie warned him. He steered Harry back to the coffee table. 'Enough banter. It's like you're in a Ben Elton comedy.'

'But Ben Elton isn't funny!'

'Precisely my point.'

Harry let out a breath as he seceded. 'You're quite right, Charlie. One should never enter a battle of the wits with an unarmed opponent. And I'm too exhausted to spar tonight. It's twenty past six in the morning. I need to get some rest. It'll be sunrise in half an hour and we can pick this up then, over buttered crumpets and scones with clotted cream like Englishmen.'

'Harry, you're exhausting,' Charlie said, looking at his friend with concern. 'And I don't know if it's a good idea for you to stay here.'

Harry's face fell. '*Et tu Carolus*?'

'I'm sorry. It's just… this is all a bit *unusual*. Even for *you*.'

'Turncoat. Iscariot. Benedict Arnold.'

'*And* you weren't invited,' Rose chimed in. 'For good reason.'

'I know, darling, and after a cup of sleep I'll find somewhere else to stay. I promise I will. I passed a charming B&B in that village down the road. But right now it's twenty past six in the morning. Don't throw me to the wolves.'

'There aren't any wolves in the Lake District—' Charlie started.

'Well the rapists and molesters, then!' he said, hotly. 'You can't tell me the Lakes don't have *those*. *Ow*, my side. I mean my leg, that's right. Leg. I need to lie down.'

He collapsed face first onto the settee.

'Look. I'll make no fuss,' Harry pleaded. 'I'll kip here a little bit and in the morning I'll make eggs in Hollandaise. I'll even do some for the caveman.'

'You don't know how to use the cooker,' Charlie told him. 'And I'm sorry Harry. You should go.'

Tom was ecstatic. He clapped his hands together and rubbed them. 'Alright then, mate. Adios. I'd say it's been a pleasure, but it's fucking *not*. You can see yourself out.'

'Fine,' Harry snarled, getting up to his feet and pointing at the group of them. 'I'll leave. But I want it in my obituary you four *bastards* killed me when I'm found frozen to death by the bulrushes, half eaten by the buzzards. Title it *J'Accuse…!* Charlie, I appoint you executor of my will—'

'Don't be so—'

'No, no, you deserve that much. Now listen up: I want black dahlia corsages and dwarf ponies for the funeral cortege and all the women under fifty have to cry.' He had his hand on the doorknob. 'I suppose this is it then. I'll be leaving now.'

'Ta-ra.'

'I suppose all that remains is to *thank* you.'

'Thank us?'

'Yes, for the whisky.'

'The *whisky*?'

Tom spun round to his box of spirits. He rifled through his stash desperately.

'Twenty-five-year-old Scotch,' Harry said, reading the label. 'Not bad at all. I prefer *Irish*, myself, but this will keep me warm out there, all the same.'

Tom's jaw twitched—if there had been even an ounce of good natured repartee before, it completely evaporated now.

'Put that down,' he warned him, sweeping up the air rifle. 'Or I'll put *you* down.'

'Thomas!' Rose cawed. 'Did we not agree only *today* that you were not to cause any more trouble this weekend?'

'I'm not causing trouble. I'm ending it.'

'Tom, I *strongly*—'

'Rose, that's a twenty-five-year-old single malt for God's sake.'

'I don't care if it's *fifty* years old and grants wishes! Put the gun *down*. I won't tell you again.'

Tom's lip curled. Harry held the whisky bottle like a batsman. He stuck his bottom out and wiggled it as he dug his heels into the ground.

'I was the Harrow's best cricketer in a thousand years,' he said. 'I've had more centuries than hot dinners. I'll bat away that pellet before you even realise you've pulled the bloody trigger.'

He ran a tongue across his teeth thirstily and his eyes glittered from the depths of two dark sockets. He looked like a vampire waiting to sink his teeth into Tom's jugular. What a feast *that* would be—the vein was pulsing like a pipe whose pressure had built to explode.

'Forget it,' Tom said, letting up. The vein softened. 'You're not worth the prison sentence, *mate*.'

'I'm impressed,' Harry said. 'It takes a lot of willpower to stop oneself from ejaculating when you're oh so near, but you have proven your manhood—irrespective of the bolt-action phallus-extender you're so quick to grab hold of with both of your great, sweaty—'

He didn't get the rest of his diatribe out. Tom had drawn the line but Harry crossed it. He swung the gun back up and fired. The pellet ricocheted off a beam, boinged from a kitchen pan and then spun straight back at Harry, who had no time to react. The whisky bottle exploded like a firework of glass and it was all he could do to jump a foot back and hold up what remained of it—the neck—like the hilt of an invisible sword.

'Bugger *me*,' he wheezed, inspecting the jagged bottleneck with a fingertip. 'You could have killed me then!'

Tom had dropped to his knees when he saw the whisky pooling away through the cracks in the floorboards. He scurried over and began mopping at it with his fingertips.

'No, no!'

Nobody else made a peep—except for Rose, who had begun a slow and sarcastic round of applause. She looked between the two boys with a quavering fury in her eye.

'Well!' she said, '*That* just about does it for me.' She looked like she might almost laugh for a second or two, but by the third she scowled. 'I don't know *what* you were thinking by coming up here uninvited, Harry. But I *do* know that if I'm not asleep within the next two minutes I'm liable to murder one or the *pair* of you and, quite frankly, it's as Tom said. I don't wish to spend my peak years in an orange jumpsuit as the bitch of some great fat lesbian with swastikas tattooed across her eyelids. So *please*, come and make yourself at home, Lord Duke Harry Double-Barrelled-Public-School! Take the settee. I'm *so* sorry we've not any foie gras or roasted peacock for your highness to sup on. There's coffee and bread for toast if that pleases your lordship's refined palette? But let me just make one thing *crystal* clear. When I wake up and come out here in the morning, I very much expect to find you *gone* and all this broken glass to be tidied away. Toodle pip!'

She spun on her heel and disappeared into her bedroom, slamming the door shut behind her.

Harry had turned as red as a post box. Charlie couldn't help but smile. He patted him on the shoulder and whispered, 'Why *did* you two break up exactly? You were clearly made for one another!'

He winked and then followed Tom and Emily down the hall. They each disappeared into their own bedrooms, leaving Harry, quite alone, to feel two-foot small.

Chapter 2

Charlie was awake for twenty minutes before he actually moved. He could hear the monotone cadence of voices rising and falling from the living room. Surely not *more* arguing?

'Another day in Paradise,' he said to himself.

When he went into the living room, Emily had her back to him on the settee. Tom was by the patio doors, staring into the hot tub outside. Charlie looked around for Rose, but she was nowhere to be seen.

'Is everything alright?' he asked.

He could see Tom's reflection in the glass. He looked tense.

'Your friend's buggered off then?' Tom said, turning from the doors.

'Where's he gone?' asked Charlie.

Tom raised his eyebrows. His stubble bled like rust across a grim face, which was set like stone below a deep brow. 'We were hoping you might know.'

'Me? Why would I know?'

There was no sign of Harry in the house. The only indication he had ever been there was the broken porthole window, boarded up with a flattened beer crate. All of the glass had been swept up by the island.

'When did he go?' Charlie asked.

'We've no idea,' said Emily. 'There's no sign of him in the house.'

'Haven't been outside yet,' Tom added.

'Where's Rose?'

Tom's brows drew closer together. 'Gone to look for Ted.'

'What do you mean?'

'He's gone missing. Funny, innit? This Harry bloke shows up and the dog's here. Then Harry disappears and the dog buggers off too.'

Charlie felt from Tom's stare as if he was being court martialled by the great stone mo'ai of Easter Island.

'You know how important that dog is to me, Charlie.'

'Of course—his collar! Did you get the—'

Tom cut him off with a warning glance and nodded secretly at Emily.

'Er, I mean your address must be on his collar, right? I'm sure someone will be in touch.'

'Aye, well…'

'I am sorry about him,' Charlie said. 'I don't know why he's here but I *am* sorry.'

'Don't be,' Tom tried to smile. 'This ain't *your* fault Charlie. But what's our game plan gonna be?'

Tom took his pack of Marlboros out and shook them like a deck of cards till one slid into his palm. He wouldn't break eye contact with Charlie, so Charlie looked outside at the hot tub. There was a cardigan drifting across the surface of the water.

'Charlie? Are you with us?' Tom asked as he lit the cigarette. 'I'm asking what our game plan is here.'

'Our game plan?'

'Aye,' Tom waved the cigarette around. 'If he comes back here, what do we do about it?'

'I'll… talk with him,' Charlie said.

'Good,' Tom said. 'Because—*and I don't mean to be rude*, Charlie—but he's behaved like an unbelievable cunt. Even you have to admit that?'

'Well,' Charlie started. 'There must be a reason for his behaviour. I don't think he'd just turn up here uninvited for no good reason.'

Emily snorted. 'Really Charlie, I only know Harry *half* as well as you, but even *I* know turning up here in the manner he did is *exactly* the kind of thing he likes to do.' She turned to Tom. 'Everything has to be a spectacle. He can't have a cup of tea without informing the local press. If he wasn't so bloody stupid he'd be a bona fide genius.'

Charlie had enough. He didn't feel like having to defend someone who wasn't even present for his own trial.

'I'm going out,' Charlie told them.

He was still in pyjamas. He went into his room and got changed quickly. When he came back to the living room to put his boots on, Rose had returned and was sobbing into a cushion.

'I've… looked… *every*where. All around the meadows. I went back to that little pub we stopped at outside of Gallows for lunch yesterday. There's not a *sign* of him *anywhere*. Not a paw print or dog hair for miles.'

She lay down on the settee with a tragic look in her eye but sprung to her feet when she noticed Charlie pulling his boots on.

'You! *Where—is—my—dog?*' she said very slowly. 'It wasn't enough you crippled my Pepper, now you've gone after Teddybear, too, *haven't* you?'

'Don't be ridiculous,' said Emily. 'Charlie hasn't got anything to do with it. Harry must've taken him out for a walk, that's all. I'm sure they'll be back shortly.'

Charlie went and picked up the dog bowl and turned it to the light. There were three dark red spots by his name. He crouched down where the bowl had been. There were five or six more of them on the wood.

'What have you found?'

'Nothing,' he said. But Rose had come over and snatched the dog bowl from him.

'Blood? Oh Teddy, what's *happened* to you? There's blood, Tom! There's blood right on his bowl! Something awful's happened, I just *know* it.'

Tom let out a deep breath. 'I'm gonna call him. What's his number, Dickens?'

Charlie shrugged. 'Harry doesn't have a phone.'

'He doesn't have a *phone*? Why not?'

'He doesn't believe in them.'

'He don't *believe* in them? Christ alive.'

'How would you call him anyway? We didn't bring our phones,' Charlie reminded him. 'That was the whole point of this trip.'

'Tom's car can ring people,' Emily remembered. 'That's what Rose said.'

'Oh,' Rose blushed, 'About that…' She slid a hand into her jeans and pulled out a great fluffy lilac thing. 'Oopsy?'

She laid her phone on the island.

'What?' she snapped at a look from Charlie. 'I am a highly in-demand actress, thank-you-very-much. I've just had a top-secret audition for something calling itself *Wizard Box* and my agent *happens* to know that's code for Doctor Who. I could be getting a call *any* moment now.'

Tom carried the phone over to the window.

'Who are you going to call?' she asked.

'Dunno.'

Rose started to pace back and forth across the fireplace. 'We'll have to call the police,' she decided.

Tom scratched his chin. 'The police aren't gonna come all the way out here for a missing dog, are they?'

'They *might*. Out *here* they might,' Rose said. 'It's not like they've got stabbings to deal with like they do in London. They're probably sat around the police station playing "I Spy".'

'Don't be so stupid,' Tom said.

'Well try the RSPCA, then!' she snapped at him. 'PETA. *Anyone.*'

Tom's temple vein was as thick as a baby's finger. He slammed the phone down on the coffee table where it sat like some dead purple creature.

'Why don't you two go out?' Emily suggested. 'You should search the woods together. Charlie and I can wait here in case he comes back.'

'In case *who* comes back?' asked Rose, sniffing. 'Ted? Or Harry?'

'Harry,' she answered automatically, and then flushed red. 'Or Teddy. Either. Both of them, in fact.'

Rose burst into tears again and leaned into Tom's chest. He put an arm round her.

'*I'll* go and search the woods,' he said, grim-faced. 'But I'll tell you this for free: if I come back here *without* that dog, I'll be going straight back out to hunt posh dandy twats. And it won't be an *air* rifle I go with neither.'

'Posh dandy twats? Should my ears be burning?' Harry asked, announcing himself into the room.

95

He had been listening from the shadows, but now strolled in, striking his palm with a rolled-up newspaper.

'I shouldn't complain,' he continued with a smirk. 'It's as Oscar said, "There's only one thing in the world worse than being talked about—and that's *not* being talked about".'

Tom stood up abruptly, almost throwing Rose to the floor.

'You've got some nerve.'

'*Moi?*' Harry said, drawing back in a facetious show of surprise.

'What've you done with him?' Rose asked. '*Where* is my Teddybear?'

'How on Earth should *I* know where your teddy bear is?'

'Teddy is their *dog*,' Emily explained. 'And he's missing. We thought he might be with you.'

'He was here last night,' Tom said. 'But after you show up, he's gone.'

'Poppycock!' Harry scoffed.

'It's not poppycock, it's true.'

'I *say*, a man can barely breathe around here without—'

'So you deny it?'

'Poppycock!'

'What the fuck does that mean?'

'It *means* poppycock! Balderdash. Hocus pocus.'

'You must've let him out,' said Tom. 'Left the door open or—' Harry slammed his rolled up newspaper onto the coffee table and it frightened everyone.

'I did no such thing!' he protested, quite angrily. 'I didn't sleep last night so after the four of you went off to bed, I tidied up in here and boarded up the window and at no point in time was there ever a *dog* with me.'

''Cause you must've let him out,' Tom said. 'When you went for that paper.'

'Ah. So despite spending several hours in this sizeable palace, you think it escaped my notice there was a dog pottering around? And then when I left to get the morning paper, somehow between my opening the door, exiting the building, and then closing it behind me, this beast slipped past and I didn't even *notice*? I take it he's a tiny little creature, then?'

'He's a Pyrenean Mountain Dog,' Charlie said.

'A perineum *what*?'

'He's a big dog, that's the point. Size of a Shetland pony.'

'Then I can assure you,' Harry continued, red-cheeked, 'a *blind* man would see one of *those* slip by.'

'He might not have followed you out *then*,' Rose said, 'but perhaps you didn't close the door properly and he got out *after* you had already left.'

'I see,' Harry said. 'You think I left the door open? Then let me ask you this. Who was the first one awake this morning?'

'I was,' said Emily.

'And tell me, did you happen to notice that the door was left wide open?'

'No,' she admitted. 'The door was closed when I got up. All of them were. And Harry had already left.'

'So then perhaps you think this dog of yours had the good courtesy to close it, after he snuck out behind me?'

Rose leapt excitedly to her feet. 'But there's *blood*,' she cried. 'Yes, there's blood all over the dog bowl, look!'

'You might recall,' Harry said, 'that I was horribly shot last night. And I bled profusely as a matter of fact.'

'Profusely?' Tom frowned.

'Yes it means in vast quantities, *do* try to keep up.'

'I know what it *means*.' Tom gritted his teeth. 'But if you were bleeding so *profusely* why is there only a few specks and not a load of blood all over the place?'

'Because I *cleaned up*!' Harry marched over to the pedal bin and dug through it. He pulled out a handful of paper towels all hardened with dried blood and he threw them into the air like confetti. 'See?'

Tom's only response was to turn a deep pink.

'Then… it was the farmer!' Rose said desperately with tears in her eyes. 'He really *did* find us and he took my Teddybear. To punish us?'

97

'Oh would you shut the fuck up about the farmer, Rose!' Tom yelled. 'He's not gonna come up here to kill us *or* take your fucking dog.'

'Don't you talk about my Teddy like that, you beast!'

'It's quite a simple matter, really,' Harry said calmly. He repositioned a bowl of potpourri on the bookshelf as all eyes turned to him. 'This dog of yours is equivalent in size to a Shetland pony. We've already established that the door was closed, and as no dog ever left with *me*, then we can only assume that one of *you four* released it.'

'Of course we didn't,' Rose said shaking her head. 'Why would any of us do that?'

'Well then if you *didn't*,' Harry countered, 'it only stands to reason that his disappearance occurred *before* I entered the property, doesn't it, since nobody else has entered?'

Nobody answered him. Charlie got the sense Harry was rather enjoying himself. He had, for example, pushed his fingertips together like some mad detective, and started pacing up and down with too much of a spring in his step.

'To ascertain the guilty party all we need do is simply retrace our steps until we know who last saw the dog.'

'Yes, good idea,' Emily said, tucking her hair back behind an ear and thinking. 'When Harry was trying to kick the door down, we locked Teddy in your bedroom, didn't we?'

'But he followed me out,' Tom recalled. 'When I went to get the rifle from under the bed. And he was barking when Harry started banging on the door.'

'But he was on the porch with us,' Charlie said. 'When you pinned Harry down out there, Tom. Teddy was jumping about near my feet and I had to hold him back by the collar.'

'So then,' Harry grinned, smugly, 'the dog was outside with the five of us. How interesting! The plot thickens and the question becomes this: Who was the last one back into the house?'

For a second, everybody looked deep in thought. Rose's face quickly turned to porcelain and then cracked. 'It was *you*,' she said in disbelief, pointing at Tom with her long pink talon. '*You* carried

Harry in behind us all and *you* kicked the door shut with your beastly size thirteens!'

Tom had gone grey. 'You can't blame *me*,' he whispered. He wasn't defensive, he was sorrowful. 'I couldn't've known the dog was still out there.'

'The *dog* has a name,' Rose screamed. 'Teddy! His name is *Teddy*.'

There was a hefty thud outside which cut any quarrelling short. Everyone looked at the door. Rose had such a hopeful look in her eye it was as if she were expecting Ted to come bounding in as if nothing had happened.

But a sense of dread travelled around the remaining group. Charlie did wonder whether Monk would be on the other side of that door, his goopy eye-socket leaking down a weathered cheek, rouged with burst capillaries.

But when Rose pulled open the door, Monk was not on the other side.

At first, it looked as though there was no one there until she looked down to her feet and emitted a high-frequency shriek so terrible it made the glass wobble.

Tom ran over and she buried her face in his chest, sobbing hysterically.

'What is it?' asked Emily.

'It's a... dead *thing*,' Tom said.

Every pulse was racing. *Not the dog*, Charlie thought, over and over.

But it wasn't the dog—and he felt some relief. Instead, he found himself gawping down at a dead blackbird. It had been savaged by something and its pink innards were pouring out below its ruffled green-blue feathers.

'How did *that* get there?'

Tom went outside into the clearing and looked all around. 'Hello?' he called.

There was no sign of anybody in the treeline.

'It was him wasn't it? The farmer?'

'Don't be ridiculous,' Tom said, pushing his way back inside and walking to the kitchen where he picked up the bin and a pair of rubber gloves. 'It probably just… fell out the sky or summat.'

'Birds don't just fall from the sky!'

'Course they do. Maybe it had a heart attack.'

He picked the bird up carefully by the body but its wound popped open and a dollop of red insides drooled out across the floor.

'I'm going to be sick!' Rose squeaked.

Tom put the bird into the bin and then took the bag out, tied it up and walked it round to the skip behind the house. The smell was something vile.

'I'm gonna go and look for Ted,' he said as he rubbed the bird blood into the cracks of the wood with his toe. 'Get some fresh air. You coming Rose?'

'Yes,' she muttered. 'I need air!' She took a jacket from the hook and they disappeared around the side of the house together.

Harry closed the door and dusted off his hands. 'And then there were three!'

'*Actually*, there was *one*,' Emily said. '*Me*. Because the two of you are to go for a walk.'

'And what are you going to do?' Charlie asked.

'Enjoy a teeny slice of peace and quiet and a rather large stiff drink. Probably out *there*.' She pointed to the hot tub.

Harry nodded. 'Come on, Charlie-Boy. We'll circle the daffodils and picnic in their belt.'

'Alright. I'll… meet you on the drive.'

Harry hopped outside, looking into the sky as if expecting birds to rain down on him.

'You know he can't stay here, don't you?' Emily said pitifully. 'I don't say it to be cruel, but Tom and Rose paid for this place. It's awkward enough that her ex-boyfriend has turned up unannounced, but I don't even think she's told Tom anything about him. As long as he stays here, this entire weekend is a ticking time bomb. Go and talk to him, Charlie. But *send him home*.'

Chapter 3

Charlie led Harry off the path and into Greenwood. A festoon of flowers formed a colourful kind of pergola in the canopy and broken light fell through like golden spears.

'Look at this place, Charlie-Boy. We walk in beauty! Shame my journey here was under cover of darkness, there's so much to see!'

'Speaking of,' Charlie said, 'you never *did* say how you got here?'

Mischief danced on his face. 'You mean you didn't *see*?'

'See what?'

'Or *hear*?'

'Hear *what*?'

Harry had a snifter of Southern Comfort with an ice cube inside. He swilled it round, pretending he was debonair. 'Oh nothing. I'll show you later.'

An image flashed into Charlie's head. An image of Richard Burden's Bell-429 in a field somewhere close by. Its rotary blades sparking while curious sheep sniff at the leaky fuselage.

—No, surely even *Harry* wouldn't be so reckless as to try and pilot a *helicopter* the length of the country. He couldn't even figure out the remote control to their television.

They pushed through a thicket where the oaks were tumorous with burr. Harry studied one queerly.

'I wonder which way they went?' he said, turning back to the dense wood. 'How are we going to find them?'

'We're not *going* to find them,' Charlie said. 'You and I are going for a *talk*.'

'A *talk*! Why don't you just take me to the firing squad and be done with it.'

'Don't tempt me.'

They ducked beneath a twisted branch and went down to the gullies and followed the rills west till the wood thinned out. A mesh fence separated it from the neighbouring field but they found a cow stile and climbed over.

Sunny Green was carpeted with bluebells. The field separated Greenwood and The Barrow from Gallows Village, with the long A-road running parallel. Some way off, the lamb-white sky touched a jagged row of greenish houses at the foot of the village tor. On the opposite side, behind a haze of mountain fog, sprawled the Yarrowmoor. Its distinctive flat top made it look as if a giant's bowler hat had been left outside to accrue a lifetime of moss.

'So how long've those two been... you know?' Harry asked about as tactfully as he was capable.

'Not long,' Charlie answered. 'I don't really know any more than you do.'

'And what's he like? A total bastard, I imagine.'

'Oh, I don't know. He likes cars and sports and stuff. He seems okay. Although, there was a thing yesterday... He got all riled up because we lost this stupid competition and he made us chase this hare with his air rifle. Anyway, he killed a cow.'

'He killed a cow!' Harry repeated. 'How?'

'It was dark. We were on a little farm a few miles away.'

'A little farm? The one in Underwood?'

'Yes, how do you know that? The one with the big red barn on the corner.'

'I passed through it, on my way here,' Harry answered, pausing to stare across at the Yarrowmoor. 'I say, that mountain is truly something, don't you think?'

Charlie had stopped a few feet behind and bent over with his hands on his knees. He'd come over funny all of a sudden.

'Charlie? What's the matter?'

Whatever it was passed. Charlie stood upright and blinked into the sun.

'I think you've given me your alcoholism.'

'Nonsense. You're merely borrowing it.'

Harry hopped onto the dry-stack wall and went along it like a tightrope walker. Charlie followed from the ground and watched a flock of gulls drift through the open sky.

'Listen,' Harry said apprehensively. 'You've no plans for today have you? I've something of a surprise for us all.'

'A surprise? For all of us? What kind of a surprise?'

'An excursion.'

'An excursion to where?'

'I can't tell you. *That's* the surprise.'

'Only you, Harry, could go out for a newspaper and wind up planning an excursion.' He considered it. 'I don't know. I don't like the sound of it. You're not exactly in anyone's good books right now.'

Harry hopped down from the wall and winced on the landing. 'You mean that great brute Kaiser Tom, don't you? God, what an enormous prick.'

'I haven't noticed.'

'What? No—not that he *has* one! But rather he *is* one, is what I meant. Anyway he's a bore. I bet he chews nails. He's like something from the Planet of the Apes—hairy and just positively *dripping* with testosterone. What does she see in him? You remember my friend from the Harrow? Boffer? He had a pet *slug* with more personality—'

'Harry, stay focussed, you're giving me a fucking tumour, right here,' Charlie drilled a finger into his temple. 'And it's not *just* Tom's bad books you're in. It's Rose's, too. They're practically in mourning.'

'They're in *mourning*?' Harry faux-gagged. 'You mean for that dog? He's only been missing for five minutes. He'll be at the foot of an old oak tree barking at the squirrels. Bosie used to run off for *days* around Blye House.'

'Yes but Blye House had twelve-foot-high electric fences and live-in staff. Anyway, that's hardly the point. You need to apologise. To everyone.'

'This excursion, you see—'

'*Even* if you don't mean it,' Charlie interrupted. '*Especially* if you don't mean it. Just tell them you're sorry and maybe we can put this behind us. You know Emily wants you to go. She thinks you're a ticking time bomb—and I can't say I disagree. If you promise me you're not here to cause any trouble, especially regarding Rose— then maybe an apology will let you stay.'

Harry seemed to consider it. 'Yes. Okay, I'll apologise. This surprise I have planned *is* my apology, as a matter of fact.'

'Good.'

'And, yes, well… I *am* sorry about their dog, too, for whatever *that's* worth. You remember my Bosie, don't you?'

'I don't believe we had the pleasure.'

Harry smiled at some unshared memory. 'He was a complete bastard, really.'

They went on following the wall for another few feet until Harry stuck his arm out like a barrier stopping Charlie in his tracks and looking round at him with wide eyes.

'Do you know, I've just remembered something quite queer,' he said. 'The man. At the newsagent this morning, where I bought my paper. *He* asked me whether there was a dog staying with us.'

'He did? Why would he ask you that?'

'When I booked this excursion, I mentioned I was staying with two couples. And *he* said four young people got onto that farm back along the main road. That was *you* wasn't it? Well the farmer who owns it, Monk something or other. He's looking for you. Or so says the shopkeeper.'

Charlie felt uneasy about this news. 'What did you tell him?'

'Well I didn't know anything about the dog. I told him he had you mistaken for someone else.'

'And did you… tell him where we were staying?'

Harry thought for a moment and then covered his mouth. 'You know, I think I must have! When I booked the trip, I wrote down "The Barrow". You don't think—you don't think this has anything to do with the dog's *disappearance* do you?'

'I don't know,' Charlie said, apprehensively. 'But let's keep this between ourselves for now.'

Harry agreed. They walked on in a more sombre silence until Charlie said, 'Harry? Why *are* you here?'

Harry didn't answer straight away. He broke eye contact to watch the grass, the bluebells, the gulls on the cowls of the chimneys. He knew that Charlie was thinking about *The Incident*. Harry had drunk a rather large bottle of something last month and

104

then, for dessert, swallowed two boxes of paracetamol. Charlie had come home just in time to see him frothing at the mouth. They enjoyed a long weekend at the Royal Brompton, then were back home by teatime Monday. They hadn't discussed it since, but it had hung over the two of them like a jet-black raincloud.

'I suppose I just wanted to surprise you,' he eventually said. 'I thought you'd be glad to see me. *I* thought "the more the merrier" was the order of the day. Clearly, I was quite wrong about *that*.'

'And this has nothing to do with, you know…?'

'What, *Rose*?' he laughed at the suggestion. 'Of course not. Barely remembered she would be here.'

'No, not Rose,' Charlie said. 'I mean… The Incident. Last month?'

Harry blushed. 'God, *that*? No! No, no, no.' He had a go at smiling.

'Okay,' Charlie said. 'And this has nothing to do with your father, either?'

Harry drew back slightly. 'My *father*? Why would this—'

'When I left Milk Street,' Charlie interrupted, 'you'd just been cut off by him. And not a *day later* you turn up here completely out of the blue. You have no money, you can't drive and I have no idea why you've come or how you got here. The only thing that makes any kind of sense is that your father helped. Maybe he gave you some money or arranged a chauffeur or something. But *why* would he do that when he'd cut you off? The whole thing just doesn't add up.'

Harry followed Charlie's train of thought and when he reached the station, shook his head merrily.

'I assure you this has nothing to do with my father,' he said. 'It was all just an ill-judged attempt at spontaneity. I misread the dynamic here. I thought you'd be hammering your head against the wall within minutes of being shacked up in that old cabin with Rosalind, the tyrant at five-foot-nought. I know she practically *despises* you for crippling her dog.'

Charlie rattled his brain.

'I just don't get you. You would've realised this was one of the worst plans you've ever concocted if you'd just engaged the thing between your ears for even half a second—'

'What, my nose?'

'Your *brain*, Harry. I assume you have one. How you travelled for several *hours* without that consideration is beyond me.'

'Sorry, Charlie-Boy. My noggin's been playing up recently. Not so certain it's on the level.'

He looked sincere. They started off again without purpose but drifting in the direction of the tor.

'I wish you *had* been to see your father,' Charlie grumbled. 'He might've agreed to pay our bills again.'

Harry smiled weakly. 'We don't need my father to survive. We're capable sorts. As long as we've got each other, we'll be okay.'

'I need to tell you something,' Charlie said, before sighing like a deflating balloon. Now was as good a time as any. 'I'm moving out.'

'Moving out? Of where? *Milk Street*?'

Charlie didn't answer him.

'Well, that's... I say, that's just... Where will you go? What will you *do*?'

'We're killing each other in that house,' Charlie answered. 'You're toxic. It's not your fault, you're immune to all intoxicants. But I've caught fourteen illnesses this year and I think I'm getting a rash from the creatures that live under the carpets. I need to get away.'

'And sleep on the spiked shop fronts of Soho with the winos? Or perhaps you'll join the Romanians in a squat? Is that your master plan?'

'No.' Charlie paused. 'I'm going to live with Emily.'

Harry went all white and turned away suddenly to vomit against the dry-stack.

'Sorry,' he wiped his mouth on a sleeve, 'that was entirely coincidental. Southern Comfort, you know what they say. "Eventually, it comes out one end or the other".'

'I was going to tell you before we left. There was just never a good time.'

'And have you thought this through?' Harry asked, desperately. '*Live* with her? With Emily? No, the more I consider it the more I'm convinced that it won't work. It won't work at *all*.'

'It will work.'

'Of course it won't.'

'I know you've never liked her,' Charlie said, feeling his heart start to whir, 'but *I* do and—'

Harry laughed and stopped Charlie short. 'No, no, *no*,' he said, waving the hands about. 'You misunder*stand*. Emily's great. She's *too* good for you, in fact. She's a doctor and you're unemployed. She's an English rose in a summer rain and you're a... withered pansy in a broken vase.'

'Well we love each other and this is just what people do—'

'It's only a matter of time until she realises your unemployment isn't a phase,' he said quite angrily. 'And when she does do you think she'll let you leech off her for the rest of your lives? It's preposterous.'

'Oh, like you did? You made me quit my job, Harry, and you made me depend on you to live on Milk Street. And look where that's got me!'

'You think I *manipulated* you? Into living with me?'

'No. You're not that clever. You just won me over through pity. But I really *am* moving out. And I'll stock shelves, or—or I'll work the drive-thru at McDonald's or something. The point is, I *am* moving in with her. A little Georgian place in Greenwich, five minutes from the Market.'

'That's south of the river! Have you gone *mad*?'

'Quite possibly! But it was two months ago when I agreed to move in with you!'

Harry sulked for a while until his thoughts bubbled to the surface and he couldn't take it any longer.

'I can't believe this,' he grumbled. 'You've absolutely nothing in common. If the two of you met today do you really believe she'd give you even a second of her time?'

'That's unfair, we—'

'You only even know her because of me. Because of Rose and I.'

'That's not true, I've known her since university.'

'Yes, yes, well, peripherally,' Harry said, waving the idea away. 'But not seriously. And Rose and I—*that* made some sense at least. Those girls and I share a similar sort of background, but *you*? You're from the north of bloody England for crying out loud!'

'There it is,' Charlie gnashed his teeth, 'truth at last. Thanks, Harry. Thanks a lot.'

'Charlie—stop!' Harry sobbed, grasping at his sleeve. 'My filter's broken. I didn't mean that. I'm sorry. I don't know what's come over me, I'm just... I'm *broken*, okay?'

He had that wild look about him that came and went as fleeting as the gulls. If the windows were the eyes to the soul, then Harry was fucking doomed.

'You know what you are?' Charlie snapped. 'You're simultaneously fascinating—and a honking great big twat!'

'I know I am. But I'm working on it, I promise I am.'

Harry slumped against the wall and leaned back so his gaze fell over the Yarrowmoor again. A film of tears bubbled in both eyes, refusing to break their dams.

'On my way here... I thought a lot about that letter. The one my father sent?' Harry said. 'And I think... I think it's *over* between us. But properly this time.'

Charlie could only sigh. '*Why* do you two find it so hard to be civil?'

'Because he's a deformity. He's got something wrong with his brain. Do you know what he said of me? He said I'm in a rebellious phase. Gah and *puke*! I could've vommed. It's like he's got amnesia of himself at my age. Believe me when I say he was no saint. He was a tyrant at the Harrow, a belligerent bullier of fags and chair of the Bullingdon at Oxford. He spent six months in a bloody borstal for God's sake. The list of his war crimes is three miles long. That great fat head of his ought to decorate some royal pike.'

108

He slid down the wall to the grass and dug his heels into the earth.

'There's four or five generations of Burden who now only exist as portraits in the family gallery. And every last one of them was as insufferable as I.'

'Nonsense,' Charlie smiled. 'That's surely not possible.'

Harry wasn't in the mood for jokes. He'd turned from sad to angry. He clenched his teeth and fists and the snifter burst in his hand. His fingers turned red with blood and the violence of it shocked him. He dropped the shards into the bluebells and bundled his hand in his sleeve.

'Harry! Are you alright?'

'I'm fine. It's nothing,' he cupped the hand to his chest.

'Jesus, you're a mess. Why don't you go back to Milk Street? This isn't a place for you. Not with Rose and all. I'll be home on Monday and we can figure something out.'

'I *can't*,' he said emphatically. The dam in his left eye finally broke and a tear escaped down his cheek. He wiped it away with his bloody palm smearing red all over his face. 'I'm a stray cat. This isn't like our other arguments. This time it's different. It's all really over. I'll never talk to that man again.'

There was some finality in his tone that unsettled Charlie. Why would he never speak with his father again? They'd had worse arguments than this.

'Of course you will,' Charlie offered. 'When we get home the two of us will go over to Blye House and sort this mess out.'

'When *we* get home?' he sneered. 'You mean when *I* get home and *you* swan off to Greenwich Village?'

'Don't be that way.'

'I don't think I can stomach London anymore. Between you and *him*, what else is there for me there? The fogs of Whitechapel have given me lung cancer and it's infested with vermin. Rats the size of men in suits, riding the tube to the office. *That*'s what London is.'

His bloodied cheeks were waxen and his hairline seemed to recede before Charlie's eyes.

'Harry. Are you *okay*?' Charlie asked again, looking him over. He meant it in the sense of his soul more than his spirit.

Harry looked up at him. His whole face had morphed, crushed under some heavy thoughts and although he smiled and although he nodded, he became, however briefly, a skeleton.

Chapter 4

When Charlie and Harry returned, Emily had slipped into a swimsuit, put on her beach hat and a pair of dark sunglasses and was nestled into the hot tub with a large glass of gin. The lattice of the trellis patterned her in diamonds of afternoon sunlight.

Charlie and Harry spoke quietly by the bookshelf before Charlie slid the patio doors open and sat on the edge of the water.

'He's still here I see,' said Emily.

'Yes.'

She drew the sunglasses down her nose. Harry was drifting coyly round the kitchen and she watched him sniff at the dog bowl then reel back.

'It's no skin off *my* nose,' she said. 'But I don't imagine Tom and Rose will feel the same. Did you tell him he had to go home?'

'I tried. But oh, he *can't* Emily,' Charlie said. 'He's got nowhere else to go.'

She tilted her head. 'You mean *besides* his father's enormous mansion, the various other Burden estates that litter half of the southern English countryside, *and* your four-bed London townhouse, of course?'

'Yes,' Charlie said, turning pink, 'besides those.'

'Why can't he go back to Milk Street?'

'He's troubled,' Charlie told her. He put a hand in the water and swished it around, watching the ringlets expand around his wrist. He hadn't told her about The Incident last month. But now he thought perhaps he should.

'Thing is, I don't want to go back home on Monday and find him hanging from the chandelier with "I told you so" written in his note. If you think he's dangerous now, you should see him when he's spent a night with Johnnie Walker. And let's just say it's a jolly good thing Mad Eric Wardle still has his great-grandfather's service revolver.'

Harry had moved on from the dog bowl to the potpourri. He knocked it from the shelf and it covered him in confetti while he scrabbled through the air to catch the dish.

'What do you mean by that?' asked Emily, more concern spreading to the edges of her face where her brows pulled back into her hairline.

'All I mean is that it might not be in *Rose's* best interest or *Tom's* best interest for Harry to be here. But it *is* in Harry's. And as his friend, that makes it in *mine*.'

Her forehead creased.

'We all just got off on the wrong foot,' Charlie explained. 'And Harry has agreed to apologise as soon as they get back. He's even planned some sort of surprise for us all.'

'A surprise?'

'An excursion. And he explained everything about last night to me just now. He was knocking for twenty minutes. We were all just too paralysed with fear to answer him. If we'd called out, "Who's there?" or just answered the bloody door, we could've avoided all this. But we kept silent and he couldn't hear us. What else could he do? He assumed the house was empty so he forced the window. He fully intends to pay for the damage. And he certainly didn't expect to get *shot* for the trouble.

'And then there was the incident with the dog,' Charlie pushed on, 'which, as we've learned, wasn't even Harry's fault. Tom locked the poor bugger out all night, and Rose didn't even notice her own dog was missing. That's just bad pet ownership, not to notice your dog's missing for—*how* long was it? Six *hours*? They have no right to be mad at him for *that*. So really,' he concluded, taking a breath, 'his only crime so far is turning up here uninvited.'

Emily slid back into the water so it ringed her thin neck. '*So far*,' she repeated. 'Just don't be naïve, Charlie,' she warned him. 'He might be troubled, but he's awfully manipulative. Just look at how he got you into Milk Street. And he's up to something. You *know* that don't you?'

'What do you mean?'

'Look at the paper. Page forty-something.'

Charlie looked round. On the table was the rolled-up newspaper Harry had bought that morning. He leafed through it.

Near the middle, a page had been torn out and he ran his finger down the jagged spine.

'Someone tore a page out?'

'*Harry* tore a page out. He's the only one to touch it. Aside from me.'

'Okay, so *Harry* tore a page out. So what?'

She pursed her lips. 'And I looked through those bloodied towels from the pedal-bin. There's *no way* he bled like that from a BB pellet.'

'What are you saying?'

She sat up and the water rushed off her. 'I'm *saying* that he's lying to you. He's lying to *all* of us. I haven't figured it out yet, but I will. Now,' she slid back down, 'be a doll and put the bubbles back on for me on your way inside, would you?'

She closed her eyes again below the dark shades. Charlie stared at the torn newspaper for a second, then up at Harry inside, who waved goofily. Charlie tried to reconcile that image with the idea of a manipulative genius, but found it a stretch.

He pushed the button on the tub and opened the door.

Charlie had no sooner approached Harry by the bookshelf than Emily appeared beside him, tying her towel around her waist. Harry curtseyed as she came in. 'Don't worry, your Majesty! I'm leaving your court. I think your dogsbody is bringing one of the stallions up from the stable as we speak.'

'Put a sock in it, Harry—my *word* you're dramatic,' she said. '*Both* of you in fact. I've never met a bigger pair of babies in all my life and I spent two years at Great Ormond Street.' She sighed. 'Here's what I'll do. I mean to speak with Tom and Rose. I'm making *no promises* you can stay. If they want you gone, *you're gone*. But I'll see what I can do. *Okay*?'

'I-I don't know what to say,' said Harry.

'Good,' she answered, pulling her jeans up over her swimsuit. 'Say as little as you possibly can for the rest of the weekend and I'm quite sure we'll all get along just famously.'

She took her jacket off the hook and then sat down to put her boots on. She noticed Harry's hand, wrapped in toilet paper and browned with his blood.

'What's wrong with your hand?' she asked. 'Is *that* where all the blood's come from?'

'No, he cut it on a glass while we were out just now,' Charlie told her.

She tied her wet hair back into a ponytail. 'Go and wash it in cold water and I'll find some bandages.'

She took out the first aid kit while Harry washed the blood off in the sink. She examined the cleaned hand in the light of the side window. When she was satisfied there were no shards of glass stuck inside it, she put padded bandages over the larger cuts on his palm, then wrapped a length of gauze from the wrist through the V of his thumb and mummified each finger.

When she was done, Harry held up his hand to the light. 'That about wraps that up,' he smiled.

Chapter 5

An hour later, Tom burst back into The Barrow and bee-lined for the kitchen, causing Harry to drop to the floor and cower behind his arms.

'You mustn't hit me, I've a weak heart,' he blabbed. 'Inherited from my Great Aunt Gertrude.'

But instead of walloping him over the side of the head, Tom only reached for the cupboard above him and took down three small glasses. He filled one with cheap American whiskey and shoved it into Harry's hand, who peered into the glass suspiciously.

'F-for *me*?'

'It's no *Scotch*.' Tom glared from under a thick, stone brow. 'But it'll do the job all the same.'

'Indeed,' said Harry.

'And since it don't look like you're going nowhere, we might as well all try and get along, eh?'

'Indeed?' Harry repeated but with an upward inflection.

'So for that, I think we need a drink, don't you?'

'In... indeed,' he said again, nodding.

The girls had just returned and Charlie cast a look at Emily as Tom filled up the other glasses. He had to wonder what she had said to change his mind like this.

'No luck finding Teddy then?' Harry asked, implying the dog-less lead in her hand.

Rose shook her head.

'Doesn't the little scamp have a microchip in him?' asked Harry. 'Connected to a whopping great satellite or something? To track him and such?'

'No,' said Tom as he topped Harry's glass back up.

'Well look, he's *bound* to turn up. I daresay he'll be at the foot of a wizened old oak, barking at the birds.'

'Can we just talk about summat else?' Tom said.

He snatched the glass out of Harry's hand and continued to fill it until the whisky was level with the edge. He didn't break eye contact until he'd handed it back over.

'Yes, of course,' Harry blushed. 'Er—the weather's been rather choice, just… Don't you think? I saw flowers the colour of gasoline puddles on my way up.'

'Are you going to tell us how you got here, now?' asked Charlie, suddenly concerned.

'Oh, of course! I'm surprised you didn't *see*.'

'You keep saying that and it's gotten me worried. *Tell* me you didn't steal the helicopter.'

'I didn't steal the helicopter.'

'Because you know your father nearly *killed* you last time.'

Harry lost some of the colour in his cheeks.

'Go on then? How'd you get here?'

'Why, I *drove*.'

'But you can't *drive*. The closest *you*'ve ever come to driving was when you took your bicycle down Brompton Road with a lance under your arm yelling "Here comes Sir Shagalot" at those terrified women.'

'Yes and perhaps according to those bureaucrats from the DVLA, you're right. But I'm a damn sight better than half the baboons monopolising the middle lanes of the M6.'

'I'll drink to that,' Tom said, topping them all back up. He already had the Tennessee glow about the cheeks.

'Go ahead. Take a look outside,' Harry diverted them round the island. 'My wheels are parked around the corner.'

They crowded a side window and Charlie parted the blinds.

'Jesus on a cross!' Tom said, open-mouthed. 'Who knew you had such good taste?'

In the gap between two trees stood a handsome motorcycle in British racing green with a sidecar attached by a clamp.

'What is she—a Triumph?' Tom asked.

'Good eye, sir. I only ride British. A Bonneville. Custom spray. Isn't she just the *ratherest* thing? Don't you just want to take her to bed and canoodle under satin sheets?'

'What's the sidecar all about?' Charlie asked.

'Storage.'

'I've gotta see this,' Tom said, heading for the door.

'No—really, there's nothing to it that you can't see from here,' said Harry.

Tom wasn't listening. He was already outside when Charlie decided to follow him into the clearing.

'Oof! What happened here?' Tom asked.

He ran a hand over a nasty scrape down the fuel tank and along the edge of the muffler where the metal was badly dented and was streaked with deep red paint.

'That? Oh, that's *nothing*.'

'Nothing? Harry, it looks like you've been in an accident!' Charlie argued. 'I knew you couldn't drive. What happened?'

His mind went back to all those bloodied towels in the pedal bin. Emily's words returning to him: '*There's no way he bled like that from a BB pellet.*'

Harry waved it away. 'Dozed off a little on the way through Windermere. But I bombed half a gram of cheap whizz and perked up at Ambleside. Say, let's head back in shall we?'

Tom shook his head. 'You went the wrong way. Should've stuck to the M6 and gone *round* the National Park. Through Penrith to Wigton. Shave an hour off your journey.'

'And miss out on such wondrous views?'

'But it was pitch black.'

'I've eyes like a cat, my good man.'

Charlie reached into the sidecar and lifted out a couple of antique motorcycle helmets with bronze goggles. Below them in the footwell were five bottles of vintage red wine and a duffle bag. Harry leapt forward and lugged the duffle bag out heavily, and held it to his chest.

'What's in there?' asked Charlie.

'Change of clothes,' Harry answered.

'Come on,' Charlie laughed. 'It looks a ton weight!'

With some reluctance, Harry opened the bag. Sure enough, it was filled mostly with clothes, but the source of the weight was a silver thing, about the size of a shoebox, decorated in gilded ivy with fleur-de-lis clasps.

'What's that? A jewellery box?'

'It's nothing,' Harry said dismissively. 'Now come, we really must go back inside. The girls will think we've disappeared like the dog—'

'Christ alive, Harry,' Charlie said, having yanked the bag from him and opened up the silver box. Inside lay two antique duelling pistols across a bed of lush red velvet. 'Am I the *only* one here who didn't bring a bloody *gun* with them?'

'What are they?' Tom asked, leaning in for a better view.

'True flintlocks,' Harry explained. He picked one out and wafted it around carelessly. 'Early seventeenth century. Decommissioned of course. Or unloaded or something. Anyway it doesn't fire. See?'

He clicked the trigger noiselessly a few times in the air.

'Where are they from?' Charlie asked.

'Belonged to a privateer-turned-pirate by the name of Edward Hickory. Ex-Navy man who disappeared in Nassau when the governor arrived to hang them all.'

'Yes—save us the history lesson,' snapped Charlie, irritably. 'I *mean* where did you *get* them?'

'Ah. Sotheby's, last year. Five K, I think they went for. They were my father's pride and joy.'

'What do you mean "*were*"?'

'I repurposed them.'

'Stolen. Like the greatcoat.'

'*Repurposed* like the greatcoat, yes.'

'And the boar head.'

'In a manner of speaking.'

'What's this about a boar head?' Tom asked.

'Long story,' Harry replaced the gun on the velvet and closed the lid.

Charlie still wasn't satisfied.

'But why have you brought them *here*?' he asked, rooting through the duffle bag. He pulled out the clothes inside—a dark tailcoat and an old straw hat. 'And what's *this* supposed to be? You realise it's not the nineteenth century anymore don't you?'

'You know me.' Harry said, placing the straw hat on his head at a jaunty angle. 'I'm eccentric.'

They carried what they could back into the house. Between them, Tom and Charlie carried the vintage wines in, while Harry carried through his duffle bag.

'So how much did that little beauty set you back?' Tom wondered.

'The bike, you mean? Nothing at all. It belongs to a friend of mine, you see.'

'What friend?' asked Charlie. 'You haven't got any friends.'

'You don't know him. He lives in Guildford. He dropped it off just after you left on Friday as a matter of fact. I'm looking after it for the weekend.'

'Not very well, from the look of that scrape.'

'It'll buff out. Now do you think you could stick the kettle on? This comedown has arrived all at once and I'm certain its intention is to kill me.'

Harry kicked off his Chelsea boots and wriggled his toes about. He had settled into the settee and didn't seem to notice, or care if he did, that it was swallowing him whole. He had a hand on his brow and his eyes were shut.

Chapter 6

After everyone had eaten at eight o'clock, Harry laid a map across the island. It showed a moon-shaped lake called *Spreywater* and he drilled a finger into the green circle in its centre.

'This,' he said with much gusto, 'is Potter Island. Over here, he moved his finger south-west, about an inch off the map, 'is where we are now. And this,' he reached into his coat pocket and took out a creased postcard, 'is what the place *looks* like.'

He laid it across the map. It showed a beautiful, white wooden cabin with its entire front-facing wall made of retractable glass doors. The views looked across the waterfront with crags and ravines and all sorts of trees and hills dotted along the distant coast reflected in the glass.

'I just don't *understand*,' Rose said as politely as she could. 'It's nice of you, Harry. It *really* is. But why would we go all that way across a freezing cold lake to a tiny little cabin when we have a place of our own right *here*?'

'Because it's a call to adventure!' he rejoiced. 'It's exciting. Don't you want to see even just *one* lake while you're here in the *Lake* District? Don't you want to be rocked by a boat as you part the water headed for uncharted lands? I'm a descendant of Lord Byron, don't you know—?'

'One of the bastards,' Charlie muttered.

'—adventure runs through his blood in *my* veins.'

The response was disheartening.

'Did I mention there's a free bar?'

Tom lit up. 'They have draft?'

'I believe so.'

'And it's fully stocked?'

'So I'm told.'

'And we don't have to pay for owt?'

'No, I've told you, I've taken care of all expenses. This is my *apology* to you. It would hardly be so if I asked you all to chip in now would it?'

'And how do we get there?'

120

Harry shuffled his watch along his wrist. 'Well bugger me, it's broken!' he said shaking it by his ear. 'What time is it?'

Rose reached into her pocket. 'Oh now *where* did I leave my phone?' she said, looking round.

'I saw it on the coffee table,' Emily told her, and Rose went off to look.

'It's just gone eight,' Charlie told them.

'Great. Our boat,' Harry said, 'leaves at *nine* from the harbour just here.' He pointed to the little port on the edge of the Spreywater. 'What do you say?'

Charlie and Emily swapped a look. Tom curled his lip. Rose pulled up the cushions from the settee looking for her phone.

'Alright,' Tom decided, nodding. 'I'm in.'

'I suppose we *should* see at least one lake while we're here,' Emily agreed.

'Rose? You in?'

'Hm?' she looked over distracted. 'Oh. Yes, I suppose I *would* like to get away for a while, now that I think about it. This house is cursed. First my Teddybear goes missing and now my phone!'

Tom turned the map in his direction. 'How far d'you say it were?'

'Not far at all,' beamed Harry. 'We just take a right by that tremendous cavity of a pothole. Then follow the road down. The man said it's a twenty-minute jaunt.'

'What man?'

'The man from the newsagent where I arranged all of this.'

'Alright. Then I s'pose we better go and get ready.'

'Excellent! But first—' Harry dashed away and plucked one of the vintage reds from the coffee table. He poured out five glasses, handed them around and held his own in the air. 'A toast,' he announced. 'To new friends! And a night of debauchery, free of disaster.'

They each raised their wine. The five glasses clinked together and the legs of the red ran down their sides like blood.

Chapter 7

It was already half past eight and Charlie was conscious the ferry would be leaving at nine o'clock. He had changed into a navy shirt and pair of dark jeans but Emily was still looking through the cupboard with her hands on her hips.

'I really don't know *what* you're supposed to wear to a party that takes place in a remote *cabin* on an *island* in the middle of a ginormous *lake*,' she said. 'Do you wear a nice *dress*? Or a *life jacket*? Heels? Or a pair of hiking boots? *What?*'

'Just put on something warm,' Charlie said. He was sat on the bed reading from a brochure Harry had given him. 'Listen to this: *Potter Island was named after none other than Beatrix Potter, who said its views, which span the Coralbell crags to the Yarrowmoor, are surely one of nature's greatest achievements. She spent thousands of pounds of her own money to preserve them.*'

'It's a bloody good thing we're going at *night* then, isn't it?' Emily said. She took a canary yellow dress from the cupboard and flattened it against her. 'What about this?'

'Yes, I like it,' Charlie said without taking his eyes off the brochure. 'How do you think Harry managed to arrange all of this just by going to get the morning paper? I think you were right, you know. He's up to something. I've no idea where that bike came from. And did you know he brought a set of pistols with him?'

'*Pistols?*' Emily looked troubled by the revelation.

'They don't fire,' Charlie assured her. 'Or so he says. But I can't imagine *why* he would possibly have needed to bring them.'

He swung his legs off the bed.

'I'm going to wait outside.'

He left the room. Tom and Rose were screaming at each other when he passed their door. He took his coat from the hook and opened the front door. The sky was charcoal but the light from the lodge bled out across the drive and he could see Harry had moved his bike. Now it stood beside the Merc. He was really making himself at home.

He ran his hand down the scrape along its muffler. But then he noticed something strange. The silver box containing the duelling pistols was still in the footwell of the sidecar. He had seen Harry bring the duffle bag inside with him. So why had he left *this* out here?

'Rupert Fiddleminster,' called a voice from behind.

Harry was leaning over the porch in his old straw hat. His greatcoat was buttoned to the chin and its enormous collar fanned around him like a mane.

'What?' Charlie asked.

Harry came down the steps, smoking the end of a cigarette.

'Rupert Fiddleminster,' he repeated. '*That's* the chap who owns the Bonneville. I met him at Lords when I was twelve.' He threw his cigarette to the floor and squished it under his toe, then leered up at Charlie excitedly. 'Do you know, I've just had a corker! What do you say I take the Bonneville to port? It's only a five-minute drive but the rush will invigorate that old brain-box of yours.' He rapped Charlie over the temple.

'No way. I mean, I would, of course. I've always wanted to er… but it's Emily, you see. If Emily wasn't here I would. You know I'd be there in a heartbeat, but—'

'Don't let *me* stop you having fun,' Emily said.

She had come down the steps behind Charlie at that opportune moment.

'Just make sure you boys wear *protection*.' She took a helmet from the sidecar and thrust it into Charlie's chest. 'Enjoy.'

Harry looked at his watch, forgetting it was still broken.

'Bugger. What's the time?'

'Quarter to nine. What happened to your watch—?'

'We ready then, fuck-faces?'

Tom and Rose had left the house. Tom locked the door and came down to the drive.

'You three go on ahead,' Harry smiled. 'I'm going to give Charlie a ride on the old Bonneville.' He slapped the fuel tank proudly. 'We'll meet you at the port in five minutes.'

Tom shrugged and he and the girls took off along The Mall.

'Get in the sidecar!' Harry said, grinning ecstatically.

Harry undid his greatcoat so that he could mount the bike and Charlie fell about with laughter.

'What are you *wearing*?'

Harry had changed into the outfit from the duffle bag. It was his old Harrow uniform. Not his daily uniform, but his uniform for best: his straw hat, of course, with its blue band, and a black tailcoat that was too tight across the breast. Beneath it, a dark waistcoat, pulling at the seams, striped trousers, two inches too short and a pair of shiny black wingtips you could almost see your face in. He hadn't worn the thing for over six years.

'What are you laughing at?' Harry asked, turning red.

'Why are you wearing your old Harrow uniform?'

'Because I'm an Harrovian,' he explained taking offence. 'Once a Harrowman, a Harrowman for life. One doesn't age out of one's institution.'

'No but one certainly *grows* out of it.'

'How dare you,' Harry snapped. He pulled the tailcoat over his shoulders and held the lapels with his thumbs pointing out. 'I've not grown out of a thing.'

'Tell that to your ankles. You'll catch pneumonia riding the Bonneville like that. You didn't pack any hiking socks did you?'

'Sod off,' Harry snarled, turning away and mounting the motorbike. The old trousers rode another inch higher and Charlie fell about. He was still chuckling when he climbed into the sidecar and had to shift the pistol box onto his lap.

'Why've you left this in here?'

Harry shrugged. 'I didn't fancy leaving a pair of *guns* in Tom's reach,' he answered. 'If I make one more off-colour joke then he— *or Rose*—may be liable to shoot me. Again.'

'You said they're decommissioned.'

'Well, they are. That is I *think* they are. They're three hundred years old. But one can never be too careful when it comes to gun safety, you know.'

'Oh yes, the motto of the Fox Hunting Guild?'

'Just pop it in the footwell; we need to go.'

Charlie did as he was told and stuffed the box awkwardly below his feet. 'I don't have much foot room, you know.'

'Well I didn't intend on giving you a ride, did I? Besides, Tom's locked the door now. It'll have to stay put.'

'There's a spare key,' Charlie said, pointing at the barrel with the lockbox attached to it. He tried to recall the code. Nineteen-sixty-six, that was it. 'Let me just pop it back inside and—'

'No!' Harry said suddenly. 'There's no time for any of that. The ferry leaves in twelve minutes and I want to beat them to port.'

'Fine,' Charlie groaned, 'Just go.'

Harry looked somewhat relieved. He tucked his straw hat into his waistcoat and they put on their helmets. The bike rumbled to life and followed its headlights, slowly at first, as he felt his way down The Mall through the wood.

'There they are.' Harry clenched his teeth. He circled the others around the pothole. 'See you slowpokes on the other side!' he cajoled, honking the horn triumphantly as he overtook them.

Once they were on the paved road, Harry let Charlie feel the true power of the Bonneville. The sidecar didn't rattle but Charlie felt the engine vibrating through the wall. The road spun by, round and wide like a hamster wheel and the white dotted lines became solid. There was a great smell of concrete and foliage and the wind smacked them in the little of their faces the helmets and goggles didn't cover. He had the strange sensation he was piloting a spitfire.

Before long, the moon shaped lake appeared on the horizon. It was a navy shimmer on a wall of jet black, but the lights of the port danced like little fireflies around the lip of the water and cast squiggly lines through the waves.

Charlie was surprised to find himself smiling. He had expected only festering neuroses but his heart was thumping with excitement. Harry, however, was reliably on-hand to put an end to that.

'I don't mean to alarm you, old thing,' he shouted over the engine, 'but I've been aware for twenty seconds or so now that the brakes don't appear to be working!'

The road began its steep decline toward the port. Harry's face was strained and the veins in his neck were moving like fried gristle.

125

'What do you mean?' Charlie shouted back. 'You can't *stop*?'

'Uh-oh!' was all Harry answered. 'Uh-oh!'

The bike appeared to be growing only ever faster but the sound of the engine couldn't drown out Charlie's beating heart. It was no longer thumping with excitement. It was thumping with alarm. He could hear it in his head. Loud, like a fucking gong, and it chimed five times a second.

'Harry you intolerable bastard! If this is one of your jokes it isn't funny—'

'It's no joke, Charlie-Boy.'

Charlie saw Harry's hands—he was opening and closing his fingers over the brakes like mad but the bike wouldn't slow down.

'Christ! What do we do? What do we *do*?' Charlie screamed. He could feel his anxious energy resurfacing like lava over hard magma, quaking and erupting all at once.

Harry nodded to the grassy banks. He veered over till the sidecar was just an inch from slipping down them.

'You're going to have to jump old chap! So sorry!'

'Jump!' Charlie almost laughed but the laugh got stuck in his throat and made him feel sick. He peered over at the grass. It was constantly being replaced by new, uneven mounds as they thundered by, while the road scrolled like a treadmill at a thousand paces a second. 'Are you taking the piss? I'll break my neck!'

'No time to debate,' Harry called back, looking to the port ahead. It was growing larger by the second. The fireflies had now become streetlights. The water was dramatic, rippling under a strong wind. Waves lapped the feet of the long wooden jetty that extended out across the ink.

'And what about you?' Charlie asked.

'I'll jump too, but I need to keep the bike going! You'll have to go first!'

'Oh, Christ! Jesus Christ! Jesus fucking Christ on a cross!'

'Pray if it helps!' Harry said with a half-smile. 'When I say "go!", go. Okay?'

Charlie tried to stand up. His legs wobbled like cooked spaghetti.

He held onto the rim of the sidecar and it felt incredibly shaky all of a sudden. His legs bowed and he sat back down.

'Come on, Charlie. *One*…' Harry called out encouragingly.

Charlie tried again. He put a foot on his seat and the other on the edge of the car. He held onto the little half-moon screen guard and faced the grass at the side of the road.

'*Two*…'

He looked back at the way they'd come. It was an endless stretch of grey road and black sky. His eyes were back on the port and then on the grass.

'Three…'

Wind bit at Charlie's face with small, sharp teeth. He braced himself to jump.

'*Go!*'

He went immediately on the word.

He threw himself from the sidecar, landed hard on the grass and began to roll. His elbow hit a rock which sent a shiver through his skeleton, while a bruising throb pulsed around his muscles. But he didn't have time to consider the pain. Adrenaline was so coursing through him that he was back on his feet and running after the bike at superhuman speed. He made it to within touching distance of the port just in time to witness the outrageous finale of Harry's stunt.

Chapter 8

At five to nine, Pebbleton Port had been quiet. Its wooden sign creaked where it swung from a gallows pole and the water beneath the jetty swished against the pilings as a small ferry was rocked by gentle waves.

The ferry was a twelve-foot aluminium pontoon with a trolling motor, dangling into the water at the stern. There were seven seats, three either side and another for the ferryman set into the transom. It was a very old thing, and rusting, with a small gap at the top of the hull where the riveting had come loose between two plates.

The lake itself glistened tranquilly under moonlight. During the day, canoes, yachts and speedboats littered the waterfront but by night it was just a dark and vast mirror reflecting the stars. It was over three miles long end to end and Potter Island was the only notable thing along it. Its little white cabin looked especially small compared with the ominous mountains, like giant lumps of coal, all around it.

There were only six buildings on the harbour front. A couple of seafood restaurants, a gift shop, a post office, a fishing shop and a ticket office. The ticket office door clicked open and the ferryman stepped out to breathe the air.

He was a short, stern fellow, with one long white eyebrow like a furry caterpillar. He had a permanent squint in one eye that made his other seem to bulge. He filled his pipe with tobacco and stuck the bit between his teeth and then leaned back against the wall to smoke.

Charlie stood some twenty feet away. His hands were clasped firmly over his head and his jaws were three inches apart.

The low rumble of the Bonneville quickly drew the ferryman's attention to the head of the road. He narrowed his bulging eye at the thick cloud of smoke. A second later, the motorbike appeared, heading his way. Its rider was screaming. He thundered down the road, whizzed past the ticket office and showed no sign of slowing as he approached the jetty. Instead, the bike leapt up over the kerb and landed heavily on the wooden boards where it bobbed up and down at ninety miles an hour, heading straight for the lake.

The rider's legs pointed outwards at first, but soon they came in close and he climbed up on the seat. His bike growled like an untamed beast. He held the handles and tried to keep the thing on course and then finally, at the last conceivable moment, leapt off. He landed on his feet and wobbled on the spot, while his bike—all three hundred kilos of it—carried on until it flew off the end of the jetty, soared through the air for three or four seconds, then landed, hard, on the surface of the water and began to sink slowly out of sight.

The ferryman watched the scene unfold and then went on smoking from his pipe as indifferent as if the bike had not crashed into the lake at all, but had slowed to a nice stop and gently parked up beside the road.

'*Tsh*,' he muttered to himself. 'Bloody tourists.'

Charlie had rushed over and stopped just an inch from him, before slowly making his way along the jetty to Harry's side. He stared open-mouthed as the handle of the Triumph Bonneville— the last part still visible—disappeared beneath the surface of the wine-dark water in a cluster of bubbles.

'Bugger,' Harry mumbled as it vanished. 'Oh well.'

He turned from the lake and left the jetty, putting his straw hat back on his head at an angle.

'"*Oh well*"?' Charlie repeated quietly. He chased after Harry. 'Oh well! *Oh fucking well*, Harry? You've done it, haven't you? You've finally lost your bloody mind! We could be dead right now!'

'Ah, but we're not!' he grinned. 'We're alive and well and in the arms of these beautiful mountains! Doesn't it feel wonderful? To be held by such warmth? Breathe in the air, Charlie-Boy. That's sea salt.'

'No it isn't! This is freshwater!'

They arrived at the ticket office where the old ferryman was smoking his pipe. His one long eyebrow rippled when Harry approached.

'My good man,' Harry said, pulling a bundle of cash from seemingly nowhere and handing over a sizeable chunk. 'Hobbs, I assume?'

'Where did you get all *that*?' Charlie gawped.

Harry stuffed the wad of money back into his pocket somewhat oblivious. 'Get what?'

'That effing tremendous wedge of dough! *That's* what.'

'It's my life's savings,' Harry answered. 'I intend to burn through it before the weekend's out.'

Hobbs finished counting the cash and stuffed it into his pocket book and then gave a short chuckle.

'Who've you come as? Little Lord Fauntleroy?'

'How dare you!' Harry raged. 'Don't you recognise the livery of the Harrow?'

The ferryman chuckled again and shook his head. 'The what? Where's rest of yer anyway? Was expecting five.'

'They'll be along shortly.'

'*Shortly*,' the man grumbled. 'Aye. Boat leaves in three minutes. With or without 'em. That clear?'

'Yes, yes,' Harry said indignantly. 'They come anon.'

The ferryman scowled. He put his pipe in his mouth and watched curiously as Harry took three fags from his pack and stuck each under his lip. He lit and then smoked from them simultaneously.

Emily, Tom and Rose appeared at the top of the road and Charlie found it a great relief to see them. He couldn't change Harry, but he could dilute him.

'Here they are!' Charlie practically sobbed.

'Mm,' Hobbs grumbled, looking at his watch.

'Oh and er—Charlie?' Harry said. 'Perhaps don't *tell* them about what just happened? With the Bonneville? They already think I'm the world's greatest nitwit.'

'Fuck-a-doodle-do,' Tom said when they arrived at the ticket office. 'Is that *it* then?'

The pontoon ferry swayed unimpressively ahead. It barely looked big enough to support them all. Harry led them over to it and chucked his three cigarettes into the lake. The ferryman grumbled again.

'Welcome, welcome,' Harry said, taking a hold of the deck

130

ladder. 'Ahead lies Potter Island and a night of liver-destructing debauchery. In that there cabin,' (he pointed off to the distance) 'is enough alcohol to flood the meres. We shall drink till Bacchus himself fears our revelry and the moon can bear to watch us no longer. Now all aboard. Er, this *is* our ferry, I assume?' he turned to Hobbs with one leg on the bottom rung of the ladder.

'Listen, soft lad,' Hobbs said, stepping between him and the boat, and prodding Harry hard in the chest with the bit of his pipe. 'Let's get one thing straight, right off the bat. This is *my* ferry, not *our* ferry. Not *your* ferry. And yer not to touch her till I've told yer to. Who's Captain here, anyway?'

The tips of Harry's ears turned pink. 'Sorry, I—'

'Who's Captain?' Hobbs repeated, pushing his pipe harder into Harry's sternum.

Harry looked at him with a sullen face. 'Well you are. *Aren't* you?'

'That's right,' Hobbs said, smiling, though with hard, cold eyes. 'Now stop being so... Stop being so *you*.'

Tom gave a hearty laugh but Hobbs cast him a stern look too and he fell silent.

The ferryman climbed the deck ladder and boarded the pontoon, mumbling to himself. 'Tourists. Always pissin' tourists!'

'Well, *he's* a charmer,' Harry muttered, turning back to the group. 'I nearly thumped him one then, did you see? I was *this* close.'

'Yes *right*,' Rose rolled her eyes. 'You fell into yourself so completely I thought you were about to *disappear*.'

'No, no,' Harry said, blushing. 'I was merely trying to remain calm. I wouldn't want to go to prison. I was the boxing champ at the Harrow, don't you know? That could've been murder.'

Hobbs stood up at the stern and leaned over the boat. 'Get on then. All of yers.'

He met them at the top of the ladder. Harry climbed on first and Hobbs put his hand out.

'Hang on. Here.' He gave him five tickets and a key to the cabin.

The others got on one by one and took their seats. There was a roof, like a metal marquee, with glass-less windows over the hull. Hobbs sat on the amidships seat, with one hand resting on one of the metal cleats that lined the gunwale and his other holding a remote to start the motor. He looked at his watch—it had just turned nine o'clock. The motor growled to life and the boat juddered beneath them all as it pulled away from Pebbleton Port and crossed the lake.

Emily pulled an information card from under her seat and read it aloud: 'The Spreywater,' she said, 'is so named because of the local ospreys that nest nearby.'

'Cor! Ospreys!' Harry said looking up at the moon, hoping to spot one.

'What's an *osprey*?' Rose asked.

'Fish-eating hawks,' he told her. 'They grow about *this* big.'

Emily turned the card around to show them a picture. '*This bird of prey reaches over seventy inches in length*—'

'I hope we get to see one,' Harry said, giddily. 'I founded the ornithology club at the Harrow, don't you know?'

'Oh aye?' Tom asked. 'Didn't know you were into birds.'

'I wouldn't exactly call myself a *twitcher* per se, but I *am* currently building a table for the crows that live in our roof, isn't that right Charlie?'

'Yes and making a racket of it.'

'Why, are you?' Harry asked Tom. 'Into birds I mean.'

Tom put an arm around his girlfriend. 'We both are, aren't we babe? Rosie here loves a cockatoo. But I don't mind ogling a pair of great tits every now and then.'

Soon enough, the pontoon reached the island. Hobbs killed the motor and unwound a rope from the cleats to lasso round the piling. He pulled them in close to the wooden promenade that squared the island and the boat bumped into the side aggressively. The water here was greyer and the froth was violent by the rocks below the pier.

'I'm going to hurl,' Rose whispered. 'I get the most *awful* sea sickness, you know.'

'Just don't look down,' Tom said. 'I'll take your hand.'

Hobbs folded the deck ladder out and Tom climbed down first. Rose covered her eyes as he reached up to help her onto flat land. The others got off and Harry had no sooner uttered, 'Thank you, Mr Hobbs, my good man!' than the motor started back up and the ferry was off in a spray of fine mist.

'If I had a quid for every miserable fucker we've met since yesterday...' Tom complained, as he led the party up the steps to the cabin on Potter Island, 'I'd have about a fiver.'

Chapter 9

The pale moonlight that fell across Potter Island caused the little white cabin to glow. It was made of birch wood and sported a white-brick chimney and a flat, steel roof. Its entire front-facing wall was made of glass And as they drew closer, Charlie saw this wall was a set of bi-folding doors that opened to a balcony across the water.

Harry unlocked the door and led them inside. Everything here was white, too. Even the little corner settee and the dining table were a pale shade of grey. The chimney turned into a fireplace with a white stone hearth and there were paintings of yachts and clouds in white wooden frames. The only thing in there with any colour was a reddish support beam in the middle of the room, which branched into rafters above.

'There's a little kitchen down here,' Rose called from a small hallway at the back. 'And a washroom to the other side.'

'It's a bit dark,' Emily noted. 'Where's the light switch?'

A sinking feeling came over Charlie. Once his eyes adjusted to the chalky moonlight bouncing off the walls, it began to grow gloomier by the second.

Emily flicked the switch up and down. But nothing happened. It was like being back on Milk Street.

Harry flushed red at once. 'The bulb must be out. Perhaps there's a spare—?'

'It's not the bulb,' Rose said, re-entering from the hall. 'The kitchen and bathroom lights aren't working either.'

'Harry!' Charlie cried. 'You're something else!'

Harry drew back. 'What do you mean?'

'Even when you try and do something nice it turns into disaster!'

'This is hardly *my* fault. I booked from a reputable source—'

'The man who runs the newsagent? He probably saw you coming a mile away, hallooing the swans, saluting the daisies. "Here comes a prized twit" he probably thought.'

'Now hold on a minute,' Emily said diplomatically. 'Let's not

134

be so quick to jump to conclusions again. That got us nowhere last time, did it? Let's look for a fuse box first—'

'Yes! Thank you, Emily.'

'And *then* we can bite his head off.'

'I've found candles,' Rose said, rooting through a draw in the bookshelf.

'Great! Set them up over—'

'No, it's not *great*,' Tom snapped. 'I'm not sitting round in fucking candlelight playing tiddlywinks all night. I want a beer and TV.'

'There isn't even a TV in here.'

'Well then I want—'

'Quiet!' Emily said before things could escalate. 'Let's just look for the fuse box.'

'Yes,' Harry agreed. 'The fuse box. We'll take a room each and look for the fuse box.' He paused with a finger on his lip. 'But first you'll have to tell me… What might it *look like*, exactly, this fuse box?'

'Like a box,' Tom spat impatiently, 'with fuses in it.'

'Well, miniature circuit breakers,' Emily corrected.

'And miniature circuit breakers are…?'

'Jesus Harry,' Charlie snapped at him. 'It's a metal box in a cupboard somewhere with switches inside.'

They split up to search. Emily walked the perimeter, Tom and Rose took the kitchen and Charlie and Harry pottered around the main room. The five soon regrouped round the dining table in the dark.

'We'll just have to try and get the fire lit,' Harry suggested. 'Then it will be light *and* warm and we can get on with the business of drinking.'

'I suppose.'

'There was a coalbin outside,' Emily said. 'I'll go and—'

'I'll go.' Tom stood up. 'Dickens, you come with.'

Charlie followed him outside. They went round to the coalbin and Tom stopped by it, staring at Charlie and tapping his fingers across the lid.

'What?' Charlie asked after an uncomfortable moment passed.

'He's now on strike one,' Tom said. 'Is that fair?'

'Strike one?'

Tom pulled the lid open and let it clatter noisily against the cabin wall.

'When Emily come to us before, asking us to give him a chance,' he said, taking a bucket from the bin and shovelling coal into it, 'I agreed on one condition. If he started acting up with all his nonsense again, I'd throw him out myself. She agreed that were fair. Don't you?'

Before Charlie could answer, Tom went on, 'I'm *try*ing to be patient with the silly prick, I really am. But this is strike one. Two more and *he is out*. And if that means I have to kick his arse into this bloody lake, I will. Here, carry this.'

He thrust the coal bucket into Charlie's chest and trod back off to the cabin. The white walls were dancing in yellow candlelight when Charlie set the coal bucket down on the dining table.

'Now, we need wood and paper to get a fire going,' Harry said.

He took off his coat and rolled up his sleeves before getting to work, prying one of the paintings from the wall. It was nailed in and he almost toppled over when it popped off. He threw it to the floor where it shattered. He slid the paper out and began tearing it up.

'Wood and paper,' he said, somewhat breathless.

'With a side dish of vandalism,' added Rose.

He stuck balls of paper round the fireplace. Next he laid strips of wood over them and scooped a small shovelful of coal across the wood and poked one of the taper candles through the grate to ignite the paper in various spots. It only took two minutes for the paper to burn up and the wood to catch alight, before spreading to the coal. Within five minutes, the whole cabin had heated up considerably and it was bright enough to see one another from more than a foot apart.

'Where did you learn to do that?' asked Rose.

'Two years with The Scout Association,' Harry said. 'Now I believe *that* deserves a drink.'

'Aye,' Tom said casting a stern look around the place. 'Where's that bar you promised?'

Charlie went off down the hall to look for it. A second later, a serving hatch in the wall swung wide open and he reappeared on the other side of a little bar. Above him were two cutlasses crossed beneath a miniature breastplate engraved with an image of Peter Rabbit. In a ribbon it said *Peter's Bar*.

'*Potter* Island, *Peter's* Bar,' Harry leaned over to help himself to a bottle of vodka. 'What next—Jemima's Lavvy? Tiggy-Winkle's Pantry?'

Chapter 10

By eleven o'clock, they were all in better spirits. They had settled in around the fireplace and enjoyed a riotous game of charades—taking a shot after each round (and one or two during)—before splintering off into smaller groups. Charlie found himself at the dining table with Tom and Harry against his better judgment. Tom brought up the Bonneville and Harry tiptoed around the subject trying to avoid mentioning the fact he had driven the bike off the end of a jetty. But Charlie doubted very much if Tom would have even heard if they outright told him; his eyes had started to lose focus and his cheeks were rouged with insobriety. It didn't take long before he threw a beefy arm around Harry's scrawny neck and pulled him in tight.

'You *are* a twat,' he slurred, 'but then so am I. We're all twats, aren't we? I'm the biggest twat here. So what I'm saying is, sorry for the way I've... y'know? Let's let bygones be gone and all that. This weekend's important to me. I've got summat big planned so I don't wanna... well... What d'you say?'

Before Harry could answer, the lights suddenly flashed on throughout the cabin and everyone blinked up like trolls who had never before left the dark of their caves.

Rose suddenly sprang back into the room from down the corridor. She was wearing Harry's greatcoat and straw hat and she began pacing the length of the hearth in a perfect impression of his pompous bounce. Charlie recognised it immediately. He had been taking a swig when he sputtered with laughter, inviting Harry to scold him with a glance.

'I say, ahoy there my old woofies!' Rose bellowed. 'I should've known it'd take a man of the Harrow to fix the lighting in here. There was a fuse box in the bathroom, and I was the head electrician at the Harrow, don't you know?'

Everyone broke up. Except for Harry, who balked.

'Is that supposed to be an impression of *me*?' he said. '"Ahoy my old woofies"? I'm not a *pirate* you know—'

'—Though I do own a ship off the West Indies and carry a

138

couple of flintlocks around,' she continued, illuminated by applause.

Harry looked firmly annoyed, which only made Charlie laugh harder.

'It's not *becoming* for a guest to insult the host!' Harry snapped. 'And I do not start every sentence with "*I say*"!'

'I say, I'm finding this whole thing evidently inaccurate, m'lady, old bean, tip-tip, tally-whack spiff-spoff!'

'Now, *really*,' Harry said, open-mouthed. 'They're not even *words*—'

'And I should know,' Rose continued, 'I was the owner of over three dictionaries at the Harrow, don't you know. I practically invented the English language.'

'I see now,' Harry sneered, sourly, 'why you're yet to receive that call from your agent.'

Rose's smile faltered—but just for a second. She decided to double-down on her character assassination and Charlie noticed there was some aggression thrown in with the act now.

'I say, it's a jolly miserable thing being so utterly wedged, isn't it? It's like I was saying to Barnaby Toffy Fudgewell the Third over at The Dorchester last week, my father would just kill me if he saw—'

'That's enough!' Harry shouted and it was clear he was sincerely insulted. It took the wind quite out of everyone's sails.

'Come on Harry, we're just having a bit of fun,' Charlie reasoned.

'Yes, fun. It's an absolute *ball* isn't it?' he sulked for a bit. Then he pointed at each of them in turn: 'You don't see me walking around pretending to be an *actress* with zero talent for acting,' (at Rose), 'or an oaf with only a muscle where a brain ought to be,' (at Tom), 'or an unsuccessful *writer* living in squalor, now, do you, Charlie?'

'Well, maybe that last one—'

'I just don't find it very *amusing*, all right?' he snapped. 'That isn't acting. And it doesn't sound anything like me and I should know a ruddy good impression when I see one—my aunt Madeline was in the Footlights with Fry and his lot. But if you mean to get personal, I can get personal, Rosalind. Why don't you tell Tom how it is you know my father owns a vessel in the West Indies? How we spent a weekend aboard it in Puerto Rico—*sans un pantalon*? *That* might be fun—'

Tom, who had been in something of a slump, sat up a little frowning. 'What's that?'

Rose shrank about a foot, swallowed by the greatcoat.

'Do you wish to tell him or shall I?' Harry pressed.

'Harry—' Emily started, cut off by a stern look.

'Better yet, perhaps *you* should enlighten him, Emily? Or Charlie? Any one of you is capable, since it's only the caveman not privy to our entwined histories.'

'History?' Tom said looking from Harry to Rose and slowly connecting the dots. '*You two*?'

Rose shrank another foot. She was looking at the floor doing a different impression now—one of a toddler being scolded. Her toes pointed inwards and she stuck her hands into the deep front pockets of the greatcoat.

'I don't believe that for a second,' Tom laughed. 'She'd have to be bonkers to go out with someone like you.'

'Funny,' Harry said, 'I could say the same of you.'

They were almost at each other's throats.

'Blimey, Harry. What's this?' Rose squeaked.

'Don't try and change the subject—'

She had pulled her hands from the pockets and held a great hefty wad of cash up in one. Almost all its notes were red.

'I knew you were rich but this is a *lot* of dosh!'

Harry turned as red as the wad.

'Yes, but that's the last money I'm likely to own,' he said dramatically. 'You'll be pleased to hear my father has cut me off. I'm poorer than Charlie, in fact, and he's the unemployed underclass.'

Charlie took the wad of cash off Rose and rifled through it.

'Christ, this must be… ten grand. At *least*.'

'About twelve and a bit,' Harry explained. 'I had twenty to

begin with, so whatever's left after getting up here and booking this place and having a spot of lunch at The Tasty Plaice yesterday and—'

'You spent eight grand in a *day*?'

'Where did you *get* it?' Charlie asked. 'When I left on Friday you didn't have a penny to your name. You haven't...' He trailed off and shook his head. 'You haven't *repurposed* this from somewhere, have you?'

'No. Of course not! Charlie, you know me better than that. This is *mine*, I told you. Truth of it is, I had a feeling my father would cut me off eventually. This was my insurance policy. Squirrelled away for such an occasion.'

Charlie gave him a long suspicious stare, which Harry couldn't take. He blushed another shade of violet and tried a smile instead.

'Anyway, er—drinks, anyone? I'll make us a cocktail each. Yes, more alcohol I think...'

He ran round to the serving hatch of Peter's Bar and rummaged through its collection of wines. As he uncorked a bottle, he kept a nervous eye on Tom, who Charlie noticed was eyeing up the pair of cutlasses above the bar.

Chapter 11

Charlie was surprised at how well Tom had taken the news that Rose and Harry had once been a couple. No, he hadn't taken it well, exactly, though he had notably not said a word to anyone other than Rose in the last hour. But he had not attacked Harry, either physically or verbally, and *that* Charlie had taken as a blessing.

Despite this reaction—or perhaps in spite of it—the evening had been mostly uneventful ever since. Tom had sat talking in a low grunt to Rose, while Emily tried to maintain some semblance of atmosphere. She found some board games which Charlie, and somewhat more reluctantly, Harry, joined in with. All the while Harry's eyes were on the back of Tom's head, as if he expected him to come over at any minute and throttle him till his legs stopped kicking.

When Emily eventually announced she was opening something called their 'wind-down-wine' it was so late as to be early and almost the second she uncorked the bottle, the electricity promptly cut out again.

'No!' Harry yelled. 'No, no, no! You utter bastard! I demand a refund, this is preposterous!'

The fire had almost died out and the sky was still asleep. Emily went to go and check over the fuse box again, but this time, she reported, nothing had tripped. The electricity simply didn't want to cooperate.

They had to put up with it. While Tom tried to instigate another fire, Harry slipped through the bi-folding doors onto the balcony looking miffed and Charlie followed him out.

'You think I'm lying don't you?' Harry asked. 'About that tremendous wedge of dough? You probably think I'm a humongous demon with big black wings or something.'

'I don't think you're a demon—'

'Good.'

'I think you're a *tosser*,' Charlie told him, only partly in jest. 'But not a demon.'

Harry smiled with a faraway look in his eyes. He was leaning across the balustrade with a cigarette in his bandaged hand. Charlie joined him so that they both had their backs to the house. Everything out there was blue; the water, the grass on the distant coast, the Yarrowmoor. Its foothills were navy and the summit was chalky from the moon.

'It's beautiful here, isn't it?' Harry said. 'There's not a city for a dozen miles. Maybe more. Look, the sky shows all the cracks and holes of the universe and with it, all of its stars. The moon is close enough to pluck, like an apple from a tree. Do you see that mountain? The big black one with the flat top? You can see it from the loft window back at the lodge, did you know that?'

'It's called the Yarrowmoor,' Charlie told him.

They looked on it. How it caught the moonlight now as perfectly as it had caught the sun the day before.

'I didn't mean to put you through it. Last month I mean,' Harry said quite abruptly. This was the first time he had so much as acknowledged the event.

Charlie had been out for lunch with Emily and came home to find him sprawled on the settee with a white beard of foam.

'Was awfully selfish of me to leave *you* to pick up the pieces, Charlie. Should've done it somewhere nobody would think to find me. Like up there.' He indicated the chalky mountaintop. 'Yes, if I could choose the time and place of my death, it would be somewhere just like that. As the sun beats down on your face, surrounded by the song of birds. Death would greet you kindly in a place like that, wouldn't it? He wouldn't come as a skeleton in bloodied robes on a pale horse. He'd come as a friend.'

'Don't talk like that,' Charlie warned him.

He was looking at Harry with concern. Warmth spread back into Harry's cheeks as he smiled.

'Sorry. A hangover of my Chelsea diet.'

'Your Chelsea diet?'

He nodded. 'Retinol, modafinil, Ritalin, Valium, SSRIs. Sometimes slithers of LSD blotter soaked in hand sanitiser. Just a little bump once every three hours. I'm off it all now. It was getting me down. You remember my rough patch in February? When I nearly burnt my manuscript in my underpants? And there's... *The Incident* last month... That was really the final straw. I'm just on the spirits and the fags and the occasional speed binge now, hand to God.'

He waved his arms around theatrically, causing ribbons of smoke to circle him. Charlie noticed the bandaged had turned brown in the palm.

'How's your hand?' he asked.

Harry turned over his bandaged hand and looked at it blankly, as though he'd forgotten it was still attached to his arm. 'I'll live.'

'Can I ask you something?' Charlie asked hoping to catch him off guard. 'Why are you here?'

Harry fidgeted awkwardly. He hoisted himself onto the balustrade so his feet were off the floor and he leaned over the edge steeply. The water was jostling round the rocks and his face was reflected in its broken lines. Charlie wondered whether he might just throw himself over rather than face talking to him. But he didn't and dropped back to his feet.

'It'll sound silly,' Harry said.

'I don't care. I want to know.'

'The thing of it is,' he started. 'The truth of the matter... I had this *dream*, you see.'

'A dream?'

Harry looked embarrassed to be discussing such hocus pocus.

'Yes, the most frighteningly realistic dream of my life. It felt prophetic.'

'I never took you for superstitious,' Charlie said.

'Nor did I,' he admitted. 'But... well, it was like this. Did I ever tell you about the summer of 1816?'

'Yes, that's the year you went holidaying with the Duke of Wellington, isn't it?'

'In 1816,' Harry went on, ignoring him, 'my ancestor, Lord Byron, wrote this fantastic poem. I must have recited it for you before, it's one of my absolute faves. *Darkness* it's called. The one about wild birds gnashing their teeth and such? No? Well, the context of it is, this volcanic eruption somewhere in Indonesia or somewhere caused a whopping great cloud of smoke to turn the skies black across London. Acidic rain burnt through the heavens. Crops failed. There was sulphur in the air, all that hoopla. And this came at an important moment in history, you see. They'd just brought a whole trunk-load of dinosaur bones to the British Museum and people were starting to question their faith! But then this volcano goes off and nobody in London society knows about the volcano in Indonesia. All they know is, the skies are tinged with yellow and great rolling black clouds have blot out the sun. To them, this is a sign from God of the apocalypse!'

Harry had worked himself up with excitement. The colour had rushed from his heart up his neck to his face. He let himself simmer and then cleared his throat.

'Point is, the night you and Emily left, I dreamt I was there. I was a scholar in Oxford and I saw this darkness blot out the sun and it scared me more than anything in the whole world could or ever has. It frightened me to my core. I woke up covered in sweat and I thought I still *was* that scholar! I ran to the window and looked outside, but, of course, it had only been a dream...'

He trailed off looking distractedly across the waterfront.

Charlie stared at him. He thought about sharing his own dream. Of the birds flooding the kitchen of The Barrow, and of the same feeling of horror he had woke with, tight in his chest like a heart attack.

Instead, he asked, 'But what's any of that got to do with your being here?'

Harry shrugged. 'Nothing, *really*. But in my chest I still feel that same, intense fear. It's like it's guiding me. I feel this impending sense of doom, Charlie-Boy. I don't understand it, but then neither did the people of 1816. We laugh now. We know it was a volcano *now*. But they didn't. Well what if that's what's happening to *me*? Is that so preposterous? Perhaps something we're just too dashed primitive to comprehend has made me come out here!'

'And it wasn't the speed you took?' asked Charlie, finding the whole thing quite implausible. Of all the excuses to come out with, this was certainly the Harryest.

145

'Last night I bombed half a gram of cheap speed, yes,' Harry said. 'It must have triggered some latent chemical reaction inside me. A hangover from the Chelsea diet, perhaps? The cogs in my brain went at double speed and I just took off, coursing with adrenaline. *That's* why I arrived so late and in such discourteous style. But the dream... the *dream* is the reason I'm here.'

He dropped his cigarette into the waves around the rocks. It bounced from every one before it disappeared forever into the turf.

Chapter 12

The bi-folding doors opened out and Rose joined them on the balcony.

'Oh, don't leave because of me, Charlie,' she said, noticing how he had started to head indoors.

He stopped and hung around awkwardly as she struggled to light a cigarette.

After a couple of minutes, Harry said, 'Do you know, I can *feel* you staring at me, Miss Seymour! Now I know this night has been mostly a disaster and partly, it's my fault. But I really don't feel as though I ought to be regarded as the... the criminally *insane* or something. I made a simple mistake regarding electricity and that's all it was. I mean who thinks to ask, "Oh and by the way—is there electricity?" when booking a holiday home? It's preposterous. But being treated like this is just—well it's just not *English*, okay?'

Rose waited until he had finished his little outburst. He had worked his face into the colour of a tulip and that made her giggle.

'Is something funny?' he snapped.

She blew a little ball of smoke from the side of her smirk. 'You do take yourself *very* seriously, don't you?' she asked.

'I do no such thing. And anyway, I *am* serious. I'm as serious as they come, as it goes. As serious as a heart attack in the chest of a very serious businessman.'

'I say, I'm just tremendously serious,' Rose mocked.

Harry was appalled. She stopped laughing and then pushed him gently on the arm. He almost leapt a foot back in shock.

'*Do* lighten up, you great *writer*, you. *I'm* the one that ought to be in a bad mood. You were quite insulting to me, you know, belittling my talents and all. But I'm not. I'm rather happy as it happens. I've had a revelation, you see.'

'A revel*a*tion?'

'M-hm,' she said. 'It regards a tower I'm building. But *mostly* I think I'm just happy to be out here in such beauty. Even if I *am* in it with you.'

'I'm not so bad, you know,' Harry told her. 'With us... it's not *my* fault you know. I can't help how... you know.' He glanced over at Charlie, with red cheeks.

'I know,' Rose said. 'You're a good person deep down. About a *thousand miles* deep. But you are. I'm probably the only person who knows it—'

'And Charlie, of course.'

'Well—' Charlie started, playfully.

'Shut it Charlie, you'd snog the ground I walk on and you know it.'

Rose pursed her lips. 'While we're *on* the subject of judging one another,' she said, '*I'm* not so bad either, you know.'

Charlie was quite impressed by her manner. Not often did someone have the gall to stand up for themselves in Harry's little sphere of chaos. Something on his face stung. It was a smile. Four inches wide from lobe to lobe.

'I know you're not,' Harry said. 'And... you're not a bad actress either. I was against a wall, that's why I claimed otherwise. Did I ever tell you my aunt Maddy was in the Footlights?'

'Almost daily.'

'Mm, well she was a ruddy good performer in her day. And if we're doing swaps, I *am* a great writer, in case that was supposed to be sarcasm. I happen to be developing a seminal work. A memoir of childhood neglect. It'll sell a billion copies and clutter waiting room tables for aeons. There's not many of us, either. Great writers I mean. Just me, Charlie and old Bill Shakespeare.'

Rose let out another puff of smoke. 'And Lord Byron, of course,' she said.

And Charlie noticed how she didn't look away from the decedent of Byron until Harry looked away from her.

Chapter 13

When Harry, Charlie and Rose came back inside the cabin, the evening had clearly fizzled to an end alongside the embers of the fire.

Emily had just polished off the end of her 'wind-down-wine' but Charlie wasn't even sure if Tom was still alive. He looked catatonic, staring with a surly irritation up at the breastplate above the bar with a hand on his chin like Rodin's *Thinker*.

'I'm exhausted.' Emily yawned. 'I think I'll get some sleep. What time is our pick-up Harry? I don't want to oversleep.?'

'Our pick-up?' Harry said, turning green.

'Yes. You *did* arrange a pick-up? She asked.

Harry nervously patted at his pockets until he found the stack of ferry tickets. He scanned one with his pulse visibly throbbing through his neck.

'Odd, it doesn't give a time for a pick-up.' He turned the card over.

Charlie took the ticket from him. 'One way,' he read holding it up for the others to see.

Tom still didn't move, but his eyeball rotated in its socket in their direction.

'*One way?*' Harry snatched the ticket back and stared at it with his nostrils flaring. 'Oh, Christ! Can't that stupid bastard from the newsagent get *anything* right? He bungs us off to this remote cabin with no electricity and fails to book us a return trip!'

'*You* failed to book a return trip,' Tom grunted.

'Nonsense. He's a saboteur that man! Trying to off us so he can paddle over in his dinghy to ply our wares from our corpses!'

'Why didn't you book a return trip Harry? How did you think we were going to get back?'

'I'm sorry,' he cried. 'Talk of a return trip never cropped up. I didn't even *think*—'

'You never do, Harry!' Charlie groaned. 'That's your problem.'

'It's okay. We can book one from here, can't we?' Harry said.

He didn't sound confident that they could, in fact, book one from there. But he was off around to the other side of the bar. 'I'm sure I saw a phone back here somewhere.'

'But there's no *electricity*,' Rose reminded him.

'That doesn't matter. Phone's don't work that way, do they?' he was desperate. 'Ah, here it is.' He lifted an old phone from its cradle. 'Phones always work in blackouts, don't they? For emergencies. Like those chaps in the blitzkrieg who carried phones across the battlefield? They run off, uh, copper wires and telecommunication masts and such, *don't* they?'

Tom had got up with a heavy sigh and snatched the phone from Harry, putting it to his ear. 'Doesn't sound like it mate. I don't hear a thing.'

Harry bent below the bar and when he stood back up, he was holding the wire attached to the cradle. It had been chewed clean through by a creature.

'Fantastic,' Rose yelled, throwing her arms up. 'This is just fantastic. So we're stuck here?'

'Are you happy mate?' Tom asked. 'You've stranded us here.'

'Stranded!' Harry laughed. 'This is hardly Robinson Crusoe. We're less than a mile from land, for God's sake!'

'There must be some flares or something around here,' Charlie suggested.

'*Flares*?' Rose hissed. 'Are you out of your stupid *mind*?'

'Don't talk to Charlie like that,' Harry defended. 'He's only trying to help.'

'Why wouldn't there be flares?'

'Because we're less than a mile from land!' Rose reiterated.

They descended into bickering until they were just shouting over one another. Emily stuck her fingers in her mouth and whistled loudly.

'The ferryman,' she said.

'What about him?'

'The ferryman knows we're here,' she reasoned. 'Surely he will *realise* and come back for us? Even a great miserable so-and-so like *him* wouldn't leave us here on purpose.'

'Perhaps, but when?' asked Harry solemnly. 'A day or two? A week? Seven years? He'll walk in here to find our skeletons with their hands round each other's throats.'

'I wouldn't count on him coming back neither,' Tom said. 'In fact, I'd be surprised if he's not having a good old chinwag to that Cyclops down the pub right now.'

'Unlikely,' Harry said. 'The pubs don't open till midday.'

'Wait a minute!' Charlie lit up. 'Rose, don't you have your phone on you?'

Rose shook her head. 'I couldn't find it, could I? I lost it before we left The Barrow yesterday.'

'Let's stay calm,' said Emily. 'You left your bike at port, didn't you? Maybe someone will see it and realise we're out here?'

Harry went a strange colour. 'The thing of it is, you see... It's just that, well, when I... that is to say, the *Bonneville*, you see—'

'What *is* it Harry?'

'Spit it out.'

'What have you done,' Tom stood up and took a step closer, 'to that bike?'

Harry bared his teeth. 'Sunk it,' he said in barely a whisper.

'*Sunk* it?'

''Fraid so.'

'What's he talking about Charlie? Where is it?'

'He drove the bloody thing into the Spreywater!'

Emily and Rose reeled back while Tom shook his head in disbelief.

'Let me get this right. First, you turn up uninvited. You break into our house. You make our dog run off. You book us a cabin nobody even wanted to come to—a cabin with no electricity. You proudly reveal you used to go out with *my* lass... That one I still can't figure out. You forget to book us a trip back. And now you tell us you sent that *beautiful* motorbike to the bottom of the sodding lake! A bike you already scraped right down the fuel tank. Did I miss owt?'

Harry thought. 'I also set fire to somebody's cardigan during the night. Almost dozed off with a cig in hand you see. I threw it into the hot tub—'

'That was *my* cardigan!' Emily gasped.

'You're unbelievable,' said Tom. 'That's it. That's strike three. You're out, mate.'

'Strike *three*?' Harry was appalled. 'When did I have a strike *two*? When did I have strike *one*?'

'Tell him Charlie.'

'He gave you your first strike when we found out there was no electricity,' Charlie sighed. 'He told me while we fetched the coal.'

'And strike two were when you booked us a one-way trip here. I'd've sooner spent the night in the fucking woods, than in here with you.'

'Then why didn't you?' Harry asked. 'Nobody put a gun to your head.'

'I was trying to be nice! Emily come sticking her nose in and asked us to give you a chance, so I did.'

Emily started. 'Well that's hardly fair—'

'Look,' Harry said, pulling out a bundle of cash from his coat pocket with trembling fingers. 'I'll make this right. A hundred each, how does that sound—'

Tom spat on the floor at Harry's feet. 'That's your answer to everything innit? Some things you can't fix by throwing cash at.'

'I know but—'

'You could have all the money in the world, but that don't stop us being stuck on an island, does it? In here, you're worth as much as the help you can offer. You wanna help us? Why don't you tie a weight to your fat head and jump off the roof?'

Harry's teeth were grinding together. 'You've crossed a line, Mr Darrow. It's a duel.'

'A what?'

Harry bolted to the serving hatch and pulled down one of the cutlasses from the crossed sword display of Peter's Bar. Everyone but Tom inhaled. Tom just wore a hungry grin and ran his tongue over a fang. He was a vampire, thirsty for blood—for Harry's blood. And he was about to get it.

Harry held the sword to Tom's neck and walked in a circle around the cabin keeping him a sword's length back as they paced.

'Wrought by the lonely maiden of the lake,' Harry smiled. 'I've got two years of fencing at the Harrow under my belt. I'll bet you didn't even finish your B.Tech.'

Tom was watching the blade carefully but he gave a loud snort. 'You're acting like a tit.'

'An inspired wit,' Harry said. 'I see they teach creativity at the same level as academia over at the School of Hard Knocks.'

'I don't need a private education to know you're acting like a tit.'

'Harry, put the sword down for heaven's sake,' Emily pleaded. 'This is ridiculous.'

Harry cast a quick glance at his audience. 'This is about honour,' he said. 'He bites his thumb at me.'

'So *what*?' Rose snapped. '*I* think you're acting like a tit, too. Are you going to behead *me*?'

'It's true, Harry,' Charlie said. It was four on one now. 'This isn't how we settle things in the twenty-first century.'

'See?' Tom grinned. 'Even Dickens agrees you're a cock.'

'He agrees I'm a *tit*,' Harry corrected. 'He said nothing to compare me to a cock.'

'Well you are one!'

Sweat ran along Harry's neck. His eyes flashed back and forth from Tom, who stood grinning at him at the end of his sword, to the others, grouped with identical looks of distress.

After a few long seconds, Harry relaxed his stance. He let the hilt swing round his hand so the blade was pointing flaccidly at the ground.

'Et vivere, reservate.'

Tom's Adam's apple pulsed while a sigh passed through the room. It looked, for a moment, like the fight was off. That was as Harry intended it to look no doubt.

But in the blink of an eye, he chucked the sword over to Tom, who caught it by the handle. Then he slid beneath him, hopped up on the other side and pulled the second cutlass from the wall mount.

The blade was raised back at Tom before anybody could breathe. Tom lifted his own sword to Harry's and Rose squealed.

The blades clashed with a satisfying metallic clang as they glided along one another.

'This is madness!' Emily cried. 'Pure madness!'

'Welcome to my world,' Charlie said.

They shuffled behind the bench as the swordsmen circled in the centre of the cabin again. Rose cowered into the corner of the room, covering her face in her hands.

Tom's jaw began to twitch. 'Just give us a reason. Give us one good reason and I'll slit your scrawny little throat.'

'Enough talk,' Harry said. '*En garde.*'

He made a fast, circular rotation with his hand and the flat side of his blade slapped Tom's down. Tom raised the sword back up uneasily.

'*Allez*!' Harry called.

He lunged forward and caught Tom by surprise. Tom threw up his sword and counter-parried the blade away. They swapped sides and stared at each other. Tom took the cutlass with both hands and ran at Harry.

He swung the sword round. Harry bobbed down and it stuck into the reddish support beam in the centre of the room. A burst of splintered wood flew out like shrapnel.

Harry threw his head back in mock laughter as Tom struggled to pull his sword free. He had the flat of his foot up on the support beam and was pulling at the cutlass with both of his great mitts. When the sword finally dislodged, he fell a step back and his elbow smacked Harry hard in the face, who staggered back himself, spitting blood.

'You'f knocked my bloody toof out!' Harry gasped.

He felt his mouth, at the gap where his front tooth had just been, and dropped to his hands and knees to look for it on the floor.

Tom put his foot on Harry's backside and kicked him over. His sword swung up and down at his side, like a bladed pendulum. Harry got back to his hands and knees and scurried off behind the bench.

'Come on then! Is this what I get fighting Harrow's champion fencer?'

Harry got back to his feet but any confidence he had in his swordplay had disappeared. Tom was no swordsman but his brute strength showed in each swing. Harry held his sword limply.

'Perhaps a duel was an archaic manner of settling our differences?' he suggested. 'Perhaps—'

The bench took Tom's swing and one of its cushions burst into feathers. Harry leapt about a foot back.

'Now really, this is silly,' he said, trying and failing to put on a brave face.

Tom swung again and Harry ran round him to the dining table. He was backed up against it and Tom prepared another two-handed attack. Harry rolled across the table as the sword came down, narrowly missing him.

Tom lifted the sword again and Harry rolled the opposite way, back along the table. This time, it came down like a spear and pinned the tail of Harry's greatcoat to the wood. He pulled at it and tore his coat free.

'You bastard!' He wailed as he landed on his feet and twirled around to see the damage to his coat. It was forked like a snake's tongue.

But there was no time to worry about that. Tom was advancing, so Harry put the table between them. They spent the next twenty seconds swapping sides, which got Tom worked up; his neck glistened with sweat and his temple's wormy vein slithered from one side to the other. He flipped the table with one hand. It frightened everyone in the room. The bowl of plastic fruit, a tray of shots, a bottle of brandy… they all flew up into the air and clattered back down in a symphony of glass and metal.

'Stop it!' Rose wailed. 'Stop it now!'

Harry backed away. He was scared for his life because Tom had transformed. If there had been even a hint of playfulness in the duel up until then, it was gone now. Tom wanted blood. His face had turned to stone—his brow and lip and jaw jutted out like a rock carving and his eyes were dead. Even the firelight didn't reflect in their ink-black pools.

Harry bumped into the support beam and slid down it in defeat. He shut his eyes tightly as Tom stood over him.

'You're pathetic,' Tom scoffed. 'You couldn't fence with a one-armed toddler.'

He pulled his sword back like a golf club and swung it at Harry. It struck Harry's blade, which spun off like a boomerang and shattered the bi-folding glass wall completely. Its crystals exploded across the balcony like artillery shells, then pooled into the cabin like waves as Harry's sword plopped into the Spreywater below.

A long moment of silence followed. Nobody knew what to say. Once that deafening silence settled in, all Charlie could hear was the hiss of the surf against the rocks—and the pneumatic pounding of Harry's heart.

'Come now, old sport,' Harry said. 'You wouldn't attack an unarmed man, would you? That's not cricket.'

Tom raised his sword as if to spear Harry like a kebab.

'Enough!' Rose howled. She leapt in front of Harry with her arms outstretched.

'Get out of it,' Tom growled. He was essentially slobbering with anger and he shoved her to the floor without hesitating.

She threw her arms out and they slid through the broken glass. It stunned her for a second. She looked down into her palms where a dozen rivers of blood started trickling to her cuffs.

'You maniac,' Emily said. 'What's the matter with you?'

Charlie helped Rose to the bench where Emily attended her and Tom watched on as if he'd just woken from a bad dream.

'Rose?'

He let his sword fall to the ground and started toward her.

Harry seized this opportunity. He dived across the glass, swept up the sword and swung it round. It sliced Tom in a vicious red line across the back of his calf. His leg buckled and he grabbed hold of the mantelpiece for support. Dark blood seeped through his fingers where he clasped his wound and he came over all shaky.

'You ready then?' Tom panted.

It was Harry's turn to go ashen. 'Ready?'

Tom charged at him like a bull. One who hadn't just been sliced across the calf.

Harry dropped the sword and tried to run but Tom dived almost seven feet across the cabin and rugby tackled him to the ground. He raised his fist but Charlie pulled at it like David restraining Goliath.

'Come on, Tom,' Charlie wheezed as he strained against the arm. 'You've already broken the glass wall. And look what you've done to Rose. Just stop all this.'

'Stop it?' Tom snarled. 'After everything *he's* done, you're telling *me* to stop it? Look around you. This is all *his* fault!'

'That's not true,' Charlie said. 'You've caused all this damage.'

Tom resisted for a second but then he looked at the crystal shards all round them and over at Rose, at the horror in her face.

Harry crawled free. 'You need to be sectioned!' He sneered, wiping blood on his coat. 'Can't a man propose a duel without the other trying to kill him?'

'I'm warning you,' Tom said. 'I'll chuck you in the lake.'

'I'll be having words with my uncle the Viscount Honeywell. This time tomorrow you'll be hanging with the nonces.'

'Final warning or I'll duff you.'

'You're nothing but a muscle in denim.'

'Better than a stick in plus fours.'

'Well *you're*—' Harry paused and a wicked smiled drew across his face as his gaze was occupied by something outside on the horizon. 'Wait a bloody moment. Stop the clocks and hold the boat! Look *there*! The ferryman! He cometh!'

He pointed at a spot on the waterfront. Everyone moved round to get a better look. Even Tom turned his neck. The muscles in it rippled like sidewinders.

'Where?' he asked. They all struggled to see on the waves.

'Over there,' Harry said, as he bent his knee and swiped the bottle of brandy from the rubble. 'Out past that bit of fog.'

'*I* don't see him,' Rose said, 'and *I* happen to have perfect eyesight.'

'He's having us on,' Tom told them. 'There's no ferrym—*ungh.*'

Harry clubbed him over the back of the head with the brandy bottle. Tom crumpled to the ground like a ton of bricks.

'That's disappointing,' Harry said studying the bottle. 'I was rather hoping it would break.'

Rose had turned only in time to see Tom slump to his knees and then hug the wood with his face. It was only after Harry replaced the bottle on the table she put two and two together.

'What did you do *that* for?' she bellowed, wild-eyed. She threw herself to Tom's side and cradled his head like a soldier's wife. 'Tom? Tommy?' she rubbed his unconscious face and blubbered hysterically. 'You've killed him! Emily, he's killed my Tommykins.'

'He's not *killed* him,' Emily said, taking Tom's pulse. 'He's knocked him unconscious.'

'A crying shame,' Harry yawned.

Rose started to growl like an engine and then the growl turned into a high-pitched scream. She was up and running at Harry like a berserker. More supercharged than Tom in a scrum. She knocked him back to the floor and clawed at his face with her talons till ribbons of scarlet swirled through the air.

It caught Harry off-guard. He had expected to be carried on their shoulders as a hero, not mauled by a manicured bobcat.

Charlie pulled her away and threw her onto the bench. She tried to lunge again but he stood with his arms out like a goalkeeper. She scavenged in the rubble for something to lug and found the plastic fruit. They soared over Charlie and bounced off Harry's bottom as he shuffled away.

'Gang of effing psychopaths,' Harry muttered to himself as he crawled over to the hole where the wall of glass had been. 'I'd be safer lighting a match in a puddle of *gasoline* than I am in here with this lot.'

He paused on the threshold. He'd seen something wedged in a knothole and pried it out.

'Aha! My tooth!' he announced, holding it to the light ecstatically.

Rose had run out of fruit. She picked up the serving tray and hurled it like a Frisbee. It passed around Charlie, smacked into Harry's wrist and knocked the tooth onto the decking where it rolled along the balcony and then bounced down to the rocks below before disappearing into the water with an unheard *plop*.

'My tooth!' he yelled again as it disappeared forever.

Rose loaded up on brandy snifters and was poised to throw one like a grenade.

'Emily, help?' Charlie squeaked.

'Rosie, come and hold Tom's head,' Emily said. She was tending him on the glittery carpet and when Rose looked over, teary-eyed, she dropped the snifters onto a cushion and went to cradle him again.

'Oh Tom, it's okay now. You're with *me*. It's Rosalind. Your little Rozzy-wozzy.'

Charlie tucked a pillow below Tom's head as his eyelids started to flutter. Two red eyes stared up at them.

'Where's he gone...?'

Rose held him to her breast. 'Oh Tommy! Are you okay?'

'He might be concussed,' Emily said. 'Stay still.'

'I'm fine,' Tom slurred, getting to his feet and swaying. 'Where is he?'

They looked around. Harry was gone. Gone from the cabin and nowhere to be seen on the balcony outside. Charlie went out and circled the house but Harry seemed to have disappeared into thin air. He even leaned over the balustrade looking into the water with a sinking feeling.

'No,' he whispered to himself, looking at his broken reflection in the lake. 'He wouldn't. *Would* he?'

'Charlie-Boy!' a voice called. 'Up here!'

Harry was on the roof. One hand was on a hip, the other was shielding his eyes as he surveyed the coast. His long tattered coat blew around him in the wind.

'How did you get up there?'

'Climbed.'

Tom had heard him and led the others outside.

'Get down here so I can knock the rest of your teeth out,' Tom called up. 'Dunno how they wrestle in the changing rooms at public school but that were what we call a blind side in Sheffield.'

'What are you even doing up there Harry?' Emily asked.

'Surveying.' Harry pointed to the horizon. 'Do you know, I think I could bloody *swim* that.'

There were squiggles of white and yellow on the distant waves like brushstrokes on a landscape. Even from here they looked rough.

'Come off it you bloody fool. You'll *freeze* if you don't drown first!'

'Nonsense. I was the long-distance swimming champ at the Harrow. Three gold medals and robbed of a fourth by web-footed Sullivan. Froggy we called him. This is nothing. Only about a mile or so.'

'You'll catch your death.'

'I'm being Byronic!'

'You're being *mor*onic,' Emily countered.

'Hey hey! I'm no moron, missy. I'm an Englishman. I'm a descendent of Lord Byron, his great-great-something-or-other, and he practically *invented* swimming. Charlie, hold this.'

He took off his coat and wristwatch and threw them down to Charlie and then started hopping from foot to foot to limber up.

'He's going to kill himself,' Charlie muttered.

'Saves me a job,' Tom shrugged.

'Au revoir, land mammals,' Harry bellowed. 'I'm off to swim with the fishes.'

And then he dived, quite expertly, and cut through the water below. A long time passed as the four islanders leaned over the balustrade and watched in stunned silence. Eventually, fifty feet out, Harry's head resurfaced. He waved at them and then headed to port.

Chapter 14

Harry's disappearance did little to quell the misery that hung around the cabin. Nor did the sunrise, which slowly filled the reach of the mountains with daylight as Charlie stared out across the waterfront. It had been almost four hours since Harry leapt from the roof and Charlie had finally started to agree that it wasn't likely he was coming back.

'You're all bloody fools if you think you're ever gonna see him again,' Tom had said before he slunk off to the kitchen to try and sleep. 'There's more chance of us getting rescued by Elton John.'

Soon after, Emily and Rose followed him through. The kitchen was tiny but the gaping hole in the side of the cabin where the bi-folding doors had been now whistled with cold sea air, so it was the only place they could hope to get some sleep.

Charlie alone stayed up. He leaned across the balcony with the collar of Harry's greatcoat turned up around his neck, watching a magnificent bird loop from the crystal firmament to its mirror in the sky. He wondered if this was an osprey.

It had been too dark to see much as Harry swam to shore. Now that morning had broken, the water was still and silent. Eerily so. With a bit of luck, Harry had made it to port hours ago and was well on his way to rescuing them. But Charlie wasn't banking on that. More likely the stupid bastard had drowned himself and was lying with the Bonneville.

Behind Charlie, the kitchen door clicked open and Emily came to join him on the balcony.

'I don't suppose there's a cigarette in there?' she asked.

He checked the pockets of the coat and pulled out Harry's Chesterfields. 'Two left. Here.' He lit one for her against the wind.

'Do you think he's all right?' she asked. 'Harry, I mean.'

Charlie squinted at the waves. 'Yes,' he decided. 'It takes more than can kill mere mortals to stand in the way of Harrington Burden.'

'What do you think he's *doing* here? Really?'

Charlie could feel her eyes boring holes into his temple—but he didn't feel like having that conversation. He pointed at the bird across the lake and said, 'I think that's an osprey you know.'

'Charlie, don't avoid the subject. Didn't you find out anything yesterday?'

'No. And I'm fed up of talking about him. Like he's a dog that needs putting down or something. If you really want to talk about someone behind their back, what about him in there? Jesus, breaking the windows like that? Throwing Rose to the ground? Tom went *far* crazier than I've ever seen Harry—and that's saying something.'

'I know,' Emily said. 'Rose certainly knows how to pick them.'

'Doesn't she have an ex in Broadmoor? Tom ought to join him. Mind you, so should Harry. *That* would be some record. Three blokes go out with her and they end up cellmates in a padded room.'

Emily blew a ribbon of smoke into the air. 'So what *did* he say to you yesterday exactly?'

'He just said he needed to get out of London so he came here.'

'And that's all? He didn't say anything about his collision?'

'His *collision*? No. What collision? Do you know something I don't?'

'Maybe,' she said, taking another drag.

'Like what?'

She placed her cigarette into a groove in the wood.

'Come with me.' She led him through the house to the washroom and pointed at the bin. 'Look inside.'

Charlie lifted the lid. It was filled with something like toilet paper, covered in red and brown stains.

'Sanitary towels,' she said. 'How do you explain that?'

'Jesus H., Em!' Charlie said, letting go of the lid and reeling back. 'I nearly touched that!'

'How do you explain it?' she asked again.

'Sanitary towels in a toilet bin? Not exactly a case for Poirot, is it?' he answered. 'I suppose Rose must have... you know... been invaded by the British?'

Emily shook her head. 'Rose doesn't have a period. It's her pill.

And they're not *mine*. And they weren't here when we arrived either.'

'So what are you saying? That *Harry* is having his period?'

'Of course not. But I *do* believe a DNA test would find that blood belongs to him.'

She led him back to the promenade and picked her cigarette up from its groove.

'He has an injury, haven't you noticed?' she asked.

'Yeah, well, Tom *did* shoot him.'

'No. That was in the top of his leg. This is on the side of his torso, just here. He keeps clutching it when he thinks no one's looking. *That's* why there was so much blood at The Barrow when Teddy went missing. And I *presume* that's why he didn't want me to remove the pellet from his leg, too. In case I saw his injury.'

'But why... how—*what's* he supposed to have done?'

'Tom said that bike of his had an awfully big scrape down its fuel tank, didn't he?' Emily answered. 'My leading theory is that Harry was involved in a crash on his way here.'

Charlie was stunned by the suggestion. 'But why wouldn't he tell us that? Why wouldn't he want medical attention?'

'Because,' she started and then paused. 'Wait. First—do you remember what Harry said, back in London at The Nag's Head? When we told him we'd been invited away on Friday, he said "My, my, what a coincidence."'

'That's right. So?'

'*So*,' she said, tucking her hair behind an ear, '*Harry had also been invited somewhere on Friday.*'

Charlie nodded. 'I suppose. But why would that mean he'd hide his injury? Or lie about being in a crash?'

'That brings me to my second point,' she continued. 'He was invited away somewhere and for whatever reason he doesn't want us to know about it. A secret girlfriend, he doesn't want Rose to know about? Or maybe he's mixed up in something he doesn't want *you* to know about. I don't know and it's pointless to try and guess. But what we *do* know is that he goes off to some kind of secret rendezvous and then turns up here, incredibly hysterical, not long after, with twenty thousand pounds, a pair of pistols and a new motorcycle. Even for Harry that's a little wild. The fact he's covering up this injury leads me to believe he's done something quite serious. Two days ago he was penniless and had been cut off by his father. So I have to believe Harry *stole* that money and then crashed into something while making his getaway. Why else would he cover up an accident like that?'

Charlie sunk a hand into the deep pocket of the greatcoat and pulled out the wad of notes. He leafed through them and felt something whir in his chest.

'Alright. I'll get to the bottom of this,' he said. 'I'll talk with him. If he hasn't *drowned* himself.'

Emily squinted at the water. Somewhere the bird caught a fish from the lake and carried it back to its nest in the mountains.

Chapter 15

'Wake up,' Emily said, nudging Charlie. He had fallen asleep, most uncomfortably, across the dining table.

'What is it?'

'Come and see.'

Halfway across the lake was a little white smear on the water. The white smear turned into a grey steamer. It was half the size of the ferry and had a smokestack in its middle pouring clouds into the sky. Two red paddlewheels at each side churned the blue water into frothy white mist. Some tiny figure leaned across the bow, dangerously close to toppling into the froth, and waving manically.

'I'll wake the others.' Emily went back into the cabin and left Charlie to stare out in a perplexed awe.

'Harry, you stupid, brilliant bastard,' he muttered.

He was not able to stop smiling. When he had looked upon the Yarrowmoor only an hour before as a pastel halo began to form around it, although he hadn't allowed himself to readily admit it, some small part of him imagined Harry had swum into its embrace and succumbed to the sirens on the rocks. Now he couldn't imagine anything more ridiculous. A life like Harry's wouldn't be wasted in such ignominious fashion.

The steamer arrived and bobbed against the rocks by the promenade below the cabin. It was driven by a young woman in cord dungarees. She called out some greeting as Charlie raced to the jetty. The boat was a tiny, laughable thing with *Sea Beast* painted clumsily down the hull.

'Ahoy, landlubber!' Harry called from the bow of the boat.

The first thing Charlie noticed was that he had changed clothes. He was in jodhpurs and white woollen socks with a linen shirt unbuttoned to the chest and its baggy sleeves rolled up to the elbows the way an Elizabethan poet might wear a blouse.

The second thing Charlie noticed was what an awful mess he looked. His head had swelled up in several places while his face was bruised and lumpy like a rotting peach. His smile was toothless, the bandage round his hand had come off in the water and a bloodstain was permeating the blouse by his ribcage—Emily, it seemed, was right about a mysterious injury.

But despite his disfigurements, Harry was radiant. He leapt with a gangly athleticism from the bow to the promenade and said, 'Would it be hubristic to declare myself a hero?'

'It would be incredibly foolish,' Charlie warned him, though his cheeks now ached from all the smiling and they hugged in camaraderie. 'You're something else entirely, Harry, do you know that?'

'My, my, did a *compliment* just sneak past the defences of your lips?'

'Let's just say it wasn't an insult. Who's that?' He meant the young woman driving the steamer. She hardly looked more than thirteen years old.

'Ah, this is Captain Kara,' Harry said. 'She and some local fishermen kindly helped me—'

'Dragged him out the water's what we did,' the girl grinned. 'Rescued him on me pa's ship.' She pointed off to a larger boat in the distance.

'*Rescued* is a rather grandiose term,' Harry objected.

'Floundering like a chimp, so he was. What were you even doing in there at that time, Mr Burden? Must've been five degrees.'

'Well I wasn't doing lengths,' Harry snapped sourly. 'Do you mind? We're trying to have a private conversation.' Harry steered Charlie away from her while the young captain chuckled to herself. 'Kara's grandfather operates a charity shop over in Mossly. He kindly let me tuck into the donations so as I could change from my wet clothes.'

'I see,' Charlie peered back at Kara, who was taking the opportunity to swig from a hipflask. 'Is she *drinking*?'

'Of course she's drinking. It's the rule of the sea, out here.'

'But it's seven o'clock in the morning. And she's about ten years old! And we're not at sea, this is a lake.'

'Say that after *you've* swam the bastard. It's essentially an ocean.'

'Well if she capsizes us after the night we've had, I'll be

166

terminally miserable. And you'll have to tell Rupert you've sank *two* vehicles to the bottom of the same lake in less than twenty-four hours.'

'Tell who?' Harry asked, scratching his chin and looking up at the cabin.

'Your friend Rupert Fiddlesticks or whatever his name was. The bloke who owns the Bonneville.'

'Oh, old Fiddleminster!' Harry looked as if he had just recalled an old joke. '*He'll* hardly much care. He owns an entire garage of them. Last time I was at his house, he crashed the Rolls into a Grade II listed building in Belgravia. Arrests were made.'

'I thought he lived in Guildford?'

'Well yes, yes,' Harry said. 'But he rents a place in London on the weekends, doesn't he? Oh crikey, here they come.' He was looking at the cabin where Tom and Rose were being led down the steps by Emily. 'Have they been sharpening their pitchforks?'

'They're not overly fond of you,' Charlie told him. 'So just *please*, Harry, *try* to be normal.'

''Fraid that's not in my repertoire, old chap,' Harry said, patting him roughly on the arm before making his way to the foot of the stairs to greet the others.

Rose approached first and she didn't look in the least bit touched by joviality. She wore a sombre expression and it was quite clear she meant to maintain it. But when she saw how Harry was dressed, she found herself simply unable to maintain the charade.

'My word! What *are* you wearing?' she giggled. 'That shirt is just *hideous*.'

Even Tom cracked a smile.

'Who's playing the genie?' Emily asked. '*You'll* be Aladdin, I assume?'

'Aye, "*a lad in*" a girl's outfit,' Tom said. 'Is that satin?'

Everyone fell about.

'I fail to see what's funny,' Harry said looking blank. 'I actually *own* a pair of jodhpurs just like these. And this shirt was positively made for the sea.'

'In 1750.'

'Yes, yes,' Harry said, rolling his eyes. 'Come on, the boat awaits. Come, ye land-dwellers and board the magnificent Sea Beast.'

He led them along the promenade and Rose groaned at the sight of the steamer.

'The *Sea Beast*?' she said. 'Is that supposed to be funny? It looks more like a sea *cu*cumber.'

'Well, she's an unsightly maiden, yes,' Harry said, looking the boat over, 'but she more than makes up for it with personality. And she'll have us back on terra firma before you can say "lickety-split".'

'Lickety-split!' she replied, staring at the thing with an unhopeful glare. 'Oh, my,' she swallowed and turned away. 'This is all I need on a hangover, isn't it? I can already feel it, right here in my throat. Three bottles of white. I'm quite sure I'll barf absolutely *everywhere* if I have to get in *that* thing.'

'You were quite capable during last night's dalliance with the waves.'

'Last night the boat wasn't in danger of *sinking* if it hit a *trout*!' she said. 'Is this old bathtub even seaworthy?'

'Aw, now, don't be so harsh on the old girl,' Captain Kara called over. She slapped the wheel as if it were the hind of a prize-winning cow. 'She's made over seven thousand return trips across this lake. That's six thousand nine-hundred and ninety-nine and a half more than the Titanic ever made and *she* weren't no bathtub now, was she?'

Rose studied the mini steamer and turned a shade of green.

'I just *really* think I'll empty my entire stomach if I have to get on that right now.'

Tom shoved past her. 'Please yourself,' he said as the boat dipped under his weight. 'But I ain't sticking round this rock another second.'

She took one long look at it and then sighed.

'Let's just get this over with.'

Chapter 16

It was mostly white wine in the vomit that pooled around the floor. It had been a mistake to watch the waves fornicate against the hull. Rose should have kept her eyes on the floor.

'Don't worry miss, worse has been inside the Sea Beast,' Captain Kara said. 'Fish guts and the like.' It was meant to comfort her. But it didn't.

More came up. Eventually it all swilled away and ran off the back of the boat. By the time they were halfway across the lake, the cool breeze and fresh air caused a wave of melancholia to wash over them like a collective comedown had hit all at once.

Nobody made eye contact with anyone. They looked into their palms or at their feet or out across the morning waves. Charlie alone was looking at their faces. *God*, they looked terrible. Like sickly creatures who had endured a particularly unpleasant night on a remote island. All gaunt and pale and lifeless with a touch of tragedy and a jot of jaundice and a dash of despair.

Rose was examining the cuts in her palms. They didn't look too bad as she traced a path over them with her pinky. Tom glanced at her but quickly looked back away to the rippling tide and Charlie thought he saw the little of his conscience, that twinkled through the blacks of his eyes, depart on speedboats.

Emily was almost asleep, sat with her eyes shut heavily, her head bobbing up and down whenever a wave rocked the boat. She alone was peaceful.

Harry was something else entirely. A tragic figure at the bow of the ship, staring at the disappearing horizon with shaking hands on the pulpit.

Yes, he was an arsehead, Charlie thought. But he felt suddenly sorry for the great big idiot. The island had been a disaster but Harry had *meant* well by this whole thing. And hadn't he just dived thirty feet into ice-cold water and then swam over a mile through jostling waves to rescue them all? Really, it was quite brave of him. And after all he had endured. Rose's palms may have been covered in scratches and Tom's calves may have stung from the blade, but

Harry, no doubt, deserved the trophy for Most Injured.

And had he complained even *once*? About *any* of it? Well yes, but—

'Not as much as *I* would have,' Charlie muttered.

'You would have what?' asked Emily, stirring.

'Oh, nothing,' he said as she rested her head against his shoulder and fell back to sleep.

Part III

Chapter 1

It felt like a lifetime ago when they had left The Barrow, but in actual fact less than twelve hours had passed. Emily suggested they all go to bed to try and recover and so they went off to their bedrooms while Harry took to the settee under a blanket.

Charlie felt as though his eyes had only just closed when he found himself being aggressively shaken awake by Harry.

'Unless you're dying,' Charlie grumbled, 'I advise you to go away.'

'It's important,' Harry whispered, so as not to wake Emily. 'Meet me in the drawing room at once. And put some clothes on.'

Harry shot out of the bedroom before Charlie could argue. Instead, Charlie looked at the time and, sighing, swung his legs out of the bed.

When he walked along the hall into the kitchen area, Charlie couldn't immediately see Harry, who was crouched by the side window peering out.

'Harry?'

'Sh!' Harry hissed, waving his arms around like he was swatting a swarm of angry hornets. 'Get down! Come here. No, don't move. Look, there.'

'Well which is it?'

Harry pointed between the trees, an enthusiastic grin on his face. 'What was the name of their dog again?'

'Teddy. Why?'

'Because I just saw the bugger!'

'You don't even know what he looks like,' Charlie reminded him.

Harry rolled his eyes. 'No, but I'd imagine he looks quite a bit like a dog. Four legs? Black nose? Stop me when I'm close. Come on. Let's snatch the little blighter before he bolts again.'

He flew off to the other side of the lodge and pulled the front door open.

'I should get Tom,' Charlie said, starting back along the hall.

'No! No time!' Harry dashed back inside and dragged Charlie by the sleeve. 'We can do this without him. Put your boots on.'

They ran around the house out of the woodland and into Umber Meadow at the back. Harry took an animated lead and crouched in the blades twenty feet ahead where he signalled to Charlie like a Commando.

There! he motioned. Do you see?

His arms flailed about like an air traffic controller in the midst of an epileptic fit.

'I don't see a thing,' Charlie mouthed back.

Just there, look! Harry pointed.

Charlie looked over the meadow. The wind yawned and made the long red grass sway. And at first, that was all that seemed to move it. But then he noticed a snake-like path winding through, as if an animal was burrowing beneath it.

'Oh!' Charlie said in some surprise.

'You see? I told you. That's Teddy all right.'

Harry was back on his feet, walking briskly in the direction of the Thing. It had stopped ten feet ahead and Harry stuck his arms up, making himself as tall and wide as he could, before leaping on the Thing.

'Huzzah!'

The Thing bucked like a scared horse and started howling. Its wiry, brown legs kicked out of the long grass and Charlie wondered for a second whether Harry hadn't caught himself a baby cow.

'Harry…' Charlie squinted through the blades. Harry continued to thrash around like he was riding a mechanical bull. 'Harry! Stop. That's not Teddy.'

'It must be,' Harry said, holding firmly onto the collar. 'Or is Gallows just a… haven for stray dogs?'

'I fear the latter. Ted is five times his size.'

'Well,' Harry said miserably, 'do you think Tom and Rose would *notice*?'

'It's quite likely,' Charlie said. 'Oh!' the Thing had turned round to face him and he recognised its dopey face. 'This is Trevor! Trevor, stop boy!'

Harry let go of the collar full of disappointment. The dog calmed down at the sound of his name and lay in the flattened grass, licking himself.

'Good boy,' Charlie said kneeling down. The dog rolled over and scratched his ears while Charlie turned over the pendant on his collar.

'Who calls a dog *Trevor*?' Harry asked.

'Mr Bramble does.'

'Who's Mr *Bramble* when he's at home?'

'Our neighbour.' There was no sign of him back through the meadow. The only sign of life at all was a murder of crows, perched on the carcass of an old tractor. 'We should take him home.'

'And you know where he lives, this neighbour of ours?'

'Bramble Cottage,' Charlie said, tapping the pendant on the collar. 'It's somewhere across Sunny Green field up toward Gallows.'

'*Somewhere*,' Harry rolled his eyes. 'How *specific*. Can't we just tie the rotter to a tree and go to the pub or something?'

'No. Anyway I'm never drinking again after last night.'

'Blasphemy. Treason. I'll have you arrested for that. Drawn and quartered in the square.'

'It can't be far,' Charlie said, bringing Trevor to his feet and looking back into the wood. 'Come on.'

They walked for close to a mile. Back through Greenwood where bluebells grew like a lilac carpet around the roots of ancient trees; then down by the rills to an embankment. They were soon at the wire fence separating the field from the wood and Charlie led them back to the cow stile they had crossed the previous day.

'This is twice now we've been here in as many days,' Harry complained. 'I sincerely hope he's home, this Bramble fellow, or I'll invoice him for some Wellingtons and a dry-clean.'

'Do you ever stop moaning?' Charlie asked. 'How can you possibly complain about having to walk through a place like this?'

Harry pulled his face. To Charlie, this was paradise: spring was rife, with primroses over the west banks and hares amongst the hillocks. Across Sunny Green, blue dragonflies raced floating pollen along the dry-stack wall. Even as far as the Yarrowmoor you could see the arctic-alpines flowering on the northern cliffs.

Trevor, at least, was in good spirits. He sprang ahead, tongue hanging out his mouth, tail wagging like a helicopter blade, chasing the birds and the bees and catching flies in his jaws.

Toward the end of the field, the dry-stack turned green with moss. Another wood, smaller than the one around The Barrow, but denser, concealed Bramble's cottage, though an avenue of tire tracks led to it.

The grass was marshy here. Spiky fingers of quillwort and shoreweed sprouted through shallow water on either side of the avenue and a pile of timber lay half-submerged in the quicksand. Bramble's cottage itself seemed to sink into the swamp. It sprawled, wonkily, with a sad look on its grubby face. In the front yard was a skip filled with tree trunks, whose roots knotted together like a mass of rattails. Beside it was a rusty bathtub and the empty shells of half a dozen cars.

'Incredible,' Harry said, stopping by a walkway of paving stones to take in the sight. 'I take back what I said. The Barrow *isn't* the biggest dump in the District after all.'

'When did you say it was?' Charlie asked.

'Lord, cover your nose,' Harry winced as he hopped over the paving stones. 'The whole place smells of mould.'

Trevor, who not only recognised the place, but had led them there, bounded up to the porch and started barking.

Charlie knocked on the door five times without reply, so Harry went round the side of the house to the window.

'Ba-loody hell,' he wheezed. 'We're truly through the looking glass now, Charlie-Boy. Feast the old peepers this-a-way.'

Charlie wiped a circle of grime off the window and cupped his eyes to it. The place was a cluttered mess: character jugs, decorative teapots, Coronation plates and other bits of porcelain tat filled every square inch of wall—from mantelpiece to skirting board. There were trophy mounts of animal heads that wouldn't have looked out of place at Blye House. There were jars of weird pickled things and overflowing boxes of rubbish: packaging, cartons, empty beer cans, newspaper… and all of it sat in stasis under a layer of grime.

'It's like a museum for ugly pottery,' Harry noted. 'Come on. Let's force the door and stick him in there.'

'Don't be stupid.'

Harry stepped back to survey the cottage. 'Do you know, I think I could climb this. I was the rope-climbing champ back at the Harrow—'

'And if you successfully climbed onto the roof,' Charlie sighed, 'what do you plan on doing from there?'

'Why shimmying on down the chimney, obviously. That's an open fire in there.'

'What *for*?'

'So I could open the *door*, Jesus. And then we could leave the bloody mutt inside and get down to the pub for Christ's sake and an ale.'

Charlie didn't respond. He went back to the front of the house while Harry followed him, complaining about something new. He tried the handle to the porch and the door opened.

'You see? It's open. Why do you always want to climb everything?'

The porch was a microcosm of the mess inside. Stacks of Yellow Pages, now green and brown from damp, rose up one wall. The other was filled mostly by a bag of golf clubs under cobwebs. The floor was littered with unopened mail and there was a hole in the tiled floor where mushrooms and creeping ivy grew.

'There you go,' Harry beamed. 'Leave him in there.'

'You can't leave a dog inside a porch. It's illegal, isn't it?'

'It's not a *car*, for crying out loud, it's a porch.'

'What's the difference? It's a glass box. He'll overheat. Even I'm sweating just standing here.'

Harry scoffed and went off. He found a length of rope in the skip, tied it round a trunk and carried the other end back over.

'Tie him to this, then at least he can roam a bit.'

'All right,' Charlie said. 'But we should leave a note, have you got any paper?'

'Yes, I carry a ream on me for whenever I find a stray dog. There, use one of his bills.'

'Okay, I'll write Dear Mr Bramble, uh, here's your dog? We found him in a meadow. From Harry and Charlie, of The Barrow. How's that?'

'Bloody marvellous,' Harry said drawing his coat around himself. 'It's your magnum opus. Come on, I'm starving.'

Chapter 2

Gallows was alive with people. Crowds filtered down the narrow cobbles and spilled onto the high street where market stalls lined the pavements around the central square, Wickham Green. The smell of food filled the air. Stews, curries, jerk chicken. Burger patties sizzling on a hot plate with onions frying beside them. Melted chocolate with fresh fruits, pooled into the centre of pancakes. Behind the stalls were street performers. Living statues, buskers, break-dancers. A man in a kilt attempted to deafen several people by blowing horrendously into a pig's bladder.

'Well this is unexpected,' Harry said, watching a magician turn a balloon into a poodle.

'Oh, of course!' Charlie said, remembering something. 'Mr Bramble said there was a market on most Sundays.'

'I wish you had told *me*,' Harry replied curtly. He was stone-faced and pulled his collar up high against his cheekbones. 'You know I don't like crowds.'

'Since when?'

'Since forever. Come on, let's keep moving.'

'Why?'

'I don't like the way they're looking at us,' Harry said of some imagined stares from a nearby group of clergymen. 'There's something sinister behind their smiles. I'll bet they go home and sodomise each other in Venetian masks.'

Charlie rolled his eyes—but then recalled having a similar thought when he arrived. There was a giant wicker pyre on a hill somewhere, waiting for him to climb inside with a couple of unsuspecting lambs.

'Alright we'll go,' he agreed. 'There's a pub—'

'Hold on a tick!' Harry said, suddenly off on heels like springs.

He landed in front of a stall and handed over some cash and then bounced back over to Charlie, showing off his new watch. He fastened it round his wrist, above his broken one.

'Why are you still wearing that thing?' Charlie asked of the broken watch.

Harry shrugged. 'I'm sentimental.'

'What happened to it?'

'Fencing accident. Lamé with sabres, last spring. I was the featherbrain who refused to wear the manchette and boy, I paid the price all right. This was my great-grandfather's, don't you know. Swiss and what not. Come on. Let's get some lunch and out of this square. I don't like the way they're watching us.'

'They're just clergymen for goodness sake—'

'Not the *cloth*,' Harry said, pointing up. 'I mean *them*.'

Charlie looked up. Every roof in sight was lined with blackbirds. Thousands of the bastards—no doubt attracted by all the food and fuss below. A shudder ran down his spine. There were even more of them in the air, like scrambled fighter jets, dipping and diving then soaring off out of sight. But the sky cackled like television static.

'Come on,' Harry urged. 'I'd give all my riches for a pot of ale.'

Chapter 3

Gallows Village's second and only other pub, The White Pony, was beyond the Wickham Green square, and down a narrow side street. Its sign showed a white Shetland pony beside a thatch-roofed pub. Harry pointed out how the afternoon sun that fell over it made the pony's coat a pale greenish colour and he asked whether Charlie thought this a sign.

They went inside and a handsome young barmaid with auburn hair seated them up on a little dais behind the banister. They ordered a pie each but before she left their table, she pointed at Harry.

'Do I know you?' she asked. 'You look awfully familiar.'

'Who? *Me*? No.' He blushed. 'Not unless you frequent the Royal Thames Yacht Club.'

'Sorry, you must just have one of those faces.' She looked embarrassed by the mistake and disappeared with her freckled cheeks turning pink.

'I say, she was a classic beauty,' Harry said, leaning across their table to watch her disappear behind the bar. 'Like Botticelli's Venus. One's heart might yearn. Wait a moment—yes. I'm in love.'

'What, with *her*?'

'Don't call the future Mrs Burden "her".'

'If you can tell me her name I'll use it.'

'She has freckles like brick dust,' Harry went on. 'Did you see? Something's a-flutter in my chest.'

'You'd need a heart for that.'

'How do I look?'

Charlie examined the specimen. He was scratched to buggery, white as whalebone and his smile drew the eye to its black hole.

'Sort of like a collapsed vein in jodhpurs,' Charlie told him. But Harry wasn't listening again.

'I tell you, back at the Harrow I would've had her like *that*,' he said, snapping his fingers in Charlie's face. 'I've been off my game for too long. Haven't so much as breathed the same *air* as a girl since Rose and she's already on boyfriend number two hundred and thirty-eight. I'll be the first to admit I'm past my peak.'

He checked his reflection in the back of a spoon, licked his palms, ran them through his greasy hair and flattened down his eyebrows.

'Alright, calm down,' Charlie said, noticing Harry gearing up for another bout of mania. 'Any more incidents today and I'll defect. I mean it, I'll join your opposition.'

Harry simmered. 'What's the matter?'

Charlie had been wearing a pained expression. Something had suddenly snapped in him. '*You* are,' he said. 'Tom is. It's everything. I was about to have a breakdown on Milk Street. I was one day away from an aneurysm. Coming here was supposed to be relaxing and it's been everything *but*.'

When Harry finally spoke, it was to say, 'You're like Odysseus aren't you?' and all it did was annoy Charlie more.

'In what way,' he snapped, 'am I *possibly* like Odysseus?'

'When he was on the Italian strait,' Harry explained. 'You're torn aren't you? Between them lot back at The Barrow and me. Like old Odysseus, torn between that frightful whirlpool Scylla and the sea beast Charybdis.'

'And which are you?' Charlie asked. 'The whirlpool or the sea beast?'

Harry shrugged. 'You decide.'

Just then, Venus the barmaid returned with their food and set the pies down on the table. Neither Harry or Charlie spoke for a while and Charlie picked at the pastry with his fork idly.

'Come on, don't be such a misery,' Harry said as he stuffed his gob with a mouthful of pie. 'It's not the end of the world, is it?'

Charlie took a bite and shrugged his shoulders.

'Cheer up,' Harry said. 'Talk to me.'

'About what?'

'Anything.'

'Alright, I'll talk to you,' Charlie said. He was holding one of the pub's red-handled steak knives and he pointed it Harry in what he thought was a threatening manner. 'What did you do to your ribs there?'

Harry paused for a second and a glob of gravy drooled out the side of his mouth. He wiped at it with his napkin for several seconds and Charlie wondered if he was stalling for time.

'What are you talking about?' he eventually asked, setting his fork down and sitting back in his chair.

'You've done something to yourself, haven't you?' Charlie pressed. 'You keep holding it like you're in pain.'

'Tom shot me didn't he?'

'Yes,' Charlie said. 'He shot you in the leg. But this is higher up. See, *Emily* thinks you got into a crash. That's why the bike's all scraped down the side.'

Harry had grown quite pale in the last twenty seconds and started drumming his fingers on the table top.

'Yes,' he said slowly, nodding. 'Didn't want to alarm anyone, but she's quite right. Gosh, *awfully* astute that girlfriend of yours. They do say opposites attract, don't they? Yes… I crashed into that red barn in Underwood. Where Tom killed that cow.'

Charlie almost choked on his pie. '*You crashed into Monk's barn*?'

'Yes, it was quite the spectacle. Through one wall, took out a supporting beam and burst right out the other. Zig-zagged between cows and then launched over the fence like Steve McQueen in The Great Escape.'

'Harry! That's got to be the worst thing you've done since you got here!'

'It's hardly *my* fault. That barn was positioned most precariously on the edge of the road. I was just turning the corner—'

'At what speed?'

'About eighty. Oh, what *now*?' Harry said, at Charlie's open-jawed stare. 'The road was empty! We're in the middle of nowhere out here. Why *shouldn't* I rev up the old engine on the A-roads?'

'Because you don't know how to drive, you fucking idiot! Christ, you crashed through his barn! Rose already thinks the man wants to murder us; you've just given him a reason to.'

'Hold on! Let's put things into perspective,' Harry said with anger beginning to spread from his face to his voice. 'I'm only responsible for a tinsy-wincy spot of property damage *and* I left a healthy stack of compensation monies behind. Whereas *Tom*! Tom murdered one of this man's livestock! For all we know that cow could have been like a child to him.'

'Alright, alright,' Charlie said trying to keep his tone even. 'Let's just keep this between us for now. There is something else I need to ask you. Emily thinks you had some kind of secret meeting on Friday. And that you stole all this money from whoever it was you met with.'

If Harry had looked ill before, he looked now as if he might just have died. Eventually he blinked.

'And?' he asked. 'What's the question?'

'Well, is it *true*?' Charlie asked, leaning in.

Harry was frowning most impressively. 'What do *you* think?'

Charlie shrugged. 'Why don't you just tell me?'

'But I already have! And clearly you didn't believe me. That money is *mine*. It's my life's savings. And I got the bike from Rupert Finklewhatever it was I said his name was and those pistols belonged to my father. That's my story.'

'And that's all true is it?'

'Certainly is.'

Harry had crossed his arms and turned his head away and he refused to make eye contact, instead choosing to purse his lips like some insolent child. He was staring at an enormous white-bearded gentleman who had just ordered a pint at the bar and crossed over to a nearby table beneath the television set and plonked down a big metal chum bucket that whiffed badly enough to make Charlie's eyelids peel back.

'Ugh, that *reeks*!' Harry snapped. 'Do you mind, Gandalf! We're actually trying to *eat* over here.'

The white-bearded man beneath the telly looked over blankly.

'Come on, Charlie,' Harry said, standing up and pulling his coat around himself in a show of disgust. 'Let's go outside.'

They went out into the beer garden. Unfortunately, they walked right into the middle of a circle of senior citizens holding acoustic guitars like tommy guns. They had just let out of church and were evidently not yet ready for the fun to end, so had started on a tone-deaf rendition of *Jerusalem*.

'Christ, let's go back inside,' Charlie whispered. 'I prefer the smell of chum to *this* drivel.'

'They're better than *that* rubbish,' Harry said pointing at the tele above the bearded man. Songs of Praise was on. 'Look, it's a choir of MPs singing *And then Jesus Came. Where* he came it doesn't specify. I bet you a tenner this lot do *Hallelujah* next.'

Charlie rolled his eyes. 'All right,' he agreed as Harry led him over to a spare table in the corner. 'But if they do *Kumbaya* I'm sticking a knife through my fucking skull.'

'Eh, lad,' a voice said as Charlie sat down, and a lumpy finger tapped him on the shoulder.

He turned round to find Mr Bramble at the adjacent table. Under his legs, Trevor lay fast asleep.

'Got yeh note,' Bramble said. ''Spose I owe you me thanks. For finding our Trevor, like.'

'What sort of a *dog's* name is Trevor?' Harry asked.

Bramble's eyebrow raised an inch and he glanced at Harry, then returned his steel-eyed stare to Charlie. 'Is he wi' you?'

'Unfortunately yes,' Charlie answered. 'How is he? Trevor?'

'He'll live.'

'We actually thought he was our friends' dog at first,' Charlie explained. 'Teddy went missing yesterday.'

Bramble looked quite surprised for a second, then a wry smile came over his face and he began to nod his head as if he had just solved a tricky puzzle.

'I see,' he said quietly. 'Listen, lad. I owe yeh one, for finding our Trev. An' I think I can repay you *right now*.'

'Oh?' said Charlie, looking up at the old man's lined face.

'Funny thing. He's a Pyrenean this friend's dog?'

Charlie was completely taken aback. 'Yes! *How* do you know that? Have you seen him?'

'No. But Fletcher Monk has.'

Charlie's heart sank a little. 'Wh-who?' he said.

Bramble shook his head. 'Don't take me fer a fool. I know all about that cow. Terrible thing to've done, but I'm not getting involved in none of that business. I owe yeh one so here it is. Not many folk round here care for Mr Monk. But he *does* have his friends. He's got people spying fer him all over the place. An' last night, Monk come raving in the pub about *four young people with a Pyrenean mountain dog*. Said two blokes with a rifle shot dead a cow of his.

'Now it's not that I'd've helped him none, even if I *had* known,' Bramble continued. 'But when he asked if I knew who might be to blame, I said "no". Course I only knew *you and that girl* were at The Barrow. Didn't know there was any more've you. Or a *dog*, for that matter. But now you say this dog belonged to a friend of yours, well—it all makes sense don't it? *It were you four what killed that cow.*'

Charlie's throat had gone dry and he couldn't properly speak. Before he had to, Bramble said, 'Monk's not a happy chappy at the minute, let me tell you. His cow first. Then last night, some idiot totalled his barn. He don't care for the damage none, but the cows inside, well he's worried about them all right. He's sayin' upset cows don't produce much milk and all this palaver.

'But what you don't know about Mr Monk is this: he's been wanting some power in this village since the day he could walk. And 'cause of all this upset, he's dangerously close to getting it! So as thing's've turned out, it's now in *my* interest to make sure you lot don't get caught. Or else *I'll* be forced to follow the whims of Fletcher soddin' Monk for the rest of me life.'

As Bramble spoke, Charlie felt something like a claw tighten round his heart. When Bramble had finished, Charlie swallowed deeply and said, 'And Mr Monk—he doesn't know where we're staying, yet, does he?'

Bramble shook his head. 'Don't think so.'

'Are you sure?'

'Well he were in here a few hours ago askin' after yehs. But listen. *When* he finds out—and that's not *if*, that's *when*—he *will* come for yeh.'

'What will he do? Shoot us?'

Charlie was suddenly reminded that Emily had asked these same words of Monk the first time they met Mr Bramble, and he had laughed at the suggestion. But Bramble didn't laugh now.

'Just do yehselves a favour,' he said sombrely. 'Stay out of trouble. Better yet, get yehselves out of Gallows. Won't be long till he figures out yehs are the lot at The Barrow, and then he'll come for his revenge.'

A long solitary silence passed, interrupted, eventually, by Harry blowing a raspberry.

'Puh-*lease*,' Harry said rolling his eyes so far back into his head that they disappeared and came back out the other side. 'You make farmer Monk sound like he's the head of the Cosa Nostra! The man's a one-eyed cripple! He can barely walk.'

Bramble stared at Harry for a long moment and then something in his demeanour softened. 'Do I know you?' he asked.

Harry didn't skip a beat. 'I'm afraid you've mistaken me for someone else. Possibly my ancestor, Lord Byron.' And then he stood up and stalked back off inside.

'He's a card,' Bramble said.

'*Card* is not the word I'd use,' Charlie told him. He was perturbed by this recognition Harry kept receiving. First the redhead barmaid and now Bramble.

'Any road, thanks for bringing my Trevor back,' Bramble said, smiling for the first time. 'Don't know what I'd do without the daft git. 'Spose I'll be off.'

Bramble finished the last of his pint and then tugged Trevor up and they left through the beer garden gate.

Chapter 4

When Charlie came back into the pub, carrying their drinks, Harry was leaning over the bar. At first Charlie thought he was pouring himself another pint. But as he got closer, he could see he was engaged in a tug-of-war with a very short man on the other side.

'What are you doing?' Charlie asked, perplexed.

'Charlie!' Harry blushed. He let go and the barman shuffled a step back, clutching a remote control to his chest. 'This bastard won't turn over the tele.'

'So what?'

'So what?' Harry sputtered, almost at a loss for words. 'I'm about to overdose on Christianity, *that's* what! We've got the Jesus Christ Fan Club out on the patio singing *Jerusalem*, and a choir of middle-aged eunuchs on the TV in here.'

'It's Sunday,' the barman growled. 'Have some respect or I'll throw the two of you out.'

'Don't exert the effort, we'll leave,' Harry snarled. 'We'll find somewhere with a little more charm to spend the afternoon. I think I saw an *abattoir* down the road.'

Mr Bramble's words were still going around Charlie's head. *Stay out of trouble. Better yet, get yehselves out of Gallows.* The last thing Charlie needed now was for Harry to cause enough trouble to summon Fletcher Monk. So Charlie apologised to the barman and quickly pulled Harry over to the side.

'Look you heard what Bramble just said,' he explained. 'Fletcher Monk is looking for us out there.' Charlie checked the time. 'It's... quarter to one. And it's still busy out there. If we leave now, anyone might see us and go and tell him. We should lay low for a few hours until the market dies down.'

Harry shook his head and his eyes flashed over to the white-bearded fisherman beneath the TV set.

'Sod this place. We should go back now.'

'No, think about it. Bramble said Monk was already in here an hour ago looking for us. It's unlikely he'll come back this way any time soon. But he could be anywhere out there. He doesn't drink in this pub either, he drinks at The Packhorse. So I think this is the safest place for us, until we can get back through Gallows without being seen.'

'We won't be seen,' Harry protested. 'They're looking for four people with a dog. We can slip back through that market and get home.'

Now Charlie shook his head. 'No, remember when we were in the market, before? You pointed out those priests were staring at us, remember?'

Harry's face contorted slightly and his bottom lip stuck out. He looked like he wanted to say something but restrained himself.

'They might've been some of Monk's "spies" that Bramble mentioned,' Charlie went on. 'For all we know, they might have already told him they saw us. He could be on the main street, waiting for us to wander by. I think it's best if we just stay here, let the lunch rush die down and then we can go.'

'There must be another way round?'

'Probably, yes, through the fields or the wood, but I don't know it, do you? I don't fancy being stuck in the wilderness for a few hours. But the only road between Gallows and The Barrow is Twin Hills, and that's where the market is.'

Harry had been staring past Charlie, back at the fisherman with the bucket of chum again. Charlie peered round at him too and frowned. Whatever it was that so fascinated Harry about him did not have the same effect on Charlie.

'No.' Harry stood firm. 'I really must protest. If this psychotic Cyclops is out looking for us and he's already been in here once today, then I think it's a stupidly dangerous thing for us to stay here a second longer. We should get back to The Barrow and tell the others. If he does see us, so what? I hold the hundred-meter record at the Harrow, I can out-run a cripple.'

'Why are you so eager to leave?' Charlie asked, frowning. He could see that Harry was holding something back in the way his entire body prickled and he had drawn his coat tightly around himself.

'I've told you,' he answered. 'It's silly of us to stay here, that's all.'

Charlie sighed. He didn't believe him for a second, but he also didn't have the fight in him to unravel the mystery. If Harry meant to be aloof and weird he could feel free to be aloof and weird.

'Alright, then. Have it your way. Let's go.'

Charlie planted his half-empty glass on the side and turned to the door. But no sooner had he reached it than Emily, Tom and Rose came waltzing in.

'Oh!' Emily gasped. 'What are you doing here?'

'Leaving, actually,' Harry interjected. 'I wouldn't stay in this place if the ale was free.'

'You can't leave yet,' said Rose. 'We've only just arrived.'

Tom grinned. 'Rose, if Harry wants to leave, please don't stop him. Charlie'll stay though, won't you mate?'

Bramble's warning circled his thoughts again. *Get yehselves out of Gallows.* But he also knew he was right. Monk drank in The Packhorse and he had already searched this pub less than an hour ago. Gallows might have been a small village but it wasn't so tiny as to warrant Monk another stop. He was certain this was the safest place for them, until the busy markets died down outside.

'Yeah, I'll stay,' Charlie agreed. 'Harry?'

Harry looked awfully set-upon. Charlie distinctly saw his eyes flash back over the fisherman, but he seemed to decide he had no other recourse but to stay and threw his arms up in surrender.

'Fine! We'll stay for *one* drink,' Harry said, grinding his teeth. 'But that's all.'

'Excellent.'

The others started toward the bar, leaving Harry to grind his teeth. A second later, he sprang over with a wide-eyed smile.

'You lot find us a table,' he said. 'I'll pay for our drinks. Least I can do.'

He pulled out a fifty pound note and wafted it around.

Tom was the first to agree. He slapped Harry on the back. They each gave him their orders and then left him at the bar. Charlie led the others back up to the dais and sat down on a table in the furthest corner, watching Harry across the room suspiciously.

'So, how's he been today?' Tom asked. 'Captain Toff over there. Up to any more nonsense?'

'No more than usual.' Charlie said, which was true. He was thinking about how to explain the situation they found themselves in delicately.

'And have you talked to him about what I said on the island?' asked Emily.

'Hm? Oh, yes.'

Tom leaned in closer. 'What's this?'

'Harry had a crash on his way up here,' Charlie grumbled. 'Injured himself. I'd like to say that's why he's been acting so weird, but… Oh Christ, what's he doing *now*?'

Charlie's heart went into overdrive at once. He knew there was bound to be more trouble this weekend. He hadn't expected it so soon.

Across the room, Harry was in some sort of slanging match with the landlord again. Charlie leapt to his feet and ran over just as the landlord started hopping up and down behind the bar, trying to swing at Harry.

'Get him out of here!' the landlord spat. He was in a rage, practically frothing at the mouth. His eyes were all a-bulge. How could Harry have caused such severe loathing in such little time? It was surely a new record.

'What has he done?' Charlie asked, trying to restrain Harry, who was hopping from foot to foot himself and jabbing at the air like a boxer warming up.

'He just asked me how much it would cost,' the landlord snarled, 'for a night with my daughter!'

He pointed at the young red-haired barmaid, Venus, with the freckles like brick dust.

'Harry, why?'

'I didn't know she was the man's *daughter* for goodness' sake. How was I to know? I just thought he was jealous. Jealous I can pull a cracker like her and he can't even pull a pint.'

'That "cracker",' the barman howled, 'is fifteen years-old!'

Harry paled slightly. He quickly regained some of his

190

composure and decided to double down on the assassination. 'Well, who isn't fifteen in this place? It's like a bloody primary school. What are you hiring fifteen year-olds for anyway? Do you get to pay them less? Child labour? Or perhaps you don't pay her at all, being family. Room and board, is that it? Oh, I get it. Now I'm building up the picture. *That's* why you were so offended by my generous offer. She's all yours, is she? A close-knit family, are you?'

The barman's rage somehow grew, like a stoked fire. His cheeks went from plum to scarlet. He vibrated like a bomb about to blow. And then, without another word, he leapt the bar, landing only feet from Harry, and stuck his dukes up.

The sight only made Harry throw back his head in mocking laughter.

'I was the Harrow's boxing champ,' he said. 'You'll need a step ladder to stand a chance against me. Even then I don't fancy your odds.'

The landlord dived forward and thumped Harry in the hip. Harry laughed at first, but then came another and the smile disappeared. By now, there was quite a crowd of onlookers. The dozen or so patrons had drifted from their tables and gathered round the scene. By the third punch, Harry turned quite pale. He held the landlord's sizzling head and the man went on swiping, but hit only air. He ducked round Harry's arm and gave chase around the tables.

It might have been comical, Charlie thought, if it wasn't Harry Burden in the middle of all this.

'Alright, little man, you've made your point, we'll leave,' Harry said, his face flushed with colour.

'You've missed your chance,' the man spat. 'I'm gonna knock you for six.'

Harry lunged across the table and pulled one of the red-handled steak knives from the cutlery tin and brandished it like a rapier.

'I bested my previous opponent in a duel, what say I best you too?' he said, pointing it at the barman.

There was steam coming from the barman's head now. He

looked like a boiled egg in a cup. He turned round, found a bottle of beer and smashed it over the bar so that he was holding the neck with its fanged edge pointed at Harry's knife.

Charlie thought there was something about the landlord so willing to cause damage and destruction in his own pub that made the scene more frightening than it otherwise would have been.

Harry clearly thought the same, because his face contorted with fear.

Charlie began to withdraw as Emily, Tom and Rose came down from the dais and joined him by the door.

'Come on Harry, let's go,' Rose hissed.

Harry looked round at the rest of The Barrow crowd behind him. He kept the steak knife held out and his eyes trained on the landlord, but began a slow retreat to the door. He took another step back and his foot plummeted straight into the bucket of chum. The gloopy red meat-drool spurted up his leg. He hopped out and shook the leg and chunks of it flicked off in every direction. A few people groaned as it slapped them on the arms and face. A whopping great wedge landed in the middle of a table of girls who shrieked.

'Sorry,' Harry said bashfully, while edging toward the door. Something of an opposition was forming now and it seemed to be advancing from the bar.

The barman was still quaking on the spot and he held onto his bottleneck with sweaty palms.

'We're leaving now!' Harry announced. 'Off to find somewhere that doesn't hire underage prossies to lure in the punters! Keep watching you charlatans. Officious fishermen! Voyeuristic tosspots! Wankers! Public masturbators! Organists! Sit and drink your livers to death while this great sack of mashed potato parades his floosie around. If she's pregnant in the next year you ought to check the baby's not got a third arm or an extra pair of eyes. I know what happens up here in the northern mountains.'

'Come *on* Harry,' Charlie urged tugging at his sleeve.

He had pushed open the door and the others slipped out behind.

The pub crowd closed in on them as they backed away to the exit. They jeered and threw nuts and beer mats. Someone had reached over the bar and scooped the ice from the freezer. An enormous clump of it shattered a painting above the door. Glass and ice rained down as they finally pushed through to the street beyond.

A thundering roar picked up inside. Any minute an army would be on them, tearing their guts out with bare hands in the middle of the road.

Stay out of trouble, Bramble had said. Good advice, Charlie thought.

'What now?' Rose asked, panicked.

'Leg it?' Tom suggested.

They looked at one another and then broke into a sprint. It didn't cease until they were on the other side of the tor, about as far from The White Pony as could be. Charlie hadn't even thought about where they were going, but he spotted The Packhorse not far ahead and his stomach flipped.

Fortunately, Rose stopped first at the head of the road, gasping for breath.

'Stop! I'm about to revisit my lunch,' she said. 'Where are we going? The Barrow's in the complete opposite direction!'

'Let's get inside somewhere,' Tom suggested, looking behind them. 'In case anyone's following us.'

'But it's Sunday,' Emily pointed out, 'everywhere will be closed.'

'Not everywhere,' Charlie said, and he pointed down the steep where The Parish Church of St Paul's nestled into the earth.

Chapter 5

The grass around Gravesend was marshy, fed from the green water that drizzled from a wide culvert at the edge of the road. The graveyard around the church was filled with ugly concrete crosses and hogback tombs and the grass was untamed and weedy. The church itself was plain and grey, built from ashlar brick, with a sixty-foot tower and crocketed spire pointing wonkily back up the steep road of the tor.

A chill ran down Charlie's spine as they looked at it from above. A trail of leaves swirled by in a breeze, rustling the branches of the trees. Birds took to the sky and dispersed and then everything fell silent and still again.

'Come on,' Tom grunted.

He led the group to the transept and two stone angels watched them enter.

It was empty inside and Emily said, 'Where is everyone for God's sake?—and I mean that quite unblasphemously.'

Charlie pointed to the clock. It was some time past one. 'Morning sermon's over.'

They walked the central aisle to a rood screen at the back of the chapel and Tom directed them to the pews, while he stood in front like he was about to give a eulogy.

'You,' he glared at Harry. 'Start talking.' He pointed at the crucifix on the wall behind him. 'And explain just what in the name of bleeding *Christ* all that were about?'

'What's to explain?' Harry answered. 'I was attacked by a violent imp, you all saw.'

'An imp *you* provoked,' Tom replied. 'I mean, haven't you noticed it's only ever you that gets into these scrapes?'

'In fairness, Tom,' Emily said, 'the last time I was forced to run like that it was because *you and Charlie* broke onto a dairy farm, executed a cow, and almost had us all murdered for the trouble.'

'Exactly!' Harry clapped. 'Your selective memory lets you compartmentalise your own discretions to paint *me* as the bearer of the black flag. It's as Byron said—'

'Never mind what Byron said!' Tom howled. 'I don't want to know what bloody Byron said. I'm sick to death of hearing about the cunt.'

'Yes and, well, I'm not *defending* you particularly, Harry, either,' Emily continued. 'I still happen to think you've behaved like an arse-headed thing from the very moment you got here. But I believe we should all regain a little perspective, that's all I'm trying to say.'

The door at the head of the church clicked open and the sound of rubber soles squeaked on the stone floor.

'Hullo,' a frail voice carried over.

A nervous-looking priest waddled down the aisle looking like a penguin in his cassock. Charlie recognised him as one of the men from the market that had been watching them.

'I'm afraid you've missed my morning sermon,' he said as he approached the pews, 'but there'll be a mass tonight at ten o'clock.'

'We're not here for your sermon,' Tom said.

'Oh?' the priest took off his glasses and cleaned them on his dress. 'Then how can I help?'

'We're just, um… we're *praying*, your holy… grace,' Rose said. 'We won't be any trouble.'

The priest drew close enough to see them and he looked a pearly sort of grey in the faded light, which fell over him through a cross-shaped window. He put his glasses back on and his smile faltered.

'N-no problem,' he said. 'I'll be in the sacristy if you need anything.'

He practically ran behind the rood screen and disappeared into a little room at the back of the chapel.

Charlie had a great fat lump in his throat. He thought about what Bramble had just told him. *He's got people spying fer him all over the place.* Emily tried to resume but Charlie cut her off—

'Look—we need to get out of Gallows,' he said in a low voice. 'Urgently.'

'Because of *him*?' Tom asked, confused, pointing after the nervous priest.

Charlie looked at the door and could see the priest's eye in the crack below the hinge.

'Not just him,' Charlie said in a lower voice still. 'It's *everyone* here. It's like all these… Gallowsians know one another. They're a hive mind. And we're going to end up burning on a wicker pyre. As we speak there's virgin girls building one while shepherds round up the lambs—'

'Calm down,' Harry warned him. 'You're getting hysterical again.'

'Yes, because of you!' Charlie snapped loudly. The priest's head popped out from behind his door. Charlie shot him a look and he went back inside. 'I came out here to get away from feeling like this, but you've just brought it all up here with you. Anyway, it's not safe. Mr Bramble told me we're being *hunted*.'

'*Hunted*?' Rose asked, sitting up. 'By who?' She looked as if she already knew the answer.

'Fletcher Monk,' Charlie told them. 'We killed his cow and uh… someone apparently destroyed his cow shed. He wants revenge.'

Harry blushed and looked down at his toes.

Rose clapped her hands together. 'Well! *That* just about does it for me. This weekend has been an unmitigated disaster from the moment we got here. It's impossible to have a relaxing weekend with *you* as it is, Tom. But oh no, stupid little Rose had to go and add *more* people into the mix. I'm *sorry* Emily, but I never should have invited you.'

'What have *I* done?' Emily asked, half offended.

'*You* haven't done anything, of course,' Rose replied. She had started tapping her nails nervously over a hymnbook in her lap. 'But if I had never invited *you*, then Charlie wouldn't be here. And therefore *Harry* wouldn't be here. And if Charlie *wasn't* here then Tom never would have brought that stupid gun with him to show off and none of this would have ever happened. I didn't even *want* to invite you. Not after… *that weekend* and all the… unpleasantness. It was all *Tom's* idea. He practically *begged* me to.'

Tom turned a little pink around the ears. Charlie's thoughts immediately fell to the ring around Teddy's neck. Tom's plan to propose couldn't have fallen further off-course.

'Well *I* hardly think that's fair,' Harry chimed in. 'You can blame *me* by all means. But to insinuate *Emily* had anything to do with all this trouble is to scapegoat her for Tom. The truth of the matter is *both* Tom and I are reprehensible. I'm a gate-crasher and he's a cow killer—'

'*Either way*,' Rose said, standing up, 'I think I'll go home now.'

'Yes, and I'll join you,' said Emily.

'No. I don't mean home to The *Barrow*,' Rose said. 'I mean home to *London*.'

'What, why?'

'Why? *Why*? Didn't you hear what Charlie just said? We're being hunted, Em. *Hunted*! And it's all because of *these two*, Tweedledum and Tweedle... *dumber*!'

She pointed at Tom and Harry.

'I wasn't even *here* when they murdered that effing cow!' Harry protested. 'What am *I* supposed to have done?'

'You can't seriously mean that?' she spat. 'Just when I was starting to think you were not *completely* unbearable, you go and cause a scene like that little thing at the pub. You really are doing just a tremendously spiffing job of making us all absolutely *loathe* you. Of making *me* loathe you. We could have been friends again, you know. Good friends, even—'

'The feeling's mutual,' he snapped back and they fired knives at one another from their eyes until Charlie whistled for their attention.

'*As stressful* as Harry has made this weekend,' he hissed, 'this has nothing to do with him—'

'Nowt to do with him?' Tom couldn't believe his ears. 'He's the nutcase who had everyone chucking stuff at us like we were in the stocks.'

'You mean the pillory,' Harry muttered.

'*What*?' Tom glared at him.

'You *mean* "like we were in the pillory",' Harry responded.

197

'The *stocks* are something for your feet. You can remember it because *stocks are like socks: for the feet.*'

'Harry, now's not the time for—'

'And how do *you* know,' Tom said, leaning in close, 'that when I *say* the stocks, I don't *mean* the stocks?'

'Because nobody *ever* means the stocks. The stocks are for feet. The pillory's for your head and arms. Like this—' Harry held his arms up. 'And I happen to know for a *fact* that the image in your head was of the five of us, lined up in Wickham Green square, in the pillory.'

'Are you really this big of a prick or am I just dreaming?'

'I don't know—why don't you pinch yourself and find out? I'll do it for you if you like?'

'You're a cunt.'

'No *you're* a cunt—'

'No *you're*—'

'*Listen to me!*' Charlie shouted, loud enough to silence everybody. 'It's not important who's done what. Stop fucking rowing with each other! It's pathetic. You're *both* cunts as far as I'm concerned—'

'Charlie—'

'No!' he shouted, getting to his feet in the aisle. 'I've had enough of going along with all this bullshit. You're all driving me mad. I've just told you we're being sought out by some psychotic one-eyed monster and all you care about is who's to blame! We've got *one night* left here. We just need to get out of this fucking village, go back to The Barrow and *stay out of trouble* until tomorrow. Then we can all get in our cars as soon as day breaks and go our separate ways.'

'Yes!' Harry said, leaping to his feet. '*Me* to Milk Street and *you* to Greenwich Village with your dolly bird!'

Charlie felt his face turning red and patchy now that he had stopped shouting. Nobody else said a word. They just shuffled about uncomfortably.

'Charlie's right,' Emily eventually said. 'Monk doesn't know where we are. We should head home right now and stay there until tomorrow. Keep ourselves out of trouble.'

'Keep outta trouble,' Tom chuckled. 'Thing is, I don't think *he's* capable.' He meant Harry. 'He'll find a way to raise hell on the walk back. Prob'ly get us all arrested for the night or piss off some landowner who'll shoot us. If you put him in an *empty room* he'd find a way to tear down the walls.'

'*This* coming from the man who quite *liter*ally brought down a wall—on Potter Island. Or have you stored that particular memory in the recycling bin of your mind, with the rest of your transgressions?'

Tom had no answer for that. Instead he just asked, 'Why are you here?'

There was something about the simplicity of the question and the earnestness behind it that caused Harry to sink into his pew. Tom stood back up and started shaking his pack of Marlboros like a deck of cards.

'You know, you might have *these three* fooled. But not me,' Tom said. 'I've been mulling it over all morning and I think I finally know just what's going on.'

Harry didn't say a word. He smiled at Tom, unafraid of whatever it was he knew—or *thought* he knew. It was Emily who interrupted first.

'What is it, Tom?' she asked. 'What has he done?'

Tom leaned in close to Harry again and said: 'Armed robbery.'

Harry balked at the idea. 'Well now *really*, that's the grand deduction of your great detective mind?'

'He left London in a hurry,' Tom explained quickly. 'He turned up at six in the morning without a word of warning. And all he's got on him are some pistols and a fuck-tonne of cash. *You* do the maths.'

Nobody replied. Emily looked over at Charlie who was staring at his toes in the aisle.

'And then there's that bike,' Tom continued. 'You said yourself Em, you'd never seen it before. Well where did he get it from? Did it appear out of thin air?'

'A friend of mine dropped it off. Rupert Fiddleman.'

'Fiddle*minster*,' Charlie reminded him.

'Yes, that's the fellow. He was going away you see, and he's between houses. Didn't want to pay extortionate Heathrow prices and—'

'Whatever!' Tom called. 'Not important. The point is, that bike was all scratched down the muffler.'

'Now really, can I defend myself in this kangaroo court? Or has Judge Mental decided the verdict already? This is tosh and drivel and—'

'*Quiet*, Harry,' Charlie said. 'For your own good. Go on, Tom.'

'You mean you're *believing* this fiction?' Harry asked.

'I've tried to get the truth out of you and been entirely unsuccessful,' Charlie reminded him. 'You had your chance, so I'd like to hear what Tom has to say.'

'Thanks, Charlie,' Tom said. 'So. You said his dad cut him off, right?'

'Right.'

'And where did you say you lived? Kensington, was it?'

'Knightsbridge.'

'Oof. Can't be easy on the wallet,' Tom grinned, elated at his newfound power. '*So*. Prince Harry's sat alone in Knightsbridge, thinking about what it'll be like out in the cold when daddy's money dries up. He's got these two pistols. All he needs is a getaway vehicle and somewhere to lay low.'

'"Getaway vehicle"? "Lay low"?' Harry scoffed. 'We're in *rural England*, you egg.'

'I don't know where you got that money, Harry, but I *know* you stole it,' Tom returned. 'Maybe you stuck up a petrol station or something, hopped on that bike and got in a police chase on your way up here—'

'A police chase! Is *all* of your evidence based on things you've seen in films? A round of applause for Thomas Darrow, QC. Oh bra-*vo*!'

'That's not *all* my evidence,' Tom said, turning to look up at Christ on the wall. 'There was that newspaper you bought, the morning Teddy went missing. You left it at The Barrow and I looked through it. I found a few pages torn out near the middle—'

'Yes!' Emily said. 'I saw that too.'

'Right. You know him better than I do, so correct me if I'm wrong, Em. But Harry don't strike me as the type to collect Pleasure Beach vouchers.'

Harry rolled his eyes. He had stretched his arms out and put them behind his head while Tom went on with his French detective routine.

'Perhaps His Majesty can tell us what *that* were all about?'

'*I* don't know,' Harry said flippantly, waving his hand like he was shooing a fly. 'I don't even remember tearing a page out. Perhaps I had a piece of chewing gum I needed to envelope before I threw it away. Perhaps there was a particularly enormous spider I was trying to squish. Maybe I *bought* it like that. I didn't realise it was a crime to tear pages out from newspapers. Particularly from The *Mail*.'

'Nice try,' Tom rebuffed, 'but... *nah*. I think it's safe to assume there was summat in there you didn't want us to see. An article about this robbery, maybe? So I'm wondering if that's why you decided your next little act of domestic terrorism was to pack us all up and ship us off to a remote island for the night? You'll all remember he conveniently "forgot" to book a return trip. I'll wager that were the real plan all along. Stick us on an island for as long as he could.'

'But Harry's the one who *rescued* us,' Rose piped up.

'Only after I nearly killed him,' Tom reminded her. 'Maybe he realised his *life* weren't worth seeing the plan through. Anyway, it got us off the mainland for a night. And more importantly, it gave him a good opportunity to do away with some evidence, didn't it?'

'Evidence?' Charlie asked. 'What evidence?'

'Oh, come on, Charlie. I thought you were supposed to be *smart*?' Tom said. 'I'm talking about the *getaway vehicle*.'

Harry stood up now and Tom turned so they were facing one another in the aisle.

'I've heard enough,' Harry said. 'You're going to burn yourself out if you keep making these giant leaps of logic.'

'Charlie, think about it,' Tom said, looking round at him.

'*Really* think. He sank that bike to the bottom of the lake *on purpose*, didn't he?'

Charlie could have laughed. He had *been* on the Bonneville with Harry when it stopped working. He told Tom as much.

But Tom looked quite angry about that.

'Brakes don't just stop working, Charlie. Jesus! Not on brand new Triumphs. He drove up here on that thing didn't he? What's that, three hundred miles? And the brakes worked fine *then*, didn't they? So what's he saying? That someone cut them? That *I* cut them maybe?'

'He never *accused* anybody of tampering with it, he just said—'

'Brakes don't just stop working, Charlie,' Tom repeated. 'Use your fucking head. That whole little spectacle was set up so he *could get rid of the evidence.*'

'But only a *lunatic* would do something like that,' Rose insisted and Tom just raised an eyebrow at her.

'I'll tell you summat else, too,' Tom went on. 'It were no accident that island had no power. He had to make sure there was no way for us to contact the mainland or else the whole thing would've been for nowt. And if he wanted us cut-off, that meant getting rid of *all* our phones.' Tom looked at Rose. 'I'll bet you anything *Harry stole your mobile.* That's why you couldn't find it before we left.'

Rose turned ghostly white and made several unsuccessful attempts at vocalisation.

'You're not *buying* this are you, Charlie-Boy?' Harry asked. 'That *I*—Harrington Burden, who can barely tie my own *shoelaces* without your help—was involved in an armed robbery with an antique flintlock, and got into a high-speed police chase at four o'clock in the bastard morning, and then orchestrated this Christie-esque island escapade in a matter of hours?'

Charlie didn't know what to think.

'If he was going to get rid of the bike,' Charlie asked Tom, '*why* would he do it with *me* on board? Wouldn't it be easier to have just dumped the thing on his way up here?'

Tom considered the point. And Harry clapped his hands, happy to accept the little victory.

'He had to make it *look like an accident*,' Tom decided, pacing up and down with his finger under his lip. 'Yeah! That's right. If he turned up here on Friday night with no hint of a vehicle we'd have been suspicious from the get-go wouldn't we? How the fuck did he get here? Did he fly in? But... if he has a plausible accident? Then bingo! All he needed was a gullible witness, right? And... well...'

He looked down at Charlie sympathetically, who felt his cheeks blush.

'Even if that's not true,' Tom went on, 'you all saw state he was in when he turned up here. And his bike were all scraped and what-not. He probably didn't have *time* to dump it then, he just needed to get here and worry about that later.

'So,' Tom breathed, 'when do we call the police?'

'The police!' Rose shrieked. '*No*body is calling the police. Not until we've sat down and thoroughly discussed all this and heard everyone out.'

'What's to discuss? He's a criminal and—'

Rose slammed her hymnbook on the pew.

'*And* what? Do you have any proof?' she screamed. 'Any *actual* quantifiable evidence other than your—*frankly*—less-than-astute observations? Hm?'

'What evidence could I have?' Tom roared back. 'He sank it all to the bottom of the fucking lake! That's my whole point!' They stared at one another furiously. Then Tom's face seemed to flicker with a satisfied smile for just a second. 'The bottom of the lake...' he repeated under his breath. He looked round at the faces all looking up at him, each in a different stage of belief. 'Fine. Fuck you all,' he chuckled. 'I'm going for a smoke.'

He stormed off down the aisle and let the church door swing shut behind him.

Charlie got to his feet at once and pulled Emily up by the hand. 'I could do with a breather, too.'

'And I'll come with you,' Rose said quickly. Clearly, she didn't want to be left alone with Harry. Not now.

Harry got to his feet too and cracked his back. 'Yes,' he stretched, 'air sounds good.'

'No. Uh, why don't you stay here?' Charlie said. 'We'll only be out there for five minutes. Just give us a breather? And for the love of *God*, stay out of trouble. You *are* in his house.'

Harry sat back down slowly and raised his arms. 'Yes. I'll be sure not to "pull the walls down" as Tom says.'

Charlie indicated Christ on the wall. 'Since you didn't immediately turn to *ash* when you came in, you might as well have a word with *him*.'

Harry looked round at the face of Jesus and rolled his eyes. Blood ran down his cheek from the thorns in his crown.

Chapter 6

When Charlie, Emily and Rose left the church, they couldn't find Tom anywhere. They walked the whole perimeter without luck.

'Where's he *got* to?' Rose asked.

'You don't think he's gone to fetch the police?'

'No,' she said, sitting down on a bench. 'He knows better than that.'

Charlie slumped down beside her and none of them said a word for a while.

'He's gone a bit *mad* really, hasn't he?' Rose eventually said. '*Tom* I mean. Harrington Burden: an armed *robber*? It's laughable. *Isn't* it?'

Emily sifted about and tucked the loose hair behind her ear. 'I'm not so sure he *has* gone mad, in all honesty Rose. I must say, I've been working on a similar theory myself.'

'You *have*?'

'Yes He had a bike accident on his way up here and injured himself,' she said. 'We know that. It could easily be part of the mystery.'

'It certainly would explain a lot if he's banged that head of his,' Rose said.

'You're right, Em,' Charlie admitted. 'Harry crashed into… something on his way here. He told me himself just now.' He thought it best not to mention Monk's barn for the moment. 'He denied any robbery took place though. But I'll tell you what. Something Tom said just now *did* strike me. What he said about Harry, hiding something from us in that newspaper. It made me think about that little show he put on at The White Pony. Before you all arrived—' (Charlie sighed as if he were about to cross the point of no return) '—he kept looking over at this fisherman who had come in with a bucket of chum.'

'And?'

'*And* I don't think he *was* looking at the fisherman at all,' Charlie explained. 'I think he was looking *above* him.'

'What was above him?' Rose asked.

'The television. Do you see?'

'No.'

'It was almost one o'clock,' Charlie said. 'Songs of Praise was about to end and the BBC Weekend News was about to start. Do you see now?'

'Oh!' Emily said, finally understanding. 'If he was so scared that we'd see something about him in the *paper*,' she explained, 'then he must have been *terrified* what we might see on the television.'

'That's why he asked if we could leave after one drink?' Rose asked.

'He had already tried to turn over the TV. And when that failed, he was suddenly eager to leave. I didn't understand it. Then you lot arrived and we decided to stay.' Charlie hung his head. It suddenly felt heavy. 'He must have caused that great big scene on purpose to get us chucked out. I *thought* it was odd he fancied that barmaid. I've never so much as seen Harry even *try* to talk to a girl before.'

Rose blushed slightly.

'Oh, Harry, what are you *hiding* from us?' Emily asked.

Before anyone could speculate, the door to the church blew open and Harry stormed out, heading straight up the main road toward Wickham Green. When the door slammed shut behind him, the wing of one of the angels cracked and fell off, sticking in the dirt like a dagger.

Charlie ran after him. 'Where are you going?'

Harry threw something over his shoulder, which Charlie caught. It was a pack of Marlboros.

'Look familiar?' Harry asked.

'They're Tom's fags aren't they?'

'Exactly. "Gone for a smoke" has he? *My arse* he's gone for a smoke!'

'Well he's probably just gone home. Had enough. To tell you the truth, I don't blame him.'

Harry's face twitched.

'What's going on Harry? Stop walking and speak to me.'

Harry did stop and so suddenly Charlie crashed into him.

'Alright Charlie. I'll tell you a secret now but you must promise not to overreact, because it's no big deal.'

'Oh, God. Tom's not... *right* about this robbery business is he?'

Harry scoffed. '*Armed robbery*, Charlie? *Me*? What do *you* think?'

It wasn't exactly a denial.

'Then what's this secret of yours?'

'Well,' Harry said. 'Thing is, I *did* sink the bike on purpose, okay. He's right about that—'

'What!'

'Look, keep walking, there's not much time,' Harry said, turning back uphill and frog-marching the whole way over. Charlie had to jog to keep up with him.

'Harry, you total bastard, you might have killed me!'

'Nonsense.'

'Why did you do it?'

'Listen, no time,' Harry said evasively. 'I think Tom's on his way back to The Barrow to try and find his precious evidence against me. We must beat him there. That's imperative.'

'Evidence? Harry, evidence of *what*?'

A car was rumbling steadily up the road behind them and Harry stuck his arm out to flag it down. It showed no sign of stopping so he promptly threw himself out in front of it, arms and legs flayed and eyes shut tight. The driver had to slam on her brakes to stop from hitting him and her car swerved to a stop. Its front bumper very gently touched Harry, who endeavoured to roll across the bonnet and fall heavily to the floor six feet away. A real thespian.

Charlie could only roll his eyes as the driver leapt from her car in horror.

'Is he alright?' she screamed, staring at Harry's body on the floor.

'I'm afraid to say he's not alright, no,' Charlie told her. 'But that's got nothing to do with you.'

Harry got to his feet and she held her chest with relief. 'Oh thank God. I *tried* to stop, I really did, but you just *threw* yourself at me—'

'I must commandeer your vehicle,' Harry said, hobbling round the side of the car. 'I'm with the Metropolitan Police. There's been a murder.'

'You silly little man,' she replied in the disappointed tone of a primary school teacher. 'You could have killed yourself! Or *worse*—me!'

Harry pulled at the car door. 'Come now, stand aside, official police business.'

She was stronger than Harry and they wrestled with the door until she got quite cross and bit his fingers. He screamed out and leapt a foot back, shaking his hand.

'What did you do *that* for?'

'Because you're behaving like a wanker.'

Harry saw he had met his match in this force of nature at four-foot-four. He looked down the long main road in the direction of The Barrow and squinted. It was some way off yet, and he appeared to come to a decision.

'Fine, fine! You win. Here.'

He reached into his deep pocket and pulled out whatever money he had left.

'Whu-what's that?' she asked, astounded.

'About three thousand pounds,' he said. 'And it's yours. For a ten-minute taxi service.'

'*Mine*? Are you crazy?' she turned to Charlie. 'Is he *crazy*?'

'Without a doubt.'

'Look, we're wasting time! Have we got a deal?' Harry was already pulling the passenger door open and climbing in. There was another vehicle coming down the road and they were blocking the way. 'Charlie, get in the back. And you there, lady, uh, what's your name?'

'Daisy,' she said.

'Daisy—you drive. But we really *must* go *now*.'

The car behind started honking its horn at them. Harry leaned over and honked Daisy's back while shouting off a reel of impressive swear words.

'Oh, what am I getting myself into?' Daisy said as she climbed inside.

The car behind revved its engine and whizzed past them, holding down its horn the whole way round. Harry wound his window down and held out a finger.

Daisy clicked her belt in and started the engine up. 'Right— where am I taking you?'

'Follow this road for about two miles and turn right at the woods. I'll point it out when we're close. Come on! Time really is of the essence here.'

The car started to move and Harry rubbed his hands together excitedly. 'Here we go!' he said. He was looking back through the rear windshield and then down every side street they passed until they got out of the village and onto the flat by Sunny Green. Only then did he seem to relax a little.

The Yarrowmoor appeared on their left. Harry reached into his pockets then and began to neaten out the notes in his bundle of cash in preparation. Daisy almost welled up.

'This must be a dream,' she said. 'Is that really for me? I'm *never* this lucky. You know what I should do? I should buy a lottery ticket!—I'm just… I'm ecstatic Mr…?'

'Byron.'

'I'm just ecstatic Mr Byron. I must be the luckiest woman on the Lakes.'

'That's right, you're very bloody lucky—watch the road now!'

She was driving blinded by tears and had veered into the hedgerow. 'I just can't believe it,' she practically blubbed. 'My Dylan and me, we can take the month off and go away somewhere for a while. Paris or Venice or Barcelona. Somewhere pricey, a European capital, you know, somewhere with those little white buildings that catch sunsets just right.'

'Yes, yes, but easy does it,' Harry said. 'You're veering into the bush. Jesus! The road! *Watch* the bloody road woman!'

They went on like that for a few minutes. Daisy blubbering, the car leaking black exhaust fumes and making a strange rattling sound and Harry, holding on for dear life as he bumped his head every time she swerved along the straight. Charlie could see Harry's eyes in the rear-view mirror. They were wide open.

'Ah, now here—at the end of this road pull in, but watch out for the—'

Pothole.

He never got the last word out. They swung with the wind; the car teetered to the left, almost on two wheels, then screeched with the slam of the brakes. It had overshot, passed round the pothole like a planet breaking orbit, and stormed onto the bracken towards The Mall, steamrolled through the untouched foliage, back onto the path and then turned just in time to smack headlong into the wooden sign, where the car crumpled round its pole like a tin can.

The sign cracked in half and the top, which said *Welcome to The Barrow*, fell off across the bonnet of the car. Underneath was the part that said *Beware of pothole!* and it stared at them ironically.

Everyone took a breath.

And then—with impeccable comedic timing—the two front air bags blew open with a bang as loud as a shotgun. White corn starch was thrown across the three of them. Harry wasn't wearing his seatbelt and he was shoved up against the passenger door with his neck craned against the roof. He fought with the nylon hopelessly until he was forced to pull out the red-handled steak knife he'd repurposed from The White Pony, and the bag finally sagged.

He rubbed at his twisted neck and glared at Daisy. She stared back at him wide-eyed.

'I'm sorry,' she panted, in a state of shock. 'Are you alright?'

Harry opened his door without a word and stood up dizzily. He threw the stack of cash into the car.

'*That*,' he said, angrily, 'is three thousand pounds more than your driving deserves! You ought to pay *me* for that fiasco!'

Daisy stared at him without a peep as he ran off into the wood, zig-zagging from tree to tree in a daze. Charlie unclicked his seatbelt and opened his door.

'I think I've got whiplash,' Daisy said.

'Sorry about all this,' Charlie told her.

He got out and set off towards the lodge. The sun was glowing strongly above the wood and it filtered through the trees in amber waves. The trunks and the leaves and the grass were all sepia. At the edge of the driveway, he found Harry crouched behind Emily's little blue car.

'Look,' Harry pointed at The Barrow. The front door was open and a shadow passed back and forth across the windows. 'How the devil did he get back here before us? Wait here and I'll—'

'No,' Charlie hissed. 'I'm sick of all this. I'm going inside to speak with Tom myself.'

Harry grabbed Charlie by the arm. His eyes were filled with tears. 'Charlie, you're my only friend in the world. I'll explain all of this to you as soon as can be, I promise. But right now, I *must* confront him. I just ask that you don't desert me. Not for *him*.'

Charlie considered it. He'd been with Harry this far. He could see Tom's shadow passing back and forth across the blinds on the window. 'Okay,' he said reluctantly. 'Fine. But I've had it to here with all this bloody nonsense. When we get in there, I want answers and I want them all.'

'Cross my heart,' Harry promised.

Charlie nodded again. He knelt at Harry's side by the front tire and felt like Odysseus on the Italian strait. Torn between the whirlpool Scylla and the sea beast Charybdis. He donned his armour and prepared to face the creature inside. It was seven-headed with ten horns.

Chapter 7

Harry and Charlie were poised to storm the lodge when the front door swung open and Tom came marching out holding a backpack.

Harry dropped a foot closer to the gravel. Charlie's heart was doing all its usual somersaults.

'What are we hiding for? Let's confront him?' Charlie whispered.

Harry shook the head. 'Hang on. Let's watch.'

They got to their knees and lifted their eye lines above the bonnet. Tom had loaded his backpack into the Merc and got behind the wheel. The engine growled and the gravel spat out from under the tires as the car howled off out of the clearing and along The Mall.

'Do you think he's given up? Gone back home?' Charlie asked.

'Unlikely,' Harry said, though he was frowning, perplexed.

He shot to his feet and then dashed off towards the lodge. Charlie followed behind.

'It's locked,' Harry noted, twisting the handle.

'There's a spare key in the lockbox,' Charlie said, pointing at the barrel.

'What's the code?'

'Nineteen-sixty-six.'

Harry punched it in, snatched up the key and flew back to the door to unlock it.

When it swung open, a strong chemical smell drifted from the house. Charlie went in, took one look around and his jaw swung open. The side tables had all been flipped upside down, the settee and coffee table were pushed back against the far wall and the cushions were strewn about the floor. It looked like they had been burgled. But the centrepiece of this disaster was a mountain of purplish foam coiled in a dollop across the hearth.

'What do you suppose happened *here*?'

'I'll tell you what's happened,' Harry said pacing around. 'Your good friend Thomas Darrow has finally lost the bloody plot.'

'It looks like a wedding cake,' Charlie said, digging through the mountain of foam with his toe.

'It's A-triple-F foam,' Harry read, rolling over a fire extinguisher with his foot. 'There must have been a fire.'

Charlie dug further through the mound. It covered the broken chassis of the plasma screen, which had come off its bracket on the wall and exploded into shards of black metal and plastic across the rug.

'Suppose it fell off,' Charlie noted, running a hand across the wall-mount. 'What's *that*?' He had noticed something through the patio doors. Some dark thing drifted on the surface of the hot tub. 'Not another dead bird?'

Harry followed him outside and they edged over. It wasn't a bird, that much was clear. It was furry, not feathered. He prodded it and then Charlie discovered, with some relief, that the fur was not black as he had thought, but purple, turned black in its wetness.

'Rose's phone!' Charlie said, pulling it out of the water. He turned it over and tried to turn the thing on but it was dead. 'So I take it you didn't leave the phone in your Bonneville?'

'No, but there was something in there.,' Harry confessed. 'Now if Tom had found *that*...' he broke off and turned white.

'Yes?'

'Come on,' Harry said, 'let's find the keys.'

He ran back inside and along the corridor to Charlie's room. It took Charlie another second to register what he had even said.

'Wait a minute—*keys*?'

Harry emerged from the bedroom, juggling Emily's car keys and then headed for the door.

'What do you think you're doing?'

'Following Tom, now *do* hurry.'

He had already climbed into Emily's little blue car and was attempting to start the engine. On the third turn it coughed, sputtered, barfed, then came to life.

'God, oh *god*,' Charlie groaned. 'You can't even drive!'

But what choice did he have? Let Harry take the car out alone? Emily would never forgive him. So he got in the passenger seat shaking his head.

The car was growling and it lurched and then stalled.

'I've never driven one of these older ones before with the lever-thingy. Why don't you do that and I'll do the pedals?'

Charlie's jaw wouldn't close. 'The "lever-thingy"? You mean the *gearstick*? Why don't you let me drive?'

'No time. Must hurry.'

Charlie put it into gear and the car lurched through the wood. They stopped by the pothole where Daisy was leaning on her crumpled car looking distressed.

'Daisy!' Harry called to her. 'Did you see a big black car thunder by?'

'It went that way,' she said pointing to Pebbleton Port.

'As I suspected,' Harry groaned, putting his foot down. The car shot off as fast as it could manage. Almost fifty on the flat.

Soon they could see the Spreywater. There were boats on the lake and it was lively around the port. People were fishing from deckchairs and, further afield, ramblers with metal detectors headed across the nature reserve.

When they arrived, Harry slammed the brakes on and the car drifted to a stop by the ticket office. Tom's Mercedes was parked in the next spot. Harry killed the engine, threw the keys to Charlie and was out of the car before he'd even caught them.

'Do you see him?' Harry asked, as Charlie caught up on the promenade. He was frantically scanning the length of the dock.

'No. No sign of him. What would he be doing here?'

Harry turned to the same length of pier he'd driven the bike off with an uneasy look.

'Hold on to this.'

Harry pulled off his greatcoat and stuffed it into Charlie's arms. The watch joined the collection. He was rolling up the sleeves and legs of his outfit now. He took off his shoes and placed them on top of his coat in Charlie's arms.

'Back in a tick, old bean.'

He sprinted off along the pier and then dived into the lake at the end.

Charlie ran after him. He hadn't surfaced by the time he got

214

there, but a legion of bubbles came rupturing the surface. Then a huge mass of flailing arms erupted from below the legion and they flapped about like giant catfish being hauled up in a net.

It wasn't just Harry, who surfaced. He was fighting with Tom. The two of them thrashed around in the water, almost in the exact spot Charlie had seen the Bonneville sink in. Eventually, the two of them grew tired. Tom put one hand across Harry's forehead and managed to stave him off while he caught his breath. Then he pushed him under the water and swam back over to the pier with one arm.

'Charlie! Quick. Give us a hand with this,' Tom said, reaching up.

Under his spare arm was the silver box. It was still sealed with its fleur-de-lis clasp. He passed it to Charlie and then pulled himself out of the water.

Charlie didn't move. He had a lump in his throat, which originated from that box.

'Open it,' Tom said, after he caught his breath. He was sat on one of the piling masts, ringing the lake from his shirt. 'Open it,' he repeated, 'before he gets out.'

Harry was flailing around the lake like a dandy prat, murmuring, 'Help me, Charlie-Boy,' between mouthfuls of the wet stuff.

Charlie unfastened the clasps and lifted the lid. Water poured out and he drained it over the edge and emptied the box. The two duelling pistols fell out heavily across the wood. But there was something else between them. A plastic Ziploc bag, rolled very tight. He held it up and let it unroll. Inside was a long, silver knife.

And it was stained with blood.

Chapter 8

Tom's Merc screamed down The Mall.

Charlie was gripping the bottom of his seat in terror. After the discovery of the bloody knife, they had left Harry at Pebbleton Port at Tom's insistence and hopped into the four by four. It quickly thundered down Twin Hills East and swerved into Greenwood round the pothole. Tom hadn't said a word the whole drive, save for a few vulgarities and a splurge of terse grunts.

Charlie hadn't spoken either. His mind was racing. He was trying to piece it all together. The twenty thousand pounds. The pistols. The Bonneville. How did it all connect? Armed robbery was looking less likely, now that there was a bloody knife involved. What was looking much more likely… Charlie didn't want to consider.

But one inescapable thought did reoccur. If Harry had not done anything wrong… If he was innocent… then why had he, by his own admission, purposely sunk the bike to get rid of this evidence? He had sealed up that silver blade, hidden it inside that box, and then dropped it into the lake.

What had he done?

When they reached The Barrow, the car lurched to a stop, spraying gravel at the house. Tom was on the drive before the engine had stopped.

Charlie got out just as Rose flew onto the porch looking furious.

'*What* happened in *here*?' she shrieked. 'The living room is positively in *bits*!'

Tom shoved past her, cradling the silver box to his chest.

'You're soaking wet!' she gasped, leaping away from him. 'Charlie? What's going on?'

Before Charlie could respond, a dog started barking at the edge of the drive. It was Trevor, leading Mr Bramble up toward him.

'Charlie,' Bramble said, looking quite panicked about something. His eyes were darting this way and that as if he was looking for something in the treeline around them.

'Is everything alright?' Charlie asked.

Bramble shook his head. He was wearing a fishing hat which he took off to rub his white hair nervously.

'Remember I told yeh Fletcher Monk had spies?'

'Yes?'

'Well one of 'em must've been at The Pony today. Saw me talkin' with yeh in the beer garden. I've just been paid a visit by one of his farmhands. Big bloke called Pinner. He told me what went on after I left the pub. *I thought I told yeh to stay out of bloody trouble!*'

'We're trying,' Charlie said. 'That's the last of it, I… I promise.'

He swallowed. He sincerely hoped this was a promise he could keep.

'Aye, well. Pinner asked if I knew where you lot was staying…'

Charlie's heart tightened for what must have been the seventeenth time that week. Any more and it'd burst. On one side of him he had Tom, racing through The Barrow with Rose buzzing around asking a thousand and one questions. Somewhere behind was Harry, no doubt running in their direction as fast as his wiry legs could carry him. And now Bramble was delivering the fantastically refreshing news that their psychopathic hunter was inches from coming to murder them all.

'And what did you tell him?' Charlie asked.

'Didn't tell him nothing,' Bramble replied, looking almost offended by the question. 'But thought I should warn yeh all the same. He's getting' close.'

Charlie's throat went dry. 'Do you think this Pinner bloke knows we're here?'

Bramble put his hat back on. 'No idea. But if he does, I've no doubt Monk's rounding up a posse as we speak.'

'A *posse*?'

Bramble didn't respond. He just tipped his hat with a worried glint in his eye and then turned and traipsed off through the bracken. Trevor remained for another second, let out a little *woof!* and cocked his head at Charlie, before following Bramble through the wood.

Chapter 9

'Where's my car?' Emily asked as Charlie walked back into The Barrow.

'It's at Pebbleton Port. I'll explain later,' Charlie said as he handed the keys back to her.

Tom wasn't in the room so Charlie walked down the hall and found him stuffing the silver pistol box under the mattress in his bedroom. Now it lay side by side with the case for his air rifle.

'For safe keeping,' he explained, pushing Charlie out of the room so that he could lock the bedroom door with its key.

He led Charlie back down the hall where the girls were waiting for some kind of explanation. But nobody had chance to discuss things further, because Harry had just burst in through the front door, red-faced and breathless from running, still dripping wet, and snarling with an animalistic fury.

'*You*,' he growled, pointing at Tom.

Tom's rugby instincts kicked in long before Charlie knew what was happening. Harry had leapt like a jaguar some fifteen feet across the room and Tom swerved over the settee to avoid him.

But Harry was wily. He charged after him, changed direction mid-run, strapped himself round Tom's midriff like an enormous backpack and stuck two fingers up his nostrils.

Tom went charging like a bull. Emily had to practically dive onto the settee to escape his wild thrashes. He spun round in circles but Harry couldn't be shaken.

'You're getting water everywhere!' Rose howled.

Tom resorted to throwing himself into the wall over and over again until Harry fell off his back and rolled across the rug, rubbing his bruised arms.

'Someone help me tie him up,' Tom barked.

'What *for*?'

'I don't trust him.'

'Hitler!' Harry spat, rubbing his back painfully. 'Pinochet! Mao! Amin! Darrow!'

'Who made you judge, jury and executioner?' Rose asked.

'I did,' Tom said. 'Since none of you lot are capable of owt. Now help us tie him up.'

'Well perhaps, Thomas, if we were given the *facts*—'

'Christ Rose, later! We need to restrain him and call the fuzz.'

'Now hang on a minute!' Harry protested, straightening up and flicking away a handful of tears with the water from his dripping fringe.

'*You* don't get a say in this,' Tom warned him. 'We'll tie him to the radiator in our bedroom and lock the door.'

'Don't you think we ought to *discuss* this first?' asked Emily.

'*After he's tied up*. Then we can discuss it till the cows come home. But I don't want him worming his way out of this like he tried on that island.'

'The *is*land! Where I *saved* us all from starvation and cabin fever?' Harry said, flapping about desperately now like the last fish in a barrel who'd just seen all his brothers get hit over the head with an enormous mallet.

'Are you alright, Harry?' Rose asked. 'You're turning green!'

'No, I'm bloody not alright! I'm very *far* from alright as it happens.'

Harry pulled himself into the space between the kitchen and the island.

'What sort of despot are you?' he howled at Tom. 'You level unfounded accusations and inflict your will on me. Well I say why aren't we locking *you* up? You're a terrific bully and I do not understand what an English flower like Rose could see in a great ugly brute like you.'

Tom cracked his knuckles but Harry had that animalism in the eyes and he filled the gap in his teeth with a quarter of his tongue.

'I've had enough,' Harry said looking dangerously feral. 'If you think you're tying me to an old radiator, you can fuck that sky high! Hit me if you—'

Tom did. He smacked him right in the jaw. It sent Harry spinning and when he looked back up he had blood dribbling from his lip. He touched his front tooth, which wobbled.

'Going for the full set?' Harry spat. He reached into his mouth and plied the tooth right out himself and slammed it on the island between them. 'Here, you can have it.'

Tom stepped closer. Harry spat like a cobra and showered him in a mist of blood.

'Go on, I'll give you a freebie,' Harry grinned. Everyone stared in horror as he turned his cheek to Tom and closed his eyes. 'Show our darling what a *man* you are.'

Tom raised his fist and stared at the cheek, but his hand shook with hesitation.

'You mustn't,' Rose sobbed. 'You *mustn't*, Tom.' She was even pulling on the bicep with little effect.

Harry opened one eye a slither. 'Go on, I want you to.'

Rose jumped in front of him. 'No, don't *do* it,' she begged.

Tom stared at her for a long time before deciding to lower his fist.

'There!' Harry grinned. 'Ladies and gentlemen, the *current* Mister Rose Seymour.'

That did it. Tom aimed a boulder at the temple and Harry dropped like a bag of coal, smacked his head on the edge of the Corian island and passed out with a two-inch gash down the forehead.

Chapter 10

When Harry woke, Emily was pouring over him. She'd wiped up all the blood and stuck a butterfly-stitch across his brow line. But now his hands were bound palms-together, against his head. He wriggled about and discovered he was cabled-tied to a radiator pipe, feet an all.

Charlie sat on the edge of the bed and found himself simply unable to make eye contact with Harry. Tom was leaning against the en-suite door, which back-lit him while Rose stood just behind Emily and was practically a sprinkler of tears.

'You're inhuman, Mr Darrow,' she sobbed. 'That radiator's boiling hot, at *least* open a window for him.'

'I've turned the radiator off,' Tom said. 'It'll be cold soon. But we're not *touching* the window. I'm not letting him escape this time. In fact...'

Tom marched over to the window and made sure it was locked.

'Good. Now let's get out of here.'

He pushed his way out of the bedroom and stood at the door until everyone followed him meekly into the hall. He had a good long look back at Harry and then he locked the door with his key and a satisfied grunt.

'Well this is *marvellous*,' Rose said, as they gathered round the island. 'We've *kidnapped* Harry.'

'Do you have a better idea?' Tom asked. 'I'd love to hear it.'

'As a matter of fact, I do. We ought to release him and stop acting like those little rotters from the Lord of the Flies.'

'If we release him we'll be aiding and abetting.'

'Aiding and abetting *what*?' Rose laughed. 'We don't even know that he's *done* anything!'

'We *do* know that as it goes,' Tom said. 'Tell her what we found, Charlie.'

'We... we found a knife,' Charlie admitted. 'It was with Harry's stuff.'

'A *knife*?'

'A long, silver blade,' Tom said. 'And it were covered in *blood*.'

'Crikey!'

'Let me talk to him,' Rose said, standing up. Tom stared at her like she was mad. 'If he will talk to *anyone* here, it might be *me*. Let me have just five minutes with him.'

Tom did not look too keen on the idea, but he saw no reason to refuse. He led Rose down the hall, unlocked the door and let her inside.

When he returned, Charlie had drifted off to the living room to think. He stared at the broken chassis of the plasma screen and wondered how it had come to be that way.

Tom, meanwhile, was squarely in favour of calling the police and tried to put it to a vote. Even Emily seemed to side with him. Rose, they knew, wouldn't. That meant the casting vote fell to Charlie.

But instead, he asked, 'When did we last have the TV on?'

It quite surprised the other two.

Tom thought for a second. 'Friday, I think. When I were fiddling with the cables. Why?'

'Because,' Charlie said, pulling either side of his forehead into the centre, '*Harry broke it.*'

'No,' Tom shook his head and smiled. 'I'd *like* to blame him for that. But he weren't here when that happened. I came back, pressed the power button and the thing just fell off the wall. Burst into flame.'

'Exactly,' Charlie said. 'Don't you see? If we're right about everything we've said so far… about the newspaper and how he caused that big scene at The White Pony… then none of that would've made one bit of difference if we could just stick the tele on *in here* and see him plastered all over the news. If he went to those lengths to keep us in the dark… it would only make sense to get rid of *this* TV too.'

'Only… he couldn't just *break* it, or it'd be suspicious.' Charlie turned to the others. 'We watched it on Friday, and it was never in danger of falling from the wall then, was it? Tom—you just said you were fiddling with the cables. I saw you, you smacked it round the side to try and get rid of that yellow hue. And it never fell off

222

the wall *then* did it? But when you got back today, you simply *touched it* and it fell off? Does that seem likely?'

Tom nodded. 'You think he *unscrewed* it from the wall?'

Charlie shrugged. 'It certainly wouldn't be the craziest thing he's ever done.'

That seemed to settle it for Tom. He was on his feet and down the hallway before Charlie could reply.

'Rose, come on, get out,' Tom instructed.

Rose reappeared in the hallway looking crestfallen. She came to sit down beside Emily without a word. Tom glared into the bedroom before shutting the door on Harry and locking it again.

'I'm gonna go and find the nearest phone to call the police,' he said. 'And I think it's best if I keep the key to the bedroom. *Just make sure you're watching that hall*. One sign of him trying to escape or owt, you restrain him, right? Can I trust you Dickens?'

Charlie shrugged. What could he do when Tom had the only key and Harry was fastened to the radiator with cable ties?

Tom took a last look at the three of them, as if he didn't trust anyone to do as he said, but then he grabbed his jacket and slammed the front door shut behind him.

Chapter 11

'I know whose blood is on that knife,' Emily said.

They had been cleaning up the place as best they could while they waited for Tom to get back. It remained a complete disaster and Charlie knew Jim Murphy would have every right to charge them an arm and a leg for the state of the place. First, there was the winged creature over the island. That had been Charlie's fault. Then, Harry had kicked in the porthole window. There was the broken television set, the black stain on the rug from the fire and the damp up the wall from the foam. But all of that suddenly seemed insignificant compared with those words from Emily.

'*I know whose blood is on that knife,*' she repeated.

'Well? *Whose*?' Rose asked, kneeling at her side.

Emily turned to them dramatically. 'It's his *father's.*'

A silence followed.

Charlie scratched the middle of his head. 'But Harry hasn't *seen* his father since... *I don't even know* when. They weren't talking when we left.'

'But perhaps they *were* by the time we got *here.*'

She tucked the hair behind her ear and kneeled upright on the rug before them both.

'Is this what you were talking about?' Charlie asked. 'On the island?'

'It was on my mind, yes,' Emily answered. 'It was only a theory then, but well...? It makes sense, *doesn't* it? Think about what Harry brought up here with him. Five bottles of vintage wine. His old Harrow uniform. Some antique duelling pistols. *All of that money*! And the bike. Where else, if not Blye House, could he have got it all?'

'So then... he *hasn't* committed a robbery?' asked Charlie, keen to have Harry exonerated. For his own benefit.

'Oh, he has,' Emily said. 'Just not the *armed robbery* Tom believes. He robbed *his own house.*'

'And that bloody knife?' Charlie asked. 'You're saying, er... *what* are you saying?'

224

'The two of them weren't speaking, were they?' Emily said. 'But we *do* know Harry was invited somewhere the same day we came here. Well what if his father had invited him back to Blye House? I won't pretend to know why, whether for an argument or a pay off or an apology or *what*. But let's say he was invited back and let's assume their reunion wasn't quite as peaceful as either party hoped. Perhaps they fell out again. And perhaps Harry, in his anger, *stabbed his father* with that knife.'

'But *murder?*' Charlie protested, standing up tall. 'That's just... just—'

'*Just* an idea,' she added.

'It's not just an idea, it's an accusation. And a very serious one!'

'I'm just trying to make sense of the evidence. *You're* the one to bring a bloodied knife into this! I was happy when we only had a couple of decommissioned pistols to contend with!'

'As was I!'

After they both cooled off, Charlie cleared his throat.

'By the way,' he said. 'It was Monk's barn Harry crashed into on his way here.'

Rose looked set to deliver a magnificent diatribe, but there was a noise outside that killed her mojo completely. Before she could faint, the door swung open and Tom returned, panting, with a large ring of sweat round his neckline. He swallowed half a gallon of milk before Rose asked, 'Well?'

Tom shrugged. 'Notified the fuzz. They'll be here when they can.'

'And?'

'*And* what?'

For a second Rose was speechless. 'What did you *tell* them?'

'Told them we've got a fugitive under citizen's arrest.'

'And did they *confirm* anything?'

'Like what?'

'Like *what?*' Rose sputtered. 'Like—*I* don't know—that he's *actually* a criminal. Like that he's a wanted man?'

'I spoke to an operator, Rose, they don't know that sort of stuff.

I just said we've got someone in our house who committed a robbery back in London. She said they'll send a car out.'

'Is that *it*?'

'Bloody hell Rose, what more d'you want? The SAS?'

'I want some sort of confirmation,' she snapped. 'I want to know we've not got an innocent man chained to a radiator in there!'

'Well *I* want to see that knife,' said Emily getting to her feet.

'The knife?' Tom said. 'What for?'

'Because it might tell us if he's—'

'Oh shit!' Tom blurted out. Everyone looked at him as he turned to the corridor that led to the bedrooms. 'I stashed it under the bed. Before we put him in there.'

'You left the *evidence* in the cell with your *prisoner*?' Rose chided. 'I *am* glad you've appointed yourself commander of our charge. You're doing a top-notch job, Thomas. Aside from breaking the Geneva Convention and stomping on his human rights, of course.'

Tom was already halfway down the corridor as she said that. She was right behind him, throwing more insults his way. He put the key in the lock and opened the door. And then froze in his tracks.

'No, no, *no*!' Tom growled.

Charlie followed him inside. His mouth involuntarily opened when he saw that the bedroom was empty.

The only sign Harry had ever even been there was the damp patch on the floor by the radiator.

Tom did three frantic laps of the room. He looked under the bed, he looked in the en-suite, he even opened up all of the draws in the dresser, just in case Harry had had the good grace to fold himself up and hop inside one.

Charlie noticed that under the bed, the silver box had disappeared. Wherever Harry had gone, he had taken the evidence with him.

'Bleeding Christ! I leave for ten minutes and he escapes!' Tom howled. 'Did nobody check on him?'

'He was chained to the radiator!' Rose reminded him. 'And *you* took the key with you.'

'And that window's still locked?' Tom asked.

Rose drew back the curtain and shimmied the handle. 'Yes, see? Still locked.'

'*Am I going mad?*' Tom asked, positively laughing. 'Can someone tell us *how* he's managed to disappear in a puff of fucking smoke? 'Cause the police will be here in a minute and they're gonna want to know.'

Nobody answered. Charlie had the strange impression that both Emily and Rose were rather impressed by the escape act. He had to admit, it did seem impossible. Tom had checked the window before they left, Harry was cable tied by the hands and feet, and the door to the bedroom was locked with a key only Tom had, who wasn't even in the building. Even if Harry *had* come through it, he would've walked right into the living room where the other three were gathered. The only explanation was that he had flushed himself down the toilet.

'Dickens,' Tom said, desperately, taking Charlie by the shoulders and shaking him. 'Did *you* let him out?'

'No!' Charlie said, annoyed by the accusation. 'I'm as stumped as you are.'

'Well *some*one must've helped him!' Tom snapped. 'He was tied to the bloody radiator. He *must've* come down this hallway, so *some*one must've seen him.'

'Nobody has helped him, Tom,' Rose said, pushing her way out of the room with an air of satisfaction. 'Perhaps he turned into a bat and flew away.'

Chapter 12

'We have to sit still,' Tom said, not sitting and not still. 'Police are en route... yep, we just sit tight till they get here. 'No more trouble,' he added, as he stuffed a clip of BBs down the air rifle's gullet and slung it over his shoulder. 'That's what you all wanted, right? To stay here and keep out of trouble?'

He slid the doors to the hot tub open and went outside to walk the perimeter. Once he was out of earshot, Rose flew across the room to Charlie, gripping his arm tightly with her claws.

'Charlie, I have to tell you something!'

She kept a close eye on Tom, who passed the side window, pacing like a lunatic.

'I think I know where Harry is. Or where he *will* be, at least.'

Charlie had been withdrawn until then, staring at the winged thing above the island as he mulled over Harry's disappearing act. But at those words from Rose, he perked up and looked round at her curiously.

She continued in an urgent whisper. 'When I went to try and speak with Harry, just before Tom locked him up, all he would say was that he wanted to live the rest of his life on a mountain. Well, I think... I *think* he might mean the big one not far from here. The Yarrowsomething.'

Charlie's mouth went a little dry. It wasn't the mention of the mountain that worried him. It was Harry's choice of words.

'*To live the rest of his life*?' Charlie repeated, with concern.

Rose looked troubled by it too. 'You don't think he's gone up there to do something stupid, do you?'

She flashed her eyes at the front door, where Tom came back into the lodge and started peering through the front blinds, muttering to himself. Rose slid herself back along the settee away from Charlie. They shared a long, disturbed look before Charlie suddenly found himself on his feet.

'I'm going out,' he announced, surprising even himself. 'You lot can sit around here all you like, but it's getting dark. I'm going to go and look for him while I still can.'

'No. You can't,' Tom said, standing in front of the door with the rifle in his hand.

'Why, are you going to shoot me?'

Tom shook his head. 'Course not,' he said, leaning the gun up against the wall. 'But we're all witnesses here. You've gotta stay for when the police come. They'll be here any minute now—'

'You've been saying that for,' he looked at the time, 'almost two hours now, Tom. They might not get here till tomorrow. And by then, Harry could be in Shanghai.'

'Tom's right Charlie,' Emily said. 'We should all give statements.'

Charlie felt himself seething. He could hardly believe it but the only person he felt had even a smidgeon of sanity left was Rosalind Seymour. He never thought he would believe *that*.

'Fine,' Charlie snapped. 'But if I *have* to stay here, I'll wait upstairs. By myself.'

Amber dust danced around the bulb as the loft light flickered to life.

Charlie navigated the maze of furniture to the round window at the other end and pressed himself against it, looking over the canopy to the Yarrowmoor beyond. It certainly looked peaceful from here, disturbed only by a swarm of birds. The pap hill was somehow round *and* flat and its summit was illuminated by the soft moonlight that was settling over the country. Charlie didn't know what he had expected to see from up here, but he certainly could not see Harry's miniscule figure scaling the mountain's backside.

He turned his attention down, at the drop below the window. It was some height and his legs quaked as he imagined himself plummeting like an acorn to the earth. Charlie had never liked heights. But fifty mils of adrenaline whizzed around the old circulatory system and gave him strength. He looked around, hoping to find a ladder in the junk, but there was no ladder. No rope, no hope of getting down to the wood floor in a civilised fashion.

As he looked back outside he noticed the skinny tree straight ahead. A face in its knots smiled and its long branch seemed to extend a hand. It was like nature was spurring him on to the breast.

'Oh, Christ,' he groaned as he realised what he was about to do.

He tried desperately to recall what it was Harry had said to him about the Yarrowmoor, back on Potter Island, in case he remembered something that would spare him shimmying thirty foot down a scrawny tree trunk. Harry had said something about choosing the time and place of his death. About death, not coming as a bloodied skeleton, but as a *friend*...? Charlie sighed. Well, if he could pull off his own disappearing act, Harry might just be right about that last part.

Charlie shook the window lock. The wooden frame had been painted a dozen years ago and thick white gloss had fused it in place. He found a fire poker in the rubble, jammed it like a crowbar in the gap and wiggled the thing around until the window popped open and wind rushed in.

'What am I *doing*?'

It *was* a long drop.

He put a leg out and reached over for the tree's arm. His eyes were tightly shut, and he scrabbled around in the air until his fingers gripped the branch. He pulled himself closer to the trunk and then threw himself, top-heavy, till his hands joined up behind it. Then he lifted his second leg over the window frame, kicked off from the pane and wrapped both legs around the trunk like a koala.

'Harry, you intolerable bastard. You better have an explanation for all this.'

He shimmied his way down using branches as rungs until his feet finally found the floor.

His heart wouldn't stop whirring.

He peeped back into The Barrow through the side window. Emily and Rose were talking on the settee. Tom was mumbling to himself by the island. The rifle was back around his shoulder. Everything was as it should be inside The Barrow. But for a split second, Charlie thought Rose's eyes fell on him. But then she looked away and continued her conversation with Emily and he set off through the wood.

Chapter 13

Charlie was exhausted as soon as he started the ascent. He wasn't athletic and the incline, though not steep, had turned his calves red raw within minutes. Now the fronts of his shinbones felt prone to snap.

He stopped against a boulder in the foothills to scour the scene. There were countless paths branching up the Yarrowmoor but it was already dark. Soon he wouldn't be able to see where he was putting his feet.

'You'd better be up here Harry,' Charlie said, as he pushed off the boulder and started through the skeletal remains of an old fence and up the most well-worn of the paths.

It took him fifty minutes to reach the top. He stopped to catch his breath and looked around the summit for any sign of life. Wind rustled through the tufts of grass that grew in mounds against purple boulders. And all along one side, down the back of the mountain, were jagged crags. There were birds, circling up above, and occasionally a couple would land on the mountain to fight viciously over some scrap before flapping off again to the charcoal skies. But there was no sign of Harry.

Charlie sat down again, sighing to himself. The oily black water of the Spreywater was beginning to glimmer with light from the harbour. In the other direction, lights wound up the Gallows tor like it was a Christmas tree. And somewhere between, he could see the faint glimmer of light from The Barrow's loft window stretching out across the Greenwood canopy.

He cast his eyes back around the mountain. And then, as his eyes adjusted to the gloom, something he had thought a white boulder suddenly turned to look at him with a long, pink tongue lolling from the side of its mouth.

'Oh! Teddy!' Charlie gasped.

It was only Ted's head, right at the edge of the mountain. The rest of him was hidden by the curve. And he hadn't come pouncing over to Charlie, as Charlie expected. Instead the dog turned back around and his head disappeared from view.

Charlie's heart sank a little and he leapt to his feet. It looked as if the dog had just jumped off the mountaintop.

'T-Teddy?' Charlie said, stepping closer to the edge.

His heart was in his throat. He could stand on the flat of the summit without much issue. He could even admire those distant views. But edging closer to the mountain's perilous crags where he could see the sheer drop gave him tumultuous waves of nausea.

He stopped five feet back as Teddy reappeared in view. And to Charlie's surprise, he was not alone. Teddy was resting, like some mystic guardian, with his head in Harry's lap.

They were down a rather precarious jutting spur, which stuck out like a lip from the mountain. Harry was cross-legged and seemed well aware that Charlie was behind him, but he didn't move or say anything. Not until Charlie did.

'Where did you find him?'

'I didn't,' Harry answered without moving. '*He* found *me*. Resilient little thing wouldn't you say? He was rambling in simple ecstasy in the hillocks with the dragon- and damselflies.'

'Well, he *is* Pyrenean Mountain Dog,' Charlie said. 'It's probably wired into him. To look for the hills.'

'Yes. But the queerest thing was what he was *carrying*.' Harry reached into his coat and pulled out the velvet box with Tom's engagement ring inside. 'You probably know why I've climbed up here? What I'm planning to *do*?'

Charlie swallowed. Harry had turned partially to him, and in doing so, had un-crossed his legs which now swung over the spur. He only had to slide another foot and he'd paint the ground pink before anyone could blink.

'N-no,' Charlie said cautiously. 'What *are* you planning?'

'To be perfectly honest I haven't quite decided yet.'

There was a lump in Charlie's throat now.

'Perhaps you can help me decide?' Harry pointed into the abyss below him. 'Should I aim for the spiky rocks or the flat slab of chalk? The slab's *guaranteed* of course, but you can't argue with theatrics.'

'Why would you consider either?' Charlie asked, taking another step closer.

'To meet the old maker!' Harry said. 'To *die*, Charlie; to sleep, perchance to dream? To shuffle off this mortal coil. You know who said that, don't you? Shakespeare, of course.'

'Don't be daft.'

'I'm not being daft. It's from Hamlet.'

'Why would you say those things? It's only a temporary bit of strife all this rubbish with Tom. It'll be over by breakfast.'

'Funny isn't it?' Harry said, in a humourless tone of voice now. 'I climbed up here with one goal and then I bumped into Teddy. Even still, I told him, "Don't think you're going to change my mind, mister! I don't care *how* cute you are!" And then the dumb mutt puts his stupid head in my hand and looked at me with those big brown eyes and I found myself scratching his chin and then this little box fell into my hand.' He ran his thumb across the velvet. 'I suppose what I'm saying is that the reason I *haven't...*' he paused. 'I haven't... *done what I mean to do* up here... is because of Tom. Tom has essentially saved my life, by meaning to propose.'

'Look, Harry, I don't think you need to worry about that,' Charlie said, hoping to unburden the young Burden. 'Rose has been your greatest advocate all day. I'm serious. While Tom—he's gone a bit zany since your disappearing act. Why don't you tell me how you did it, hm?'

Harry craned his neck, confused. 'What do you mean, *how I did it*? It's hardly on the level of Houdini is it?'

'Well, you still have the spare keys from the lockbox, of course. I know *that*,' said Charlie. He thought if he could just keep Harry talking... 'But we would've seen you come down the hall, surely?'

Harry smiled and it looked genuine. Even his eyes twinkled. He stood up and Teddy whimpered and Charlie reached out automatically. But then Harry turned away from the edge and stepped up onto the mountain with a wicked grin on his face.

'This is fantastic!' Harry beamed, which threw Charlie for a loop. 'I hadn't meant for my escape to be a mystery! When I tell you what happened you'll see the simplicity. But there's something I don't understand myself in it all. You mean to say that room was all locked up? And the window?'

'Yes it was basically hermetic. Are *you* saying you left through the window?'

Harry laughed a jovial laugh. 'I'm envious of you Charlie. You were there to witness the look on Tom Darrow's face as he pulled open that bedroom door! Was it marvellous?'

'He was not very happy.'

'Good, good!' Harry said, grinning up at the moon and rubbing his hands together.

'Well? Are you going to tell me how you did it?'

'I didn't do it,' Harry answered. '*It was Rose.*' Charlie would cop to being incredibly confused by that reply. 'When she came to speak with me,' continued Harry, pacing briskly along the crag's edge, 'I asked her to cut my hands free. Made a fuss of how tight the binding was and pointed out that I was hardly likely to go anywhere, locked up in that room. I still had that steak knife from the pub in my coat pocket, remember? She used that to cut the cable ties. And then Tom came back to the doorway to tell her to leave and I just sat there against the radiator with my hands by my ears so he wouldn't know I was free. Once Rose left, he locked me in there again and I got up and opened the window with the spare keys. You see, this is why it was not meant as a mystery! I never locked the window behind me—I *couldn't* have, they only lock from the inside. But you say the window *was* locked? *That*, my friend, is the real mystery!'

Charlie thought back to the moment they discovered the empty room.

Tom had asked if the window was still locked.

Rose, who was nearest, had drawn back the curtain to shimmy the handle. '*Yes, see?*' she had said. '*Still locked.*'

Charlie felt himself fizz with excitement. 'She was lying!' he burst out. He explained to Harry what had happened. 'She knew full-well that window would be unlocked, so when Tom asked, she pretended it wasn't.'

'Those years at Italia Conti have paid for themselves!'

'And I'll *bet* she snuck back in to lock it again later.'

'My, my, how clever she is!' Harry said, impressed. 'You were not joking when you said she was my greatest advocate. I doubt whether *you* would have thought of such a thing.'

'You doubt right. I had no idea how you did it. She's sharp. It was Rose who told me you were likely to be up here. She said you told her you wanted to live the rest of your life on a mountain.'

'How astute. I hadn't even decided myself where I was going to go at that point. But I was annoyed I never got to see these splendid views. When I got out of that wood, I meant to go into Gallows to rent a room at The Wood House for the night. But I looked back up at this mountain and do you know what? This mountain looked back at me. I knew at once I should *come up here* to do the deed. Wouldn't want to scare the poor maid of The Wood House with such a grisly sight tomorrow morning.'

Charlie watched him carefully. Harry had been momentarily enthused by the idea of his daring escape, but the look of excitement was already fading back into a stone-faced scowl.

'It seems Rosalind Seymour knows me better than I know myself.'

'Is that why you're here, Harry?' Charlie asked. 'Because of Rose?' It was a theory he had been developing for a few hours now. 'It took you *months* to get over her, it's no wonder you've butted heads with Tom so much. It all makes sense. It must have *killed* you to find that engagement ring—'

'What?' Harry spun round looking immensely surprised by the idea. 'You think I'm still *in love*? With *her*?'

'Well aren't you?'

Harry's face became very tight and his eyebrows slid back into his temples.

'I *am* in love, but not with *her*!' he said. 'I'm in love… I'm in love with *you*, you stupid bastard.'

'With *me*?' Charlie repeated, reeling quite far back in shock. 'But… how—*what*?'

A tear ran down Harry's cheek. Teddy could sense his misery and tried to revive him with affection.

'It was an accident,' Harry said. 'I didn't *mean* to fall in love with you, look at you for crying out loud! You're a wreck of a man.

A penniless proletariat from the north of England. And you're ugly. Why would anyone *choose* that? I don't know why it couldn't have been a supermodel with killer legs that go all the way up to there, and with breasts like ginormous zeppelins—but it *wasn't*. It was *you*. And I've felt like this ever since I found out you were leaving Milk Street to live with the doctor.'

Charlie's eyes flitted back and forth as he took in the revelation. 'Hang on, I only told you I was leaving yesterday.'

Harry wiped his tears on his sleeve. 'No. I've known for months. An estate agent called the house back in January.'

'I told them not to use the landline,' Charlie said. 'I wanted to tell you when the time was right.'

'It's destroyed me. Didn't know I loved you. Didn't know I even cared all that much for you. Until I thought of living without you. I'm despondent Charlie-Boy. You understand it's not romantic love, or anything of the sort. I don't *think* it is at least. It's… *I don't know what* it is. "The love that dare not speak its name." And I don't expect you to love me back or anything like that. I suppose that's what makes it all so unfair.'

'I… I had no idea. I don't know what to say. I'm sorry, I suppose?'

Harry looked on him favourably and smiled through the sheen of tears. 'I know you are.'

'So is *that* why you broke up? With Rose?'

'I was having… feelings,' he said looking quite uncomfortable about the subject. 'She's the only one in the world I told. She was wonderful about it.'

'So what now?' Charlie asked.

Harry shrugged and slumped down by one of the purple boulders. It was better than him being on the crag. Charlie sat down opposite and Teddy came to lie in between them.

'You're not going to go through with this, are you?' Charlie asked. 'I'd hate for it to be on my conscience.'

Harry chuckled and wiped away the final tears from his eyes. 'Wouldn't want to give you the satisfaction,' he said.

'Then will you come back to The Barrow with me?' Charlie

asked. 'I know it's spring but it's not exactly warm this high up.'

'As a matter of fact I mean to stay here and watch the sun rise.'

'But that's not for about ten hours!'

'Don't feel obliged to stay with me,' Harry said. 'But I know you will.'

Charlie rolled his eyes. 'I'll stay. But I want you to tell me once and for all just *what* has gone on these past few days.'

'That sounds fair.' Harry smirked. 'Exactly how much do you already know?'

'I know you drove through Monk's barn on your way here. I know you wounded yourself doing it. I don't know why you've kept it a secret that you're hurt, but we *do* know you've got a pretty serious injury and you've been stuffing it with tampons and what-not.'

Harry smiled behind the eyes.

'And we know whose blood is on that knife,' Charlie said. 'The one you tried to get rid of in the lake.'

'Oh, yes? And whose blood might that be?'

'Your father's.'

Harry didn't respond. He just stared down at the dark body of water with a wet film over his eyes.

'You went to visit him on Friday, didn't you?' Charlie pressed. 'After we left London?'

'Yes,' Harry admitted at last.

'Then *tell* me, Harry. What have you done?'

'Alright.' Harry sat up straight against the boulder. 'While you and Emily were at The Nag's Head earlier in the week, my father telephoned to invite me to Blye House on Friday. He was throwing a party and had decided to offer me one *final* chance at redemption.'

Part IV

Chapter 1

The previous Friday, Richard Burden had installed himself behind an enormous and powerful desk in his study. He had just had a tray of tea brought in and he noticed that his man Sallow had put the mail beneath the saucer.

He took the letters out from under the cup without paying them much attention. He was instead preoccupied by something dark on the lawn. He crossed over to the bay window and rifled through his pockets for his glasses.

The door was still ajar and Richard heard the butler walking back to the kitchen. He called him in and the butler reappeared in the study.

'Sir?'

'Come here,' Richard barked. 'What's that out there? On the lawn.'

'Well, sir, if I'm not mistaken,' Sallow replied without so much as a glance through the window, 'some wildlife have taken a fancy to the garden. On account of the carrion.'

'On account of *what*?'

'The carrion, sir. Over by the guesthouse.'

Richard took the glasses off his face and squinted with his naked eye. Blye House sat on almost two hectares of green lawn. Fifty feet from the main house was a flat white building. Halfway between the two was a flock of black-winged birds, flapping violently in a huddle.

'Well why the devil is there carrion out on my lawn?'

'Well sir, as you may recall, during the evening's revelries on Friday of last week, there came a family of creatures over the lawn.'

'Creatures?' Richard struggled to remember. He'd seen off the end of the Chivas last Friday.

'Foxes, I believe, sir. And they repeatedly triggered the flood lights.'

Something started to reappear through the haze of memory in Richard's head. Foxes, yes, that was right. Three of the scrawny buggers, galloping like ponies.

'It was on the third such triggering, sir, that you bellowed at them.'

'Bellowed?'

'Quite, sir.'

'Bellowed *what* for goodness's sake?'

'You bellowed, if I remember rightly, that the next time they set off the trigger to your flood light, you would not be dissatisfied by setting off the trigger to your blunderbuss.'

'Hm.' Richard pursed his lips. It didn't sound as if he had been at his wittiest on Friday evening. He wasn't quite sure that even made sense. 'And then?'

'Well, sir, when such a time came as the flood lights were quadruple-triggered, you disappeared a snifter of brandy—'

'*Whisky.*'

'Whisky, sir, my apologies. And then you went after the creatures—'

'The foxes?'

'I believe so, sir, yes. You went after them with your decorative blunderbuss and massacred them by the guest house.'

Richard made a strange sound as he tried to reconcile the butler's story with his own mangled recollections. The last thing he could recall was watching a low-ranking member of cabinet try to fondle some pretty young thing by the billiard table, while that squeaky-voiced teenager talked business at him. The whisky, he remembered fondly, was wholly necessary.

'Massacred, what?'

'I'm afraid so, sir.'

'Well what the piss are they still doing on my lawn?'

'As you will no doubt remember, sir, I attempted to scoop the kit's brain matter from the patio when you stopped me. You insisted I keep the remains there as a warning for any other feral beasts that "dare trespass", as you put it, "on Burden property".'

Richard looked back out at the blackbirds; now he could see long strings of red sinew among all that black. And though he couldn't possibly have, from all the way inside his study, he was quite certain he could hear them.

'Well go and clear it up,' Richard demanded. 'I'm sure I don't need to remind you, with your fantastic memory, I'm having a party tonight. There's venue dressers due any damn minute now.' He looked down at his watch. It was quarter to three. 'They're erecting a marquee for the marquees and a duke box for the dukes. You know how huge these things of mine are.'

'Yes, sir. You demonstrably have the biggest balls in London.'

'Oh and pick me up a bottle of Chivas Regal,' Richard continued, returning to the tea at his desk. 'Or… better make that three bottles. How's the bar looking?'

'I'm afraid to say rather sparse, sir. From Friday evening's revelries.'

'Then have it replenished. I've invited the boy and as you know, he can outdrink a whale. He can certainly outdrink me. Hah.'

'The boy, sir?'

'Yes, Harrington.'

'*Harrington*, sir?' The butler looked surprised to hear it. 'So soon after you had me cease all direct—'

'Yes, *yes*,' Richard waved it away and pulled a face. He sipped his tea and then set the cup down. 'I was drunk when I wrote him that letter and drunker still when I had you mail it. As you are no doubt waiting to remind me! But I'm seeing clearer now.' He put his glasses back on and squinted. 'I telephoned him on Wednesday afternoon as a matter of fact.'

Sallow was quite taken aback. 'Sir?'

'What? I had to, so I could invite him over here tonight.'

'Pardon my prying sir, but what did he say?'

'He said he'd be here.'

'And do you believe he will be well behaved?' Sallow asked and Richard could see the deep displeasure in his face. 'You know how he likes to show off, sir, and in front of your distinguished guests…'

Richard laughed. 'He'll be well behaved, Sallow. That letter we sent wasn't for nothing. He's been without electricity for almost two days now. If he's not already regressed into infancy, I'll bottle my piss and drink it.'

'Very good, sir.'

'Have faith,' Richard smiled. 'You underestimate him. I think this has been good for the boy. We've made him independent.'

'For two days, sir.'

'Yes, for two days. Now I'm not welcoming him back with open arms, you understand. And I'll make damn sure he knows I'm not going to spoon feed him for the rest of his life.'

'If you say so, sir.'

'Yes, I do say so. Now don't you have fox skull to scrape up?'

The butler bowed his head and closed the door behind him.

Richard sighed and sifted through the letters on his desk. One of them looked as if it had come from some depth of hell. Creased, greasy, with miniscule spidery handwriting in pencil. He didn't recognise it, so he pulled open the draw and took his ruby inlay letter-opener from the desk. He ran it through the envelope and slid the letter out, reading it over with a look of exasperation.

Dear father, it began, *What a funny little man you are. Sincerely, Mr Burden, your son. Dictated but not read.*

It was dated two days previous.

'Oh Harrington,' Richard mumbled to himself, 'I *do* hope you'll behave tonight.'

Chapter 2

The venue dressers had done a tip-top job of the place. The estate was in the regency style and covered in ivy, but they had carefully maintained the vines when lacing little pink and white flowers over the entrance. The rain that had saturated the grounds just days ago had become a distant memory now. It was spring in full effect across London, and Blye House in Kensington appeared to be right in the warpath.

Sallow had had someone take care of the carrion. The patio around the guesthouse had been jet-washed and the lawns were freshly mowed in stripes of alternating green.

Inside, three tables stood in the atrium, covered with linen and canapés, aperitifs and seventy champagne flutes ready for pouring. There was a hustle of bodies carrying things back and forth, tidying up, moving the expensive paintings to an upper room. The maids were almost done and the purple of their uniforms began to be diluted by the starched white of the waiting staff.

'Second party in eight days,' a young blonde-haired boy said as he helped an older man with a pencil moustache ferry a display cabinet in through the back door.

'You wasn't here on Frid'y was you?' the pencil 'tache asked him.

'Only till nine. But I hear the old nutter went stark raving bonkers?'

'If Bonkers had a baby with Deranged, and then that baby gone and got a job at the loony bin, *that's* what he went like. Bonkers don't cut it. *Jesus,* watch it!'

The blonde boy had banged the display cabinet on the doorframe and chipped a corner.

'We'll 'ave to put that side at the back.'

'Where are you taking that?' Sallow asked as they got through the patio doors and into the kitchen. The blonde boy covered the chip with his hand.

'The old geezer's asked us to set it up in the ballroom. He's got some antique pistols or summink he wants on display.'

Sallow rolled his eyes and led them into the ballroom. The venue dressers had been to town in here. Most of the furniture had been pushed aside or else removed, while portraits had been rehung around the walls. There were three mullioned windows on the left wall while on the right, a trestle table had been temporarily opened and was littered with Richard's eclectic collection of what Sallow thought to be 'tat'.

The two men set their display cabinet down beside the trestle table, just as somebody else whizzed by with an ornate silver box. They opened the cabinet, set the box inside with its lid lifted to reveal two true flintlocks lying over red cushions. Somebody else flew over to set a little information card down in front of it, like a museum exhibit, while another had just connected a spotlight into the roof of the cabinet so that it lit up the guns. They had been expertly polished sometime prior to this arrangement and they dazzled behind their glass. The rest of the items from the trestle table were positioned around the pistols and then the glass door was closed and locked.

The blonde boy let out a whistle. 'Bet all that's worth a few bob.'

'Thank you gentlemen,' Sallow intoned.

'Go on,' the pencil 'tache said, nudging the boy out of the way.

Sallow turned on reception of a deep rumbling laugh as Richard Burden strode in accompanied by three assistants, taking note of his whims.

'Splendid, splendid,' he said looking round. Then he frowned, spun on his heel three hundred and sixty degrees and shook his head. 'No, no, no. *Where's* the Caravaggio. I *specifically* said to hang the Caravaggio, *not* the Canaletto.'

One of the assistants rapidly leafed back through a book of notes. 'Caravah... Caravadge?'

'*Vaggio*, vaggio!' Richard boomed, 'What *do* they teach at comprehensive schools? Honestly. Canaletto paints *vedute*, Caravaggio paints *scenes*. I asked for his King of Thebes to be the centrepiece. It was the *one* thing I insisted upon. Where is it?'

The assistant had come over all flustered. He snapped some instruction to an underling who ran off to fetch it at once.

'God almighty, if I could stomach the smell I'd hire apes instead. Sallow! Sallow!'

'Right here, sir,' said Sallow, who was already close at Richard's side.

'Where are we with the bar?'

'The delivery arrived not twenty minutes ago, sir.'

'And have you—'

'Being stocked as we speak.'

'Thank God. Sorry for shouting, Sallow, I'm glad you're here.'

'That's quite alright, sir. Now there is another matter I wish to discuss with you, if I may.'

Sallow indicated the corner.

'Wait there,' Richard said to the assistants. He followed Sallow over to the glass display cabinet. 'Well?'

'It's your son, sir. He called to ask whether he might be permitted to stay. I thought the guest house would be suitable, since we have already begun stripping his old room.'

'Fine, fine,' Richard said snappily. 'Have it prepared.'

'I have, sir. There is one other thing.'

'Yes?'

'While I had him on the line, I did enquire as to whether I should prepare myself for any misery at the expense of his good fun, and when I enquired as to this, the young Mr Burden told me that I had "no idea" what he had in store.'

'So, trouble, then?' Richard asked, gruffly.

'I expect so, sir.'

'Well you've dealt with him and his trouble before. What's different?'

'Well, desperation, perhaps, sir. As you'll recall, we have, for all intents and purposes, severed ties with him completely. He may view this, not as the olive branch you intend, but as *salt*.'

'Salt?'

'Salt, sir. To rub into his wounded pride.'

'Bah,' Richard felt like chuckling. 'What pride? We Burdens are built of such stuff as iron beams are made of.'

'Indeed, sir,' Sallow remarked. 'But Harrington is not yet as robust as you yourself. He is erratic. Irritable. If you will, irascible. He is easy to offend but difficult to convince of kindness. He treats the most minor of discretions as great acts of war. He is, perhaps, therefore dangerous.'

'Sallow,' Richard said and this time he did chuckle. 'Are you *scared* of the boy?'

'I am, sir. Though not for *my* sake.'

'Mr Burden,' the assistant called over. Richard looked round to see the underling had returned with the large framed Caravaggio.

Richard fixed his man Sallow with a long and strange look as he tried to figure out just what could be troubling the man this way. In twenty-six years of service he'd never seen a look like the one working its way through the whites of his eyes.

'Don't fret, old bean,' Richard said, trying to hide his own worry behind a false smile. He slapped the butler on the arm gently. 'I'll make sure I clear the air the minute he arrives. Have him await me in the guesthouse. I'll nip any tomfoolery in the bud.' He made his way over to the assistants in the middle of the hall. 'Tonight will be one of the more memorable of my life,' he insisted. 'I promise you that *on my life.*'

Chapter 3

Harry had been standing on the pavement outside of the twelve-foot electric gates for so long his legs had fallen to sleep.

He could see the house lit up across the lawn. The party was in full effect with dots of movement around the patio and flash cars parked all along the resin driveway around the fountain.

He wore a velvet, bottle-green dinner jacket with a gold flower on the lapel. He had a frilly undershirt with Montblanc cufflinks. He had meant the ensemble to be vulgar and garish and was disappointed to find himself look so damn fetching.

A car honked behind and startled him. He grasped his satchel close to his chest and nervously moved out of the way as somebody buzzed the car in. The gates slid apart electronically and Harry decided now was better than never. He followed the lights to the house and felt something between nostalgia and déjà vu envelope him.

He had no sooner approached the fountain when the front door burst open and Sallow came charging over.

'Oh, Christ, *you!*' Harry squawked. 'Has my old man not binned you off yet? Upgraded to the latest model?'

'Your wit is, sir, as acerbic as ever,' Sallow smiled politely. 'Now if you'll come with me.'

'How did you know I was here? Has he got me microchipped?'

'No, sir, we are using a new technology you may not be aware of, called closed-circuit television.' Sallow indicated a camera on the corner of the house. 'Now do come with me. You're awfully late.'

'Are you going to try and touch me up in the broom closet? I'll cry murder and have you tried in The Hague. My uncle's the duke of High Wycombe, you know that.'

'Sir, I really am frightfully busy tonight. It may have escaped your notice, but there is a ball in progress.'

'A ball? *Really*?' Harry feigned surprise. 'Am I underdressed? Only I hadn't known there was a party or else I would've splashed out on a bit of eau-de-something. I'm only wearing Lynx.

Honestly, a ball. I didn't know that, Sally. Nothing gave it away. Not the fancy cars or the epileptic clusterfuck of spotlights and *particularly* not the awful sounds that lot are making inside.'

The butler sighed almighty. 'As I believe I said, sir, *acerbic* is your tongue. And as you know, my name is Sallow, *not* Sally.'

'Yes, yes, but *really*, now,' Harry said. 'what *are* those sounds they're making? Is my old man hosting an orgy of farm animals? I knew he was sick but that is *sick*.'

'You're to enter round the back,' Sallow said, thoroughly ignoring him. 'There are some ground rules he wishes me to go over.'

'Oh, bore-you, Sally, you old slave, you used to give me a run for my money with the old one-two of verbal bickerage, but I see you've gotten old. Too old for young blood.'

'Yes, sir, perhaps unlike the rest of humanity, you are able to prevent yourself from ageing; certainly mentally that appears to be the case. But I have grown older since you last graced us with your presence, and with that age I became weary of what you may call: bullshit.'

Harry sniggered. 'There he is. That's the old Sally-Wally I know.'

'Now please do come round the back, sir.'

'Ooh-er.'

Sallow didn't wait for any more parries of the tongue. He closed the front door and headed around the side of the building knowing very well that Harry would be close behind.

'Where are we going?' Harry asked as they crossed the lawn, away from the house.

'I'm showing you to your quarters, first.'

'Right-O. He's got me in the outhouse has he?'

'The guesthouse, sir, yes.'

'What happened to my old room? Let me guess. Converted into a squash court or a sweatshop or a sex dungeon the very moment I left?'

'Not quite, sir. I believe the master sleeps there on occasion.'

That took Harry aback. 'In my bed? *Why?*'

Sallow looked as if he were abstaining from a large and sly grin. 'While I cannot say with any certainty, one would hazard a guess that it's an attempt by the master to feel close to you in your absence.'

'What makes you so sure? He's not the sentimental type. He probably just got abso-blotto one night and collapsed there.'

'Perhaps, sir, but that wouldn't account for the embarrassment he showed when I discovered him. I discover him "abso-blotto", as you put it, with increasing frequency, and never with the satisfying side dish of embarrassment.'

Harry chewed on it for a moment. He didn't quite know what to make of the butler's revelation. That's if it was even true of course. Sallow was a devious type.

'I suppose he got fed up of sleeping in a tomb in the family crypt,' Harry suggested. 'Not good for the back.'

'No doubt, sir.'

'Come on then, Sal. What are these ground rules?'

They had reached the guesthouse, but Harry had lit a cigarette and Sallow fixed him a look.

'First of all, you are not to smoke in here—'

'Bollocks, the old man doesn't know I smoke. That's one of yours. Thrown in for good measure to needle me.'

'You are right, sir, that the master didn't mention smoking. However, "no-smoking" is a house-wide policy that extends to the guesthouse. So I'm afraid I must insist on it.'

Harry rolled his eyes as he returned the put-out fag to his cig box. 'Well?' he said. 'Go on then, I know you're just *dying* to boss me around, so get on with it.'

'You are to remain civil and convivial at all times,' the butler began, struggling to hide his gratification. 'You are to engage in the spirit of the evening without causing Mr Burden any embarrassment. That means no excessive drinking. As Mr Burden pointed out to me just earlier today, you can outdrink a whale, sir. You are to pace yourself and set a limit. You must not mention that you dropped out of university and you *especially* must not mention that you dropped out of one *up north*.'

He unlocked the door to the guesthouse and led Harry inside. The settee had been made up into a bed. Harry flicked on the lights, chucked his satchel to the ground and jumped onto the bed, up and down like a yo-yo.

'Please, sir, I *do* hope you're paying attention.'

'The utmost, Sally,' Harry said. He stopped jumping in mid-air and fell like a plank of lumber on the mattress.

The butler cleared his throat and went on: 'You are not to swear and in particular: *no blaspheming*. Mr Burden has specifically asked that you refrain from using the words "Jesus" and "Christ". He knows you're fond of them. He is expecting a bishop tonight.'

There was an ice bucket on the bedside table and Sallow went about unwrapping a bottle of Champagne. He poured Harry a glass with a desperately short measure, and then handed it over reluctantly.

'Is everything clear, sir?'

'As carbon,' said Harry, taking not the glass from Sallow's outstretched hand, but the bottle from his other and swigging with a mischievous glint in his eye and a wink for the butler.

Chapter 4

The door clicked open and a young porter popped his head inside.

'Mr Sallow? He's coming, sir.'

'Thank you, Joules. Tell him we're ready.'

'Yessir.'

'Tell *who* we're ready?' asked Harry, feeling his neck go all blotchy.

'Your father, sir. He wishes to speak with you before you enter the main house.'

Harry had lost something in his countenance. Sallow seemed to enjoy that. He was straightening the corner of a pillow and wearing a subtle hint of pleasure.

'My... he...? That is to say—*why*?'

'Is something the matter, sir? You appear to be choking on your vocabularies.'

Someone knocked on the door and then it opened. Harry didn't need to turn. He could feel who it was in the air. From seventeen degrees to ice.

'Good evening, Harrington,' his father crooned. 'My, that's quite a dinner jacket.'

'Good evening,' Harry replied, finally able to turn and look up at his father's face. 'I thought I'd make an effort.'

There was an unmistakable similarity between them, from the strong Roman nose to the cold, steely eyes, to the set of buck gnashers like horse teeth. But the similarity transcended the physical, something in their gait, in their hesitant and awkward formality. Even their hair fell in the same way, though the old man's, Harry couldn't help but notice, looked suspiciously healthier than it had this time last year. Still, he didn't feel it wise to enquire about the possibility of a transplant as his opening gambit.

'Sallow tells me you've converted my bedroom into a sex dungeon,' he opted for instead. 'Is that why the bishop's round? Does he pay you for an hour with a choirboy?'

'Well, I see you're just as delightful as ever. How've you been?'

'Cold. And hungry.'

'Are you working?'

'No. It's this market. London's oversaturated, there are no jobs left.'

'I recall,' Richard said stroking his chin, 'setting up a job for you last summer.'

'Yes,' Harry snarled, 'with that filthy pervert van der Sar. He stroked my leg the minute I sat beside him. If I were naked, his last two fingers would've been right up my—'

'Yes, yes,' Richard interrupted. 'I'm sure, Harry, you're so irresistible that Mr van der Sar, a man of thirty-eight years wed, could not resist trying to molest you within moments of your meeting.'

'Well he did. So... you know. There.'

'Acerbic, as ever, Master Burden,' Sallow chirped.

Harry felt his cheeks burn up. He'd lost his ability to spar verbosely. He was a shadow of his previously sassy self.

'So are we going to this sodding party or not? I didn't come all this way to stand around the guesthouse all night talking about how I was almost whored to a paedophile by my own father.'

'In a minute,' Richard said, taking the glass of champagne from the bedside table and sipping it. 'First of all, I need some assurances from you. The last time I let you loose around my friends, three people wound up puking in the parlour.'

'It's not my fault they can't hold their drink.'

'One of them was *you*.'

'Then it's not my fault *I* can't hold my drink.'

'And the time before *that*, you spilt an expensive Margaux across a very senior member of Parliament.'

'That was an *accident*.'

'Then it was an accident that occurred five times.'

Harry stuck his tongue out.

'Listen to me, Harrington,' said Richard. 'Are you going to behave? Hm? *Are you*?'

Sallow made a noise like some air had escaped him.

'If *you* behave, I will,' Harry answered like a petulant child.

'I'm afraid,' Richard said sternly, 'that's not how it's going to work any longer. I cut you off this week to teach you a lesson. You are here tonight to prove to me that you have *learnt* that lesson. *If you do not do that* I have no qualms about cutting you off for good. Do you hear me?'

Sallow made a slightly longer version of the previous sound and then quickly pretended to busy himself removing the creases from the bedding.

Richard, meanwhile, was staring at Harry with such fierce sincerity that Harry did not doubt him at his word.

'Yes, yes, all right!' Harry said at last. 'I'm going to behave. What are you expecting me to do? I've not brought any firecrackers or whoopee cushions—you can have the staff search me if it'll make you feel better. But can't we make some sort of arrangement?'

'Arrangement?' Richard crossed his arms.

Harry shrugged. 'I've got no job and it's not escaped my notice you very cleverly bought the Milk Street property because it's close enough to you *here* that you could keep an eye on me. But that *does* unfortunately mean it's in one of the most expensive places to live in the entire world. If I behave tonight will you continue paying for it? At least for a few more years. Otherwise Charlie and I will be thrown onto the streets like urchins.'

Richard frowned. Harry knew his father despised Charlie and he regretted mentioning him in his plea.

But fortunately his father waved his hand through the air and said, 'Fine. I will resume our previous arrangement regarding that house, yes. *But only for one year*. That's more than enough time for you to pull your socks up and sort your wretched life out, wouldn't you say?'

Before Harry could answer, Richard stuck out his hand. Harry stared down at it for a long second and considered what shaking it meant. It meant not being himself. It meant compromise. It meant tailoring his personality for an audience of wine-soaked right-wing bigots. That wasn't the way of the iconoclast. That wasn't the Byronic way. That wasn't the way of the Burden—or not the *younger* Burden at least.

So then why in fucking hell did he shake it?

Chapter 5

Sallow led Harry and Richard into the house through the east wing door, down a long mahogany corridor and into the ballroom.

It was alive with spectacle. Beneath the windows, a string quartet played to eighty guests who, between them, owned half of southern England and a few dozen yachts off Monte Carlo. People turned to say 'Hello' and 'Good evening' and 'Blimey, Harry, int'cha got big?' as Sallow led them through, while whiteshirts buzzed around with trays of canapés. Sweet chilli prawns in spring roll pastry, fried calamari with tartare sauce, fig preserve on ciabatta with Parma ham and goat's cheese.

The long banqueting table had been removed and eight circular dining tables had popped up in its place. Nobody had yet been seated. The guests were split into twenty or thirty smaller groups and dotted around the hall. They were all in their finery, though nobody, Harry thought, looked particularly fine. The men were all fat and balding and wore over-sized suits and the women looked as if they had been dipped in fondant.

Sallow bowed away and Richard pulled Harry into a quiet corner by the display cabinet that housed his spoils. Harry wondered why they had come to this isolated corner of the room for a moment. But then he saw the trepidation on his father's face and how he was sweating around the temples of his suspiciously thick mane. Clearly he meant to keep Harry from his other guests for as long as possible.

Harry just rolled his eyes. He couldn't imagine *what* Richard thought him liable to do that had him so riled up. But he didn't stress the matter. Instead he preoccupied himself by looking into the display cabinet.

'What's all this rubbish?' he asked as casually as he could.

'Hm?' Richard looked out-of-sorts, as if he had forgotten the cabinet was there. 'Oh, er, my recent haul. Pirate memorabilia. From Sotheby's.'

In the centre of the cabinet was a box of duelling pistols. On a velvet bed around it were several other trinkets. A chalice, something that looked like a tin flute, an old leather-bound diary…

'Jesus H. on the cross, father, you *do* buy some tosh.'

'Watch your language,' Richard hissed, looking round to check that nobody had overheard. 'There's a bishop here.'

'I'm sure he'll forgive me,' Harry said, yawning. 'That's his whole racket. Now, I say!' His eyes lit up. '*This* is more like it.'

At the back of the cabinet Harry spotted a dagger; a long and slender blade of silver with a dull green gem embedded in its handle. He would cop to being fascinated by it; daggers are always fascinating.

'What is it?' he asked.

'Hm?' Richard repeated, turning. 'Oh. That's a sixteenth-century stiletto. Italian, I believe.'

Harry read the label behind the glass. It talked of piracy in the Bahamas. 'This Edward Hickory chap sounds an absolute riot!'

'Oh he was,' Richard said, beginning to ease up. He looked on the cabinet fondly. 'Hickory was instrumental in the Nassau revolution, you know. Those pistols are true flintlocks. They are the pride of my collection. Only cost five thousand but I would've paid a *hundred* to own them. Their material value is of no consequence, you see? It's their history. They were used in combat in the golden age of piracy. *That* is what's so fascinating about them.'

Harry thought it was funny—and a little sad—how his father looked on that pair of old pistols with more fondness than he had ever once looked on *him*.

'You ought to take them out for a slap-up meal,' he said, dryly. 'Look—there's the bishop. I'm sure he'll marry the three of you if you ask nicely. You could be consummating the affair before midnight.'

'Harrington,' Richard sighed, 'I thought you were going to behave?'

Harry made a show of rolling his eyes. 'I *am* behaving. They're only *words* father, lighten up. It's not like I've *killed* somebody.'

Richard scoffed. 'Yes,' he said, 'and *should* the urge prop up, you'd do well to ignore it.'

Sallow scurried back into the room just then to ring the dinner gong. The quartet started a lively ditty as the guests took their seats. Harry found himself ushered to the central table along with his father and six others. He was wedged between a ruddy-faced man in a red military jacket who smelled of booze and a plump woman with a teetering blonde beehive and a hideous cackle that she did not use sparingly.

Harry looked the rest of the group over and found he did not recognise a single face—though undoubtedly he would have been introduced to at least half of them at some time or other.

'Dickie!' bellowed the ruddy-faced man in the military jacket, pointing so closely at Harry's face as to touch his nose. 'That's *never* your wee lad, is it?'

'Indeed,' said Richard with a magnetic smile. 'Some of you, I'm sure, will know him already. To the rest, may I introduce my son, Harrington.'

Every head whipped round in Harry's direction.

'My *word*, Harry, m'boy!' the military jacket boomed. 'Last we met you were down *here*!'

'Yes, I'd rather not talk about *that*,' said Harry, to a titter of laughter.

'Ha! Such wit!' the man returned. 'No doubt you give your old father a run for his money, eh, lad? You remember *me* don't you, sonny?'

It was clear that Harry had no clue who this whisky-soaked codger was, so Richard cleared his throat. 'Allow me to make the introductions. Harrington, this is the Right Honourable John Howard—'

'Please, *please*,' said the man, shaking his hands about in protest. '*Lord* Howard will suffice.'

Lord Howard then barked with laughter and he was joined by the raucous cackle of the blonde beehive. When the two of them had collapsed into a state of wheezing and wiped the tears from their eyes, Richard went on.

He introduced the rosy-cheeked man to Lord Howard's left as Simon Oliver, a barrister for the High Court.

'Demoted, actually,' Simon said matter-of-factly and with something of a twinkle in his eye. 'Ugly business. Some tart filed a suit against me. Completely unfounded of course, but they thought I should step down until it blows over. She's the judge, you see, this tart.'

'Right,' Richard said and then he cleared his throat again and moved on swiftly.

The smart gentleman beside Simon was Dr Kapoor from St George's.

'I've a friend who works there,' Harry said, pointing at the doctor with a breadstick. 'Emily Seymour. Do you know her?'

'Er—I don't believe so.'

'Mm. S'pose you wouldn't. She's the most frightful bore.'

Richard was seated beside Dr Kapoor, and to Richard's left was a man with an egg-shaped head and van Dyck beard, complete with a fantastic set of curly moustaches. This was Mr l'Hiver, a publisher from Kent-ways.

The buck-toothed man to his left was an old Harrovian buddy of Richard's. And the plump blonde was his wife.

'Tell me Harry, what do *you* do?' she asked. 'The son of Richard Burden must be quite something!'

'I'm between jobs at the moment,' Harry said. 'It's this market, you see. Although I have this whizzo idea for a line of mittens for dogs—'

'*Actually*,' Richard said purposefully, 'Harry will be working under Gus van der Sar in the summer, isn't that right?'

'Yes, if he has it *his* way,' Harry mumbled.

Richard flushed slightly. He sought to change the subject by pointing at Harry's wrist. 'I see you're wearing my grandfather's watch,' he said.

'Never take it off,' Harry answered, turning his wrist to the show the group.

'It belonged to my grandfather,' Richard explained. 'Passed down from father to son. *Mine* wore it through the war.'

'Yes, and it was *so* good of the Luftwaffe to kindly return it with his Iron Cross,' Harry added.

A team of waiters came to break napkins over their laps. A starter quickly followed and by the time their third glass of wine was poured, Harry had the table in the palm of his hand. He was telling his fantastic rowing story and the woman with the beehive cackled inanely at his every word.

'...and after they dredged the lake and got the oar out of his waistband, old Froggy rolled over and coughed up a smelt!'

The table erupted.

'I say, your son is a *riot*, Dickie,' the old Harrovian said. 'Would've fit right in with our lot, don't you think?'

'Tell me, Harry, have you any *political* aspirations at all?' Lord Howard asked. 'Destined for a top position, no doubt.'

'You're an absolute *dish* too,' added the beehive. 'I wonder where you *get* it? They *do* say it skips a generation, don't they, Dickie?'

'Tell me about your time at Harrow, lad,' the old Harrovian said, leaning over the table to help himself to a bread roll. 'Is Father Fodersham still pottering about? He must be two hundred now. Was already ninety-seven when I was a boy.'

'Yes, 'fraid the man's mind went long ago but his body won't give up. I thought I killed him once, you know? A prank of mine backfired when the chaplain came marching through the dorm and slipped on a carpet of Vaseline I had spent the night laying. Crashed into Julian Carraway's easel and burst head-first from his canvas. Julian was working on a piece called *Pregnant Nude with Legs Akimbo* at the time so I'm *sure* you can guess where old Fodersham's wrinkly noggin came bursting from?'

'*Where*?' guffawed the beehive. '*Do* tell us Harry.'

'He burst right from her hairy—'

'*Dog*!' Richard bellowed, very suddenly, slamming his hands down so that the glasses and cutlery jangled.

The entire table looked round to find him red-faced and sweating.

'Her *dog*?' The beehive frowned.

'Burst from her *dog*, Richard? Are you sure?'

'Her... her *dog*,' said Richard, faintly. 'There was a... a *dog* in the painting, isn't that right, Harrington?'

He was glaring at Harry with caution in his eyes.

'A dog…' Harry said, trying the word out in his mouth while Richard mopped his forehead. Harry could see Richard meant to have him bent over, trousers down, cane in hand. 'You'll have to excuse my father's outburst,' he told the other guests. 'He's embarrassed by the miracle of birth the way he's embarrassed about the Persian in him. A sixteenth, isn't it? He thinks they'll rescind his subscription to The Sun if they catch wind. But, yes—I *do* recall the dog now, though. A Labrador I believe? Her birthing partner.'

'What? Oh. A Labrador, yes, that's right.' Richard could barely keep up. It was a mile-a-minute, the whirlwind that swirled around the table. 'A Labrador like Bosie was.'

'Bosie was *our* dog,' Harry explained. 'He was accidentally mistakenly locked outside when he had chewed through my father's golf bag and we never saw him again, isn't that right father?'

'Richard, how *could* you?'

'It wasn't on purpose!' Richard barked defensively. 'Anyway he swallowed a tee. Poor beast probably lacerated itself.'

'I had *wanted* an Alsatian originally, but father wouldn't let me,' Harry continued, enjoying himself.

'You're so *cruel* to the boy, Richard!' the beehive cajoled. 'Why didn't you let him have a German Shepherd?'

'Because he doesn't speak the language and we don't keep sheep!' Richard snapped, throwing his napkin on the table and standing up. 'Excuse me.'

He strolled over to talk with someone at the next table along.

'Oh, "*doesn't speak the language*,"' the blonde giggled. 'I just got it! What is he *like*? A hoot, he's an absolute hoot.'

'Say, Harrington,' the Harrovian said conspiratorially, leaning across the table. 'What party are you with?'

'Party?'

Lord Howard turned keenly. Harry took a roll from the breadbasket and bit into it.

'Well atta moment—' He swallowed, 'I'm chair of the North London Communist Society.'

The Harrovian lost his pallor.

'*Gimme socialism or gimme death*,' Harry went on, digging into the roll with his finger and scooping the doughy insides out.

'Er... I see,' the Harrovian said, looking down at the table.

But Harry was only paying half of his attention to the group now. The rest was still fixed on his father who was meandering through the tables, half-heartedly chatting with whoever tapped on his arm.

'Are you on a debating team?' The Harrovian asked. 'I was the head when I was your age, you know.'

'Hm?' Harry asked looking up at him.

'I was just wondering if you debate at all?'

'Only when it follows *mass*,' Harry said, placing his napkin over his own plate and standing up. 'Excuse me.'

Chapter 6

Harry slid his chair back and walked over to his father, who was looking rather strained in the corner of the hall.

'Are you alright?' Harry asked.

'Just peachy.'

'Good. I think I'm doing rather well with your crowd.'

'*My* crowd!' Richard laughed, once. 'They haven't been *my* crowd since quarter to nine.'

'What's wrong?' Harry snapped. 'For God's sake, I'm doing what you asked. They love me over there. Why are you all flustered and wearing that frightful scowl?'

'Because you're a loose cannon,' Richard hissed through clenched teeth. He looked around nervously and led Harry back to the display cabinets by the elbow. 'I never know what you're going to say next! If I sit at that table another minute, you'll give me a God damn heart attack.'

'Language, father, there's a bishop around.'

'Oh, bugger the bishop!' Richard howled. 'I need another drink.'

Harry couldn't believe his father. He had done all he asked— and more—but it still wasn't enough to please the old dragon. He felt like throwing a tantrum and only restrained himself with a tremendous difficulty.

He even managed to push the word '*Sorry*' from the back of his throat, up past the lips and out of his mouth. Richard seemed as surprised as Harry at the word. It hung in the air between them.

'I'm just trying to be entertaining,' Harry explained. 'That's what dinner parties are for, isn't it?'

Richard straightened himself up and nodded. 'Quite right. I suppose *I'm* sorry, too.'

They stood together awkwardly, both a little red. Harry observed his father, who ran a hand gently over the back of his head.

'I wasn't going to say anything but are you wearing a *wig*?' Harry asked.

'*What*?'

'It's better than what some of these baldies are trying to get away with, I'll give you that. Cor! just look at *that* one. But it's hardly subtle, father.'

'I've no idea what you're talking about,' Richard said, patting the side of his head with a palm.

Harry stared at his father's hair, unconvinced.

'Look, our mains are coming,' said Richard gruffly and he led his son back over to their table where they took their seats silently.

Richard poured himself an enormous glass of brandy and drank the thing in damn near one swig. And he kept the bottle in his hand for good measure.

For the most part, the main course was uneventful. They ate slow-cooked duck in an orange sauce with something that looked like a roasted doily on the side.

Harry ate miserably, picking at his food and trying to be as uncontroversial as possible. His father seemed to bear down on him like some monolithic bastard. Always glaring or scowling or sending whole clouds of steam from his nostrils at the slightest provocation. But by the time the whiteshirts had cleared away the dessert plates, it was a different story entirely. Harry had mentally checked-out and become the background to his father's charismatic raconteuring, while the old Burden himself had crossed the threshold of insobriety. He had almost emptied that bottle. His cheeks were aglow with brandy and the suspicious rug on his bonnet was starting to stand to attention.

'Tell me, Harry, where are you living these days?' Simon Oliver asked. 'Not still *here*, I assume?'

Richard overheard. '*Here?*' He laughed. 'No. Harrington lives in Knightsbridge.'

'Rath-er!' Simon beamed. 'Tell me. Chap like you must have *bus*-loads of girlfriends. Do you live with anyone special?'

Richard grunted and a few heads looked at him. The beehive frowned and turned to Harry decidedly, waiting for his response.

'I live with my friend Charlie,' Harry said. 'He's a writer.'

'A bloody bohemian layabout is what he is,' Richard scoffed. 'From Manchester, no less.'

'What of it?' Harry said. 'He's a damned genius, I'll have you know.'

Richard scoffed again. 'I've no doubt he is a genius. He's found a way to live in north London for free and with no job, hasn't he?'

The table fell quite silent, sensing the kind of awkwardness that comes as a precursor to family arguments. Harry ground his teeth together. He felt the attack on Charlie was an attack on himself.

'If it hasn't escaped your notice,' Harry said, bitterly. '*I* live in north London for free and with no job. So you can hardly blame Charlie for *that*.'

'What've you against the boy, Dickie?' The beehive asked. 'If he's a friend of Harry's I'm sure—'

'You're sure *what* exactly, Vera?' Richard snapped. 'What could you *possibly* know about anything?'

The beehive withdrew with a little squeak, and her husband, the old Harrovian, said, 'Come now, Dickie, old thing. There's no need for—'

'Hugh, there is *every* need,' Richard insisted. 'You haven't the faintest idea what this situation is like. I buy a place for my son so he can focus his attentions and ambitions on a career and what happens? He invites this… stranger into *my* home and they tear the place asunder—'

'You don't know what you're talking about,' Harry shot back. 'Charlie was an innocent first year who'd never touched a drop of hard liquor till I corrupted him. And where do you think *I* got it from?' He indicated the empty bottle of brandy that Richard was failing to pour a glass from. 'You've only met him twice, so what *is* it exactly you've got against Charlie?'

'I've nothing against him *personally*,' Richard said, calmly. 'But you have to wonder about a man like that. Someone who latches onto a person like you, Harry, and sucks the life from you without you even noticing. Takes away your sense of value. You would be heading *somewhere* right now without his influence. This Charlie character—why he's nothing but a festering maggot of a man! He has more in common with the amoebic parasites of the benthic zone than any human I've ever met. A blood-sucking leech with his damn fangs penetrating your impossibly thin skin—'

Boof!

A bread roll flew across the table and hit Richard firmly in the forehead. The shock was visible on his face.

'How dare you!' Richard said, 'Have you no respect?'

'Not for you,' Harry returned. 'Not anymore. You're an old fart in a bad toupee.'

Richard went the colour of a plum. The beehive giggled and then slapped her hands across her mouth in suppression.

'*This*,' Richard hissed, '*is not a toupee.*'

'Alright, alright,' Harry said. 'Keep your hair on.'

The beehive erupted. A few other jitters passed around the table, including a surprising little sound from Lord Howard, which was quickly disguised by a cough.

'You arrogant little shit!' Richard slammed a fist on the table.

The laughing stopped. So did the string quartet. The nearby tables had noticed the commotion by now and they all turned as one. It suddenly felt eerily quiet in the enormous hall.

'Get out of my house,' Richard growled. 'You are never welcome back here again. Our little deal is *off*. Do you hear me?'

Harry was too angry to be upset. He was bubbling under the skin as if the spirits that tend on mortal thoughts were filling him with direst cruelty. But at surface-level, he was like a pool without ripples.

The two men glowered at one another for a long time. Richard was deep purple with his hair all askew and his saliva had dried down the sides of his mouth. Richard hadn't noticed the silence but when he did, he looked around and somehow flushed deeper, if that was possible.

Harry made a show of sliding back his chair, letting the awful screech of chair legs ring out around the hall. He stood up very slowly and was well aware that every set of eyes was on him.

He meant to leave. He meant to walk straight out the door and not look back. But somehow, he felt to make a show of it would be more befitting his final moments at Blye House.

So instead, he climbed onto the platform by the string quartet and faced the crowd.

'I'm sure you all heard just then. I'm no longer welcome here,' he said, faintly. 'And after this announcement I'm sure I won't be welcome across half of London, either, considering how, you know… you lot *own* it.'

Ordinarily there would have been a ripple of laughter, Harry was certain of that. But the room wasn't in the laughing mood. The faces looked on him sombrely.

'I *would* just like say it's been a wonderful evening spent in the company of terrific people,' he gazed over at his table—at Lord Howard and Simon Oliver and Mathieu l'Hiver. At Hugh and Vera. 'But *that* of course,' Harry snarled, 'would be disgustingly untrue. You lot are the most *boring* bunch of senile old codgers I've ever had the displeasure of performing for. And *that's* why I have no shame in doing *this*.'

He turned around, pulled down his trousers and wiggled his naked buttocks across the room. A wave of gasps rocked through the crowd and Harry was quite sure he heard the shattering of at least one glass.

He didn't say another word after that. He pulled up his trousers, hopped off the platform and walked the length of the ballroom to the mahogany doors. He snatched a glass of champagne from a table, swallowed it and chucked the glass over a shoulder. A tray of canapés had the misfortune of crossing his path. He grabbed five or six of them and stuffed them all in his mouth, spraying crumbs of pastry behind him like a vapour trail.

As he strolled from the room, he heard the flurry of every single head turn in unison, like a flock of a thousand birds, and he imagined the look on his father's face—all red and mangled as he straightened that wonky hairpiece.

The final thing Harry heard as he reached the front door was the quartet begin on Saint-Saëns's *Danse Macabre*, and he chuckled to himself.

'That quartet have a terrific sense of humour,' he said, as he ran his fingers along the grooves of the wood panelling and wished that his father would choke to death on a salmon and horseradish crispbread.

Chapter 7

Harry sat out on the lawn and bawled his eyes out. He could see both houses from his spot among the foxgloves yet he remained invisible in the dark. There were members of staff flittering between the guesthouse and the main with torch-beams criss-crossing as they searched for him. Sallow even appeared by the fountain for fifteen minutes, scanning the driveway with calculating eyes while whiteshirts buzzed like bees.

'What have I done?' Harry grumbled to himself.

He had just seen off the last of a bottle of pink gin and it had turned his misery back to anger.

'I'll tell you what I've done,' he snarled to a hedgehog in the soil. 'I've mooned myself out of a will.' The hedgehog wasn't interested. 'That must be the most expensive moon in history,' Harry continued. 'And besides, Hedgey, I meant every word I said in there, you know. And I'm thrilled I got to embarrass the cocky rotter in front of that lot. I'd be a bloody fool not to be happy by the shade of magenta I got out of him. You should've seen it, Hedgey. Wouldn't believe your eyes. No human should become a grape, it was unprecedented and Lord knows I've tried it on before.'

Harry was upturning the soil with his fingers nervously. His companion scurried back into the hedge. Harry left the gin bottle in the dirt and got unsteadily to his feet.

He had developed a plan for revenge. Well, *plan*, he would be the first to admit, was a rather grand name for the scheme. He hadn't quite decided the finale of the thing, but to begin with, he meant to jolly-well return to the main house and stir up a fair bit of trouble. Nothing major. A piddle in the plant pots, salt in the sugar tin, a nice amendment to Richard's portrait. The word *Nob* across his forehead or a greasepaint moustache, perhaps. That sort of thing.

The ideas were brewing in his head as he crossed the lawn. He had witnessed most of the cars depart while he'd quaffed down the pink gin. The party had come to an abrupt end, presumably on account of the mooning. But he was stopped in his tracks before he got within a hundred feet of the back door. Sallow had stuck two whiteshirts on every entrance, posed like bouncers.

Bollocks. There was no getting in there. And even if he did, he wouldn't succeed at anything cunning. Sallow would be on to him like the old bill. He was sneaky like that.

No the plan needed further development. Harry drew back into the shadows of the hedgerow and creased the brow in concentration.

There was a spare key, he recalled, secured in a lockbox inside the guesthouse. He could wait the whiteshirts out and let himself in with this spare key. They had to go home at some point. *That* was his way inside.

The floodlights flashed over the patio like searchlights as more staff pottered round the back door. One of them started across the lawn at the back of the guesthouse, looking through the bushes. Soon they would be headed his way.

Harry laughed drunkenly to himself as he staggered towards the guesthouse. He had just conceived a most brilliant finale to the break-in. *He would steal those pistols his old man loved so much.* What had he called them? His pride and joy? If Harry was out of the will, Richard could jolly-well leave his enormous fortune to the flintlocks. That rosy-cheeked sex-pest barrister Oliver something-or-other would probably agree to the paperwork. Harry could imagine the scene now. In the morning, Richard takes the Bentley to the lawyer's office to write Harry out of the will and when he gets back to Blye House—shock! The display cabinet is empty. No windows are broken. No sign of forced entry. The house would be just as he left it, sans his pride and joy. It would be the perfect crime. That would show the old bugger a thing or two.

Richard would *know* Harry had taken the pistols, of course. It would be the most logical conclusion to draw from the scheme. But he wouldn't be able to *prove* it. Not if he did the thing properly. Not if he took the spare key, snuck in and then left without being seen.

But Sallow presented another problem. Not only did the butler live in a room on the upper floor of the main house, he was also actively searching for Harry and he must know he was still on the property, no thanks to that CCTV camera. That's why the Gestapo were still going through the foxgloves.

'One thing at a time,' Harry said as he crept up on the guesthouse. Two whiteshirts followed their torchlight back toward the main building and Harry pinned himself to the wall until they had passed. He was a cold war spy at the Wall.

When the coast was clear, he opened the door, snuck inside and flew to the lockbox on the wall. His heart was in his throat. The two porters were still close-by and he could hear their muffled voices outside. He imagined air raid sirens and gunfire cackling over artillery.

The lockbox sprung open and the spare key was still hung up inside. He took out his own house keys for Milk Street. Both were identical to the naked eye. Richard had *insisted* they install Safe-T-Bolt, 12 pin-double sidebar-locking mechanisms at all of his properties. He claimed they were the most secure in existence. *Ironic that added security will be his ruin*, Harry thought, and then sniggered.

'I'll just check again,' came Sallow's voice on the other side of the guesthouse door.

Harry choked. He stuffed the Blye House spare key in his breast pocket, hung his Milk Street key in its place inside the lockbox and shut its little door. Then he dropped to the floor and rolled under the bed.

The guesthouse door clicked open and in walked the butler. He flicked the lights up and Harry saw his feet walk into the bathroom. Then he came back into the main room and Harry heard him investigate the lockbox. He heard the clink of the Milk Street key as Sallow removed it. Then the lights went back out and the guesthouse door slammed shut.

'Now *that* was some timing!' Harry gasped, barely able to believe his luck.

He rolled out from under the bed and crept over to the window, careful to stay low, and peeped outside. One of the porters was lighting a fag on the lawn, but nobody appeared to be looking in.

'Go on, get going you silly man,' Harry muttered.

'I would say, sir, that it was *you* who was rather silly,' drawled Sallow. His voice was instilled with indelible annoyance.

Harry spun round and found the butler, still inside the guesthouse, sat on an armchair. The only thing missing was a Luger at his hip. Sallow clicked on the bedside lamp and smirked.

'Jesus, Sallow, you old prune, what are you doing in here. That's how you give people heart attacks.'

'I was dispatched to search for you, sir, to ensure there are no further... *announcements*... you wish to make to Mr Burden's guests.'

'Yes, well, fat chance I'll ever step foot in *that* place again,' Harry snarled.

'Quite right, sir. But just to be certain, I've been instructed to remove the spare key. Mr Burden had not forgotten about it.'

He looked pretty pleased with himself as he held up the key from the lockbox.

'Fine by me,' Harry replied, 'because as I said, I have no intention of returning to Blye House.'

'But you intend on sleeping here tonight, still?'

'Haven't decided. Would you have a problem with that?'

'I'm sure I would have no opinion on the matter, sir. I just question whether *you* think it would be wise.'

Harry shrugged. 'I suppose not. I suppose I'll be off then. I'll go and visit the midnight pharmacist; I'm in need of a big dose of something. And I suppose there's nothing else for me here, is there, Sallow?'

'I suppose not, sir.'

'Goodbye then, old Sally.'

'Goodbye, sir.'

'For what it's worth,' Harry said, 'I don't hold any of this against you. I know you're a big softy really. You just like to *pretend* you're the devil's arsehole.'

'Of course, sir.'

Harry opened the door.

Sallow said, 'Sir?'

'Yes?'

'Your bag, sir.'

The butler indicated the satchel on the carpet.

Of course! That was how he had known Harry was still on the property. He probably didn't expect him to roll out from under the bed, of course, but he would have expected him to show up back in the guesthouse.

'Thanks,' Harry said, slinging the bag around his shoulder.

Sallow stood up. 'I should see you out, sir.'

They walked in silence back across the lawn and down the resin path to the gates. Harry looked back up at the front of the house and at the CCTV camera on the wall over the fountain.

'Just taking one last look at the place,' he said, trying to make his face look full of upset. 'You'll have my things sent to me?'

'Of course, sir. As a matter of fact, we have already begun packing your things into storage boxes. I know your address.'

'Number six, Milk Street.'

'Yes, sir.'

'Right-O.'

Sallow punched in a code and the gates slid open. Harry crossed to the other side and headed down the road without looking back. He could hear the electronic mechanism as the gates slide shut behind him.

Chapter 8

Harry didn't have to wait long to put the next part of his plan into action. Sallow, the old bean, had only gone and helped him with the plot. He had needed Sallow to see him leave, of course, to remove himself as a suspect in the grand pistol larceny.

He walked away from Blye House for only thirty seconds before he was confident the butler had stopped watching. He doubled back along the road and stood twenty feet from the gate by the hedge.

After another group of guests departed, he checked his watch. It was just after midnight. Soon they would all leave. The gates opened and cars whizzed out one at a time. The drive started to clear up, lights started going off in the windows and eventually the whiteshirts departed for the night.

At quarter to one, a private car appeared at the head of the road. Harry jogged over to it and the driver rolled down the window.

'My good man,' Harry said, 'I'm Mr Sallow, the butler of Blye House. May I enquire who you're here to collect?'

'Ah, Mr Sallow! Er, lemme see,' the driver said, reading something on his dash screen. 'Bloke called Montgomery.'

'Ah, Monty, excellent. I was asked to meet you at the gate, do you mind if I hop in the back and you can drive up to the house?'

'No problem, sir.'

Harry opened the back door and climbed inside. The car rolled up to the gate and the driver pushed the buzzer. After a few seconds the gates clicked open and slid apart. He drove on up the resin driveway while Harry crouched down in the back of the car.

The driver looked at him funny in the rear-view mirror.

'You all right back there, sir?'

'As all right,' Harry said, 'as a man with no left.'

Harry peeped through the windshield. The CCTV camera at the top of the house was pointing down at them. He stayed low until they had circled the fountain, stopped at the front door and the camera was no longer in sight.

'Perfect,' Harry grinned, hopping out. 'Er, I'll just go and fetch old Monty. Back in a tick.'

He got out of the car and then quickly marched round the side of the building and into the dark. His heart was back running up and down his chest again. But once he was leaning against the cold brick, he knew he had done it.

He stayed there for some time. Eventually the driver had to get out and knock on the door and then a few minutes later, a drunk old man was escorted to the car by his wife. They got in the back and it disappeared from the property.

By one, Harry trusted that everyone had left. There hadn't been a peep in twenty minutes and while there were still a few cars on the drive, he assumed they belonged to the guests too drunk to drive. Taxis and hire cars had been up and down all night ferrying people. But now everything was still.

Harry slipped round to the back, took the Safe-T-Bolt spare key from his breast pocket and slid it in the lock. He turned it very quietly, the door clicked open and he snuck inside Blye House for one last time.

Chapter 9

The abrupt ending to the party had clearly extended beyond the guests to the staff, because the place was left a complete mess, as if everyone had up and left without lifting a finger. Harry entered through the kitchen and saw it was in disrepair. It was like being back on Milk Street. Hundreds of plates of half-eaten food were hastily stacked in teetering columns and there were bottles and glasses sticking up through the gloom like the tombstones of a glassware graveyard.

It didn't matter that it was dark. Mess or no mess, Harry could navigate that place with his eyes shut, like the Minotaur in his labyrinth. He reached the pantry door, felt his way along the wall, moved down the hall and then wandered for twenty yards until he reached the ballroom.

The doors were ajar. He slipped around one and allowed his eyes to adjust. Three mullioned windows pooled cool, pastel light inside. It sparkled off the glass display cabinet opposite.

It was a lot eerier than Harry had anticipated. He was quite alone in the enormous room, wandering through the abandoned hall like the sole remaining human of a world-wide rapture. And though he was not a skittish person, if Sallow had popped around the door and said, 'Hello, sir,' he was quite certain he would have a massive stroke and die.

He reached the display cabinet and looked inside. The pistols took centre place on the velvet mound, but they were surrounded by a chalice, a tin flute, an old diary and, at the back there, the long stiletto blade.

Harry clicked the case open and ran his hands along the contents. He had a good mind to steal the whole lot. He shut the pistols into their box, fastened the clasp and stuffed it in his satchel. He turned to leave just as a glint of moonlight caught the emerald in the handle of the stiletto blade.

Harry stared at the dagger for a second longer.

'Well,' he whispered, 'in for a penny…'

He snatched the blade and slipped it delicately into his suit pocket.

As he left the ballroom and tiptoed back to the kitchen, Harry felt quite pleased with himself. He had expected more from Sallow. If it was this easy to break into the place he was surprised it had never been attempted by proper burglars. They'd have a field day with the collection of tax-free art.

He continued feeling pleased with himself right until he reached the back door when the kitchen lights flashed on. Then his heart stopped in his chest and all he thought was: *Sod it*. The great pistol larceny, thwarted at the last hurdle.

He turned round and was surprised to see it was not Sallow, but his father, who stood in the doorway. Richard was in a dressing gown and looked just as surprised to find Harry there as Harry did to see him.

'Harrington!' he said. 'What are you doing now?'

Harry had no smart retort. 'Hullo father,' he said, his voice lost in a swelling throat. 'I, er... must have been sleepwalking.'

'Don't be ridiculous. Sallow said he saw you out. I hope to God you didn't break a window to get in here.'

'Ta-da,' he brandished the Safe-T Bolt. 'Spare key.'

'Sallow said he removed the spare key.'

'Yes, well *Sallow* was mistaken. He removed something he thought was the spare key but was not.'

Richard let out a long, extended breath. 'I came down to make some tea. Why don't you join me for one in my study and we can talk?'

Harry sat behind the desk in Richard's study while his father made the tea. The desk was very neatly arranged. On one side, a golden Parker in a pen-canoe was carefully laid beside a notepad of letter-headed paper. To the other was a handsome green-glass desk lamp. The only mess came from a stack of opened mail, which Harry leafed through idly with the letter-opener. He recognised the handwriting of one and slid it out to read through.

Dear father, the thing began. *What a funny little man you are. Sincerely, Mr Burden, your son.*

Suddenly Harry didn't find it as funny as he had when he composed the piece.

276

He heard his father coming down the hall and quickly scrunched the letter up and threw it into the waste-paper bin.

'So,' Richard said, setting down a tea tray of china cups beside the mail-in. 'What do you *want*, Harry?'

'I don't know,' Harry answered, honestly. A tear had just rolled down his cheek and it surprised him. 'I've come without hostile intentions but they have a way of finding me, you see.'

'Please. Do you recall last summer when I said you have that rebellious streak that blossoms in the afternoon hearts of young men, but wilts by a quarter to nine? Well I was *wrong*. I admit it. It's already nine and you're as stubborn as ever—'

'Please,' Harry blurted out. He was shaking, hand and voice. It was involuntary and the words that came out of him weren't his own. 'I'm awfully sorry. Awfully. I was out of control.'

'*Was*?'

'Am.'

'Always *are*.'

'That's not fair. I'm a strange mélange of good and evil, I admit—'

'Well you're too late!' Richard barked. 'About *five hours* too late!'

'No, no,' Harry blubbered, looking at his great-grandfather's watch. Five hours ago was pre-mooning. He shook his head rapidly from side to side and wiped his nose across a sleeve. 'I *know* you said it was my final *final* chance, but let me have one *final* final *final* chance. I beg you, you'll see a marked difference in my attitude—'

'Unless you've fathomed time travel,' Richard said, 'there's nothing more you can do—'

'Please, please, *please*…'

Harry had fallen to his knees. He was sobbing with tears now and clutching at the bottom of his father's dressing gown.

'You're embarrassing yourself. Get *off* me. I've already told you, *you're too late*. We're done.'

Richard forced Harry back. That only made Harry bawl harder.

'It doesn't have to be over,' Harry pleaded, desperately. 'You can put me on probation. You'll see. You don't have to give me any money or anything at all. Just don't say it's all over. You can keep tabs on me and, and, yes, you'll see how well I do. I'll… I'll work for van der Sar. Or I'll speak with Mr l'Hiver, I know that's why you invited him tonight. You want me to publish something—'

'Ha!' Richard bellowed. 'You really think l'Hiver wants *any*thing to do with you? Like every bridge I've ever tried building, you've burned it to the docks.'

'I know. I know I do that,' Harry said, with his head in his hands. He thought he might be able to plug the leak with his fingers, but his face glistened from the waterfall and it spurted out between his knuckles. 'You just don't understand. Your interference. *That* is what puts me off. If you just let me do things by myself… And now with van der Sar… It's all for *what*? Certainly not *my* benefit. It's only your reputation you care about. Come on. Deny it.'

'*Yes*, all right, *it bloody well is*!' Richard agreed. 'Do you remember what I said to you, years ago? Before you went off to Harrow? I told you the most important thing you could do there was to make friends with a future politician. Do you remember that? And you asked how you were supposed to know *who* would end up becoming a politician—?'

'And then *you* made the dramatic revelation that was precisely your point—I should whore myself to everyone to ingratiate myself to the elite.'

'Harrow isn't a place for education,' Richard went on eruditely. 'These schools are the most expensive and exclusive boy's clubs in the country. How do you think *I* got started in business? My company was only six months old with *one* client to our name when it was picked up in a governmental contract. And do you know *why*?'

'Because one cold winter's morning in eighteen eighty-something, while the gang were off playing ruggers, you took the future Prime Minister's chief financial advisor off to the stalls for a quick blowie?'

'*Because*,' Richard said, ignoring Harry, 'I made friends with the *right people*. But *you*? Not only did you drop out of Harrow when you were a toe's width from the finish line, you decided to read *literature* or some such dagger to the heart at the country's lav, where I assume you attended roughly *zero* lectures from the distinctly average grades you came away with. And did you make any friends of importance while there? Did you buggery! Instead you came away knowing precisely *one* creature, who you then had the *gall* to sneak into the house *I* pay for, free of charge! It is preposterousness itself that you think I would be anything other than outraged at such an arrangement.'

Harry didn't know what to say to that. In the end he just said, 'I want my money.'

'What money?' Richard spat.

'The money my mother left. Fifty thousand pounds if I'm not mistaken.'

'*That* money was for investments or property. Or a *wedding*, if such things from you are likely. If I give you that money now, I know just what it'll go on and—'

'I am not a child!' Harry screamed. 'I *demand* my money.'

'Even if I *wanted* to give it to you, I simply don't keep that kind of money in the house.'

'Then give me what you have and you can send the rest later. Sallow told me you've already started to pack up my things for storage. I'm sure you can just add it to the junk pile.'

Richard looked set to argue but decided not to. He walked over to a safe in his desk draw and took out three stacks of neatly wrapped bills.

Before handing them over, he said, 'If your mother were here now… she wouldn't even recognise you.'

There were tears rolling down Harry's cheeks. He pocketed the cash and the cold metal of the stiletto grazed the back of his hand. He thought about taking the dagger out and inserting it right into the top of the old man's backbone. He'd have to find one first, of course.

'Now,' Richard said, turning his back to Harry. 'If we're done here, I want you to get out of my house.'

'Your house. *Your* house…' Harry swallowed. Those words didn't sit well with him. The stream dried up and he was angry now. He was looking quite firmly at the top of his father's spine. The stiletto would decorate it so nicely. 'But this *isn't* your house. It was my *mother's*. It should be *mine*.'

Richard growled, 'This house has belonged to me for twenty-four years! And let me tell you something else, when I change my will in the morning, I'll make sure it's iron-clad Harry-proof at that!'

'You can't!' Harry's lip was quivering. 'Take everything from me but my house.'

Richard spun round and his face was more serious than ever. 'And it's not just *this* house I'm pulling from your greedy little claws either! I'm taking the house on Milk Street too. So you can go and tell that little faggot you live with to look for someone else to leech off of!'

Harry had no words. He could hear a whistling in his head and his vision became blurry. He charged at his old man, knocked him back across the desk and wrapped his hands around his throat, squeezing as tightly as he could.

Richard's face was one of purest shock.

They writhed around the desk, scattering the papers and sending the glass lamp and tray of china shattering across the waxed floor.

Richard started to sputter. His eyes bulged and his hair, whichever part of it wasn't glued down, was coming off at an angle.

Harry's teeth were clenched as he violently strangled his father. His face was almost as red as Richard's, and a huge vein was bulging at his temple, threatening to pop.

Richard's hands scavenged across the surface of his desk in desperation. Almost everything had been knocked to the floor and all he could feel was the tray of opened mail. He reached into it and felt something solid among the paper.

It was the handle of his ruby inlay letter-opener. He swung it at Harry, three, four, five times as he continued to retch and choke and wheeze. One swing caught the back of Harry's forearm. Harry flinched but adrenaline was coursing through him so aggressively that he did little else. Another swipe found its way to Harry's wrist where it struck his watch and shattered its glass face. And then came the sixth swing. The blade lodged itself between two of Harry's ribs with a surprising crackle.

Harry let go of his father's neck at once. They both looked down at Richard's hand which held the blade, now deep in Harry's side. Harry promptly turned chalk-white and staggered a foot back.

'Oh *well* done,' Harry gasped. 'You've killed me.'

Richard let go of the handle and the blade slipped out from the wound. Harry felt it. The full four inches of metal, leaving his body. It slid out through the moist warmth of his insides, scraped against two rib bones and a burst of cold air rushed in.

A great spatter of blood spurted out and painted Richard's horrified face. Harry fell another step back and slid to the floor.

Part V

Chapter 1

The Barrow had been silent for some time. Rose and Emily were asleep at opposite ends of the settee while Tom had his back to them both, tucked beneath the kitchen island, still with the rifle slung around his back.

Rose stirred. It was almost daybreak outside and the cabin had filled with soft pastel light. She looked at her watch—it was six o'clock on Monday morning. They had been waiting for the police to arrive all night.

She had to laugh. Tom heard her stirring but didn't move more than his head, so she got up and stretched and yawned and went through the patio doors for a smoke. All the while she stared at the back of his head through the glass and she struggled to find anything in her heart where love ought to be. She could only think a monster of him.

Not long after Charlie went up to the loft last night, she had told Tom just where Harry was.

She couldn't keep it in. Not when he had been going on and on the way he had. The police, he had reminded them for the fiftieth time, were en route. And they'd search the heavens and the oceans to find him.

'Well you needn't bother!' she had snapped, fed up with it all. 'I know just where Harry is, he's up on that mountain the Yarrowsomething. If you're so keen why don't you go up there yourself and arrest him?'

She had known he wouldn't. Of course he wouldn't—he was more mouth than muscle. But she enjoyed pushing those buttons all the same.

Tom had just mumbled something about 'waiting for the fuzz' but she could see the cogs in his brain were in overdrive. Something sparked out one ear and smoke billowed after it. 'How do *you* know where he is, anyway?' He had asked it with suspicion flashing in his eyes.

'He sent me a postcard,' she said facetiously. 'He probably assumed *you* can't read.'

Tom grunted. '*However* you found out,' he said, 'it weren't very clever of him to let *you* know where he's gone. You've got one of the biggest gobs in all of England.'

'Yes, second place only to you,' she said, studying her nails.

'Why are you acting like this?'

'Like what?'

'Like you're in fucking *love with him* or something?'

'Because you're a beast. And I *do* love Harry. More than I could ever love a disgusting creature like you.'

'What? You *love* him? How can you be in love with that anaemic stick insect?'

'I'm not *in* love with him, you pathetic man. But Harry is a sensitive and intelligent person and I just think he deserves so much more than all of this!'

'Deserves more?' Tom was seeing red again. She might as well have just told him the two of them were having an affair.

He took a long look at the fury in her eyes and it looked to Rose that he could finally see now that she really meant what she said about him. These weren't the hurtful words of the hurt; these were real feelings, nudged to the surface after being pushed deep down into the Earth for too long.

'What's the matter with you?' he asked more calmly.

'You are!' she squeaked. 'I've had a think. About everything. And our tower of resentment has just about reached its limit. The final brick has caused it to collapse. It's debris now. That's what our relationship is. Debris!'

'What are you on about?'

'Oh nothing,' she had turned to the window to avoid looking at his stupid, concrete face, but she could still make it out in the reflection. He was unavoidable. 'I'm just having some very serious reservations about you.'

'You're having reservations?'

And Rose just threw her head back and laughed bitterly, shaking her blonde hair down her back. They didn't speak after that. Tom sat at the island, she on the settee and the next thing she knew she was waking up on Monday morning.

Presently she stubbed her cigarette out and threw it into the hot tub where it floated with all the other creatures the water had consumed that weekend, while a tear scrolled down her cheek.

Chapter 2

When Rose returned to the lodge, she was poised to say something to Tom. She didn't know if she wanted to scold him or apologise. Fortunately, she didn't need to decide on either course of action because she was interrupted by a heavy wrapping at the door.

Emily, who had been sleeping still on the settee, sprang to her feet. A look of trepidation flew from her to Tom. Tom, in particular, looked unsettled.

Rose, on the other hand, looked positively delighted.

'That must be the police,' she said giddily. 'I *must* see their faces when you tell them you lost the prisoner *and* all of the evidence. Perhaps *you* will be the one that ends up in a cell. For wasting police time.'

Tom ignored her and pulled the door open. But as they crowded round the door, they saw that it was not the police standing out on the porch.

Fletcher Monk grinned up at them and his teeth niggled like loose tombstones.

'You've got some bloody nerve,' Tom said, stepping onto the porch.

'Yer know me, then?' he smiled.

'Aye,' Tom answered. 'You're the cheeky fucker who tried to flood me X200.'

'Flood yer *what?*'

'The Merc.'

'Ah. That I am, aye,' Monk admitted, scratching his wiry beard and looking round at the car on the drive. 'An' you're the bastard who *put a bullet through one of me cows*. So I'd say we're about even, wouldn't you, big boy?'

Tom scowled. Rose briefly thought he might thump the farmer round the side of the head. But Tom pointed to an enormous shadow lurking in the treeline. And the shadow was holding a Winchester repeating rifle.

'If we're even,' Tom asked, 'why are you here? And why've you brought back up?'

'His name's Pinner,' Monk said. 'He's a big thing i'nt he? Even fer you he must be pretty imposin', eh?'

Monk walked along the porch and stooped to look in through the window and he wrapped on the glass with his cankerous knuckles.

'Get away from there and tell me what you want.'

'Tell yer what I want,' Monk repeated, standing back upright, with all the humour evaporating from his face and his tone. 'I'm lookin' fer a friend of yours. *Friend by the name of Harrington Burden*. Is he home?'

Monk stood wonkily inside The Barrow, with a hand resting on the top of his leg brace. Emily and Rose sat quite stiffly on the edge of the settee, staring at him as he leered back.

Tom read through the newspaper article that the old farmer had given to him and his face transformed into disbelief.

'Listen to this,' he said. '*Harrington Burden, aged twenty-four, has been missing since Friday evening. Following a lavish ball thrown at the heir's family home in West London, the young man has not been seen since leaving the gated property. Several witnesses claim there was a heated argument between the young man and his father—controversial contractor, Richard Burden— but that the young man was seen to leave the property in the early morning. A close friend of the family said they are particularly concerned about Harrington's mental state as his disappearance follows a recent suicide attempt.*'

Tom slammed the paper on the coffee table. A black and white photo of Harry in his cricket garb was smiling up at them.

'Is that *true*? Silly bugger tried to off himself?'

'Charlie *did* suggest something along those lines,' Emily said carefully. 'But that was only on Saturday and it was the first *I'd* heard of it. But... well it makes *sense*, I suppose.'

'No it doesn't make sense, not one *bit*,' Rose said, failing to understand anything about the article. 'Harry wouldn't do that. And I don't see why they're only *looking* for him and he isn't a wanted man. If they're only *looking* for him, then that means he couldn't *possibly* have stabbed his father.'

'*Stabbed* his father?' Tom repeated. 'What are you on about?'

'That was simply *one* hypothesis,' Emily explained. She had noticed Monk's interest piqued and he swapped a dark look with Pinner that she didn't understand.

'Well it's a hypothesis you didn't bother to share wimme,' Tom said.

'And this article makes barely *any* mention of his father at all,' Rose went on, reading through it again with interest. '*Surely* if he had *killed* the man, it would be the central feature of the piece?'

'You think he *killed* his old man?' Tom said, trying to catch up. Then he shrugged. 'Summat like that can tank a company's stocks,' he said matter-of-factly. 'If the old man were dead, they might keep it hush-hush for a bit.'

'Anyway, even if he *didn't* stab his father, that doesn't make Harry *innocent*,' Emily explained. 'And likewise, just because they're *looking* for Harry, that doesn't mean he's not wanted by the police either. All this article tells me is that Harry went to Blye House on Friday evening.'

'I suppose,' Rose said, frowning. She looked up at Monk and snarled: 'I fail to see what any of this has to do with *you*.'

Monk smirked. 'Has more to do wi' me than you know, missy. See, early morning' Sat'day I get woke up by a great bleedin' crash. Some bastard has ploughed through me barn. Took out one wall, then the supportin' beam, an' then come crashin' right through the other. An' d'yer know what he left behind?'

'No.'

Monk took something from his coat and shuffled over to the coffee table where he placed an envelope on top of the newspaper.

For your barn, it said in black marker. *Ever so sorry.*

Inside was a thick wedge of cash.

'It's true that I *were* looking fer you lot after what yers did to me cow. But that were just a minor bit o' hassle compared with what *he's* done round this village. An' that envelope of cash… it's an insult, is what that is! Even if I were to accept it as apology, that won't go nowhere near coverin' the cost o' the damage.'

'How did you find us here?'

289

Monk chuckled. 'Wasn't too difficult. Though I can't say luck din't have nowt to do with it.

'After I found that envelope in me barn, I put a call out. Asked round the village if anyone'd seen a lanky streak of piss on a motorbike, parading through town like a bat outta bleedin' hell. Nobody had o' course. That is, *not until this afternoon.*'

Monk had shuffled over to the bookcase and taken an interest in the bowl of potpourri, picking it up in his grubby fingers.

'I got a call from Allan Hobbs. *You lot* know Hobbs o' course. He's the ferryman what took yers off to Potter Island t'other day. Well I'm sure yers know what *he* had to say?'

Tom felt his neck turning red.

'What did he say?' Rose squeaked.

Monk stuck a piece of potpourri in his mouth like a crisp and chewed on it undecidedly. 'Said he went back there yesterd'y to fetch yers. Only when he gets there, he finds the island empty. An' the whole bleedin' cabin's been destroyed. Furniture broken, windows all smashed... But sittin' on that mountain o' glass, he finds an envelope. Just like *that* one.'

Rose looked back at the envelope.

For your barn, it said in tall black letters. *Ever so sorry.* Harry, you rascal, it reads like utter sarcasm!

The red had worked its way up Tom's neck and was starting on the face.

'An' d'yer know what else Hobbs tells me?' Monk asked. His voice had grown louder and he had a more animated look in the madness of his eye.

'No,' Rose whispered. It was all she could muster; her throat had closed for business.

'He said the oddball what booked the trip arrived there by *motorbike*. An' he said he drove the bleedin' thing into the lake. *Like a bat outta bleedin' hell.*'

Monk snorted with disgust.

'*Well*, I thought, *that sounds like my barn-wrecker all right*!' he continued to anger. 'The real bombshell came from what he tells me next. Y'see Hobbs tells me there were four others with the barn-wrecker. Two bits o' totty,' he eyed the girls, 'one big lad and one skinny'un,' he said turning the eye on Tom. He looked round for Charlie too.

'He's upstairs,' Tom said. 'But I'm still waiting to hear how you found us here.'

'I'm gettin' to that,' Monk said. 'But ah! That were a nice little coincidence, I thought. The same kids what killed me cow and the bastard what destroyed me barn are all up here together. That would make things nice an' easy fer findin' yers.'

'But you said you're not after us!' Rose piped up, on her feet with some strength she didn't know she possessed. '*You* said you were only after Harry!'

He stared her down for a moment until she felt the weight of his gaze on her shoulders and sat back down in her seat.

'I'm not after yers,' he said. 'Not anymore, at least. Not since... well since sommet else come up. But I *was* this afternoon. When Hobbs told me all this on the blower, I had a good mind to put that dog o' yours down, fer what yers did to my cow.'

'You monster!'

Monk didn't like that. He grew very serious and his lip curled. 'I am no monster, missy. I'm about the only one in here who isn't!'

'Get to the point old man,' Tom said.

Monk let himself calm down and continued. 'Aye,' he said. 'Aye. Well after that little scene yers caused today at the pub, I got me second call. This one was from Nelson—the barman at The White Pony. He told me about what happened there. An' he figured this fella what caused all the trouble might jus' be the same bloke I were lookin' fer. He didn't know where yers were staying, unfortunately. But he did tell me sommet interesting.

'He said he'd seen that skinny lad upstairs talkin' with someone we know.'

'Charlie? With *who*?' asked Rose.

Emily put it together. 'Mr Bramble,' she said.

'Aye, Mr Bramble,' Monk nodded.

'Right, so *Mr Bramble* told you where we're staying?' Tom asked.

291

'Peter Bramble din't tell me bugger all,' Monk wheezed. 'That old sod's as stubborn as a dead mule. Pinner paid him a visit an' all Bramble would say was he'd never heard of yers. It were his *fridge* what betrayed him.'

'His *fridge*?' Rose scoffed. 'What *are* you going on about you strange little man?'

His lip curled again. 'Show 'em, Pinner.'

Pinner moved for the first time. He bounded across the room and placed a scrap of paper by the envelope of cash.

Dear Mr Bramble, it said in Charlie's spidery handwriting, *here's your dog. We found him in a meadow. From Harry and Charlie, of The Barrow.*

'The old bugger might've thought he didn't sell yers down the river,' Monk grinned. 'But he did. Pinner found that stuck to his fridge.'

'Alright,' Tom breathed. His mind was in overdrive as he thought his way out of this. 'I'm not gonna defend him. Harry's been bulldozing his way round Gallows since he got here. And he's dragged us into it with him. Let's say I knew where he were—what are you planning to do with him?'

Monk's eye sparkled.

'I'm the Alderman of this village. All's I want is to bring him to the police.'

'Bull-*shit*,' Emily said accusingly. She almost laughed. 'You're not the Alderman. Charlie heard your little meeting when we arrived here. The people don't *want* you in charge.'

Monk's lip curled a third time and he looked round at Pinner under a long rippling caterpillar of eyebrow.

'Aye, when you lot arrived, I weren't Alderman, it's true,' he said, with the caterpillar returning to a flat line. 'But a lot has happened this afternoon. When I called a meeting an' told everyone all about this Harrington bloke, they agreed sommet needed to be done. I told 'em how he wrecked me barn, dumped a bike in the lake, levelled the cabin on that island. What he did in Nelson's pub and how he leaves these parcels of cash behind, like he can do what he wants on our little side of paradise an' jus' buy his way out. They finally saw things my way.'

'What, just like *that*? They say you're the Mayor of Trumpton and you're suddenly free to go rounding up undesirables like you're the SS?'

'No,' Monk admitted. 'Weren't that easy. Might surprise yer to hear but they don't like me very much, the people o' Gallows. But Bill an' Jane Corkington? They *do* like me.'

'And who are Bill and Jane Corkington when they're at home?'

'Bill an' Jane Corkington happen to be the owners of that cabin what yers destroyed on Potter Island! They also happen to own several other buildings round here an' are very well liked. *And* they happen to be very well connected. Particul'ly with the local councils. And they *do* have that type o' power. So with their backin', an' with that of some important pillars of the community you've managed to upset over the course of this weekend, *yes*, I've been given the job of Alderman.'

'*What* important pillars of the community?'

'List is practic'ly endless. There's Nelson fer one. Yers caused a right scene in there. Called his kid a prossie, I believe. Then there's Reverend Dobson—'

'That weird vicar? What've we done to *him*?'

'He tells us yers barged into his church—the House of the Lord, need I remind yers—only to bicker an' fight. On a Sunday! An' when yers left, yer snapped the bleedin' wing off one of his angels! D'yer know what sort of a sin it is to break the wing off an angel?'

'No.'

'Type that condemns yer to Hell.'

'So let me get this straight. All this bullshit is your way of saying you're here to arrest us?'

'No,' Monk said. 'Yer not listenin'. I'm only after this Harrington.'

'Why?' Rose asked suspiciously. 'We were all there when he caused all the trouble you've mentioned. We're just as guilty.'

'That may be,' Monk said, 'but I'm Alderman now. I'm actin' on behalf of the community. An' they say this Harrington's the ringleader an' they want him. So he's the one I'm after.'

'He's got a point,' Tom said.

'No he hasn't got a single point in the world,' Rose snapped. 'He's essentially a circle. Why do they suppose Harry is the ringleader? Why do they even *need* a ringleader, why don't they want to see us all strung up in that village square?'

'Shut up,' Tom said, 'can you give us a minute?' he asked the farmer.

Monk shrugged and retreated to the corner with Pinner.

Tom turned back to Rose and spoke in a whisper. 'We might've been part of all that trouble but Harry *is* the one to blame for it. Mr Monk here's offering us summat like a, whatdjacallit—? A plea deal, right? And all he's gonna do is hand Harry over to the fuzz, which is what we were gonna do ourselves until he disappeared into thin air. If helping him means *we* get let off, then so be it. Harry's getting off light as far as I'm concerned.'

'You despicable coward,' Rose said, trying to restrain him, with tears in her eyes.

He had turned back to the little farmer a final time and Rose's efforts, tugging on those marble arms, were futile.

'If I take yous to him, all you're gonna do is take him to the police?'

'Aye,' Monk said.

'And you're not gonna press charges against any of us four?'

'Not a single charge.'

Tom swallowed. 'I can take your word on that?'

'Tom, *no*, of course you can't!'

'Quiet,' Tom snapped.

'What are you *doing*? You're making a deal with the actual devil. Look at him for goodness's sake, Tom. He has hoofs for feet.'

'Shut up, Rose,' Tom said, looking Monk squarely in the face. 'I don't *need* help overpowering Harry. But he *is* a crafty bastard and he's escaped us once already tonight.' He looked up at Pinner. 'A bit of extra muscle couldn't hurt, could it?'

'Tom, think about this,' Emily said. 'Whether you're right or not, we really shouldn't be letting *this* man make that decision.'

Monk and Tom were still staring at one another intently.

'If you take us to him,' Monk said, holding out a hand, 'we'll help yer bring him in. Nowt more. I'm the *Alderman*. I want justice, that's all.'

Tom looked down at the hand. It was filthy. The skin was yellowing and calloused and the nails were an inch long. Something like maggots appeared to squirm beneath the flesh. Then it disappeared beneath his own great mitt.

Chapter 3

On the Yarrowmoor Mountain, Charlie's head was exploding.

'So then your father...' he began. 'Your father... *He...* stabbed *you*?'

'That's right.' Harry answered.

'So then that knife? It was the letter-opener? And all that blood...'

'Mine.'

'And I suppose you didn't crash through Monk's barn after all?'

'Oh, I crashed through Monk's barn all right. I was driving with a head full of snow, old thing. But that isn't how I injured myself. I've just been bleeding from the old stab wound.'

He patted at the place the blade had been.

'Is it bad?' Charlie asked.

'I wouldn't exactly say it was *good*. But I didn't die, so there's that. I just feel awfully woozy which might account for my behaviour being more unusual than usual. I'm not quite on the level, you see.'

Charlie couldn't believe it. He had to take a seat. They'd been up on the hilltop for hours as Harry struggled to tell the full story. The wind had whipped up something fierce. Teddy sat and chewed at a tuft and though Harry was on his feet, he was still feet from the crag.

'It's outrageous! It's madness...' Charlie paused, thinking it all over. 'It's impossible to believe, but... Well, but... *but...*'

'*But?*' Harry asked, frowning.

'But—well I should say, I'm *relieved*,' Charlie responded, and he could almost have laughed.

'*Relieved?*' Harry looked appalled by the statement.

'Of course I'm relieved. All this time I thought you'd done something awful. We've discussed armed robberies and *murder*. And all this time *you* were the victim.'

'Is that how you see it? Charlie *I tried to kill him*! I tried to choke him to death.'

'Oh you never would have done it.'

Charlie started to laugh for real now. He had been so full of tension, so filled with turmoil, like his stomach was a cauldron of electric eels, that to hear Harry Burden's story was to become un-Burdened.

'Why do you say that?'

'Because I *know* you.'

'You might know *me*, but you don't know the person I became with my hands around my father's throat. *I* don't even know that person. I've never been so angry in all my life, Charlie. I wanted him dead and I think… I think he *would be* if he hadn't found that letter-opener.'

Charlie found it difficult to imagine the Harry he knew capable of murder. But Harry looked deeply troubled.

'Still,' Charlie said as cautiously as he could, 'it's hardly worth *killing yourself* over now, is it?' he asked.

'Didn't you hear the bit about the lawyer and what-not? I'm written out of the will. And on account of a mooning.'

'Do you really think he's going to write you out of his will after he stabbed you like that? And anyway, even if he does, who cares? You're *alive*, Harry. You could be in a coffin in the drawing room of Blye House with a powder-white face and pink cheeks and a giant knife sticking out of your guts. But instead you're threatening to chuck yourself off a mountain in the most beautiful place on Earth. I think that's worth celebrating, don't you? What did Shakespeare say about England? It's another Eden and er, something about a spectre?'

Harry answered quite automatically: 'He called it a royal throne of Kings, a sceptred isle, an earth of majesty, a seat of Mars, and on and on.'

'Exactly, and wait! Do you hear that?'

Harry listened. 'Birdsong isn't it?'

'Birdsong indeed. Nature's alarm clock. The dawn chorus, spreading wherever the sun hits.'

Harry rolled his eyes at the phony optimism. '"*Such little cause for carollings of such ecstatic sound*",' he droned. '*That's* Thomas Hardy.'

But he had to admit there were a lot of birds out for this time of morning. They hurried to and fro in mad disquietude. Rooks and choughs and carrion crows in murmuration.

Charlie was still figuring things out. There was so much clanging around in his head, and he was pacing up and down like a prison guard, that he hadn't noticed the birds.

'And all this stuff with the news?' he asked. 'You hiding the papers from us. You're not a *wanted man*, you're a *missing person*?'

'Children disappear every day and nobody cares,' said Harry glibly. 'And when you're an adult you should be lucky to even get a report filed. But *my* father happens to be a multi-billionaire, which means I *did* make the paper—a whopping half-inch of article and on page forty-seven. And let me just point out, my father stabbed me before two A.M. on Saturday. By the time the papers were out that morning, I was already in it! *That* is his influence, once again, engulfing my life.'

'And the TV?' Charlie asked.

'I doubt I made the *TV* news,' Harry said, reasonably. 'But I didn't want to risk it. If you saw my face pop up on there you'd be liable to start all this lark and nonsense. So I unscrewed it.'

'And at The White Pony?'

'What do you mean?'

'You caused that great big song and dance to get us thrown out because the Weekend News was about to start. Didn't you?'

Harry smirked. 'You think I'm *that* wily?'

'You're not *that* wily, but you're wily.'

Harry looked disappointed by the reply.

'While I would *like* to say that my behaviour at the pub was the workings of a meticulous ploy timed to the second,' he said, 'that little performance was merely a symptom of my bombastic personality.'

'I just don't get you Harry. The only reason to keep *any of this* a secret is to protect your father. But you *loathe* your father.'

'I'm complicated,' he said. 'And anyway it wasn't to protect him. I tried to bloody throttle the man! You seem to be under the ridiculous assumption he suddenly regrets what he did to me and is out to make things right. But I know my father better than that. If he knew where I was right now he would have me arrested for attempted murder.'

He looked back down at Teddy.

'Then what happened next?' asked Charlie. 'After he stuck you one?'

'I picked up the letter-opener and I'm not sorry to admit that I considered sticking the thing right between his eyes. But only for, oh, *half* a second. I was too shaken to follow through on the endeavour even if I'd really wanted to. Instead I put it in my pocket and ran out of the room. And that was the last time I saw him.'

'He didn't follow you?'

'He was more shaken than I was. He sat down behind his desk looking like a ghost after he stabbed me. I doubt he could muster the energy to give chase. Anyway I had left the property within ten minutes.'

'Right,' Charlie nodded, 'you got on the bike and headed up here?'

'First I staggered back to the kitchen. The pantry keeps a fire extinguisher and a medical kit and such. I cleaned myself up and wrapped bandages around my ribcage. It was while I bandaged myself that I decided I would come *here*. My mind was all over the place. I knew I needed to get far, *far* away from London, and I didn't want my father to find me. Milk Street would be the first place to look. And then I thought of you, here in this splendid isolation. I even had the Post-It Note you'd given me in my pocket. *The Barrow, Fri-Mon* so I knew how to find you.'

Harry drifted from the ledge and slumped down beside Charlie on a boulder and they watched the sun rise together.

'Before I left, I thought about those duelling pistols,' he said. 'The look on my father's face as he talked about them. He had never looked at me that way. I was angry again and decided that I may as well finish what I'd come to do. I took the box and started for the garage where my father keeps all the sports cars he never drives. The Triumph, I knew, would be sitting there.'

'Go on?'

'What I also found in the garage were all my things Sallow had been packaging up. Boxes and boxes of them. All neatly arranged and labelled against the back wall of the garage.'

'I see. So that's where we get your Harrow uniform from, I assume?'

'I felt that to leave it would be like leaving a piece of my soul behind. There was a duffle bag among the boxes and I just stuffed it in there.'

'And the wine?'

'The wine was among a small collection of his best wines, at hand for the party.'

Charlie flicked a pebble off the mountain. 'What about the money. How much was it?'

'Twenty, give or take.'

'Twenty thousand! And now you've blown it all in a single weekend.'

'Not a weekend, a *lifetime* dear boy. This is the end of the road, I've told you. That money lasted me to my final day. A grey cloud has been following me my entire life and I've constantly tried to mine it for its silver lining—but all I get is rain. But don't worry, Charlie-Boy, the worms come for us all eventually.'

'Stop talking like that. It's starting to annoy me. You're not about to kill yourself because I know you're not that selfish.'

'*Selfish*? I'm doing the world a favour. Might be the most selfless act a Burden's ever performed.'

'And what about me?'

'What *about* you? For five years, I've dragged you into the murky depths of my weird world and refused to let you surface. You've a house now, south of the river. You can go and live your life with the doctor. I don't fit into that jigsaw.'

'It doesn't matter where I live or who with,' said Charlie crossly. 'I'm not going to stop being your friend and it isn't the end of the world. You didn't think we were going to live together *forever* did you?'

'No,' Harry admitted.

Eventually, the sun creeped in across the clouds. They sat and watched it without another word until the bruises in the sky disappeared.

Chapter 4

It was around seven o'clock in the morning when Charlie stood up very suddenly and walked a few feet across the mountain.

At the bottom of the hill were several figures. A painful lump rose in his throat as they started the climb.

Charlie groaned.

'Let me guess,' Harry said, without moving his eyes from the water on the other side of the world. 'Thomas Darrow is heading this way—no doubt with a mob of angry villagers in tow?'

He was half right. Tom's enormous shape leading the pack uphill was hard to mistake. The two slender figures behind him must have been Emily and Rose. And behind them were two others. The bent-backed wiry character at the back, who dragged his caged leg heavily behind with each step, was undoubtedly Fletcher Monk. The giant man before him, Charlie assumed, was the same man who had visited Bramble. Pinner, he had said his name was.

'What are they all doing together?' Harry asked, standing beside Charlie now.

'Must've found out where we were staying,' Charlie said.

'But what do they want coming up *here*? That old farmer can barely walk.'

It was true that some distance had fallen between Monk and the figure in front of him. Tom, in the lead, was close enough now that Teddy had stood up, evidently smelling his musk on the wind.

Charlie had a very strange feeling settle over him. A feeling that a showdown was about to take place. The sun was rising. The sky was filled with hundreds of birds. The wind was up and rustling the long tufts of grass between the boulders. And now Charlie's heart was hammering away in his chest.

The dog began to bark as Tom lugged himself up onto the summit. Teddy ran over and Tom threw himself to his knees to rub the dog's belly in the dirt.

'Teddy!' he cried in shock.

Charlie could see Tom was checking the collar for his engagement ring.

Rose's voice (complaining bitterly about the wind and the mud and the birds) came up the hillside before she did. When she did appear, Teddy leapt ten feet into the air and charged at her, licking her as she broke into elated sobs.

'Where was he?' Tom asked.

He was brown-faced and glistening and tried not to smile too much, but the sight of Teddy had betrayed whatever anger he had meant to show.

'He was down there,' Harry pointed. 'Found me when I slipped on a thing and landed in another.'

'Did you er—'

'Yes,' Charlie assured him. 'It's safe.'

'Cheers.'

It was awkward then. However Tom had envisioned this scenario playing out, it was clearly not like this. He didn't know what to do next.

'Who are your friends?' Charlie asked.

The two figures were closer now. Pinner, taller even than Tom, was helping Monk traverse the rocky incline.

'Look, it's not what it looks like. They just wanna take Harry in, that's all.'

'What for?' Charlie said, finding himself standing between Tom and Harry defiantly.

Tom looked at him pityingly. 'Charlie, we know things you don't. He's in the paper. People are looking for him for God's sake—'

'He's the victim!' Charlie protested.

The girls had reached them by now.

'Charlie!' Emily cooed, almost toppling him in a hug.

'Are you all right, Harry?' Rose asked, standing up beside Teddy. 'No you mustn't be, must you? He went quite barbaric back there and essentially kidnapped you, and oh, I just want you to know that we had *nothing* to do with that, we didn't *want* to lock you up or anything, we all just feel absolutely *awful* about the whole thing. You see, I don't even understand what you're supposed to have even *done* in Tom's little fantasy. You didn't stab your father did you? *Tell* me you didn't stab him, Harrington Burden, because that would break my heart.'

'Actually his father was the one to stab him,' Charlie told them.

'What!' Emily and Rose said together.

Rose covered her open mouth with her fingertips. 'Harry! You've been *stabbed*? Is that *true*?'

'Yes, awful thing to be stabbed by one's father. If you don't mind, I'll sit now, only I'm not so sure I can quite take all this standing malarkey.'

It was true that he looked like a medical skeleton from a science classroom.

'Well, *where*? Are you okay? How did it happen? Do you need to go to a hospital? Have you *been* to a hospital? What—'

'Jesus, let him sit down,' Tom said. 'The poor bugger's got a stab wound.'

'*Poor bugger*?' Rose howled. '*You* were the one who locked him up! You were the one who meant to come here to, oh I don't even *know* what, to *shoot him*, I suppose? With that penis enlarger you've been carrying around.'

Tom looked at his air rifle coyly. 'Yeah, well, if he had just *told* us what happened one of the fifty times we've asked this could've all been avoided, couldn't it?'

'Why are they here?' Charlie asked, nodding down the ditch.

Behind them, Monk was barking something at Pinner while he tried to steady himself against the edge of a rock.

'Tom made a *deal* with them to bring Harry in,' Rose explained and Tom's cheeks went red. 'Monk's the Alderman of the village now. He's here acting on behalf of... well *everyone* really. You've upset quite a lot of the locals this weekend.'

'I see,' Harry said, turning round painfully on his boulder. Charlie couldn't help but wonder if this new agony he appeared to be in was a part of the Show. He hadn't seemed in pain two minutes ago and they had been up here together all night.

'You're not going to give him to Monk, are you Tom?'

'I—well, we had a deal I suppose.'

'Yes but now we know Harry's *innocent*.'

'We know he didn't stab his old man, but Monk doesn't care about that. He wants him for the barn and all the carnage and that.'

'Don't let him take him Thomas, I beg you! It's not right.'

Tom looked torn as Monk finally arrived on the flat, staggering and wheezing and nearly gagging on his own phlegm.

'Are you okay old man? You look like you're about to die.'

'Am fine,' he coughed. 'Got gyp in the joints. Like ter see you lot all try an' do what I've jus' done with a bad leg an' a dead arm an' a hip from nineteen forty-sommet, an' only one eye. Loses the depth perception yer know. Yers should be praisin' that little feat of endurance. Clappin' an' so on.'

Harry clearly didn't make much of this grand threat he had heard so much about. And Charlie doubted the old farmer would survive the downhill climb.

'Now then, this me charge is it?' Monk said, returning Harry's gaze and getting a good long look at him for the first time. 'Don't look like much ter me,' he said. 'Sort of a... sickly looking thing, aren't yer?'

'I suppose I am,' Harry agreed. 'But as it happens I've been stabbed, shot and punched. I've been involved in several high-speed crashes. I've had a sword fight and several teeth knocked out. I almost drowned yesterday morning and I've drunk enough alcohol to kill four men. I'm sure I'm missing something, for which I apologise, only I've been hit about the head a fair bit, you see. So if anyone's handing out whopping great trophies for reaching this summit, then I rather think the beneficiary ought to be me—and especially as I did so in the dead of fucking night.'

'Well lar-de-da,' Monk grumbled. 'Sorr-y, Sir Edmund.' He leaned forward and spat on the ground and his spit bubbled over with little yellow pustules.

'Look, there's been a misunderstanding,' Tom said.

Monk squinted up at him with a lecherous grin. 'Oh, aye? Yer not about to flip-flop on our deal, are yer?'

'I thought he'd done summat illegal, but it were a misunderstanding. Look he paid you for your barn, whatever else he's done is just an accident.'

305

'An accident what cost me a cow!'

'I killed your cow, not him. And we can work that out later. Right now we should all just get off this mountain—'

'I shouldda known yer'd turn like this. Pinner!'

Pinner stepped forward and pointed the Winchester at Tom.

'Come off it,' Tom laughed. 'You're not about to shoot us on some hillside in fuck-knows where just so that *he* can get his grubby little mitts on Harry. It doesn't make any sense.'

Monk ran his tongue across his teeth. 'He's right. Yer not, are yer Pinner? So give it here an' *I'll* do it.'

He snatched the rifle and it pointed up the hill at his opposition. It was on Tom, at first, but as he hobbled higher up the mound, he pushed aside Tom and kept slowly on up the hill.

Monk wasn't grinning anymore. His lips drooped in a snarl and his empty socket seeped a viscous white liquid down his cheek as though he was crying pus.

'Stay back you bastard, I know Krav Maga,' Harry warned. 'My cousin's involved with COBRA. He'll send your arse to Porton Down for human experimentation.'

Monk passed the girls and approached Charlie next, who felt his insides begin to crawl and he came over all woozy at the sight of the rifle's barrel.

'H-Harry,' he uttered. 'I'm shaking. Jesus all the blood's just run from my face and is making its way to the heart. I think it's going to overload like a bomb. Oh Christ, he's pointing that thing right at me...'

Harry put a hand on his shoulder. 'Alright,' he said. 'Enough's enough.' He stepped around Charlie so that the gun was fixed solely on his own chest. 'Step aside Charlie-Boy. This is between me and Polyphemus here. Let's get on with the whole *Sumer is Icumen In* business so the credits can roll.'

Charlie collapsed to his knees on legs like jelly and could only watch through the gaps in his fingers. Harry came face to face with Fletcher Monk at last and everybody around them watched the standoff in silence.

'I hate to inform you,' Harry said, staring into Monk's grimy little face, 'that I have no intention of following you down this mountain. I came up here to chuck myself off it so if you mean to threaten me with *death* by pointing that thing at me then I must inform you that you've chosen quite the wrong day to do it.'

Monk didn't bite. Charlie practically sobbed as he saw the defiance on Harry's face. Monk thought Harry was bluffing and Harry thought Monk was. It was a disaster. It was a stalemate.

Monk fired his rifle. Rose screamed, Teddy barked in fright and even Harry faltered, looking down to check if his internal organs had been blown through a hole in his chest. Fortunately, they hadn't. Monk had only fired into the clouds. A warning shot, that was all. A flurry of birds squawked and flapped around overhead. There was an awful lot of them.

'That's to show I mean business,' Monk said. 'If yer take one more step without my say-so, I'll blow yer bloody head off.'

'Come now, old thing, we both know you've not the 'nads to kill me over all this nonsense, so why don't we just talk this over?'

Monk's eye was doing a thing—swivelling around like mad as he thought about what to do.

'Please, Mr Monk,' Rose began, noticing his hesitance. 'We can settle this here and now between us.'

'Alright,' he said. The eye stopped spinning. He had an idea. 'Yer refuse to come with me, yer break yer promises, yer treat me like a laughing stock. But yer want to settle this do yer? Then here's what I'll do. I'll shoot yer dog!'

He pointed a rheumatic old sausage finger in Teddy's direction and a rictus spread below his steel-wool beard.

'Aye,' he grinned. 'Yer right, I'm not goin' to murder none of yers up here over it. I'm Alderman now, I've a reputation I'm nay willing to lose on you lot.'

'But he's *my* dog!' Rose howled. 'You won't be hurting anyone except *me* if you do such a cowardly thing!'

'An eye fer an eye!' Monk snapped at her. 'Yers are all in this together as far as I'm concerned. Yers lost me a cow! Yers destroyed me barn! Don't yer know cows stop producin' milk when they're stressed? Eh? You lot've lost me more than a bloody shed this weekend! So what do I care if it's *your* dog? I'll shoot his soddin' tail off an' work my way along the body, pumpin' him fulla daylight till I get to the head. *Then* we'll be even fer all the misery yer's've caused.'

'You're a monster!' Rose sobbed. She spun to Pinner, with tears flying from her eyes. 'And *you*! Why are *you* going along with this? Don't you see what a monster this man is? You'd let him hurt a defenceless creature so he can get his petty revenge? This is your Alderman!'

Pinner didn't move a muscle. He just opened his mouth in a gormless leer.

'So what's it ter be, laddy?' Monk hissed. 'Are yer willin' to come down this mountain wimme? Or am I gon' 'ave ter shoot this dog?'

A long ribbon of breeze whistled between them all while Harry made up his mind.

He noticed a long black cloud on the horizon writhing as if it were alive. It seemed to grow larger as it approached.

'You're bluffing,' Harry said. 'You will no sooner pull that trigger than I'd take your hand in marriage.'

'Stupid boy,' Monk said.

He swung the gun around and blasted from the hip. Sparks blew out as the shell ejected from the back. And as the gunshot reverberated around the moor, it was drowned out by a pained whine from Teddy.

Chapter 5

There was mostly silence on the hillside. The only sounds were the gargled whimpers that came from Harry. He was sprawled on the grass with both hands clamped firmly around the top of his thigh as his leg spasmed beneath them. His eyes rolled back into his head and a line of blood dribbled from the corner of his mouth.

The BB pellet had been but the warm up. Now he found he didn't much care for the headline act.

Warm, sticky blood was spurting through the small bullet hole just below the pelvis, and he failed to successfully plug it with his useless hands. Emily sprang into action. She pulled off her cardigan and wrapped the sleeves like bandages around his thigh.

Charlie was barely able to look through the gaps in his fingers any longer. He was murmuring something like '*Oh God! Oh God! Oh God!*' under his breath.

Monk was stunned. He was holding the smoking rifle with his jaw wide open.

The thing about having only one eye, he tried to explain as he stepped backwards and stumbled down a ditch, is that it affects the depth perception.

He had *meant* to shoot the dog, of course. That was only fair. An eye for an eye. A cow for a dog. It was a pure accident he had missed and instead blown Harry ten feet across the hillside.

The slug had burst into twenty strips of shrapnel, which tore their way through his body. Emily did her best to assess the damage, but there was no way she could do anything about it from up here. Harry needed airlifting to a hospital.

'I came here to kill myself,' Harry muttered, 'but I couldn't even do *that*.'

He was waxy-skinned and saliva ran down his chin, mixing with the blood. His heart hammered and he could feel his surroundings swarm as he grew delirious. Faces flew in and out of focus around him. Then he felt a giddiness ascend. He touched the wound and looked at the blood on his fingers with confusion. He had forgotten it existed.

'Wha's all this?' he asked.

'He's bleeding out,' Emily crowed. 'There's not enough pressure on the wound.'

'Oh I can't stand to look!' Rose wept. 'Will he be okay?'

'We need to get to a hospital. Now.'

'I'll take him,' Tom said. 'Nearest phone must be at that port. I'll meet yous there. Here, Charlie.'

He slung the air rifle from over his shoulder and pushed it into Charlie's trembling fingers. Then he knelt down beside Harry.

'I'm gonna pick you up now, Harry. Can you hear me?'

Charlie couldn't concentrate on what was going on around him. He was numb with fear and paralysed with shock and trembling with all his usual neuroses. He looked at the gun in his hands and then up at the bright hill where the sun was causing long morning shadows to point at him from two figures thirty feet away: Monk and Pinner had started to flee.

Without thinking, without being in control of his own body, Charlie was on his feet and after them. His legs were still jelly. He could feel the cold metal of the air rifle and the burn of his calves, but not much else.

'Stop!' he heard himself call out.

Monk and Pinner didn't stop, so he lifted up the rifle and fired it their way. A pellet hit the farmer in the middle of his back and he stumbled a foot forward. He didn't stop running though. He saw Charlie pursuing and pushed on. He even managed to overtake the giant.

'Stop!' Charlie called again and fired. This time the pellet whizzed by the giant's ear and disappeared into the sky. 'I'm warning you!' he called. 'I'll shoot you both for this!'

It suddenly grew quite dark. A cloud must have crossed the bleary sun. Charlie didn't turn around. But by now all seven of them, with Teddy in tow, were racing down the mountainside just as the dark shadow of the cloud completely cloaked them.

Charlie stopped every ten feet to shoot from the air rifle. The occasional pellet would stick one of them. In Pinner's leg or in Monk's shoulder or graze the edge of a neck. They would react with a jerk, but both kept on without stopping. Momentum had kicked in. They were limping but pumped with adrenaline.

Over in Tom's arms, Harry drifted in and out of consciousness. He had become aware of the great shadow that had come from nowhere. There had been few clouds and no planes, no vapour trails; just pure white sky. Except for that swirling black thing he had seen—*what had that been?* Now there was *only* black. Like a volcanic eruption had blown in from the east. And the darkness brought a cold that cut right to the bone.

Then came the noise—or perhaps it had been there for a while. It was so deafening as to be almost silent. Like white noise, underscored by a deep and rumbling bass. It started as a gentle whistle that built and built to this deafening wail. The sheets of Atlas rippled in a furious wind like the sails of an enormous ship.

'Tom!' Rose shouted across the sound. There was fear in her voice, haunting and shrill.

She was pointing at the sky—

Emily's ears bled. Her screams were silenced by the monopoly from above. She held the sides of her head in pain—

Charlie couldn't even swallow. He felt his stomach twisting. Every part of him shook and his skin crawled across his muscle—

Harry struggled to keep his eyes open. But he did manage—for a moment—long enough to see the sky and to see the cause of such sounds and darkness—

It was alive. It was swirling. It was filled with birds. A thousand birds. More than a thousand. More than a million, maybe. Ten million. Swarming in violent chaos. They numbered so many as to completely blot out the sun and turn that pure-white sky to black, like time had skipped fifteen hours ahead—

Nobody moved on the hillside. Nobody could. Everyone trapped in a hypnotic spell, watching the phenomenon but not understanding it—

The birds were loud, not only with their wings, but their voices. They were squawking and howling and shrieking. They were fighting. They were pecking at each other, pulling out chunks of meat and causing ribbons of blood to snake through the black.

Feathers were flying everywhere and birds even fell from the sky, lifeless and heavy, crashing like meteors across the mountaintop, digging up mounds of earth with their weight. Dozens of them rained down in incalculable order.

Rose squealed as one hurtled right for her. She leapt aside and it carved a crater by her feet. Dust exploded out from it like the detonation of a mine. When it had settled, she could see the thing was still alive, twitching, with its beak parted and an eye spinning round—

It was a war above. Biplanes roared after one another, machine gun fire cackled; the Battle of Britain—with birds. An osprey soared up from nowhere and screamed across the sky like a dragon. It swooped low against the rocks on the crags, looped round and picked up one of the blackbirds by its neck. The neck snapped and the osprey dropped it where it splattered against the flat face of the crag and exploded like a meat grenade.

Monk ran so fast to the bottom of the hill that he lost his footing and rolled over a ledge falling fifteen feet onto his back. He tried to get to his feet but was quickly surrounded by a convoy of birds of prey. He flailed as if he were on fire but his efforts were in vain. The birds forced him back to his knees where he cried as they clawed at him. They used his outstretched arms like branches, with their long razor-sharp talons tearing into him. They pecked at his head, nipped his skin, drew blood and howls of pain. One even tried plucking the good eye from his socket. Eventually, he was forced onto the ground where he was unable to move. They swarmed his body like hungry vampires and he disappeared beneath the flurry of their wings.

Harry lifted his head to his chest. Vomit poured from the corner of his mouth. The swirling black sky was sickening. And it crackled like television static, all the while underscored by that awful sound.

'What does it mean?' Emily howled. She had her eyes shut tight and her hands still cradled bleeding ears—

Charlie's eyes filled with tears. He dropped to his knees and let the air rifle roll off the ledge—

Rose was in hysterics. She had taken hold of Emily's hand—

312

'So much darkness…' she whispered. 'So much darkness…'

Harry started to mumble. Tom looked down at him darkly. 'D'you say summat?'

Harry inclined his head. 'An'… as they hurried… to and fro…' he breathed, 'with mad disquietude… on the dull sky… they gnashed their teeth and howled… The wild birds shrieked. That's Byron.'

He looked back at the sky. Another comet plummeted a few feet away. More were raining down all around. Through the dust and dirt, he saw Charlie across the mountaintop. They briefly made eye contact, before the earth began to shake.

About the Author

Christian Lea is a writer and illustrator from Manchester who works in academic publishing.

Where Wild Birds Shriek is his first novel, which was written with a coupe in one hand and a snifter of Bailey's in the other by typing with his nose. This process was made trickier by the fact he could only see straight by squinting through his nostril.

He also writes detective fiction and is currently locked away somewhere plotting another twisted murder for his shabby little sleuth to untangle.

Please Leave a Review

Reviews are so important to writers. Please take the time to review this book. A couple of lines is fine.

Reviews help the book to become more visible to buyers. Retailers will promote books with multiple reviews.

This in turn helps us to sell more books... And then we can afford to publish more books like this one.

Leaving a review is very easy.
Go to https://smarturl.it/ybn93o, scroll down the left-hand side of the Amazon page and click on the 'Write a customer review' button.

Other Publications by Bridge House

Christmas at the Cross

by Maeve Murphy

Blaithnaid's relationship with Kieran is not good. She has allies in Nadina the prostitute who soothes her with potatoes and Yoichi a Japanese neighbour who offers tea but only a little sympathy. David a neighbour supplies something approaching a festive Christmas with plum pudding and White Christmas. There is snow, there are Christmas lights and there are friends meeting for drinks. There is violence, there are threats and there is heartache. How will Blaithnaid find her way through all of this?
Christmas at the Cross – a Kings Cross story – is a novella in five parts from Bridge House Publishing. Maeve Murphy creates a compelling text, an authentic voice and a real sense of place.

"This short novel is gripping, action packed and surprising. Thought provoking and honest. Kings Cross before the face lift." (*Amazon*)

Order from Amazon:
ISBN: 978-1-914199-06-6 (paperback)
978-1-914199-07-3 (ebook)

Resilience

by Jim Bates

Remembrance Day is special for one grandfather. Which story of him and his brother at the lake will John remember today? Blake loves his garden but he's not so sure about the rabbit. Tyler stands up to his dad while hunting crows. What really did happen in the room at the Inn on the Lake? Why doesn't Quinn run away anymore?

"*Resilience* is an absolute gem. A collection of twenty-seven beautifully written short stories that deal with the central theme of its title."
(Amazon)

Order from Amazon:
ISBN: 978-1-914199-00-4 (paperback)
978-1-914199-01-1 (ebook)

Fresh Beginnings

by Leela Dutt
illustrated by Kate Attfield

An intriguing mixture of stories, all in Leela Dutt's inimitable style – something here for everyone, and beautifully illustrated by Kate Attfield.

Some are short and funny, some poignant – Leela Dutt's collection *Fresh Beginnings* will warm your heart and stay in your mind – it might even make you laugh!

"If you like short stories, if you like good stories, then *Fresh Beginnings* is for you." (*Amazon*)

Order from Amazon:
Paperback: ISBN 978-1-914199-12-7
eBook: ISBN 978-1-914199-13-4

www.ingramcontent.com/pod-product-compliance
Lightning Source LLC
Chambersburg PA
CBHW070220260626
47160CB00002B/611